T0329242

Meet the Women of the University

SALLY JO—

a self-proclaimed "perpetual virgin," a pampered Southern belle who adores all kinds of men—as long as they're white.

LAUREL

her happiest memory is the night she was "devirginated"—she's been struggling to find herself.

ESMY—

a dedicated teacher, devoutly religious, terrified of becoming a "frustrated old lady."

INGE—

a clown in the classroom, a heavy drinker at home, living in a fantasy world full of handsome, willing men.

CONNIE—

a nice girl in nasty company, strung out on heroin and divorced at twenty-one.

JENNIFER—

a traumatic childhood left her a prudish "straight arrow"—but a tall, handsome black athlete changed all that.

They're The Girls on the Campus, and they do a lot of things you won't find listed in any college catalog!

THE GIRLS ON THE CAMPUS
is an original POCKET BOOK edition.

Books by Jack Olsen

The Girls on the Campus
The Girls in the Office

Published by POCKET BOOKS

 Are there paperbound books you want
but cannot find in your retail stores?

You can get any title in print in **POCKET BOOK** editions. Simply send retail price, local sales tax, if any,
plus 25¢ to cover mailing and handling costs to:

MAIL SERVICE DEPARTMENT
POCKET BOOKS • A Division of Simon & Schuster, Inc.
1 West 39th Street • New York, New York 10018

Please send check or money order. We cannot be responsible
for cash.   *Catalogue sent free on request.*

Titles in this series are also available at discounts in quantity
lots for industrial-or sales-promotional use. For details write our
Special Projects Agency: The Benjamin Company, Inc., 485
Madison Avenue, New York, N.Y. 10022.

THE
GIRLS
ON
THE
CAMPUS

by

JACK OLSEN

PUBLISHED BY POCKET BOOKS NEW YORK

THE GIRLS ON THE CAMPUS

POCKET BOOK edition published April, 1974

ᴌ

This original POCKET BOOK edition is printed from brand-
new plates made from newly set, clear, easy-to-read type.
POCKET BOOK editions are published by POCKET BOOKS,
a division of Simon &. Schuster, Inc., 630 Fifth Avenue,
New York, N.Y. 10020. Trademarks registered
in the United States and other countries.

_____

ISBN: 978-1-5011-1923-1

Author's Note

The Girls on the Campus is about fourteen women at a midwestern state university of excellent academic reputation.

As in a previous study (*The Girls in the Office,* Simon and Schuster, 1972), the subjects speak for themselves, and I am reluctant to add colors or shadings of my own.

A condition of each interviewee's cooperation was anonymity, and I have respected that condition, primarily by changing all names except those of historic personages.

Like Blanche DuBois in *A Streetcar Named Desire,* nonfiction authors "have always depended upon the kindness of strangers," and in this case I have been totally dependent upon the women of the university. I thank them once again for their frank and sometimes painful cooperation, and I dedicate this book to them with sincere admiration and gratitude.

Jack Olsen

The Girls on the Campus are:

D'Angelo, Carrole, 28, senior in performing arts, mentally disturbed, but determined to become "a degree person" in between electric shock treatments.

Engemark, Ingeborg, 42, assistant professor of English, an inspiration to her students, but something less to herself.

Leblanc, Bonnie, 19, sophomore in psychology, male-oriented, the prototype "teenybopper" of the sixties and seventies.

Lee, Sally Jo, 26, assistant instructor of library science, misses the Greek life, fifteen-cent beer, and blacks who know "their place."

Martin, Consuelo, 21, sophomore in education, a Mexican-American divorcee who slips almost unwittingly into heroin addiction and burglary.

Milne, Laurel, 19, sophomore in political science, precocious and peaceable revolutionary, sharply at odds with The College and the establishment.

Ronson, Riva, 20, junior in performing arts, a talented student fighting to recover from a torturous childhood.

Scott, Jennifer, 18, freshman in arts and sciences, described by a teacher as "a straight arrow," in love with a black athlete.

Smyth, Nathalie Seymour, 22, senior in education, blessed by reasonable parents who accept everything up to (but not including) her living arrangements.

Snowflake, 22, senior in theology, an early-blooming "flower child," determined to love mankind and pursue her own life-style.

Stults, Ann, 23, instructor of English, a child of Catholicism and parochial schools, wry and realistic, wonders where the boys went.

Taylor, Rebecca, 53, associate professor of sociology, sometimes thinks of The College as "a strange, retarded place," but seems to have found her niche.

Vander Kelen, Anita, 34, former faculty wife, former "beatnik," battler against her own addictions.

Wilson, Esmerelda, 25, instructor of English, devoutly religious, constantly trying to reconcile the church and her physical impulses.

LAUREL MILNE, 19
Sophomore, Political Science

Somehow we all must learn to know one another.
Harvard psychiatrist Robert Coles, 1971

Riva Ronson, one of Laurel Milne's roommates, says:

Wow, I can still remember the first time I met Laurel. All I could notice was her immense boobs, you know? Like it was phenomenal, this tall, skinny chick with like 38D-cup boobs, you know? I mean, it seemed so unfair. Why can't they spread it around a little, you know? Like me, I got stuck with a skinny, bony body and like *no* boobs. I mean, share the wealth, you know?

Well, anyway, when I first saw her it was when we were being assigned our dorm rooms last year; she was wearing this really stylish short dress with heels and hose, and she was looking fantastic. Her parents were with her, and her mother hovered over her like a mother hen. It was "honey" this, and "honey" that, and "honey, do you think you'll like it here?"

They obviously had money. I mean, I couldn't tell if they were rich or not, but I could certainly tell they weren't poor. The way they handled themselves, you know? And I looked Laurel over and I thought, Hmmmm, I wonder if she's a jock. She has a little bit of that California jockstrap bullshit to her, at least when you first meet her and she comes on with that "Hi! How are *you?*" bullshit. So sincere, so honest, so smiley. Now I just sit back and laugh at my first reaction to her. Laurel a jock! Whoo-ee, what a joke! She's into revolution, she's into women's lib, she's into child-care centers, she's into everything good, and she's just an amazingly good person. Laurel a jock. Oh, what a stupid impression! She's so *un*-jock. Oh, I really dig her!

Bonnie Leblanc, Laurel Milne's other rommate, says:

I really have a fine feeling about Laurel. She's really a loving person. Amazing! She really honestly cares about people and loves herself enough to be able to show it, and I really feel that she loves me and she'll always be there when I need her. She just looks at me when I'm feeling depressed and she says, "Well, I love you," and that's enough for me.

Ann Stults, an English instructor, says:

Yes, I remember a student named Laurel Milne. She was one of the teenyboppers who used to slouch into my eight A.M. classes looking more dead than alive. I taught her English One, composition, and she never showed the slightest interest or enthusiasm for anything I did or said. She sat back there in the last row, and you could almost see the fumes of marijuana swirling above her. I only had one conversation with her. I asked her how she felt one day because she was looking so bludgeoned, and she said, "Wrecked." I asked her what that meant, and she said, "Well, just wrecked, you know?" and walked away. She did ten compositions, five at home and five in the classroom. She got ten A's. Figure that out.

There are a lot of armchair psychologists who say that you become a revolutionary by hating your parents, but then how do they explain me? God knows I've had my share of problems with my parents, and you might even say that my problems with my parents are the most important factor in my life. But you could never say that I hate them, or that they made me into a rebellious little revolutionary, because it's just not true. I love my parents very much; I see the beauty in them, and I see how they tried hard to give me a nice life.

Like when I was a kid. I was happy. We did things like camping out; we did good things, healthy things. I had far more than my share of sickness: scarlet fever, very complicated German measles, rheumatic fever. In some school years, I was only there two-thirds of the time. My parents were very good about it. They made my bedroom into a creative place where I could read and compose music and paint. They went far out of their way, and I will never stop loving them for all that they did.

But I also see how hopelessly they're entrapped in the system. Like, we went to the Methodist church for one reason: because my mother figured it was *the* social church. We didn't go there out of conviction, but just because it was the best.

I was raised to be a good little hostess and a good little guest. I'd be told how to pass the hors d'oeuvres when the guests came, and take the coats upstairs and lay them on the bed properly, and show the way to the ladies' room, or the little girls' room, as they called it. I used to lead three-hundred-pound tubs of lard, fifty and sixty years old, to the Little Girls' Room. How stupid! My mother would say to them, "Would you like to use the powder room?" And I had an urge to holler, "Hey, fatty, you wanta piss? Well, it's upstairs." But I never had the guts.

Politically, my parents were always one hundred years behind the times. They'd have given anything to be able to vote for Chester A. Arthur. The only time I ever saw my father excited about a candidate was when Goldwater ran. My father is so unthinking that it scares me. When my brother got into a civil rights demonstration in college and my father found out about it, he threatened to throw him out of school. It was a simple sit-in for black workers, but my father wouldn't stand for it. Well, he's frustrated in his job. He loves us kids, but he doesn't understand us. He's not demonstrative, but I am, and he returns my affection in a really uptight, nervous way. I hug him all the time, and he always smiles and lights up, but you can see he's also uptight. And he doesn't initiate affection, he's too businesslike. But he's beautiful inside. He would never do anything wrong, he would never lie. Both my parents are heavy drinkers, typical California suburbanites. My father drinks so much that I cannot talk to him on any level at all after he comes home from work. He starts downing martinis. He can handle them physically, but his mind goes. He's a very intelligent man, but the more he drinks the more conservative he becomes, a stickler for conservatism. And after a couple of martinis, he turns into Ronald Reagan on wheels. His mind gets pickled!

Anytime you sit down to talk to him seriously, he goes out and gets a drink first. He seems incapable of speech without a drink in his hand. So you rarely get him sober. And the drunker he gets, the more he holes up in this little circular, conservative logic, and says that everything else is crap, he won't listen, and he leaves the room.

My father has negated his most beautiful assets because of his belief in the system. He's a stockbroker, and for about two hours a day he makes the hot-cold, crowded, dirty frustrating commute to and from San Francisco. He reads the *New York Times,* the *San Francisco Chronicle,* the *Wall Street Journal.* Imagine this man who loves the outdoors so much, loves to hike, loves to fish and hunt, riding in those crummy commuter trains eight to ten hours a week. It's twisted him.

Both my mother and father hold in their emotions. They deny their sexuality, like most of their generation. They think sexuality is fine within marriage, but no place else. I think they see me as a fallen woman. They probably have a very normal healthy sex life together, but when I catch them hugging or kissing, they get all embarrassed. I say, "Hey, man, that's neat!" But they turn away. I come up and try to hug and kiss them, too, and they get all embarrassed, tied up in knots.

My mother isn't quite as out of it as my father; in fact, she thinks of herself as a good liberal. That means she has very generous and outgoing ideals, but she won't do anything about them. She just *thinks* about them. That's a good liberal. She wouldn't dream of marching. She wouldn't dream of telling a stranger how she thinks. Her ideas are very comfortable for her. She says, "Nixon's a bad president, but maybe we need him to bring back law and order." She says integration is a good idea, but you can't cram it down people's throats. I say to her, "What's the use of having ideals if you don't do anything to implement them?" And she says, "Well, I'm just not a marcher." And I say, "Well, mother, then you may as well be a Fascist."

They both freak out when you mention drugs, even though they're both nearly alcoholics. In their heads, marijuana leads to heroin, etcetera. Whenever anything goes wrong in my life, I know they blame dope.* But dope has nothing to do with it.

And yet within all these sick, unhealthy attitudes, there are a couple of cubbyholes of reasonableness. I don't know how to explain it. For example, my family always respected nudity. My father went around the house nude and so did my mother. Of course, they didn't do this when Chad and I were little kids, that would have scared us to death, or anyway that's what my parents thought. Personally, I think that's bullshit. I think you should start going nude within the family as early as possible. I read about this little two-year-old boy who played with his father's penis and gave him an erection, and it was really good, really healthy. People go around naked in the communes and it's not a sexual trauma for the kids. The kids go around with their hands on their penis a lot, but no one says anything to them about it. They'll probably grow up adjusted to their bodies, accepting them, better than those of us who went around as if all kinds of dirty disgusting things were growing under there.

But while my parents accepted nudity and were very natural about it, they didn't feel the same about sex. Somehow sex was regarded as something entirely different from all the other body functions. They made a big thing about it in a negative way. They couldn't accept it as a normal pubescent functioning.

When I was around six, I asked my mother how they made me and Chad. "Your father and I decide we want to have a baby, so we get really close at night when we're

* "Dope," to Laurel Milne, means marijuana only.

in bed, and the baby comes later." So for about three months, I wouldn't touch my father. I felt I was too young to give birth. All through those years, my mother inculcated the idea that you had to be married to have sex, and you had to do it to have a kid. She left out the idea that it was fun.

When I was eleven or twelve, we had a sex education program in school, and we learned how other animals did it, and we kind of figured out how to do it ourselves. I told mother about it, and I asked her how often she and dad did it, and she said a couple of times a week. This made me glad. I figured it would help their marriage.

I guess through the adolescent years, I was sort of intoxicated by sex. Most kids are, but they won't admit it. I masturbated before I knew what it was. I didn't even know the word for it, but I knew it was sexual and I knew it was giving me pleasure, I knew it freaked me out. By the time I was sixteen, I wanted sex in the worst way. I dreamed about it every night, and I thought about it during the day. Every day! Doesn't every young girl? It dominates your life. I was popular with boys, and for a while I got into a so-called fast group—beer parties, drag races—but then I realized that they were assholes, and furthermore they were the kind of assholes who would stay assholes. So I dropped out of that group. Some of them are here in Collegeville now. They're very into fraternities and football games, things like that.

Once in a while I petted pretty heavily, but until I was sixteen, no one had ever been in my vagina, in any way at all. Then in camp I met a boy named Lem, and he blew my mind. It was total infatuation for me. We were both counselors. He was nineteen, and I put him on a pedestal. I wanted to be his mistress, I really dug that role. Sometimes it seemed that I was the only person in the Methodist church camp who was not having sex, but now I was going to correct all that. It would be good for Lem, because he needed a summer chick. I was like a convenience to him.

Once a week at this camp the counselors had beer and wine parties in the woods. I'd tasted both before, but I'd never been drunk. One night I got drunk with Lem and we talked about having sex, and I asked him to explain to me when it was safe for us to fuck, about my period, etcetera. He said it was always safe because he used condoms. I said that was fine because I really wanted to start doing it, and especially with him. It took the beer and wine to make me say that, but I didn't regret it.

There was a fine freak nurse in the camp, and when I told her about wanting to lose my virginity, she told me not to do it unless I really wanted to. "Don't do it for pressure. Do it for yourself, or don't do it at all."

I said, "I *want* to."

She said, "Okay, I'll help you then. You can use the infirmary."

What a place that infirmary was! The nurse was busy turning on my friends—acid, marijuana. She got them stoned all the time. She'd just been married, and for their honeymoon, they'd gotten two kilos of marijuana, and they'd stayed up all one night rolling joints. And they still had a lot of them left. They were hidden all over the dispensary.

Anyway, the fine freak nurse moved all the patients into one wing, and let Lem and me have the other for the occasion. A couple of Lem's campers were in the dispensary, and they saw us coming in that night, but he told them to stay in the wing and keep their mouths shut.

We turned off the lights, drank a little wine, and talked for a while. Then we went to bed. Lem said he'd have to do *coi-shus interruptus*.

I said, "What's *coi-shus interruptus?*"

He said, "I'm gonna withdraw."

I said, "Oh. Cool!"

So we did it, and we stayed there until six A.M. It was fun and good—nothing perverted or anything. It wasn't terribly painful, but on the other hand I didn't feel any great sensations. Mostly, I enjoyed his enjoyment.

At six o'clock I sneaked back to my cabin. My roommate woke up and whispered, "Laurel, did you do it?"

"Yeah, man."

She jumped up and said, "Oh, far out! I'm gonna do it too!" She got devirginated a few weeks later.

For the next couple days, I felt really neat. I could still feel him in my vagina a couple of days later, and it was a nice warm little hurt. I just walked around sort of half-assed beaming. We didn't fuck again for about a week 'cause I couldn't have handled it, but after that we did it regularly all summer.

When I went back to high school I got my first taste of what men were really like. I heard *nothing* from Lem. I would cry myself to sleep. He was a bastard. Finally, I got a letter; it listed all the people he was fucking in Arizona.

I don't know what happened, but something went wrong in my sex life after that. I had no sex with anybody in my whole senior year of high school. And I couldn't masturbate anymore. I was full of hangups. I could fantasize sex, but I couldn't masturbate.

I had a friend whose day wasn't complete without at least a little acid, and once when he couldn't get acid, he bought a jar of codeine cough syrup and drank the whole thing. First he puked, and then he had an amazing high for three hours. He turned me onto dope, and I did dope off and on in high school. I smoked marijuana and hash, but I took no chemicals. I was afraid of them. I wanted to take them, but I was afraid. The most I did was smoke some opiated hash, which gave me hallucinations and made me feel the vibrations between people much more acutely. It gave me very positive vibes.

At the beginning of that senior year I was the typical suburban San Francisco school kid. I wore thirty-dollar sweater outfits and Jonathan Logan dresses and Gucci shoes and junk like that to school. French knits, etcetera. But then my head changed. I switched over to jeans and sweaters and stuff. The change in my attire paralleled the change in my head. I was really getting into politics. We decided to turn that school upside down, and we did. And they were glad as hell when we graduated. The principal openly hated me. I've never had anybody make snide remarks to me the way he did. When I graduated, he said, "Are you gonna come back and agitate some more?" I said, "Fuck you!"

I was having the same kind of fight at home. When I first started getting political, my parents freaked out. They told me, "You go to school to learn and read your books." They ordered me to stop demonstrating. But when I kept right on they could see that they couldn't change me, and my mother even tried to learn a little bit about ecology herself. She came up to me one day and said real proud, "I bought white toilet paper today."

I said, "Far out, mother. But it's perfumed!"

"Well, honey," she said, "I'm trying to learn."

Another time she said, "Well, honey, our generation went through World War Two, and we fought so hard emotionally that we spent all our energy for society. Now we're too tired to do anything." A lot of adults talk like that. But what they really mean is that by the time you're forty you're supposed to be enjoying yourself, not committing yourself anymore. Your energy has been spent making your money, and living within the system, and if the system isn't meaningful, then your whole life isn't meaningful, and who can face that?

We had these endless arguments. I'd say, "Mother, if you agree with us about ecology, you've got to help us."

She'd say, "Well, I'll do what I can, but I *can't* demonstrate with you. I'm too tired for that."

I'd say, "Mother, the movement needs both the generations. We need all the ideas and energies and experiences of both. We *need* you!"

"Well," she'd say, "honey, I'll try, but really it's all *so* tiring. Don't you find it tiring?"

It blew the principal's mind when I got absolutely straight A's on every report card through the whole senior year, even though I was busy with my radical, evil, disgusting politicking. I got every award there is. A National Merit Scholarship. A California Jaycee award. The DAR tried to lay something on me, but I told them to stick it. I wasn't interested in accepting an award from those senile old Fascists.

My valedictory speech was against bombing in Camin my life, I got into chemicals. A guy came around the dorm with MDA, which is a really fine drug, a mellow drug. It makes your body feel drunk, but without any of the bad aspects of drunkenness, and it makes you love everybody. It's a mellow, fine drug, and I recommend it to anybody. After I began taking MDA, I smiled and laughed a lot and loved the world. Walking downstairs was like being a superball. Bouncing down the stairs, ring-a-ding-ding, on each step. Fun! I used to bounce up and down the steps for hours.

The nice thing about taking drugs in our dorm was that it was the accepted behavior. Our dorm was one of the best places on campus to trip. You found people wandering around stoned all the time. Everyone was smiling at you, and you knew they were stoned, too. You'd have people doing their laundry at three o'clock in the morning, just sitting there watching the suds whirl around. One of my friends told me about seeing a fish walk out of the wash water and talk to him for three hours. I said, "Well, okay, right on, man. Crazy, man! Tell me more." Good vibes!

We had a couple of ODs in the dorm, but no deaths. We handled the freak-outs ourselves. I was working at the clinic, and I had some experience with freak-outs, so I was considered one of the more helpful people on our hall. One night a girl came into my room, and she said she'd taken a bunch of pills, uppers and downers and everything else, and didn't know what she'd taken all together, and she was really freaking out. She said, "I think I'm gonna die. Laurel, I think I'm freaking out. I just don't know *what* I've taken."

After a while she began having trouble breathing, and I had to hold her and tell her how to breathe. I said, "Just sit there and suck in the air, and now—let it go out! Now suck it in again." The simplest things! I called a number in The City where they could help me figure out what she'd taken. I got her to describe the pills, and then I told the man over the phone, and he tried to put it all together. She'd done reds to come down, and when you fight reds they work as uppers—and so in effect she had had a double load of uppers, and her heart couldn't take it, and she was freaking out. Also, she'd done some mescaline, and it's really dangerous to do mescaline in Collegeville because the pushers will hawk *anything* as mescaline. Sometimes it's as much as one-third strychnine. So you can see the problem we had.

I just kind of stayed with the chick through the whole freak-out. I let her stay in the room all night. I held her. I let her cry. Toward the end she wasn't saying much because her mind was going twenty times faster than she could talk. I talked to the doctor in The City several times and he told me what to do, but nothing seemed to work. Sometimes the chick would be passive, and sometimes she would scream out the window and rip at her clothes. It was terrifying. But after about twelve hours she seemed to be okay.

It's hard to describe all the doping that went on in our dorm. After the school year they took a survey and found out that 50 percent of our kids had used drugs *before* coming to Collegeville, but now 75 percent of them were users. And almost everyone had been approached by dealers *in* the dorm. *Everybody* was into dope. Aline, an engineering student, told me that even engineers smoke it, but they keep it quiet. They're so straight and crew cut, but they're busy smoking in their rooms. She told me that one of the engineers had even turned on his father, and now the old man loves it.

One reason that drugs are so common on this campus is that they're so cheap. In one way or another, you can get a nice four-hour high for $1.50 or $2.00, much cheaper than liquor. Marijuana is the cheapest and therefore the best seller, but chemicals like MDA and LSD and THC are sold cheaply too. Or mescaline. Or reds.

You always hear that these are the things that lead you into the heavy stuff, but on this campus heavy stuff is looked down on, and there's not much smack used. Even those few who are into it curse it. There was a little smack in our dorm, but no one was hooked on it. I wouldn't try it myself, it's too frightening. I did get into speed for a while, Dexedrine, and that's just really nice.

send me to one of those Japanese hymen-makers, the ones that sew them out of silk and insert them into women on the wedding night. The Japanese even have publicly accepted dildoes. They have some real *good* ideas. Later in the day, my mother said, "Don't *ever* tell your father. He'd be heartbroken, and I promise I won't tell him. He'd just—God knows *what* he'd do."

Talk about hypocrisy; talk about burying your head in the sand! Who should come to see me a few weeks later but the devirginator, Lem, and my mother treats him like a long-lost son! She apparently didn't know that Lem was stoned out of his mind from the minute he arrived until the minute he left. One night we went out, and he said to mother, "What time should I have Laurel back home by?" And mother put her hands on his shoulders, and said, "Oh, Lem, we don't care, we know we can trust Laurel when she's with you."

I said to myself, "Oh, you're kidding!" She'd always told me how much she hated him for devirginating me. This shows the capacity to fool your own self. People of my parents' generation have to say the right thing, even if it's a lie, and they *know* it's a lie, and they know that *you* know it's a lie. Suburbia! Ugh! It blew my mind.

You know something weird? My mother now seems to think that I'm a virgin again. Yeh! She has such a capacity for self-deception, and it was so hard for her to accept the idea that little Laurel fucked anybody, and now she indicates in every way she can that she thinks I'm still a virgin. It blows my mind! What they can't accept just can't be true.

I told you that my mother and father liked the outdoors, and I guess they decided that maybe it would help me to get my shit together if we went up into the mountains for the last week before I embarked for Collegeville. Off we went to the hills, and it was hell. On the way my father said, "We're having our doubts. We wonder if you shouldn't stay home for a few months before you go off to college. We don't think you can handle yourself on your own at Collegeville."

I said, "Oh, come on! I've *got* to get away from this place."

The discussion continued all through the vacation in the mountains. I just didn't like *anything* they did or said. Every night they drank themselves drunk, casting agonizing glances at me—the cause of all their trouble. It was weird—we weren't communicating; the whole thing was too heavy for them to talk about.

Every night we'd get a motel and sit by the swimming pool and my parents would get so drunk that they couldn't enunciate. They'd kind of weave back and forth. On a lot of nights I just went off and cried by myself because I didn't want to be with them.

The night before the wonderful vacation was over mother and I were sitting out by a motel swimming pool, and she began talking about how alcohol served many good purposes, it was a good calming agent and it was medicinal, and then she turned to me and made me promise never to smoke dope again, and never to be in the presence of it again, to get away from it whenever I smell it, and never to associate with anybody who smokes it. "Because if you smoke marijuana, you're *automatically* a terrible person!"

I looked at her, tears were streaming down her face. "You've *got* to promise me!" she said. "Promise me!" I couldn't believe it. I just stared at her. She grabbed me and began to shake me, so I said, "Okay."

But she wasn't finished. "And you've got to promise me never to have sex before you're married!"

I said, "Mother, get a grip on yourself." But I decided, okay, I've always been honest with my parents, but now I can't be. I'll promise; I *have* to promise, so I will. I joined in their little game, and I said the right thing. This enabled them to keep on loving me, to retain their image of me, to see me as they desperately needed to see me.

Mother said, "Well, I'm glad you've promised. You know I haven't been sleeping nights at all. I wouldn't be able to go on living if I knew you were smoking and having sex. That's why it's so important."

Man, I wasn't in Collegeville two hours before I started smoking dope pretty heavily. And it wasn't long after that when I started sex again, and I got into that pretty heavily too. I just decided to let myself go, to forget all the politicking that I had done. I was exhausted from fighting the high school administration anyway. I said to myself, "Give it a rest for a while." So all I did was join an ecology group, and after a while I began to work for a clinic where they treated a lot of dopers. But I didn't go around fighting city hall like I had in high school.

My dorm was coed and mostly governed by the students themselves. It was open twenty-four hours a day, and anybody could come in and out at any time. Of course, we were watched closely. There were cops around all the time trying to bust people for dope, but they never busted anybody because we were too smart. Screwing was acceptable; they just didn't seem to care about that anymore. It was the freakiest dorm, the most together dorm, the druggiest dorm on campus, but it was also the most intelligent. Of the freshman honor students, more than half were in our dorm. And as you might expect, the outlook in our dorm was far more relaxed. Word got out to the street people that if you needed a place to crash, you'd go to our dorm. Some nights the population of the dorm was doubled by crashers and hitchers and street people.

I can't speak for most freshmen, but in our dorm there was a stigma against virginity. We had a couple of virgins, but they got that over with fast, you know? It's bad to be a virgin. The guys think you're just a dumb chick, because screwing's really *fine*. One of our chicks made a New Year's resolution not to be a virgin; she went out and found a guy and lost her virginity on January the second. One day a girl named Annie came running into my room. She was ecstatic, jumping up and down. "I've finally been fucked! I'm not a virgin anymore! I've been fucked, let's have a party!" So we all got stoned in honor of her devirginizing. She'd been working on this guy for a month and she finally got him to do it.

After a while, I got a room of my own. I had a lot of crashers, and sometimes I'd have sex with one of them. It was a rowdy time. I was finding myself. Everybody has to fuck around like that for a while. There were only a few hassles.

I had one pair of crashers in my room for five weeks, till I couldn't handle them any more. They were very self-sufficient people, you had to admire them. They'd roll out their sleeping bags and go to sleep. If they needed food, they'd rip it off at the cafeteria or we'd rip it off for them. We didn't consider it stealing, it was just taking what's there. It would have been thrown away, otherwise, and it was shitty food anyway. We'd take whole loaded trays up to the crashers and nobody'd ever pay for it.

Riva Ronson says:

Laurel really *cares* about people, you know? I mean, like she'd have these marathon encounter sessions with her crashers—she'd get the whole story of their lives out of them, as if anybody gives a shit about hippies. I mean, you very seldom meet a crasher who's even worth five minutes' talk, you know? But Laurel would sit there and rap with them all night, digging out the facts, showing her *concern*. And it's *real* concern, real love for her fellow man, you know? She doesn't fake it. Give her the slightest excuse, and she can run down the whole town type by type, and what made them all that way, and how we have to help them, raise their level of consciousness. She ought to hang out a shingle and go into practice.

I learned a tremendous lot about people on the campus in that first semester of my freshman year. I found out there are basically three types of students: the conformists, like my first roommate; the nonconformists, like me; and the anticonformists, like most of the crashers. The conformists look for acceptance in the Greek areas, in the fraternities and sororities, in the rah-

rah shit—football, sports. The anticonformists look for social acceptance in drugs and sex and in being cool, or in the useless types of political activity, like the Abbie Hoffman and Jerry Rubin type of action. They're like running around making noise, you know? They're into anticonformity because they think that's where it's at, that's where they can find the greatest acceptance by the greatest number of people. But they lack genuine ideals.

These anticonformists are the largest single group on campus. To the unhip observer looking at the college scene, they may appear to be a huge mass of radicals just waiting to disrupt our society, but they're not that at all. They're just the other end of the establishment circle. I mean, you start at A on the circle and follow all the way around, 360 degrees, till you get to Z, but Z is right next to A. Z *is* A. These anticonformists *are* the campus establishment.

So while the fraternities and sororities are dying, you don't find in general that the campus people have a higher consciousness at all. They have practically the same consciousness and the same mores as the Greek society people, only it's translated into, "Oh, man, I'm so ripped! I'm so stoned!" instead of "Hey, man, let's go to the football game and drink beer," you know? It's the same chauvinism, the same chick-chasing mentality, the same low consciousness as the old fraternity people, or maybe a little lower, because the anticonformists aren't even into scholarship.

In its own way the square establishment is just as bad or worse. Nothing *real* gets done. For example, there are so many women here with children and no husbands, and they desperately need a day-care center for their children. The College keeps talking about it, but that's all. But at the same time they're building this asshole sports center and spending about three million dollars on it. They actually had a telethon to raise some of the money. While children in Bangla Desh are armless and blind! I read somewhere that four thousand children a day died of starvation in Bangla Desh. *A day!* Pure genocide! But we're building a fucking sports center for three million dollars! Lunacy! My friends and I are stricken by the asshole stupidity of the administration.

I look around me on campus and I say, "Who supports this kind of action?" I don't know *one* student who supports it. Maybe the fraternities and sorority groups do, but they're down to less than 10 percent of the total enrollment. No, I'll tell you who supports it. It's the trustees, the alumni, the ancient and elderly. The world's completely changed, and our trustees are still putting up new sports centers for the fucking basketball team. And they don't even fill the stadium for football. They used to fill two charter planes for away games, and now they have a hard time filling one, but they're still acting as though sports is where it's at.

Well, anyway, all these ideas were developing through the first semester of my freshman year. I started out to avoid politics, but I wound up in politics up to my ears, and then I got so frustrated by the general lethargy that I began doing dope in a big way. I was stoned throughout my whole second semester. I did it for an escape. I was facing a lot of problems over my parents and my discontent with The College. By now I could see that I was going to be a member of the counterculture all my life, and it would be an uphill fight the whole way, prosecutions, persecutions, and a lot of shit. It was hard to face this, so I just stayed stoned. I couldn't stand the dichotomy with my parents: They thought I was innocent, naive, not responsible, a child; and I knew different. It was all a lie, hypocrisy. I had terrible dreams about my parents. I'd slit my mother's throat and get blood all over my hands. It was really gory. One time I was having sex with my mother in a dream, and I was doing it to ridicule their own sex act, and my father walked in, and he said, "See, you're all fucked up." I took a knife to him and opened his stomach.

I had a couple of bad spiral depressions, and I considered suicide, buying a bottle of reds and just doing it. I felt totally worthless. Somehow I got through my exams, but I was stoned the whole time. For the first time in my life, I got into chemicals. A guy came around the dorm with MDA, which is a really fine drug, a mellow drug. It makes your body feel drunk, but without any of the bad aspects of drunkenness, and it makes you love everybody. It's a mellow, fine drug, and I recommend it to anybody. After I began taking MDA, I smiled and laughed a lot and loved the world. Walking downstairs was like being a superball. Bouncing down the stairs, ring-a-ding-ding, on each step. Fun! I used to bounce up and down the steps for hours.

The nice thing about taking drugs in our dorm was that it was the accepted behavior. Our dorm was one of the best places on campus to trip. You found people wandering around stoned all the time. Everyone was smiling at you, and you knew they were stoned, too. You'd have people doing their laundry at three o'clock in the morning, just sitting there watching the suds whirl around. One of my friends told me about seeing a fish walk out of the wash water and talk to him for three hours. I said, "Well, okay, right on, man. Crazy, man! Tell me more." Good vibes!

We had a couple of ODs in the dorm, but no deaths. We handled the freak-outs ourselves. I was working at the clinic, and I had some experience with freak-outs, so I was considered one of the more helpful people on our hall. One night a girl came into my room, and she said she'd taken a bunch of pills, uppers and downers and everything else, and didn't know what she'd taken all together, and she was really freaking out. She said, "I think I'm gonna die. Laurel, I think I'm freaking out. I just don't know *what* I've taken."

After a while she began having trouble breathing, and I had to hold her and tell her how to breathe. I said, "Just sit there and suck in the air, and now—let it go out! Now suck it in again." The simplest things! I called a number in The City where they could help me figure out what she'd taken. I got her to describe the pills, and then I told the man over the phone, and he tried to put it all together. She'd done reds to come down, and when you fight reds they work as uppers—and so in effect she had had a double load of uppers, and her heart couldn't take it, and she was freaking out. Also, she'd done some mescaline, and it's really dangerous to do mescaline in Collegeville because the pushers will hawk *anything* as mescaline. Sometimes it's as much as one-third strychnine. So you can see the problem we had.

I just kind of stayed with the chick through the whole freak-out. I let her stay in the room all night. I held her. I let her cry. Toward the end she wasn't saying much because her mind was going twenty times faster than she could talk. I talked to the doctor in The City several times and he told me what to do, but nothing seemed to work. Sometimes the chick would be passive, and sometimes she would scream out the window and rip at her clothes. It was terrifying. But after about twelve hours she seemed to be okay.

It's hard to describe all the doping that went on in our dorm. After the school year they took a survey and found out that 50 percent of our kids had used drugs *before* coming to Collegeville, but now 75 percent of them were users. And almost everyone had been approached by dealers *in* the dorm. *Everybody* was into dope. Aline, an engineering student, told me that even engineers smoke it, but they keep it quiet. They're so straight and crew cut, but they're busy smoking in their rooms. She told me that one of the engineers had even turned on his father, and now the old man loves it.

One reason that drugs are so common on this campus is that they're so cheap. In one way or another, you can get a nice four-hour high for $1.50 or $2.00, much cheaper than liquor. Marijuana is the cheapest and therefore the best seller, but chemicals like MDA and LSD and THC are sold cheaply too. Or mescaline. Or reds.

You always hear that these are the things that lead you into the heavy stuff, but on this campus heavy stuff is looked down on, and there's not much smack used. Even those few who are into it curse it. There was a little smack in our dorm, but no one was hooked on it. I wouldn't try it myself, it's too frightening. I did get into speed for a while, Dexedrine, and that's just really nice.

I did Dexedrine for about a week, and I'm glad I had the experience, but when my body began to feel like it was full of crap, you know, I stopped it. I could tell it would really fuck me up in the long run. So I took a couple of days to get all the poison out, and I had residual effects for about a month. My mainstay was dope, marijuana to you. Every morning I'd get up and start smoking and chewing. I even got into dealing. Almost everybody in the dorm dealt at one time or another. We were getting it for our friends. That's one thing about the marijuana scene: It's a very social scene, and it brings people together, and it's a really nice, together thing to do. Once somebody turns you on, you can always go back to him and say like, "Hey, man, can you tell me who your dealer is, because that was really good dope," and things flow easy between people, and they'll tell you, or they'll get it for you. Sometimes I think most students at The College get their money from dealing. It's an amazing thing, how many are doing it. And it's socially acceptable, it's cool, as long as you're fair about it and as long as you deal good dope.

My first sales were to my close friends, but then I began selling to others. It gave me extra money, and I made a lot of good friends. After I began to build up my contacts, I would buy three or four bags at once and sell them. The only thing I didn't like about it was going into a wholesaler's house. The vibes were weird. You could tell instantly that you were in a wholesaler's house. Wiggy! They didn't see people as people; people were all marks. The Mafia controls these wholesalers, and they make sure the dealers sell certain amounts or they take it away from them. It gives you a sick feeling to come close to a wholesaler.

In our dorm dope was sold door-to-door, the way kids used to sell magazines. People I never saw before would knock and say, "Hey, want a lid?" You could roll about forty joints from a lid. Grass is really cheap. And so is hash. Two or three grams of hash would stone about eight people, and the cost is low.

Dealing is so socially acceptable in Collegeville that

you don't need to go around ashamed of yourself like a Harlem heroin pusher. You are a part of the structure and you are respected, even admired by some. There was a camaraderie. Like the other day a chick came up to me and said, "Hey, sister, do you know where I can score some grass?" I sent her to a place. I told her, "There'll be cops in the neighborhood, but there'll be dealers too. You won't have any trouble." I saw her a few hours later, merrily stoned, weaving down the street. Really, it's hard *not* to get dope in Collegeville. Everybody's selling it. A friend of mine was walking home one night at three A.M. and he walked across the quadrangle and passed one guy standing there, and the guy said out of the corner of his mouth, "Dope and hash and LSD, I've got the best, try me and see!" *Three A.M.*

At first I had very little to do with the crashers in my room, but then I realized that everybody else was fucking them, so why shouldn't I? But they seemed to be a pretty boring class. Most of them were high school dropouts, traveling around the country seeing the sights, avoiding responsibility. You'd talk to them, and you'd always wind up talking about dope and sex, because that's all they knew anything about. It was very unromantic.

One night I met a new crasher in the ironing board nook. He was reading a very bright book about creative teaching and organic reading, and so I realized that he must be interested in education. We began to talk, went out for a walk and really started digging each other. I said, "You could stay in my room tonight." So we went upstairs and made it. He was inside me and on top, and suddenly he started singing away at the top of his lungs. An operatic aria! Bellowing like a hog! He said, "Isn't this wonderful? It just makes you want to sing."

So, of course, I lost all my excitement and arousal, with this mad tenor singing on top of me. I'd already had to concentrate hard on staying aroused—I always do—and this just broke it off completely. The singing fucker! He looked down at me and said, "Hey, what's wrong?"

I said, "I can dig what you're doing, but my body can't."

He said, "I'm sorry." So we just went to sleep.

He stayed about two weeks, and we made love a few times, and then he drifted off. He didn't do an encore with the singing. But I just couldn't get interested after that. This was typical of the crashers. It wasn't enough fun to ball them because there was no real emotional commitment. This was always the problem in the dorm. It didn't trouble me morally to do things like this, but it was frustrating, because there was no love.

But at least the singing fucker was gentle. Not all of my lovers were. One night we were having boogies out on the side lawn, informal unadvertised music and dance sessions, where people would bring their own instruments and play, and some would bring booze and dope and get high. It's great. It's better than formal dances. You get stoned and drunk and dance all night, and some people go off in the bushes and fuck.

This night the music was provided by the Freezones, a bunch of crazy guys who mostly play music and deal dope. They live in a couple of communes around The City. Most of them are gone now, they've been busted for their heavy dealing.

Tom was a Freezone. We just kind of met. It was a happy, tacit thing. Your eyes catch, and you look at each other, and you say, "I dig it!" He says, "Come on over to the house and I'll turn you on to some mescaline."

I said, "Far out."

So we trucked over to his house and he turned me on to some mescaline and some MDA, and then we smoked some hash and some weed, and I was *really* stoned. Then he took me into his bedroom and we fucked, and we fucked, *and we fucked*. Violent! If I hadn't been high, I couldn't have stood the pain. It's really amazing that I could stand it at all. I was ripped and sore, but I didn't even know it. The next day, I really hurt. I was coming down from all the drugs, and my vagina was so sore, it was incredible. He must have been superhorny that night.

I realized later that he wasn't a person, he was pretty fucked, and I felt sorry for him.

I guess I must have balled about ten men during that rowdy first semester, and I never had a single orgasm. I still didn't realize that orgasms are emotional as well as physical. Don't be shocked by the number of men I balled; I was just another normal freshman in our dorm. Later, when they sent around questionnaires, 80 percent of the kids admitted having someone of the opposite sex spend the night with them at least once, and they were *not* there to play frisbee.

To tell you the truth, the sex never really bothered my head, during that period. Everybody else was doing it, and we didn't worry about it. I was more fucked up over my parents. I saw a psychiatrist for a while, and he said at one point, "When you're going through troubles, you have a lot of tensions, and a lot of girls can release those tensions sexually, and that's perfectly healthy. Just make sure you're taking some kind of birth control pill." Now that I looked back on it, I was using sex to escape from myself, trying to avoid knowing myself. Anyway, sex comes naturally in a dormitory, especially in a coed dorm. That's one of the things you can't avoid—because you're always talking to the girls about how horny you are, about how bad you want to sleep with somebody, how the guys in the dorm are all a bunch of fuckers, but you do want some ass. So fucking becomes a social thing, an extension of these friendly talks in the dorm. It gives you something to share.

I also realized later that my promiscuity was meant to punish my mother. When I realized that, I cut it out, or cut it down. I'd say to myself while I was being fucked, "I wish she had a TV camera and she was watching this right now. I wish she *had* to watch it, I wish someone was *making* her watch it, and saying to her, 'Look, your daughter's getting fucked in the ass right now! *Now you watch!*' "

Toward the end of the semester I met a boy named Jack, and we had good feelings for each other, and I had good sex with him. It lasted for a month or two, and when it was over we stayed friends. It was good that I met him and began to enjoy normal sex, with emotional involvement instead of just fucking, because if I had kept on that way, I'd have really fucked myself over something awful. I did it just long enough to learn something from it. What I learned was that I wasn't an animal, that I couldn't fulfill my needs like an animal.

Jeanne Miner, one of Laurel Milne's close friends, says:

If I had been Laurel and my parents ever treated me like that, I'd tell those motherfuckers to fuck off, you know? I mean, slavery is dead, right?

About the middle of my second semester I went into a heavy depression. One night I tripped on mescaline and MDA, and I was up for three days. Coming down from my trip I just didn't think I could go on. One of the girls in the dorm told me that the Institute for the Study of Nonviolence was opening a ten-day session over the Easter vacation, and that I should go, and I figured, what the hell, I had to do something or else just kill myself. I floated into the session, still a little high on drugs, and it turned into ten days of just a beautiful love celebration. After a couple of days of study together, everybody at the session just realized we all loved each other, and we just celebrated this joy, and talked about it and tried to work with it, and tried to figure out what it meant, how we could retain it after we left the place. It was an unconditional love for each other. A few of the people at the institute were Quakers, and I wrote my parents and told them that I had decided to go to the Quaker traveling school, Friends World College. The way my Quaker friends described it, it was a great way to learn. You don't spend much time in the classroom; mostly you go out and just do what you want to do, practice nonviolence. Most of the students are freaks, and they talk to people and share with them what they've learned. It's active learning. You study what you want. There are no required courses. They have resource centers that give you lists of names and addresses of people you can go live with and be with, all over the world.

When I wrote and asked if they would support me at Friends World College, my parents freaked out. They wrote me, "There is *no way.*" They said, "If you want to go, then drop out of school and earn the money and go. We're not going to have anything to do with it." They'd visited one of the Quaker centers in California, and they saw that the place was very unfancy, because the Quakers don't have much money, and mostly their institutions look like army barracks. My parents freaked out. They'd expected a lovely little entrance hall, covered with ivy, and someone rushing out with hands outstretched, gushing, "Why, Mr. and Mrs. Milne! *Do* let me show you around the campus." Instead they saw a bunch of freaks with rolled up shirtsleeves, and somebody said to them, "Hey, man, there's some coffee over there, if you want it." My parents had never heard of a college like that.

I wrote back and asked them why they thought I was in college in the first place; and they wrote that people who graduated from college got better jobs and made more money, which is bullshit. Then they sent me a clip of a magazine article—they send me about two clippings a week, most of them from the *Reader's Digest*—and it said that people who graduate from college tend to lead more satisfactory lives than dropouts. Which may be true, but the fact that they went to college had nothing to do with it. The study turned things around all backwards.

So my parents and I compromised, and they told me not to worry about preparing for a career, just study the subjects I'm interested in, the things that turn me on, and sooner or later I would straighten out. So I wrote back that I was taking drama, ecology, and music, and I had joined an encounter group. Mother wrote back and said, "Oh, that sounds fun. But *what are you studying?*"

I freaked out! Just when I thought I'd communicated

some of my values to them, they had to do something like that to prove that they had no idea of what my values are.

So I just turned away from them for a while and began spending more and more time with a girl I had met at the Institute for the Study of Nonviolence. Her name was Jeanne Miner, and I just fell in love with her. She was from a poor, working-class background in New York City, but all her attitudes were in the right place. She was a radical politico, a counterculturist, and we dug each other at first sight. Jeanne was the first female I'd ever loved physically, the first one I ever had any sex with. We never gave each other orgasms, but we enjoyed each other's bodies, stroking each other, hugging and kissing, massaging each other. She moved into my room with her freaky dog, Tolliver, and she stayed with me for five weeks, until final exams. Jeanne helped me to put my head together more than anyone else. She'd been through all this shit with her own parents. We stayed very heavy into dope. We'd smoke when we woke up, smoke all day and be really stoned all the time, and I would drag myself to class. What a joke this college life is! I made the dean's list because I knew exactly how to be tested and how to feed their personal prejudices back to the teachers. And while I was making the dean's list, I wasn't learning a fucking thing. That shows how stupid it all is. My science course was astronomy, which is a really nice thing to know, and someday I'd like to know it. I went through the course and got an A-minus, in a class of four hundred, and I hardly remember a word. I don't know Betelgeuse from beetle juice. I don't know the difference between a meteor and a meteorite. Isn't one of them a crater?

One day I visited a commune, and while I was there I realized what I could be: a good worker, a good communal sharer. My parents had raised me to be a good little hostess, and a good little guest, which is a pile of shit. When I got back to school, I went to visit an old friend from home and I started to clean the ashtrays and she said, "Oh no, you sit down over there, you're the guest." I said, "What?" I just totally freaked out! I said, "Listen, you've got to get over that hostess bullshit. That just isn't where it's at. From now on people are working together, and *fuck* who's the hostess and who's the guest! There'll be no more role-playing. We'll just be ourselves. We'll just be people."

I wrote my parents a long happy letter, telling them some of my new ideas, how I had worked at the institute and visited the commune, in great detail. I didn't hear from them for two weeks, and then they telephoned. My father was drunk, and my mother was well on the way. My mother opened up by saying, "You still haven't told us what you did over the holidays."

That blew my mind. I *had* told them—in detail. But I said to myself, well, they're both drunk, as usual, so I'll tell them again, and I began the whole long description of what I had done. When I had almost finished, mother broke in and said, "Oh, yes, I remember now. You wrote us something about that, didn't you?" *Something* about that? I wrote them six fucking pages about it. But I already told you: My parents completely space out things they don't like, or things that reflect on me and therefore they think reflect on them, just as if they never happened.

On the next school vacation who should show up but my parents, suggesting that we spend a lovely time together, driving around the country. With them they had their old reliable portable liquor cabinet, supplemented by three or four extra bottles, jiggers, ice breakers, and enough of everything to totally stone Napoleon's army. We went off on our lovely drive and, just as I expected, they were drunk every night. They seemed to need it to relax themselves. They couldn't just be relaxed by the lovely scenes. One night I got to thinking how silly it all was. Here's my mother and my father, sloshed out of their skulls, they can barely talk and walk around, they're sloppy-ass drunk, and yet if I pulled out a single joint and got just a little high, they'd freak out! They'd explode! They'd call the fuzz! How in the world can you explain hypocrisy like that?

Night after night I tried to get them to talk about something meaningful. One night we had a short rap about political action. They said they were too old and tired to do anything about it. Imagine? They're both in their early forties, but they're too old. They just couldn't understand me; I couldn't reach them. I was trying so hard to get through to them that I started crying. I kept telling them that I didn't enjoy college, I wasn't learning anything, I was learning much more outside the school, and I thought I should take a semester off to get my head together.

My father gave me a silly rap about how I would lose my student status on the insurance and tax forms.

I said, "Well, forget the insurance and tax forms! I need a rest."

My mother chimed in, "But, honey, it's so important that you retain your student status."

I said, "What's important is that I'm going out of my skull. I'm confused, I'm frustrated, I'm crying myself to sleep every night over that stupid school, and the only satisfactions that I'm getting are completely outside the campus. That's what's important. Not student status."

My mother patted me on the shoulder. "You can stick it through, honey," she said. "We have faith in you. Just take a few courses less. Maybe you're working too hard."

A few days later we were rambling all over the countryside trying to find a motel with color TV. That pissed me off. I said, "Mother, stop trying to convert the whole United States to San Francisco. We can do without a TV for one night." But we couldn't.

Finally, we found a place, and as usual they pulled out their liquor cabinet and got stoned. The ritual was always the same. They turned on the TV, but didn't watch it. It seemed to comfort them, the magic eye. When they had reached the point where they could hardly talk, they began telling me that they didn't like Jeanne Miner's influence on me. "We've only barely met her, honey," my mother said, "but it's obvious there's something wrong. We think she probably takes drugs and we think she's trying to get you into the counterculture and away from all the good values we've taught you."

The real reason they didn't like Jeanne was because she'd slipped and said *shit* in front of them. She just forgot herself. Well, my parents are hell on bad language. I mean, they'll rationalize burning and mutilating Vietnamese children, but don't say *damn!* Once I used damn in a letter home, and I got back this formal business letter from my father, saying, "Young lady, don't you *ever* use language like that!"

I don't know how people get so fucked up about words in the first place. I don't see how you can straighten out your mind just by avoiding certain words. My generation just uses them; they're useful words, we're not afraid of them. Shit, piss, fuck. What's wrong with them? Say them over and over: piss, fuck, cunt, shit, soon they'll lose their bite, and they'll just be basic and simple words about basic and simple things. There's no reason for them to be considered dirty. Your mother fucked, right? Is she dirty? Nowadays, we're trying to make those words as useful and ordinary as they were in Chaucer's time. Trying to take the filthy connotations off them. Like the word motherfucker. The way we use it now it can mean superlatively good, like, "Hey, man, your bike's a real motherfucker," which means it's a really fine machine.

On that whole two-week vacation with my parents I could only remember one really nice thing happening. My father and I were hiking together, and we were on a clear trail, with no trees or bushes or anything. And while we're rapping, my father just turned around and pissed on the trail. I was right there with him, and we just kept on talking just as if it were a perfectly ordinary occurrence. That was incredible. It was so *nice* to have happen. I just loved it. It was so *natural*.

But their final farewell was hypocritical again. Mother said, "Ooooh, darling, we're *so* glad you're here at The College. We wouldn't want you to be on any other campus in the country, not even Smith." She said, "Good-bye, good-bye, we'll miss you *so* much." I was glad to see them go. I was high within an hour. Such phoniness! Such hypocrisy! I know they thought I was completely totally lost and yet they put down this bull-shit about how glad they are to see me here. How can anybody get behind thinking like that?

In the summer vacation after my freshman year, Jeanne and I decided to rent a house and start a commune of our own. Jeanne went home to visit her parents, and I rented us a big old ramshackle house just off the campus. But, of course, I couldn't spend the summer relaxing and enjoying myself, that was completely against my parents' ethics. They used some influence and got me a summer job in a big department store in Collegeville, and wasn't I lucky?

Well, I didn't have much choice. I had to take it. I can't for the life of me explain the reasoning behind it, but my parents send me a good healthy allowance and pay all my expenses, but only on condition that I'm attending school *or* working. In other words, if I don't have a job or any source of income whatever, they'll send me nothing. So you can see, I simply had to take the job, even though I detested the department store and everything it stood for.

My mind died while I was working there, it was so unpleasant. I was all alone in the big house waiting for Jeanne and some other kids to move in with me, and I just spaced things out. The store broke my back. Everyone was so hypocritical and sweet. I was told to wear my hair up, because it looked too freaky when it was long and frizzy. I had to curl it and wear little ringlets and wear makeup and high heels. It was all too hard for me! I'd go to work and come home to an empty house and cry and cry. I had a kind of walking nervous breakdown.

Every morning I'd go to work, hoping for a miracle. But nothing changed. I couldn't relate at all to the other workers, except a couple of young girls who planned to go to college, and I could say fuck in front of them and they'd laugh. Finally one day I went to work and I said,

"I can't stand it today. I'm just gonna go home today." I stuck it out for awhile, but then one of the little old bitches that run the floor told me to be careful, because my underpants showed when I leaned over. Right there in the middle of the store, as dozens cheered, she gave me a demonstration of how to lean over. "When you bend down, I want you to do it like this," she said, and she went into a squat position. "See? With your knees together."

I thought, what an unusual position for a body to get into. People came around and watched, workers and customers alike. Then the old whore stood up and said, "Now you try it, my dear." So I had to squat in front of all those people. I finally cried and left.

When I got home there was Jeanne with her boyfriend, Sonny Minelli. I was so thrilled to see them I started crying and fell into Jeanne's arms, and we just rolled on the grass together. The first thing Sonny did when he got inside was to bake some bread. Sonny bakes fine bread. From that second on, we started getting it together in the commune.

Sonny moved right in. He's a complete draft resister. He won't even be a conscientious objector. As a result he's a fugitive, and he has to live anonymously. I wrote my parents that Jeanne and I had taken an apartment and that another girl moved in with us, Sunny Jones. I hated to lie to them, but it was necessary. I also wrote them that I was quitting the store, that I had enough money to support myself for the rest of the summer, and that I was going insane, I just couldn't hack it.

A few days later my telephone exploded. They said that it was irresponsible not to be either working or going to school. These two things were okay, everything else was immoral. My father talked as though I had just blown up the world. I told him it was cool for me to relax a little. I told him I was going to take some courses at the Free School, read some books, ride my bike and relax.

"*Relax?*" he said. He sounded as if I'd said "motherfucker." He said, "The Milnes don't relax. Relaxing is for losers. Do you think we got this big house by re-laxing?" Yes, daddy, yes, daddy. No, mother, no, mother. Period.

They went on and on about how disappointed they were, how could they explain to the neighbors, to the relatives? Everyone had thought everything was going so well, and now I was quitting. It was the end of my life. My father said, "Every morning I go to work on the commuter train, and I don't like it, but I do it. Of *course* I don't like it, but I say to myself, 'This is an-other humpty-hump amount of dollars to make sure that my baby gets through college.' And now you do this to me! Well, I guess I'll just stop putting so much heart into my work, if this is the reward I'm gonna get."

My mother said, "Well, if your mind's made up, you'll just have to learn right here and now that life is real and life is earnest. You'll see! We're not send-ing you a penny till you get a job or go back to school."

May I remind you that all of this was about the fact that I was taking off one month? *One month!* Other kids took off the whole summer, *every* summer, swim-ming and traveling around the world. But if I took off one month of the summer, for the first time in five or six years, for the first time since I had started working as a counselor at summer camps, why, I was a dirty rotten no-good schmuck. Soon after the telephone conversation, I got letters from both of them confirming their attitude. My mother said, "You're doing a terrible thing, and you will live to regret it."

Well, I love my parents very much, and I just couldn't do this thing to them. However screwy their ethic might be, it was plain that I was hurting them badly, so I went back to the job, and my head kept on spinning with the stupidity and hypocrisy of the whole commercial world. One night I came home from work very tired physically, and on the way I ran into a kid I knew, and he said, "I've got some Orange Sunshine, and you can have it cheap."

Jeanne Miner says:

The big head-change for Laurel came after her trip on Orange Sunshine. I date *everything* to that trip. I mean, until she tripped and freaked out, I wasn't too sure that Laurel was even gonna make it. Her parents and all that, you know? But the trip—as bad as it was, and as frightening as it was, especially to those of us sitting around watching her and wondering if she was gonna die—the trip changed her head completely. People who put LSD down—I mean *completely* down—should hear what it did for Laurel.

Let me tell you about Orange Sunshine. It is very fine LSD. I didn't know it at the time, but Orange Sunshine is one of the most superconcentrated of LSDs. It costs two dollars a hit, two dollars a tab. They're little teeny things, about one-third the size of an aspirin, and each of those little tiny tablets will provide at least four fine trips. Unfortunately, I didn't learn all these details till later. I bought three of the tabs and went inside and discussed the matter with Sonny. We both agreed that it would be a great escape from all this shit that we were going through. He said he'd never tripped on LSD, and I said I hadn't either. We looked at the little tablet and decided we'd better break it in half and see what happened. But then he said, "No, let's not be chicken." So we both dropped a full tab, a really big load for beginners. It was a really, really big load for *anybody!* We didn't know it, but we had already OD'd.

We dropped at about five in the afternoon, and when nothing happened after twenty or thirty minutes we smoked some dope. Then the rush began, and at first it was nice. We sat outside and watched the sunset. I really started coming on, things began to look crazy. Cars would go by and they would look as though they were made of bubble gum. They'd go along—blub, blub, blub, blub! And the tires would assume weird shapes, fat bolognas, like the tires in the Sunday cartoons. People came down the street and they looked like they were in a slow-motion movie, they were going *so* slow, and some of them looked like they had rainbows around them.

I went into the backyard and began to feel how my hair felt. I was so *tactile*. My hair felt wild! Electric! There was tremendous energy in me, all electric. Then I started touching Sonny's hair, and I dug that. It was still light, but I decided to go around naked. I was really getting into my body. I was feeling my breasts, and touching everybody. It wasn't sexual, just tactile and physical. Like that's a lot of me, anyway, LSD or not.

For a while I just wandered around the backyard naked, touching a rose, running under the sprinkler, and feeling my hair, and then I looked up and saw the guys next door watching through the fence. They were a bunch of jocks, fraternity types, and usually we were in a state of war with them. But I tiptoed over to the fence and kissed one of them. He said, "Hi," and I said, "H i i i i i!"

He said, "Are you tripping?"

I said in this little girl voice, "Oh, yessssss. Oh, yesssss. Thank you."

I hugged him and tried to climb over the fence. I said, "I can't get over the fence."

He said, "Well, that's too bad."

That early phase of the trip lasted about four hours, and it was all beautiful—sensual and sensory, eyes and ears and hands, feeling and happy and loving everybody and just digging the whole scene, the whole world!

By nine or ten o'clock I was really flying, but I was also getting a little tired. I must have been peaking, right at the top of the trip. When the freak-outs happen it's usually right after the peak, and that's how it was with me. I started coming down, but I had dropped so much acid that I still didn't know what to do with myself. I decided I wanted to make love with Sonny, because I really felt like I loved him.

Jeanne said it was okay, but Sonny said he wouldn't do it. Jeanne is a very nonmonogamous person; she doesn't want to own anyone or be owned by anyone. She doesn't need the false security of one person. So she kept telling Sonny it was okay, but he still wouldn't do it.

I said, "Oh, come on, Sonny! I just want to make love to you, because you feel so good!" I was still using this little girl voice. "And I want to feel so good, Sonny."

I was literally insane for a while. I began to black out, and I imagined that I was representing everyone in the world of acid, and if I kept going backward in time, I would perish and the whole world of acid would perish, and I would be responsible for this disaster. I began hallucinating; I saw giants and dragons coming to attack me. My mother and father chased me with axes and knives and guns. They were trying so hard to kill me, running after me with blood pouring out of their eyes, screaming at me.

Around midnight I woke up and wanted to make love to everybody, the whole world. At one point I ran into the kitchen, and there were Jeanne and Sonny, and I said, "I'm gonna put you all inside me." They said, "You can't do that. It's impossible physically."

"Oh, yes, I can. I've complete control over space and time and size and everything. And I'm gonna put your bodies inside of my body."

I wandered outside and I saw the sun shining bright. I ran back into the kitchen, and I said, "Let's all get together. The sun's coming up." It went on and on, hallucination after hallucination, and the recurring dream was the nightmare about my parents coming back for me with their knives and guns and axes. Many times I woke up screaming, and then I'd go under again and I would see my mother and father and the old bitches from the store and the police and all the authority figures in the world advancing on me, with knives and spears and every weapon imaginable. Sometimes I would back off and scream at them, tell them what I thought of them. Other times I would beg for mercy, and tell them how I apologized for my life and my faults. All my true fears, everything that I had repressed, came out. Around three in the morning, Jeanne shook me awake and told me I had to quiet down. The people next door were complaining. She said, "You've been jumping around and screaming a lot, and the police are coming. You'd better fuck off!"

But I went under again. The room became the universe, and I was in control of it, but I was letting it all slip away, and I would be responsible for this terrible loss, and all my friends would hate me, and the only people left would be the authority figures, those terrible monsters, and it would all be my fault. But I didn't have the strength to save the world. I woke up screaming, "Oh, my God, I'm letting down everybody!"

I finally woke up at dawn with Sonny and Jeanne sitting on top of me on the living room floor. Sonny yelled in my ear, "You're under the influence of a drug. Nothing is trying to get you. It'll all wear off soon. You're imagining these things. You're going to be all right!"

I was confused; I had blown it, the whole world. I said, "You've got to kill me. I did it! I did it! I ruined it for all of you. You've *got* to kill me." Later on, Jeanne and Sonny told me that they were glad to hear me say that, it was an improvement on all the screaming and hollering I'd been doing.

Later on, I looked over at the clock on the wall because there was something in my nightmare about stopping time, but the clock just kept twisting in and out of shape, it wouldn't let me read it. Then another scary thing happened. I began hearing things wrong. Jeanne's mouth would move, but she wouldn't say what her mouth was saying. Her lips and her words didn't go together. This terrified me. I went under again, and slept for an hour or so, and when I woke up the freak-out was over. I had to get up and go to work, and you can imagine how I looked and felt. I was back in the world that had created all those fears, I was *really* terrified. I stumbled to work and they sent me home. For a couple of days I was in a haze. I walked around panicky, the sky was falling. I had confronted all my fears on one night. I was so frightened I couldn't even talk about it.

Jeanne said, "We were so worried about you, we were really scared."

Sonny said, "I worked in a free clinic for a while, and yours was the worst freak-out I've ever seen. We just didn't know *what* to do."

I felt the acid in my system for three days. I was just a piece of jelly. I couldn't think, couldn't coordinate, couldn't sleep. Then I began thinking over the implications of the trip. I realized what had happened. By confronting all the authority figures that terrorized me, I had begun to see reality. Reality was that all the people at the store were a pile of shit, handing out shit to people. I didn't want to be a part of that, so I called up and quit. My mother had told me that I would just have to go along with what the store said, since there was no place in the world that would treat me exactly as I wanted it to. To them that meant that I had to adjust to the store. To me it meant that I'd *never* work for a commercial company again, and I won't. That was the first good thing that came out of the acid trip.

The second good thing was that my freak-out made me realize that I hated my parents at the same time that I loved them. I had never confronted this before. I realized that I could love them and hate them at the same time and accept both feelings, I could treat them as people, I could come across to them as an adult woman, and ever since then that's been pretty true. I wrote and told them that I had quit my job, that there was nothing they could do about it, and when they called I simply said, "Look, I don't think that my quitting this job is such an important thing. The summer vacation's almost over anyway. I believe I'm being true to myself. I *need* this rest. I *am* a responsible person. I *know* I am, and somehow or other I'll prove it to you."

It was amazing; *I* was playing the role of the adult in this conversation, and they were the sniveling infants. They whined and fussed, and I answered them calmly and rationally. I felt so good about this. I carefully explained to them that they were too immersed in the work ethic, the Protestant ethic, but that I wasn't, and that they would simply have to respect my ideals and ethics because they were just as good as theirs, and we didn't all have to be carbon copies of each other. They said I was being irresponsible again, and I said I certainly was not, and I refused to discuss it any further. I was able to talk to them like this because on my trip I had faced what I most feared about them, their authority over me and within me, and now I knew I could handle it.

Jeanne Miner says:

Laurel is the one who made our commune go. She's not aware of it, but she's copied one thing from her old lady: they both want to be mother hens, clucking around and raising about fourteen children and watching over them every second. Like we never had any real bad hassles over doing the dishes, making the beds, cleaning up, and shit like that because Laurel would rather do those things than hassle it, you know? Like one part of her treated us like a bunch of children, and a mother doesn't mind cleaning up after her brood.

Now that my head was on a little straighter, the commune really began to grow. Soon there were five or six people living there, plus three dogs, and it was really cool. We asked only one thing of residents, that we all commit ourselves to be honest with each other and to confront one another whenever necessary, and to show our true feelings and talk about them. Whenever we felt it was needed, we'd have a meeting, and we'd let it all hang out.

The cooking and cleaning and household chores were never designated. Dishwashing was done like every couple days. Most of the work got done, but sometimes somebody would fuck off, and we'd get pissed, and we'd say so. A few of the men had a sexist tendency to let the women do the dishes and clean the house, but we quickly let them know where it's at. The rent was shared out; money was communal. I had the most money, so I paid the most, and I went all the way through my savings by the end of the summer. Sonny had money that had been given to him, and he went through this quickly. But it all worked out, because basically we didn't care about money.

There were occasional problems, but we handled them communally. There was one cat who was always high, and whenever it came his turn to do some work he would beg off and say, "I can't, I'm all fucked up." So we had a meeting, and we said, "Hey, man, we don't care if you're fucked up or not, *you do your share!*" We put a sign up on the refrigerator, "These words are not to be said in this house: *Please. May I? Thank you. I'm fucked up. You're welcome.*"

We tried to be as natural and normal as possible. The bathroom door was never closed. That was the most public place in the house. We took showers together to conserve water. If the lack of privacy hassled anyone, they could close the door, but hardly anyone did. In fact, we had some of our greatest talks in the bathroom. One person would be on the john, and the other would be sitting on the side of the tub. I mean, what's more natural than bathroom functions? You have these two reciprocal acts, eating and shitting, and one we consider respectable and one we consider dirty. Why? Maybe because the sex organs are down there. Probably if we shitted through our big toes, we wouldn't have this problem.

So many crazy things happened that summer it's hard for me to remember them all. For one thing, I found out that the mattress in the back room had crabs. This was one of the shitty things the shitty landlord did to us. It was all his fault. Jeanne and Sonny both got crabs from it, and for a while we thought the whole house would get them. So we had a meeting. We sat down and worked out who could possibly have gotten crabs from whom. And we got a whole bunch of lice soap and handed it to everyone who came in the house, and everyone took crab showers for a couple of days, and we did nothing but clean the whole house and sit around naked searching our crotches. There was one chair reserved for those who thought they had crabs, and nobody else could use it. It was a panic! Funny! And no one was all that upset. We were a very clean commune.

We also tried to be open sexually, but that was harder, because we were still hassling values that had been laid on us as children. We knew that jealousy had no part in a communal living arrangement, but there were still jealousies. Some of the men were very sexist, too. Most of our sexual activities were individual, but we left everything up to the participants. Sometimes, Sonny and Jeanne and I would make love together, and there was always somebody sleeping with me, and somebody sleeping with Jeanne, or sometimes all of us in the same bed. But it was nothing like the sex orgy that most straight people would imagine. I mean, people like my parents would probably think we were wild, stoned, freaked out, having big orgies every night, but we just weren't. None of us were that thrilled about sex. We drank or got stoned now and then, but like it was never a case of twenty people in the same room with a bottle of Wesson Oil. Oooh, how oooky that would be! Sure, sometimes somebody would be making love in the front room, and we'd all pass in and out and see them. But that was just from necessity. They were crashing there.

Jeanne and I, of course, we were lovers from the beginning, physical from the beginning. I touched her body a lot, and she touched mine, and we touched supposedly erogenous zones, but that's mostly garbage about erogenous zones. I mean, I would touch her breasts and she would touch mine, or like the small of our backs, or between the thighs or, like that, just in the course of massaging each other or lying next to each other. Our hands would just fall there, because we were always caressing each other. I never had any guilt feelings from it, and neither did Jeanne. It was all just love, affection. My attitude was, "That's all Jeanne and I love her!" None of it was centered in my vagina. I felt, "I love Jeanne and I want to give my whole body to her." And she felt the same way.

After a while a woman named Karen moved in and

introduced the first strong ideas of bisexuality to Jeanne and me. I mean things like giving each other orgasms. I wasn't too interested because I had too much work to do on my heterosexual side; I was having *enough* problems with that. It turned out that Jeanne and Karen had feelings for each other, and they had some intense sexual experiences, privately, and with others. Karen and Jeanne and a man named Bill would all make love to each other, because they loved each other. Why shouldn't they make love with each other?

Personally, I found that having sex with a woman is an entirely different type of sexual experience than with a man. Women are more sensitive creatures anyway, they don't have to be phony strong and tough, like men. So when you get women loving women it's two very sensitive people giving and taking in very subtle ways. An orgasm is an orgasm, if you reach it, but it is not so necessary in a woman-to-woman relationship. Like I've *never* had an orgasm with a woman, but I have had very enjoyable sexual experiences with them, ranging from very intense, with a lot of physical manipulation, to just lying in bed and feeling each other's warmth, the way Bonnie and I still do a lot. You don't always have to touch erogenous zones.

For a while a friend of Jeanne's named Doug Miller lived with us, and he and I became interested in each other, at least sexually. So we lived together in my room for a couple of weeks. Once we spent a whole day in bed making love, and everyone else knew we were doing it, and they dug it, and thought it was far out! They would come in and talk with us now and then, watch us, and then we'd all rap, and then make love again. All day! But it was a very open and honest sharing thing.

But there was also a lot of time that we just went around horny, because Jeanne and I had developed very strong feelings about not balling people unless there's a genuine human relationship there. We don't believe in just fucking. Sure, there was a time when I did fuck a lot of guys I didn't like and didn't know, and I found out there was nothing to that. So now I prefer to be horny because otherwise the emotional injury is too over-powering. It shouldn't be that way, but it is. For myself, most sexual pleasure is really emotional, and if I don't have a feeling for the partner, the man or woman I'm making it with, most of the pleasure is missing anyway. I guess the whole point is, we communal women are not some new kind of females who operate entirely differently from the others.

In the long run, sex was really a very minor part of what our commune was all about. The whole idea of a community together is so that you can accept people for their human worth, and the sexual aspect is only a small part of that, smaller than any other part. For most people who live in communes, the sexual need is replaced by a general loving and kindness and consideration and real physical affection and caring for each other on a considerate basis. When you reach that point, you don't need a sexual partner to get your gratification.

We were also pretty casual about dope. I mean, it wasn't on our minds constantly, it was not the reason for the commune's existence. Some evenings we would have an evening smoke or an evening drink, with wine. But on the whole we didn't do much dope. None of us were interested in getting stoned out of our minds, we were too interested in making the commune work. Of course, when crashers came we'd sometimes let them turn us on if they had some hitching dope* with them. One night Jeanne and I did some mescaline and a little MDA. And there was another night where a crasher turned us all on with opiated hash.

You never knew what your crashers might have with them. Most of them were experts at ripping off; they ripped off *everybody,* and they didn't care what they got. One crasher showed up with a box of a dozen Timex watches, and another one had ripped off a bunch of expensive lenses for cameras. To tell you the truth, ripping off was a very important part of our culture, so let me explain it and how I feel about it.

I don't believe in ripping off as a revolutionary gesture,

---

* Marijuana carried by hitchhikers.

because part of the reason we need a revolution is because there's so much distrust and hate and anger, and by ripping off you're just furthering all these negative things. But I do applaud people who rip off really capitalistic stores like the one I worked in. Personally, I'm too chicken to rip off a big operation like that, because I know I'll get caught, because I look like I'm there to rip, my face betrays me. But today I ripped off a nineteen-cent pen from The College bookstore because I was pissed at The College and I got even. Imagine that silly thinking: I'm gonna shut them down by ripping off a nineteen-cent pen!

The way I feel about ripping off a capitalistic store is, well, they have money in their budget just for rip-offs. Their markups are like three hundred percent, so they can afford to be ripped off. They're perpetuating a selfish capitalistic setup anyway, and therefore it's good to rip them off. It's also good to rip off the government whenever you can. The money only goes for napalm.

I'm of two minds about ripping off our neighborhood supermarket. It's an ecologically conscious place, but still they're making money off their ecological preachings. On the other hand, they're a damn good supermarket, so it's hard to figure out whether to rip them off or not. I end up ripping them for their vitamins, because they're marked up so much, and anyway I figure they're making enough money off the other things that I buy, so if I rip them off now and then it's cool, it doesn't bother me, I've got it *coming*. But I get pissed at the freaks that rip them off for twenty dollars worth of food at a time and never buy anything from them. I'm a regular customer; I think I have a right to rip them off once in a while. Anyway, I don't think of it as stealing or ripping off. I think of it as getting something for the apartment.

One thing we won't do, Bonnie and Riva and me, my new roomies and me, we won't rip off co-ops. I hate to see freaks rip off freaks. There's a freak co-op downtown that gives away food when they have any left over, and yet freaks consistently rip that place off. That's immoral. I'm also not too crazy about the rip-off morality among the street people. Their ripping off has nothing to do with the revolution or taking care of others or being Robin Hood or anything like that. It's just, "I want something, so I'll steal it." They'll steal from anybody, rich or poor. They'll roll somebody that's out on smack. It's inhuman. It's an animal level of existence. They stop thinking, but they still have needs, so they rip people off. And once they get hooked on smack, why, ripping off becomes a way of life with them.

Well, as I was saying, we had to do a lot of different things to keep our commune going, and ripping off was one of them. But as the weeks went on, we could see that we were a viable operation. We were making it. We were coming out even, a little bit ahead. Then the shit hit the fan.

My uncle called up, and he said that my parents had gotten a long letter from the landlord, making all kinds of ridiculous accusations. He said, "They're all uptight about this, Laurel, but they were afraid to call you and confront you directly, so they asked me to call. They want you to call them back and talk it over."

I couldn't imagine what the letter was about or what the charges were, so I called my parents right away. They were freaked out! I'd never heard my mother so irrational; she sounded like a wild jungle beast. My father had it together a little better, but he also sounded his usual self, which means he was drunk. He said, "We don't want to believe this, but the landlord's right because it's his house and why would he lie?"

Shit! Of course they'll believe the landlord before they'll believe me. They believe *property*, money, authority, and it just seemed natural to them, as it did to the landlord, that if we were in the house unchaperoned with a lot of men, why, of course, there would have to be gang bangs and daisy chains and orgies every night. Why else live together with both sexes? They're locked into that old style of thinking. And of course they believe that if you take drugs you become raving sex maniacs. That's why my mother was so hysterical. She has the Art Linkletter approach to drugs.

My father said, "I'm ready to fly out there tonight and take you home." I could hardly hear him, mother was yelling and screaming so loud on the other phone. I said, "Mother, I can't get through to you. Just get off the phone and let me talk to my father!"

She kept saying, "Remember, the police are watching you! Get those men out of that house!" About twenty times she made me promise that all men· would leave the house right away, there would be no males on the premises at any time. I promised and I promised! But she wouldn't shut up. She was just admitting her paranoia over the phone. Finally I said, "Look, can I hear the letter?"

My father read it over the phone. Here's a copy he sent me later:

   Dear Mr. Milne:

   As you are aware, your daughter Laurel is a tenant at————High Street. We think there are a few things that you should know about your daughter's behavior. Laurel and her friend Jeanne Miner have been cohabiting with males and violating their lease in many other ways. As you know, you are legally responsible for anything that goes on in this house, as you have jointly signed the lease as guaranteeing the rent. Therefore, we feel you should know about these goings-on.

   There have been as many as six to nine men in your daughter's house on more than one occasion, and we have every reason to believe that drugs are very much in evidence. On any given night, you can find men who are not on the lease sleeping on the floor of the house. We have brought this to the attention of the Collegeville police, and they are watching the property closely for narcotics violations and other violations. They tell me that they are very close to making arrests.

   Let me remind you again, *you are responsible* for everything that goes on in this domicile. I regret informing you of this information, but I feel there is no other way to combat the low morals and lack of appreciation for property values that is being shown by your daughter and her cohorts.

Very truly yours,
Jason F. Burns

cc: Chief of Police, Collegeville, and District Attorney, Collegeville.

When my father had finished reading the letter, I was stunned. I couldn't believe the language. Such exaggerations! I said, "They've got to be kidding. Do you really believe what they said in there? Why, their language gives them away!"

My father said, "Well, we'd like *not* to believe it, but it *is* a landlord speaking, and he's got to have some basis for these charges."

So I said, "Well, read the charges one by one again."

So he did, and I answered each charge, or tried to, but it was so incredibly noisy and emotional on the other end of the phone that it was almost impossible. I denied everything. I said we had a few friends in from time to time, but there were never six to nine males there. At least not overnight. And even if there were, so what? They were charging that all sorts of immoral things were going on, which was ridiculous. About taking drugs, I just lied. I said no. I explained that we often burned incense, and I guessed that the landlord mistook it for drugs.

All this time, my mother was weeping and wailing like a banshee. She kept screaming, *"Get those men out of the house!* You're not only violating the law, you're violating your body."* Her paranoia was hanging out all over the place, especially about men. To my mother, all men are inherently bad. All they want to do is fuck you, take advantage of you. I remembered how she would dress me in beautiful bras and sexy dresses, but then I couldn't let a man touch me. Incredible! It blows your mind, the contradictions in the older generation. She'd buy me the sexiest things to wear, and when I put them on, she'd say, "Oh, honey, you look so cute, but if anyone lays a hand on you, scream and run, and kick them in the crotch!" What she's really saying is that males are bad and they'll fuck me over and I've got to admit this and prepare for it and never trust a single living male. Her barriers are amazing!

Toward the end of the conversation, she was coming on so loud that I had to scream back at her. "Look," I hollered, "I *love* you! What do you want me to promise? What are you trying to do to me? I told you that the men are gonna be kept out of the house about ten times already! Now I'd rather talk to my father." So finally she got off the phone. I guess she went to the bedroom and had a small nervous breakdown. What I learned about my mother from that talk! She's more freaked out about men than she is about drugs, which blows my mind. Men are *people!* But her attitude is that men are animals. Drugs can be flushed down the toilet, but a man's *there,* and he'll stick his penis up your ass! That's how she thinks. She's incredibly freaked out.

After that wonderful fun discussion, I freaked out myself. Jeanne and I kicked all the men out of the house. We took our stash box to friends to keep for us. We just said, fuck this, and changed our whole way of life. I wrote my parents that the landlord was a Goddamn liar, and that I was going to take the whole situation to the housing commission on the campus and prove that the landlord was wrong and had overstepped his bounds and libeled us. I made so much noise about being angry, being hurt, being victimized, that I gradually convinced my parents that the landlord was wrong and I was right. Once again it was a case of them *wanting* me to be right. That worked in my favor. It always does.

Soon after that, the commune broke up. With big brother watching us, the fun went out of the whole operation. Also, winter was coming on and some of our crashers were heading for warmer places and some others were going back to other schools. But it was a heavy place while it lasted. Someone was always confronting you with something, and you'd have to work it out with them, which was good. By the end of the summer some had blown their mind from the intensity, and had to have a rest from all this truth and honesty. That house taught me so much about life. It gave me entirely different attitudes. It made me love naturalness and hate artificiality. It changed me from the neat little hostess of the suburbs into what I am today. For one thing, I became a vegetarian, although I'm not compulsive about it. Living frugally in the commune, I found that I didn't need meat and I didn't desire it. Our meat's basically unhealthy in this country. It's highly treated with chemicals and hormones and it has a high concentration of contaminants, plus it's full of heavy, animal fat, which is the worst kind. I'll eat meat, but only under certain conditions. Like if I go to your house for dinner and you serve me meat, well, that's a form of love. You're saying, "Partake of my love," and if I refused it, I'd be refusing an offer of your love, and I wouldn't do that to you. The strict vegetarians believe that violence and aggressiveness are caused by the meat we eat because it's too yang. I don't see that. But I do see it as unhealthy. Meat and booze are killing my father. He eats something from the meat group—meat, cheese, or eggs—three times a day. His body is incredibly soft, he had high cholesterol, he huffs and puffs, eating all this mucus food. His body's just rotting. I tell him, "You're poisoning yourself! Let me tell you what you're doing to your body tissue and your heart." But he won't listen. He says, "My mother taught me what a good diet was, and I'm sticking to it." Sure, when he grew up during the depression the ideal was to eat meat three times a day—because you *couldn't*. Now that he can afford it, he's killing himself with crap like that.

Another thing that I learned in our communal life was the stupidity of things like deodorants. They're just pure sexist. In America we've correlated our societal facade, our polite cocktail party fronts, with our bodies and our fashions. Our mass mind is correlated in our mass fashions. "Hey, girls, here's a new thing from Paris, let's all do it, so that no one *won't* fit in." This is the attitude that keeps American women together in their sexist pigeonholes. A lot of it is hiding what you really are, what you really have. By dressing and acting like everybody else, you're not only concealing what you really think, but what you really are, and that includes things like what you really smell like, your own personal individualistic smell or aroma or stink, whatever you want to call it.

I'm not against body aromas, including my own. I shower every day, I can't stand smelling shitty, but I don't believe in adding unnatural artificial smells to my own. Do you want to smell Arrid Extra Dry, or do you want to smell Laurel Milne? I'll admit, sometimes my underarms really raunch me out, when I'm really working hard physically. I tend to have a strong odor, see, and it gets into my clothes sometimes and I can't get it out. So when I have to relate to older people who don't understand things like this, I use a little deodorant, but I never use it routinely.

Something else that's stupid and sexist is shaving. It's so unnatural. It clogs up the drain. It's a pain in the ass. When I shaved my legs, I'd get cuts all up and down, terrible rashes under my arm, and for what? For a social thing that's meaningless.

But my mother is still so concerned with what's on the outside of a person. Last summer when I saw her I was wearing sleeveless things and she said, "Oh, honey, you have *European* underarms." She tried to joke about it, but I could see that she was freaked out. She said, "Honey, people are going to think you're a foreigner."

I said, "I don't give a fuck. What's bad about foreigners? So what if they think I'm from Bavaria? Is that so horrible?"

She says, "Well, honey, I'm sure there's *some* reason you stopped shaving. I guess it's 'cause you used to get such terrible rashes."

I said, "Sure, that's it."

She said, "Well, if you want me to, honey, I'll shave your underarms for you." She was absolutely hellbent to get me shaved! Her ass was completely out of shape about it.

I said, "Well, mother, if you really want me to do it, I'll do it myself." So I did, because I didn't want to hassle.

She said, "Oh, now, honey, doesn't that feel much better?"

I said, "No, it stings."

"Well," she said, "at least you don't look as if you just got off the boat. Except your legs———"

"Well, I'm not gonna shave my legs, mother. I'll wear dark stockings."

"It's the middle of the summer. People will think you're crazy."

So she went out and bought me a pantsuit, but I wouldn't wear it. I don't wear dumb fucking pantsuits.

Well, these are some of the things that we spend all our time screaming at each other about. At least it keeps her off the subject of sex. I know how she's worked it all out in her mind. In the front of her head she knows I'm not sleeping with anybody because I promised her, and I'm her dear little darling. But in the back of her head she thinks I'm sleeping with *everybody* and performing all sorts of weird Arabian sex acts with them.

Well, I can't help her. I feel sorry for her because now that I've moved into this apartment with Bonnie Leblanc and Riva Ronson, I'm enjoying sex *very* much, and I refuse to be ashamed of it. Why should I? I *am* a sexy person. I have a curvy, voluptuous body, and I don't do anything to down-play it. Physically, I like the image I project. Some women with figures like mine go out of their way to project a cold image, but I've accepted my womanhood. I'm a woman, and I try to give that out. It doesn't mean I'm going to sleep with everybody. Some people may think I'm a loose woman, but I don't really care. My sexual activities are not what earlier generations would call conventional, but to me they're quite normal and natural. Like one night we had six or eight friends over, both sexes, and we all got stoned and drunk, took off our clothes and went in on the bed and jumped up and down. Then we went to the shower and showered together. Sure there was some sex that came out of it, and why not? It was very enjoyable and no harm done. A few months ago I met a very intense and brilliant young man named Michael Gold, and he and I are very much in love, and he's moved in with Riva and Bonnie and me.

Bonnie Leblanc says:

Sometimes I think Laurel and the rest of us spend too much time sitting around trying to *figure sex out*. Like, she and Michael'll discuss the subject for hours and hours, and then when they go into the bedroom to do it, they're all turned off. Amazing! That's one thing I'm learning in my therapy group, or *trying* to learn, anyway. When you feel like fucking, why, fuck! Don't sit around talking about it all night.

Mike and I spend a lot of time working on our sexualities. In both of our heads, we've had some trouble enjoying it. We were both brought up to think it's the wrong thing to do. I've been having sex since I was sixteen, and I'm still trying to get over the guilty feelings. Frankly, I almost never have orgasms, and I find that I must get my pleasure vicariously, through the male's pleasure. Michael and I still feel little jealousies sometimes, but maybe that's because we're in a stage right now where we're deeply in love and we're perfectly satisfied with each other as sex partners. My real desire is for him to find other women too, but right now our love is so powerful that we just can't see going with anyone else. We're basking in the light that we're making now, but we wish each other some new relationships. I *want* him to find other women, and I *know* I'll find other men. What we have to avoid is falling into the domestic role, but it's so hard. We both have too much to do to be domestic, too much to do to play games instead of going out into the world and realizing our potential as individuals.

There are things going on in the world that need Michael's and my attention, things that tear us up. The other day he came into the house and held up a newspaper that told all about Belfast on the front page and he started crying and he didn't say any words. He just broke down, and after that we went into my room and held each other for about half an hour. I was really stoned at the time, and I said that I would hate to see him cry or get upset every time someone was killed. But he said he just couldn't help it. I said I really feel strongly about war, things like that, but I can't let myself empathize as purely as he does. He's so involved in life that it hurts him personally.

When something horrible happens, like the Northern Ireland thing, it just goes to the ends of Michael's fingers and toes and he's sad with his whole body. It's the grief that parents of dead children must feel. I don't get so sad; I just get bitter toward the abstract and impersonal institutions that keep the disasters happening with horrible regularity, that keep the wars going. My father once said that if he had a son of draft age he would expect him to go to war. "After all," he said, "I went to my war, didn't I? So my son should go to his war."

Isn't that beautiful? Every generation has its own war to be proud of, and already my generation's had two, and maybe some more coming. I'm seriously getting just fed up.

Well, there's no use pissing and moaning. You've got to make your move. I'm not getting any nourishment out of college, but I'm getting plenty of nourishment out of my political activities outside the school. That's where it's at. I'm getting real excited about how much I can accomplish once I quit school. Like we started a good co-op. We buy food from the same wholesale outfits as the big stores, and yet our prices are one-third to one-half off. Twenty-four cents for a dozen eggs, ten cents for a bottle of milk. Different cells run the co-op, it changes off from one cell to another each month. A cell is a house where one commune lives. All we handle is organic food. It's cheaper and better for you. Fertilized eggs, whole unpasteurized milk, things like that. I got more satisfaction out of helping to start that co-op than I did when I made the dean's list in my freshman year.

This sophomore year, my mind has been blown from the first day. In every single class the first things we talked about were how the grading system worked, how we would be tested, *all the least important things.* Nothing about the sheer beauty of learning, the usefulness and practicality of the courses, how we could apply what we were learning to life and do something with it. All they were interested in was the horseshit fucking mechanical things like how we'll be graded, as though the objective is to get an A, rather than to learn. Well, this college is only furthering decadent competitive aims, getting us ready for a job in corporate America, preparing us to do nothing useful, to amass possessions, to rip off yourself and everybody else. I wanted to get up and say, "This grading system is bullshit. Why are you making me do this?"

I realized from the very first day of school that the university uses me for its own ends and for the stupid competitive ends of the United States. The university dictates *how* I think, *what* I think, but it tells me nothing about how *to* think. It's only teaching me how to be competitive. By grading us A to F it sets me up against my fellow students, when I should only be competing with myself. It tells me exactly how to learn and how to be tested so I can get a nice grade, to keep up a nice front. It keeps me in this nerve-wracking competition with the rest of the class, where everyone gets panicked every six weeks by exams.

Well, I got through the first semester this year, but it's absolutely the last one. I was excited about a few of my courses to begin with, but that excitement soon died. I realized I was different from the other students. I relate so differently to the world. I realized that there was a complete world with a whole lot of problems that needed to be worked out, whereas the university just thinks that Collegeville and the campus are everything. Who cares about that? They're just not sensitive. The persecution in Goa doesn't exist for them, but it keeps me awake at night.

So I'm backing off. I'm dropping out. Nothing I'm studying relates to where my head is, to what I want to do. I would like to work politically in communes, in communities, in free schools, and all the places where people can come together to help each other. Competition is passé, it's no longer a viable factor in society. The wave of the future is sharing and being together and working and living together toward the common goal of happier lives. I see that clearly. The university doesn't. So I have to leave, back off, gain a new perspective. If I see how I can use the university toward the proper ends, toward humanitarian and meaningful ends, then maybe I'll come back.

But that might be never.

SALLY JO LEE, 26
Assistant Instructor,
Library Science

Esmerelda Wilson, an English instructor and friend, says:

Men are on Sally Jo's mind *all the time,* ad nauseam. She's the classic southern flirt, it's the only thing she seems to know how to do. She's a regular *professional* at it. When we're together and a man appears on the scene, I just stand there like a repressed little person and keep my mouth shut. I know when I'm in the presence of a master.

She's a stunning girl, but I also think she's frigid. She finds men and then turns them off. She just won't let them get *any* place. She had one fairly long relationship here at the college, but that only worked out because he was seeing her in the middle of the week and sleeping with another girl on weekends, or else he'd have gone crazy. Sally Jo told me that they had "a good animal physical relationship," which turned out to mean that they kissed once in a while. An animal physical relationship! She's the very opposite of me. I may go to bed with a man I'm interested in emotionally, but on the outside I seem very austere and unapproachable. Sally Jo comes on like a free-and-easy type, flirting outrageously, and then she makes the boy fight for a goodnight kiss. It's a southern cliché type of woman. The spoiled, daddy's girl.

She has very few women friends. That's why it was hard on me when she selected me as one of the lucky ones. I found out later that she chooses female friends who she thinks won't give her competition with the men. She thought I wasn't competition, and I wasn't.

She has to be in the limelight all the time, and men friends are all that matter to her. She seems to have been brought up to entertain men. My goodness, a southern geisha girl!

We used to have these long talks, and they'd always get back to the men she'd dated in the south. All the men were in love with her. She *never* mentioned a girl friend, only men. And yet she's still a virgin, and proud of it.

Sometimes I wonder why she's teaching here and working on her doctorate. Why isn't she back home at the cotillion ball? Maybe some secret part of her is afraid that she'll never find the right man and she'd better pick up some tools and skills just in case. Or maybe she came to The College *just* to find a man. It's possible. If I had to make a guess, though, I'd guess that she's thinking about a career as a librarian, but in the back of her mind she's hoping she'll be saved by marriage. Saved by the bell!

I have to laugh when I think about her religious attitudes. She says *her* God is the God who should be finding her a husband. The helpful, *utilitarian* God. I suppose if she thought God wasn't going to help her find a husband, she'd drop him cold. Well, for my money, she's a humanist, a materialistic humanist. She's too much involved in her own life, her own myths and legends, to be anything else. She went to my church one Sunday, but it didn't seem to touch her. She said she liked the stained glass window.

Now write this down, hear? "Sally Jo Lee comes from an old southern family. On her father's side, she goes back to Robert E. Lee. On her mother's side, she goes back to Simon Beauregard. Sally Jo Lee is a *happy* person with a *happy* upbringing. A happy, roisterous family of ten children. No hangups, no problems."

Well, no, it's not *totally* true. Nothing is *totally* true, is it? You darn better believe it! But it *is* true that I've had very few hangups, very few mental problems. One is about my appearance; I've only ever felt attractive one time in my life, and that was at a New Year's party where I had on a black midi and pants, and I felt really good, really attractive, for the first time ever. Yes, I *know* I'm attractive, I *know* I'm considered better than average looking, but I'm not fully convinced way down in here, where my main gears are turning. You understand? The mirror mirror on the wall may say I'm gorgeous, but I say the mirror's a liar. A damned liar! It's just something ingrained in me. You know? I look at my appearance and I say, "What's the deal? *What is the deal?* Why do I look so grungy?" Well, thank you. It's very gracious of you to say that. I hope you mean those words, kind sir, and I surely do thank you.

Church? Oh, yes, I'm *highly* involved in the church. You won't find very many of us East Texas girls who've embraced godless atheism; you better believe it. I was brought up a Baptist, but I've lost some of my fundamentalist impulses. I could *never* be like Esmerelda Wilson, hearing voices and all. But I'm religious enough to teach Sunday school. I always write home and tell mother, "Mother, I still teach Sunday school religiously." Get it? Teach Sunday school *religiously?* Oh, you! You really know how to hurt a girl, don't you?

Yes, I've heard girls like Esmy Wilson and Ann Stults complain that there's no men on the campus and their lives are so lonesome, boo hoo! Well, I haven't found it that way at all. *Not at all!* There are men around, even for virgins like me who intend to stay virgins. Of course, I did lose five years of my dating life going steady with one boy from Missouri. Five years! Gone but not forgotten. That set me back a little in my program to get married and settle down by the age of thirty, you better darn believe it!

Yes, that *was* a long time to go with one boy and still remain a virgin, but I did it, and I intend to continue doing it. It's just ingrained in me. Just like the black-white thing. Certain things are ingrained in you, and there's no rhyme or reason for them. I don't know that it's important to take virginity into a marriage. I'm not convinced that men even *care,* but that doesn't help me,

because *I* care! I think it's important! I'm not staying a
virgin just for my prospective husband; I'm staying a
virgin for Sally Jo Lee, *that's* who. My friends say, Well,
Mr. Right'll come along and he'll unlock your key, he'll
break your little bubble. Maybe they're right. He almost
came along last spring. I met this wonderful man and I
really liked him. But I was so hung up about being
messed on that I couldn't make anything physical out of
the relationship. I was so afraid I'd be hurt if I gave into
him. He kept saying, "What's the deal, Sally Jo? *What's
the deal?*" And I just couldn't give in to him.

There's one old boy I used to date in high school, and
now he's married. He's a tremendous person and I really
did like him. I kept running into him at parties and
he'd always comment, "You know, I really did love Sally
Jo. She took a really big hunk outa me!" Imagine! I just
said to him one night, "Wilfred, why do you keep saying things like that? Who pulled your chain, anyway? I
know *I* didn't!" I think it's extremely odd of him to go
around expressing *personal* thoughts about me. If I were
his wife, I wouldn't like it. But men seem to do things
like that after they've gone out with me.

I'll run into old boyfriends like Len Sommers, and
he'll begin telling me how bad things are between he and
his wife, and how he's never been able to get over me,
and on and on. It really hurts me to hear all this. What
about his wife? Why, that old gal's gonna pummel my
ears, she hears that! But I do seem to have a collection
of men in my past that wish they'd married me. Or
maybe it's just talk? Talk's cheap. When they come on
like this, I just wonder, What *is* the deal?

I also seem to have a knack for breaking up marriages
without in the slightest intending to. There was this
boy I'd gone with, and then we broke up, and then I
ran into him and his fianceé in the street, and he introduced me politely, and then we went on our way. The
next day I was coming down the steps and somebody
whistled. Well, I never pay any attention to that, because
I figure it's gonna be at somebody else anyway, and I'm
not fixing to turn around and embarrass myself. Then

somebody comes running up behind me, and he hollers, "Howdy, Sally Jo," and it's this same boy. And I said, "Oh gee, I'm glad to see you, because I just wanted to tell you I was terribly impressed with the gal you're gonna marry," which I wasn't, really—I didn't think she was nearly as cute as she should have been, for him, and she was two years older, and that's extremely bad. I said, "She's every inch a lady, isn't she? And very much in love with you. 'less I miss my guess."

"Well, you miss your guess," he said. "She broke our engagement last night, called off the whole wedding."

"Why in the world would she do a fool thing like that?"

"She thinks I'm madly in love with you."

I said, "Why, you must be out of your mind! What's the deal, anyway? Did you tell her that there wasn't anything to it?"

He took my hand, and he said, "I told her that there *was*."

Isn't that awful? Isn't that just horrible? I'll *never* forget that scene. And that same thing's happened to me about five times. At least. I hope it isn't something I'm trying to do subconsciously. Breaking up marriages is just *not* my thing, but I seem to keep on doing it. It's probably related to one other personal phenomenon, and that's the way I seem to encourage married men to make passes at me. I can't believe it! I don't mean just hugging. *Everybody* hugs in the South. But I mean trying to go beyond mere hugging—and with their wives in the next room! It must be something in the way I come on. Me, the perpetual virgin! Can you imagine?

When I first came here to teach at Collegeville, I really felt scared. It's a big, beautiful campus. but there's something frightening about being completely alone in a place where you don't know a soul or where you are or where you're going. Why, I could be murdered in cold blood in the middle of the night and it'd be two weeks before anybody even knew it! That's what I was thinking. I felt so alone? You know?

But then I met Esmy, and she introduced me to

this tall, blond, brown-eyed teacher who just spun my gears. Something indefinable inside me just went "Zzzzzzzz," and I knew that all the main gears were turning. Esmy talked to him about me, and he told her that I spun his gears, too, but then he also said, "But it's just the wrong time, Esmy. I'd love to go out with Sally Jo, but I can't 'cause I'm living with this girl. I'm really sorry because it would have been a very good deal."

That was my first romance in Collegeville; it lasted about an hour. And it was a sign of things to come, too. In the South, things were different. If you met a man who spun your gears, you had a reasonable expectation of going out with him. But here in Collegeville you have to ask first if he's living with somebody. *Everybody's* living with somebody. My laws, it's an epidemic of living in sin! I guess I'm hopelessly behind the times. Why, just yesterday a man walked up to me at the pool and started a conversation, and before five minutes had passed he wanted to know if I was living with anybody, and would I consider the possibility of living with him? I said, "What's the deal here? *What* is *the deal?* Are you all crazy around here?"

He said, "Well, I just thought I'd save a lot of time, eliminate the red tape," and then he walked away. He just wasn't even interested in talking to somebody who didn't want to live with him.

Well, I just have to accept the idea that I'm different, my southern background and my southern culture and manners stamp me as an oddity around here, and that's just fine with me. I *know* I look different. I'm not cut out of that same cookie cutter—sweatshirts and jeans and no shoes and no bras. Why, in my whole long life in Texas I only ever saw one girl without a bra, and she probably was just passing through town from New York. But in Collegeville they turn around and stare at you if you're not jiggling all over the place.

Of course, there are *some* moral people around, but not too many, I can assure you. On one of my first nights here, I was talking to some young, single girls, and they told me that they were absolutely *expected* to go to bed with their boyfriends on the first date. It was *routine*! If you didn't do it, they assumed you were a lesbian and you'd never have another date. They told me that fourteen- and fifteen-year-old girls were doing it regularly; they told me about one fifteen-year-old who'd counted up thirty-seven times she'd had sexual intercourse in a month. It's become just as casual as kissing, I suppose.

Another thing that disgusts me here: I never see one black male who isn't with a *blond* female. Bwaaaaaah! You want to throw up. Why, the other day I saw this old gal walking down the street leading a strange little baby, with blond kinky hair and dark skin. Revolting! I just couldn't imagine them in bed! I tried to, but I couldn't.

My attitude toward blacks is simple: I have a lot of classes with them, and I teach with a lot of them, and all I say is, "Look, if you're smart enough to compete with me, why, go right ahead! Compete with me *because* you're smart, *because* you're intelligent, because I'm smart and intelligent, too. But don't say I owe you anything just because you're black because listen, buster, I don't owe you anything!"

I'd be the first person to admit that I'm not relaxed on the subject. I don't want to be! A black guy and a white girl live next door to me, and I just cringe! But then I couldn't imagine going out with a Chinese, either. All that sallow, yellow skin! I'm a liberal, but that's just the way I feel.

Once I had some friendly conversations with a group of black teachers; it just happened that we had the same free period together, and we'd meet in the faculty lounge and rap, as they put it. But lookee here at what happened: One night one of the Nigra males called me on the phone and said that some of the others were saying that there was something between him and me. That *really* made me uncomfortable! He said, "Has anybody said anything to you about something going on between us?"

I said, "They certainly have not!"

He said, "Well, people are beginning to talk about the

way we look at each other, and for your sake and mine we better cool it a little."

You better darn believe I slammed that receiver down damned fast! "Cool it a little!" Can you feature that? Why, *there was nothing on God's green earth to cool, and he knew it!* They're violently attracted to white girls, and a white girl with very light blond hair like mine is always a special target.

That little incident worried me for weeks. I wondered if I'd been unconsciously showing some feeling for him. I mean, you have to be honest with yourself, no matter how abhorrent you find it. Well, *did* I have some feeling for him? *Ooooooh,* it made me shudder! And I finally decided that the whole thing was just an attempt by him to create a false familiarity, based on nothing. But I *still* think about it. I *still* wonder. Would I date a black guy? Never! The reason is simple. I'm a bigot. I admit it. I was brought up a bigot and I'll die a bigot. It's a terrible thing to say, I know. Sure enough, a lot of white gals go out with Nigra men, but it's just so they can say, "I'm not prejudiced." But I *am* prejudiced and I admit it. I don't have to put on any damned show. That black teacher who called me up was a good-looking man, looked a little like the black teacher in "Room 222,"* but there wasn't a single chance in Hades that I would have gone with him to the corner store, let alone out on a public date. I guess he realizes that now.

The thing that keeps coming back to me is that line in Yeats about the center not holding. This campus is a perfect example. There's simply no center to hold anymore. No traditions, no culture, no rules, nothing! All the good old things about university life are dying or dead. People don't go to the football games anymore; we're lucky when we get seventy-five percent attendance. Why, what's the matter with football? What's the matter with school spirit? Cheering and getting all excited, and being one fine unit of people, all joined together in a

---
* A television program.

common cause? I *admire* that. Singing the alma mater always made me cry.

The fraternities and sororities are dying, too. The good values? Things you can depend on? Why, *drinking's* dying, can you feature that? What's wrong with going out drinking? You get to know people, you lose some of your inhibitions, and you enjoy yourself in the company of others. How I do miss fifteen-cent draft beer! We used to have it back where I took my B.A. Somebody asked one of my old Sigma Delta Chi boyfriends what was the *most* important thing on our campus, and he said, "Fifteen-cent draft beer!" And he *meant* it.

I suppose if you asked some of these hairs around the college the same question, they'd say, "Good hash!" or "Good LSD." All they can think about is chemicals, chemicals. Why, their idea of heaven would be a night watchman's job at the Squibb factory! They'd give up *everything* for a chance to wallow in those awful chemicals.

I don't know where all this decadence is leading. Except for me. About one more semester of this crazy place and I'm on my way back to Texas. Back to fifteen-cent beer, cultural values, traditions, football, and men that are *men,* and no pushy Nigras drawing unwarranted conclusions. I'm practically on my way home.

BONNIE LEBLANC, 19
Sophomore, Psychology

Ann Stults, a young English instructor, says:

I know this is supposed to be a swinging generation, the generation of the teenyboppers, but they don't look happy or fulfilled to me. For one thing, they all look alike, with the long pressed hair, the Ben Franklin glasses or "wires" as they call them, the bare feet or sandals, slacks, loose sweaters or work shirts over no bras, no makeup, and pierced ears. I have a *lot* of trouble telling one girl from the other in my classes. But the main thing I notice is their long faces. They look so unhappy, almost miserable. I guess they would tell you that they're upset about the world, about war and ecology and hypocrisy, but I wonder if every one of them has to carry the whole world on her shoulders. Probably that's why they turn to narcotics and chemicals so much. They're completely miserable the rest of the time.

Laurel Milne, one of Bonnie Leblanc's two roommates, says:

Bonnie's one of the most together people I know, one of the most consistently happy. She has an ability to cheer you up, the big smile, the big robust laugh, the arm around your shoulder. She's never given me a second's negative feelings. I've never felt anything for her but an intense love. Sometimes we just lie next to each other naked in bed, just to feel our bodies. We love each other so much.

Riva Ronson, Bonnie Leblanc's other roommate, says:

I just can't tell you how much I love Bonnie, how totally I admire her. She's everything I'm not, you know? She has so many boyfriends she has to name them with Roman numerals: Tom I and Tom II, Ray I, Ray II, Ray III. It blows your mind! I'll bet she has a hundred boyfriends. I mean, really a hundred!

The first time I met her was in the dorm, when she was assigned to share a room with me. Wow! I felt so inferior! She looked so terrific, so Miami Beach, and I looked so Collegeville Hills, you know? So *dumpy*.

I just stood there. Bonnie walks over to the dresser, and she says, "All right, this'll be my drawer! This'll be yours!", and she comes on all authority, all order and efficiency, you know? The exact opposite of me. So I go, "Sure, that's fine." I tried to get my shit together, to be a little neat, you know? Because I didn't want her to find out right away what a slob I am. I was thinking of finding a hole and maybe hiding in it for the first week.

I loved my mother and father, but sometimes I get so sick of hearing their 1950 prejudices. My father would flip out if he knew I dated a black person, which I did, here at college. My father never said much on the subject of race, but my mother served as his mouthpiece. "Let the Nigras pull themselves up by their bootstraps, the way we whites did. *We* started out poor, and look at us now. The Nigras can do the same if they want to. The trouble is, they'd rather collect welfare. If you redistributed all the money so that everyone started with exactly the same, within a year we'd all be right back where we started, the blacks on welfare and us with the money, because your father works, and the Nigras don't." Etcetera, etcetera, etcetera. That's all I heard, the old tired clichés.

People like my parents just can't see the hypocrisy in their lives. Both of them swear, sometimes pretty extremely. But if I say "shit" it's a federal case. This summer my dad had a long talk with me and he said,

"Just what *are* your standards? Do you have *any* at all? Do you condone dope? Do you condone living together out of wedlock? Do you condone people swearing in public?"

I said, "Of course I condone swearing, dad. I condone you and mother, don't I? They're just words, dad. They'll never hurt anybody."

The only thing they think about is how things *look*. What's happening underneath is unimportant. Like the neighbors across the street sometimes leave trash cans out. That upsets my mother. She actually intended to go over and throw their trash cans on top of the roof. She really gets silly sometimes, like a kid! And everybody in the neighborhood freaks out over lawns. Lawns, for Christ's sake, *fucking grass!* One guy had his whole front lawn cemented over and painted a weird green. Now he's out of the lawn competition. Amazing!

They gave me my sex knowledge slowly and stupidly. My mother warned about menstruation, but that was the only sex education she gave me. She just said, "Be careful!" But she never told me what to be careful about, so I didn't know what she meant.

Well, I'm making them look bad. They really weren't. Even though they were cold and demanding, I could always feel their love. I remember when my mother had an automobile accident, and how gentle my father was when he told me she was in the hospital. I never had any really big fears, because my father calmed them all. I was a pretty happy child. I pretty much accepted what my parents said. I suffered from homesickness when I went to camp. And when I came home I was terrified that our family would break up. My parents fought almost every night, and I'd hear it right through the walls, and it would freak me out. They'd just *scream* at each other. My mother would lose all her composure, and become almost hysterical. Almost all of the fights were about money, money, money. Once I got so upset I went in their bedroom and said, "Please, stop fighting!" But they sent me to bed and went right on. It was the consuming fear of my childhood: that they would split up, and I would be alone.

Anyway, in junior high school I found another way to torment myself. Males! I was amazed by the things you could do with boys, the fun you could have. In church camp my girl friend and I used to sneak out at night and meet boys. Or we'd go down to the beach and pick them up, and we'd make out with them right there, or see them later on. Real cool! I started liking a boy named Tim, and we went steady for three months. We used to write each other love notes. "Oh, I love you so much." Amazing! He was the first boy I let feel me up, go to second base with me. I was about twelve.

One night Tim's parents were out for the night, and we started making out, and he gave me all these hickeys, sucking my neck. He just gave me *all sorts* of them. And also—I almost let him get to third base, but I didn't quite. All week long I had to hide the hickeys with cover-up makeup. My mother finally saw them after they were pretty light, and I told her I did them tumbling in gym. She pretended to believe me.

Later on, after I stopped going with Tim, he told some of my friends how I nearly let him go to third. Mean! I was so embarrassed! I was really into a morality trip in those years, that there were good girls and bad girls, and that I was a good girl. At least I appeared to be. But this showed that I wasn't a good girl underneath.

I had a girl friend named Tina, and she was pretty speedy. Her parents went out a lot at night, and we used to go over to Tina's and make out with the boys. Sometimes we'd mix crazy drinks from her father's liquor supply, and then go out and TP* people's houses.

One night when I was thirteen, we drank a whole bottle of Scotch, with two boys. We thought we were pretty cool. The boys left, and Tina and I went to bed, but she got up in the middle of the night and threw up in the bathroom, and her mother realized what had happened. Her mother came in and woke me up, and I proceeded to throw up all over the floor. So her mother

*TP... toilet paper on.

freaked out that we'd been drinking and she called my parents. I was so wiped out that my father had to carry me to the car. Amazing!

You can imagine the repercussions. I was grounded for the whole summer. Both my parents did the we-have-failed number for weeks.

Anyway, one night when I was twelve or thirteen, there was this terrible misunderstanding. I was over visiting a girl friend, but my father thought I was out with a boy. When I came home, he had this angry look on his face, and he said, "Go in your room!"

We both went in, and he started yelling, "You're lying to me! You're nothing but a Goddamn liar! Where were you? What were you doing?"

But he wouldn't give me a chance to answer. Before I could get the words out he'd be asking me another question. He didn't care whether I was right or wrong. He was just angry, and he was out to punish me. Finally he said, "Aren't you going to say anything?"

I said, "What can I say?"

I was kind of a small child, maybe eighty or eighty-five pounds, and he picked me up and threw me across the room into the wall. I hit hard. Nothing was broken, but I had a terrible bruise all down my side. Later that night, my mother called the girl I had been visiting and talked to her father and found out that it had all been a misunderstanding, that I hadn't done a thing wrong. But my father doesn't apologize, and he didn't. Not to this day!

You can imagine how freaked out I was by high school. I was still playing my parents' game, keeping up appearances, into the grooming bit and all that, but I was also beginning to get a little freaky myself. All the social clubs rushed me, and it was a good ego boost, badly needed at the time. I joined the Royalites, and we had a lot of good times, parties, meetings with other clubs, rushing new members, going on trips, singing, and skipping down the street singing, "I'm Off to See the Wizard."

Oh, I went out with so many boys! I couldn't remember them all. I met all types. The ones who wrecked my ego. The ones I wrecked. The love-'em-and-leave-'em types. The ones I brushed off. Red was one of the nicer ones. He was homely, but sweet and quiet. He was a really nice person, but he was really, really insane, almost too intense. His family was pretty fucked up, and this made him terribly insecure. We never had any sexual relationships, except kisses good-bye, which were all he wanted. He had me up on a pedestal, he worshipped me, and kissing was plenty for him. One night he came over and said he couldn't handle me going out with other boys, and I said, "Well, Red, you'll just have to forget it then. I don't go steady."

It broke him up, and he acted so freaky that I was afraid for his life. Late that night one of his friends called and said, "Red's okay, don't worry. He pushed his hands through the window and tried to cut his wrists, and he had to have some stitches, but I'm with him now, and he's okay. He wanted to drive his car into the canal, but I wouldn't let him do it." That's really a heavy thing to have on you. But it wasn't really my fault. I don't know what else I could have done. I really don't know. Oh, wow! I was so young, I was just into breaking hearts in those years.

Around my senior year I began hanging around with longhairs. By this time I was lying to my parents about everything. I had to. They forced me to lie, and then they'd bawl me out, and I would lie all the more. I'm not saying that lying's good. No, it's really bad, but it's become a habit to me, and it's hard to get rid of. Parents should be a lot more permissive and understanding and then their kids wouldn't have to lie. A lot of the experiences I learned the most from and enjoyed, I would never have done if I'd had to follow the rules of my parents. So I had to lie, and it was a good thing.

Anyway, one weekend in my senior year, I went away on a trip with the hairs, and my parents found out about it. This was only the second time I'd ever seen my father really blow his top, although his violence was never very far from the surface. He took me into his room and he said, "Why do you have to go around with

freaks like that? They're all dopers! They're the ones who
are responsible for your bring-down on standards. . . ."

He just screamed accusations at me for an hour. I didn't
try to explain because I knew he couldn't understand
my priorities. If I'd done something that was immoral,
it would have been different. But all I'd done was go
camping with three boys who were my friends, none
of them lovers even. What is immoral about that? Someone's ideas are just fucked up. And it wasn't even that
my father didn't like those three boys; it was more that
they had long hair, and they were embarrassing to have
around the neighborhood.

My father screamed so loud I thought he would throw
me across the room again, but my mother came in, and
he just turned to her and said, "Well, I don't consider
her my daughter anymore. *You* just take over. She's
your daughter. I will have *nothing* to do with her. And
I don't want to hear any more about her!"

On the outside I was still the clean-cut Miss America
when I met Salter in my senior year. I was proud of my
virginity, it *mattered*. I was going to present it to my
husband when we married. But Salter was twenty-one,
and a very appealing, winsome person, and he was just not
going to sit still for me being a virgin. Salter was into a
heavy LSD thing, and other stuff. He took LSD three
or four times a week, and he got into two automobile
accidents because of it. He was immature, but he was
a kind, good person. He let me know that he cared
about me. I didn't care that he was fucked up; I just
wanted to be with him.

The only trouble was that he constantly wanted to
ball me. It didn't matter where we were. He always
wanted to ball. I held him off for three months; I told
him I wasn't ready for it. But I never liked to hassle, so
I finally gave in. It was the lesser of two evils. But we
kept on hassling after that. He couldn't get enough sex.
He wanted to do it all the time. At night, he would want
to do it on the beach, where eighty thousand people
could stroll by. Once we were in the park, and he said,
"Wouldn't it be lovely to make love out here in nature?"

I said, "No, there are too many people hiking here." But he insisted. I really didn't like making love with him anyway, and I certainly didn't want to do it with twenty people watching.

I never had an orgasm with Salter, there was too much resentment and I didn't have the courage to tell him to knock it off. I was never strong enough to say no, absolutely no, and to let him know that I was beginning to hate sex, that I had separated it from good feelings, that he was making it bothersome and boring and something to get over with as quick as possible.

Laurel Milne says:

Sometimes Bonnie comes on all happy and bubbling, and this has given her a lot of shallow relationships because she's so easy to get along with and there's no need to plumb her depths to be her friend. And so many of the men in her life can't seem to see past the beauty, past the surface, into a fine, complex human being. This has given her problems with a lot of men, but she's aware of it now, and she's demanding fuller and more meaningful relationships.

A lot of her problem is her Miami Beach background. She's been a sex symbol all her life, a Florida beach cattle type. And she played the role willingly for a long time. She liked the role, because she was just a dumb high school kid, and what did she know? She wore the right clothes, the right hairdo, the gloves, etcetera.

Bonnie developed a lot of facades, but now she's finding out that the facades are insufficient when she wants to express her true self. Like she's trying to stop being surfacely beautiful and cute and clever, like Doris Day, and she's trying to start showing her real self to men, so that they'll stop saying, "Oh, what a cute chick!" and start saying, "Oh, what a beautiful human being." She hasn't found herself yet, but she's working on it. So maybe men will stop fucking her over so much.

* * *

When I first came to the campus, I went into a terrible tailspin. I felt so alone the minute my parents dropped me off. I felt really . . . Wow! Like here I am by myself, and who do I know on this huge campus? Things got a little better when I began going out with Ray. But after two weeks he became superpossessive, and I couldn't handle possessiveness after Salter. I just didn't want *anyone* to possess me. I really really liked Ray a whole bunch, and he was good looking, and nice to me, but possessiveness was out.

Then I met another Ray, Ray II, at the coffee shop, and started seeing him, but he ended up being too weird. He practically raped me. It freaked me out. It turned out that he was heavily into dope. He'd been doing heroin, and he couldn't control himself. I found all this out later, after I'd stopped going with him.

Anyway, I was living in a coed dorm with my assigned roommate Riva Ronson, and there were males all over the place. One night I met Jules, and we got hold of some mescaline and dropped that and goofed around on the front step, and then we started riding bikes late at night, and it was so much fun. Amazing! We ended up getting really stoned, sitting in his room most of the night, laying next to each other and talking. This was one of my best trips. I just felt real close to him. I really liked him.

There were plenty of good times, but usually they would only last a day or a night, when I would let things happen spontaneously. One night I was walking on the campus and I ran into Ken Inman, a boy I was really attracted to, *such* self-confidence, *so* good looking. I met him and I went, "Oh, wow! Oh, wow, he's so good looking!" The trouble is, that attitude blows it right there, because you start off relating to his good looks instead of to his maleness. And you have trouble talking to him and stuff.

But that night we were sitting around and talking, and we went to a birthday party at somebody's pad. There were a whole bunch of beautiful people, and Ken and I drank some mescaline punch and climbed up a hill and got really stoned, and we came down and goofed around all day long. Oh, wow, what a nice day! Then we went to a rock concert, and there were all these bands there, and bonfires and tents, really fine, really a neat thing, a full moon and rings of color around the moon, and stars out. It was just really amazing, especially since we were so stoned.

Ken and I spent the whole second night together, dancing, getting high. There were people huddled together all over the place, too high, freaking out, and it was really a weird atmosphere, and we slipped out into this field in back, just the two of us, and hugged each other and really felt close to each other, and it was really fun to trip with him. But he wouldn't let go his deepest inhibitions. He never kissed me. We'd hug and smile and be close, but he never kissed me. I wanted him to, so bad! But he never did. I still see him around the campus and I get really good vibes from him, and I want to get to know him, but nothing happens. Amazing! It blows my mind!

Then I met Piero, but we didn't get close for a long time, because we were both into a sarcasm trip, where our big number-one front was that we would be sarcastic to each other and we'd get into these sarcastic hassles, you know? We were both not into feeling and we couldn't really relate as good friends because we wouldn't allow ourselves to. The only time we really related was when we were drunk or stoned, and then we'd be affectionate toward each other and talk as friends, have a really good time. Come to think about it, that's the way it was at home. The only way we really related was through sarcasm. The rest of the time we were hassling each other. This is a way to cover up feeling.

Anyway, Piero went to Europe the next semester, and I wrote him and he wrote me back, and I could tell that he was changing, because instead of getting a typical sarcastic letter, I'd get a really fine letter. It was much more open, much more honest. These are the things you must work on twenty-four hours a day: being your real self, being open and honest in all your relationships. This is my constant endeavor: to *relate*.

After Piero, I began going with still another boy named Ray. I call him Ray III, because of the other two. He was one of the few male friends who showed me love in little ways, and we became really good friends and I let him know from the beginning that I didn't want anything else and I'm really glad I did that with him because I probably would have fucked him over otherwise. I mean, I was into friendship and not into sex, and I wanted him to know that from the beginning. But one day I was reading the local paper, and I saw that they'd arrested seventeen people for dope, and I started to read to see if I knew any of the names. Then I saw Ray III's name and it really blew my mind, and I called his house and his roommate said, "Oh, didn't you know? Ray got busted last night."

Ray told me the whole story later and he said he felt really fine about the whole thing. He felt good that the dope was at last out in the open and his parents knew about it now and the worst thing that could happen to him would be a short suspended sentence. He also said that he felt that I was his friend, and that he could love me as a friend, and he even wondered if our relationship could go further. We really kissed, you know, *really* kissed for the first time. I'm really confused about the whole thing. I love Ray as a friend, but I also feel very strongly that in order to be physical lovers, people have to be mental lovers first, and for a long time. I wonder if I'm really ready to be his lover.

Anyway, back to my freshman year. I tried sniffing some cocaine, and eventually worked my way through just about all the psychedelics. I even ate some peyote with my friends. It was awful tasting, and I don't think I'll do it again. I *do* like psychedelics. I take them because they help me to live the way I want to live, even if it's only for a short period of time. Psychedelics give me a real idea of how I could live totally. Like walking is so great when you're tripping, looking at trees and mountains and sky. Everything is so intensified, because of the psychedelics. And the pleasure of just being with friends is extra special, even their *dogs* are special. A day under psychedelics teaches me about the intensity of living, the joys, the perceptions, the excitements that come from heightened awareness. Now if I could only heighten my awareness without taking psychedelics!

The only trouble with my freshman year was that I was having a lot of good times, but they only seemed to come when I was tripping. When I wasn't tripping, I felt depressed and down. I couldn't seem to find any happiness outside of drugs. And my relationships with men didn't seem to be leading into anything. I longed for something deeper and more meaningful. Unfortunately, it was just about at my lowest point that I met Moon at a party. He was blond, twenty-three or twenty-four years old, the son of a rich man who gives the university a lot of money. At first he was good to talk to and impressive to be with.

Well, I was in a strange stage. I'd been having trouble relating to good men. I could relate to them as friends, but not as lovers. I suppose it was that strange period of a girl's life where she's sort of attracted to assholes. Like Moon. A girl gets involved in the whole mystique of the nasty snarling type of sadistic man, the *macho* type who treats you rough and makes demands. I'm over that now, thank God, but at the time I was real negative about myself. I was thinking about all the things I didn't like about myself, and unconsciously maybe I couldn't relate to good men because I didn't think I deserved them, and I was trying to punish myself with men like Moon.

We started sleeping together after about six weeks. He had wanted to from the beginning. The whole thing was so negative. I wasn't passionate enough, I wasn't this enough, I wasn't that enough. I knew I didn't love him, but there *was* an attraction. He was such a male chauvinist. If I was at his place he'd insist that I cook for him. The woman cooks! One night he told me he wanted a partner who would come over almost every night of the week because he was a very sexually frustrated person and he needed a lot of sex. But he never *ever* made any reference to what the woman needed.

In bed he would take care of himself first, except that it bothered his ego that I didn't have orgasms. It was a big ego trip for him to give orgasms to girls. He was really sick! Amazing! He was the devil. He wanted a *complete* sexual trip out of me. He wanted a constant sex partner. He never mentioned love or feeling. What an asshole he was! I must have been on a real weird trip, to take the shit that he put out. I had no orgasms, and I began to think that I was incapable of having them. I was so unhappy.

At the time I was taking birth control pills, but I forgot them one night. That's all it took. Soon I realized that I might be pregnant, but I went to the doctor to make sure. The doctor confirmed my fears. I told Moon, and he said, "Aw, you're not pregnant! No *way!* You're just using that as an excuse not to sleep with me!"

I said, "Aw, forget it!"

When I finally convinced him I was pregnant, he said, "Well, we've got to work out an abortion." There was nothing about how I felt, or whether I was in any danger. He simply said, "I've got some doctors that'll do it. I'll go make some calls." He split, without even asking me how I felt.

Moon arranged for the abortion in another state. Just before I went away, I started to write him a note. I wrote, "I'll be aborting *our* baby." But I threw the note away. How could I connect him, Moon, and me, Bonnie, into *our* and then into *baby*. How could such a deathly relationship with one dead person, Moon, and one dying person, Bonnie—how could this relationship produce a life?

Moon seemed to think that his job was done when he found a doctor to perform the operation. I had to find the money. When I couldn't get it all up, Moon fussed and hollered and finally *lent* me a hundred dollars. Mind you, he had just bought a new Harley to go with his TR-6 and his Jeep, so he wasn't hurting for money. But he's such a bastard.

The abortion was easy. In this little country hospital there were a bunch of girls having them. There was one girl about fourteen, holding her mother's hand. I was glad when they finally put me under to perform the operation. I woke up in the recovery room and this hip young nurse said, "You must be into marijuana or something, because you came out of the gas so fast. Look at all these other people, they're not awake yet." And I looked around and saw all these bodies, out cold. The fourteen-year-old had been under for three hours, and they were trying to wake her up. I guess my experience with drugs paid off.

A few days later I went back to school, and my mother and father were waiting for me at the dorm. Somehow they'd gotten the word. I just broke up. My mother said that she loved me, not to be upset, she understood. I felt, "Ooooooh, how *strange* I feel about this."

But my parents were fine. They treated me great. After all our troubles, I figured they'd kill me for something like this, but instead they were perfect. They paid me back all the money that I'd spent, and my father said he guessed he'd repay Moon, too. But later on he decided against it. He said it would teach Moon a lesson to lose his hundred dollars.

Anyway, a week later Moon came over and demanded his money back. I was amazed! He said he felt he had it coming. I was really pissed! I told him what an insensitive jerk he was. He was standing there in the middle of the room shouting how good he'd been to me through the whole thing, and how *sensitive* he was. He screamed it out, "I'm sensitive, I'm *so* sensitive! Goddamn it, I'm the most fucking sensitive person you know!" Screaming and yelling out of control. Amazing!

I said, "You're not sensitive, you're just fucked! Get out of here!" But he wouldn't leave. He just kept yelling and screaming and telling me that I had to give the hundred dollars back, he *had* to have it, and my parents owed it to him. He demanded their phone number in Miami Beach so he could call them and ask for the money. Oh,

I should have given him the number! I told my dad later, and he said, "Honey, you made a mistake. You should have given him the number. That's one phone call I'd have enjoyed getting."

The whole thing blew my mind. First, that Moon was such a fucker; and second, that I could ever even have talked to a man like that, that I was *so* stupid. But I was in that dumb stage where all you're looking for is a big, dumb, dominant type of male.

The worst part of it is, Moon almost made me lose my whole philosophy of life, which is that people are all good underneath. But I concluded that he was just fucked up. A falsely strong man, a fuck-'em-and-forget-'em type, covering up his weaknesses. I knew that if I scratched deeply enough I would find good in Moon, too. But I just didn't feel like going through the process.

Well, since then my whole sexual life has been aimed at overcoming what I went through in negative relationships with men like Salter and Moon. I'm learning slowly. I've gone with fifteen or twenty men since then, and I'm just barely beginning to learn to have orgasms and to enjoy sex. My generation is still trying to get over the idea that sex is dirty. We want *your* generation to be the last one that goes around with that stupid idea. Loving is the thing. It's not dirty. Oh, how much I want to love! *So* much!

I know I've just let my parents down terribly since I've been in college, but there was just no other way. Our values are so different. Like they desperately wanted me to join a sorority. It blew their minds when I didn't. My mother said, "Well, we really *want* you to. It'd be so important for you."

I said, "Mother, the whole idea with sororities is to maintain the status quo, so that society will never change, never grow up. It's a way of teaching girls to be exactly like their mothers. It's just not for me."

She argued on, and I finally told her, "Mother, stop having all these expectations of me. Just let me be me, then everything will work out all right." I told her. "I have to negate everything about myself to find myself.

I hope you understand. I have to negate my looks, how I dress, all the worries about how I appear to others." I said, "Mother, you can't consider me as your representative forever. I'm only representing myself from now on. It doesn't matter anymore what your friends think of me or even what my friends think of me, but only what *I* think of me."

Anyway, in the summer after my freshman year, we had some pretty hairy talks. At one point my father said he would cut off my finances completely if I continued to live a life-style that he didn't approve of. One night he said, "Why do you always lie to me?"

I said, "Because I fear you. I'm afraid that you'll just cut me off and say that I'm not your daughter anymore. You already said that once."

He said, "Well, that won't happen as long as you conform to our life-style." Which means it *is* going to happen, because I'm not changing life-styles, and they're not either.

The talks got hot and heavy. My mother freaked out a couple of times. She started screaming and saying she wanted to kill herself. And she gave me a guilt feeling that I was causing all this. Then she calmed down and said maybe we all needed to go to a psychiatrist. That takes the heat off her personally, see? We *all* need one. All emphasis is no emphasis. And anyway, my father doesn't think he needs a psychiatrist. It's everybody else that's out of step.

I went back to school for my sophomore year and moved into this apartment with Riva and Laurel, and for awhile I didn't see my parents. Then my mother wrote that she was going to a psychologist and I was amazed. One night I called her and told her that I had met a boy named Phil, and I was going to Chicago to visit him, and I thought, "Well, now she'll freak out over this."

But she said, "That's wonderful!"

I said to myself, "What?"

She said, "Why don't I send you a hundred dollars for the trip?"

I said, "Oh, mother, you don't have to do that."

She said, "I *want* to. Oh, by the way, I'm not gonna tell your father, because he's been going through some really tense times."

"Oh," I said.

She said, "One thing, just be careful."

"What do you mean, mom?"

"Don't get pregnant. Take precautions."

I thought, my God, this doesn't sound like *my* mother. I wonder what's going on. She must have sensed my confusion, because she said, "I know I'm suddenly sounding like a liberal mother, but I'm having hard times myself, and I realize that I can no longer dictate to you."

Well, I found out what it was all about when I went home over Thanksgiving, and mother picked me up at the airport, and she was acting real peculiar. I said, "Mom, something's on your mind, isn't it?"

She said, "Yes but it'll wait till we get home."

On the long drive she began talking about life-styles. I told her she'd never understood what was going on inside me, she was always so concerned with all the extrinsic things like my friends, how we dressed, how we talked, etcetera. She started crying. She said, "Yes, I can see what we did to you, darling, and I feel bad about it. We put you through a lot, didn't we?" The tears were streaming down her face as she drove.

At home she poured herself a drink and told me to sit down and started rapping. She said she'd been suspicious that my father was going out with another woman, a woman in their bridge club. She was sure that my father and this woman were making weekend trips to other places. He would always say he was going on business but he would never leave a number, and he would come home and act distant and strange.

Mom told me that when he came home from one of the trips, she couldn't stand it any longer and she said to him, "You've been seeing Felicia, haven't you?"

My dad said, "Yes I have."

Well, they sat right down and talked the whole thing over, and now both of them were seeing a psychiatrist, and trying to hold things together for the sake of me and my sister.

My first reaction about my father was, "Why, that fucking hypocrite!" He'd given me all that shit about, "What are your standards? Do you condone living with people out of wedlock?" Bah, bah, bah, and all that shit, and even while he was telling me this he was running around with that bitch down the street.

But I got over that attitude quickly, and I decided that I'm more *sorry* for him than anything else. I realize that he's kind of lost inside, and his outer-strength trip, his big manly muscle, his big manly authority, his big loud voice, and his authoritarian style are all to keep him from revealing the truth to himself. He's sad and lonely. It sort of relieved me to find out.

Anyway, there's been an improvement in the relationship between me and my father. The last time I went home he was real careful how he treated me. He must have realized how hypocritical he'd been. One night I was going out with my old friends. Tom I and the hairs, and he knew it, and he said real brusquely, "Where are you going?"

I said, "Out with the freaks."

He said, "Well, let me tell you one thing, younglady—" But then he said, "Oh, never mind," and he walked out of the room. I think he's begun to realize that I'm an adult, and that what I do is my own business.

Laurel Milne says:

The only trouble with Bonnie is that sometimes she's not direct and open about showing her love and affection. I mean she puts it through some kind of filter first, and it comes out as cutesy, sweetsy, "play" type thing. Personally, I don't mind because I know her and I know how she feels about me and Riva—she loves us *completely*—and the affection is no less real, no matter *what* filters she puts it through. But to an outsider. all this cutey-cute stuff might not look honest, it might turn some people off.

Bonnie's sexual problems are inside herself. I mean, she just doesn't enjoy plain fucking. She would enjoy it if she could find somebody to love and fuck at the same time, but she keeps concealing her real self from men, and so she doesn't get involved with real love. If she would just open herself up. But she won't.

Riva and Laurel and I have been having some great times together here in our apartment. Like we're always learning, experimenting with each other. Like the other night five or six friends came over, and we dropped some psychedelics, and we got into seeing how many of us could kiss each other and touch at the same time. Amazing! We wound up on the big bed, rolling around hugging and kissing each other and feeling good about each other and just letting our hands move over the bodies, the crevices, the valleys of other people's bodies, not knowing who it was or what it felt like, just knowing that it was being human and alive. Then Laurel came in and took off her clothes and then Tom II and I took ours off and everybody took their clothes off, and then we did the same thing, hugging and kissing, kissing girls, kissing males, males kissing males, girls kissing girls, and just hugging or loving and feeling good about friendships, feeling good about a sense of community. Then we all took a shower, and went to bed, after a lot more hugging and kissing.

Just after midnight my new boyfriend, Swede, wandered in, and I threw everybody else out of the room, and Swede and I slept alone, and hugged and just felt good, feeling each other's nude body without the need for sex. Other people wouldn't understand, but we're all born with a body, without the clothes and ornaments that we wear, and somehow when people are unclothed around people, it helps them to break down some of the barriers that they have and just to be human beings, without sex roles and without games and without all the shit we put in front of us, without the paranoia about what other people are thinking. The more time I spend

naked with males, the easier it gets to be, the less paranoid, the less afraid, the more loving.

About the only discordant note in the apartment—and
it's not really his fault—is Michael Gold, Laurel's boyfriend. He's so pathetic! The other night we had a house
meeting. We needed to get some things out into the
open, and Michael really blew my mind. He started rapping about his hangups, and they're so complex. He's
really messed up. He feels that people don't love him
so he hides it by developing intellectual friendships that
conceal the lack of love. But his number one problem
is that he doesn't love *himself* enough, so naturally he
wouldn't feel that others could love him. He has the
most terrible blocks to feeling. As he spoke, I felt so
helpless, there was *nothing* that I could say or do. He
has *so* much to work through, just *so* much. The only
help I can give him is to let him know I care about him.

The amazing thing about Laurel is that she can stay
with Michael, because he's so fucked up. It's amazing
that she can show him so much love, that she doesn't
get terribly, terribly frustrated about how he's not changing. because he really isn't. He has huge blocks to changing. He keeps trying to find himself through reading,
through babbling, but it isn't there, it's in his head. I
hope that living in this house will help him, because all
three of us honestly love him.

But he does get on our nerves. When I'm feeling
harassed or feeling down, he *really* gets on my nerves.
He plays little child games, things I did when I was
younger. Like he's on a sibling trip, competing with
siblings, and not trying to reach out to people. He re-
minds me of things I used to do with my sister. He's
trying to work through his sibling problems with us because he never had any siblings of his own, but I told
him, "I'm *not* your sister, and I won't play the sibling
game with you."

There was a scene awhile back when I started to put
on our Cat Stevens record, and he said, "Oh, don't do
that!"

"Why?" I said.

He said, "The equipment isn't working right. You'll wreck the record."

I said, "Well, it's *my* record, and it's my apartment, and I *want* to listen to it."

He said, "Well, it's my opinion that you shouldn't put it on."

I said, "Well, I'm putting it on."

He said, "Well, if I were you I wouldn't put it on." And that was like the last word, from the oracle, you know? So I went ahead and put it on. But the overtones were very bad. Do you catch the bad vibes? He has this thing about getting his own way, even when he knows that his own way is not my way or not even necessarily the right way. He just *has* to make his point, and even after he's made his point, he needs to keep expanding on it, pushing it into you.

He did a scene with Riva, where she started out by saying how neat it was that her parents had finally joined the Republican Club. Michael said, "Well, I don't think that's so neat."

Riva explained that it was neat because at least they were getting involved in *something*, even if it was on the wrong side.

Michael would just not leave her alone. He kept pecking away. She finally said, "Well, I understand how you feel. Now why don't you just drop the subject."

He said, "Well, this is something *very* important." He kept making his point over and over, sticking it into Riva until it really must have hurt. She was just on her back. pleading, saying, "Look, enough is enough," over and over. He was just really screwed up about it. It blew my mind, I could feel Riva hurting.

Laurel Milne says:

That time when Bonnie got physical with Michael and gave him an erection, wow! That was one of the high points of our life together. We all felt so happy and *natural* about it! I was *so* happy for Michael, because I *want* him to get involved with other females. And we all three got in bed together afterwards, because we were so happy and open about it. Get Bonnie to tell you the whole story; I'm sure she'll be glad to.

Sometimes Michael's just so pathetic and sweet, you want to hug him. One night a whole bunch of people were here, and we all dropped some woodruff and went to see *2001*, and it was fun, a real space trip. We walked home together, and it felt like good times. Michael was complaining about the cold, and I was cold too, and we rushed home ahead of the others and jumped into my bed, getting warm and talking. Because we'd tripped on the woodruff, our capacity for being out in the open was expanded, and I could see my blocks and Michael's blocks just floating away. I felt really close to him as a friend. I could see his loneliness and my loneliness, and I could see our strength, too.

We took off our clothes, and soon we were hugging each other. We were hugging like friends, you know, not with sexual overtones, at least not on my part. I know Laurel told all about this, and she told me I should tell my version of it too, and I'll be glad to, but how should I begin? Well, we talked, and—I don't know—well, we held each other, and—we—talked some more, and looked—at each other, and—I don't know—Michael just got a hard-on, and Laurel came in right after that, and I hadn't even noticed the hard-on because I hadn't even been thinking about sex, believe me! And I didn't notice any sexual overtones, and it wasn't any big deal anyway, just something that happens to males sometimes, and they have trouble controlling it.

I thought about it later and I wondered if Michael hadn't felt ugly and like a duck all his life, and here he was with me, the beach beauty, the social person, and that might have hit him and given him the hard-on. Here he was with a person he admired and envied, him, the ugly duckling, and it sort of overwhelmed him, and he got hard. But all I was thinking about was friendship.

Anyway, when Laurel came in, it was no big deal. I mean, people sometimes get hard-ons, and it doesn't imply that we were having sexual attraction or anything. And anyway it doesn't matter, because if people are secure enough with those they love, they're capable of having multiple relationships, so it was all cool anyway.

The important thing is, living in this house with us three women will help Michael because we all do honestly love him and he needs that security of love and none of the other false securities that he gets behind, like talking your ear off or running back to his books. The three of us can give Michael a very, very deep love, and no one else can. I wonder if he knows how lucky he is.

NATHALIE SEYMOUR
SMYTH, 22
Senior, School of Education

The only true education comes through the stimulation of the child's powers by the demands of the social situations in which he finds himself.
John Dewey, 1897

I use two family names because I had two fathers, Thomas Llewellyn Seymour and Lucius Smyth. I loved them both very much. I have very few memories of my biological father, Tom Seymour, but they're good memories. He was studying to be a doctor, and the family didn't have much money when I was born. I was the fourth child; three brothers were spaced two years apart, and we lived in a Quonset hut on the hospital grounds in Chicago. There was still a housing shortage, and student doctors didn't make much money, but we were a happy family. The family joke was that we kept our silverware in the sandbox. We didn't have much money for toys, so my mother let us take the silverware out to the sandbox, and sometimes she'd have to come out and borrow an extra piece if anyone came to dinner.

I remember my first father as a strong, gentle man, really not that much different from my second one. He came home for lunch most days; that was a luxury. My brothers and I used to play a game that we called "Daddy and Indians." We'd go into his bedroom on Sunday morning and tie him to his bed, and then we'd all run and hide, and he'd try to get out of his knots and chase us, and we'd have a great glorious wrestling match.

He was like a big kid in some ways, my first father. He had this lock of brown hair that fell over his forehead. He could never control it. Sometimes it seemed that he and my mother were always laughing. Maybe they knew they had to get their laughs in while they could. My father had had severe rheumatic fever as a child, and he'd always been told he wouldn't live a normal life-span. So maybe he tried to squeeze some extra life into his allotted years. I don't know. But I only have good memories of him. I remember after he got pneumonia, he was in bed next to the door of the Quonset hut, and mama was taking care of him, and he was lying there with his head propped up and telling me a story and laughing his head off, and the next thing I knew he was gone. They took him into the same hospital where he was taking his residency.

I guess I should feel all broken up about it, but I honestly don't. My first father was a good man, a happy man, and he lived a good and rewarding and useful life. Later on his colleagues told my mother that he was a marvelous diagnostician, and that he would have made a brilliant doctor. I'm proud of that.

I know that all the details of his death are buried deeply in my brain, where I can't get at them, and it's probably just as well. Sometimes I wonder if I remember his death at all, or do I remember the memory of the death, or do I remember what other people have told me since? I don't know. I do remember the great chill that came over the house. Friends arrived and talked to mother, and they all spoke in hushed voices. My brothers sat quietly, and my mother tried not to cry. I remember that scene better than I remember the loss of my father. It must have been a terrible blow to my mother to be left with four young children. My father lingered on for five weeks in the hospital, but toward the end there wasn't any question what would happen. One night my mother came home from the hospital and she had a gift for each of us, a little thing to take our minds off what was happening. She gave me a child's set of needles and thread. I still have it.

In some ways I learned from my first father's death. When someone close to you dies, you think the world will stop, but it never does. It keeps right on turning. As soon as you realize that, you're ready to go on yourself. You stop wasting your time with morbid thoughts, you stop brooding. It's hard to lose your father when you're five years old, but there's a positive aspect to it, because you learn a difficult lesson at a very early age: that death is inevitable, that it's natural, that it's *bearable*. I know kids who go ten, twenty years without experiencing the death of a loved one, and they worry about it, and they dream about it, and they say, oh, how will I *stand* it if I lose my mother or my father or my boyfriend or my husband. They don't know what I've known for seventeen years: that you'll stand it, that you'll even grow from it, and it's not the end. There was a time in my teens when I tried to relate everything that happened to me to the death of my father, but I think I exaggerated. The loss was sad, but it didn't create a terrible childhood. I had a lovely childhood. I was a very happy person. I was also lucky.

My father died in the fall, and that Christmas I can remember waking up to find four bikes under the tree in the little Quonset hut. My mother must have used some of her insurance money to try to lift the cloud from the house. These are the things that you remember long after you forget the death: little proofs of love.

There was a time in my childhood when I might have been overinfluenced by the loss. I was always afraid that someone else in my family would go to the hospital and die. I'd get up early in the morning to walk my big brothers to the school bus. It was terribly important to me. One morning I got up at the last minute, and by the time I got dressed, they'd already left. That terrified me. So the next night I slept in my clothes so I'd be able to jump right out of bed in the morning and go with them. Somehow I felt that I had to walk them to the bus or I might lose them. I was very protective of what family I had left. I still am.

At the same time I was always very affectionate to older men. I was cute, a little redheaded girl with pigtails and freckles, and I exploited it. I got to know a German boy down the block, and through him his father, a strange, lovable man who still had shrapnel in him from

World War II. I loved his accent and the funny things he used to say. I would ask him if his shrapnel hurt, but he wouldn't talk about that. Once or twice he told me the story of how he fought for the Germans, and how he married an American WAC and came to this country. He told me that the German people were good people, and that they had a culture that went back two thousand years, and he told me that a group called the Nazis wrecked everything. More than once I saw tears in his eyes as he told me about his homeland, and even as a little kid of five or six, I was interested in going to Germany and meeting the people like him, except that I didn't want to meet any of the people he called Nazis.

The real strength in those years was my mother. She and I were as close as twins. When I could barely hold a needle, she taught me how to sew. She could knit sweaters almost as fast as a machine, and she taught me to knit before I went to school. She took me into the kitchen and showed me her recipes, and I was making full meals for the family by the time I was eight years old. Complicated things like spaghetti and meatballs, macaroni and cheese, fried eggs and toast! I loved it, and I loved the feeling of being the lady of the house, even if I was only making some silly thing like macaroni. My mother always told me how delicious it was and compared me with the *cordon bleu* chefs. I almost believed her.

My mother knew exactly what we needed, and she gave it to us. Our house was always full of rabbits and gerbils and white rats and cats and fish and dogs. I never remember having less than three dogs. We had a warm and happy house, and we were warm and happy people. My father's death only brought us more tightly together.

I suppose there was a time when I overreacted to the suffering of others, probably because I was feeling sorry for myself, although I really had no reason to be. I remember that there was a girl in my kindergarten class with a deformed hand. It was almost as though she was born without a hand, with just a few fingers an inch or so long. I related to her and identified with her terribly;

there were times when I felt she was me and I was her. I was terrified that people would insult her or humiliate her and make her feel bad. One day a little brat of a boy was walking around her, holding his hand in a twisted shape and looking at her and leering, and she started to cry, and I whaled into that kid and knocked him down, and I remember that I was screaming and crying myself. I had the strength of ten, and I beat the crap out of that little brat.

When I was seven or eight, I became very conscious of not having a man around the house, and I began to bug my mother about finding someone. I must have driven her nuts. Once she asked me what I wanted for Christmas, and I said, "To see you in a wedding dress." What a little brat!

One day I came home from school, and this beautiful guitar music was coming from our house, and a strange man was sitting in the living room playing. The sound fascinated me. It sent shivers down me. My mother introduced me. She said, "Nathalie, this is Luke Smyth. I met Mr. Smyth playing bridge."

A few days later I found a box of candy by the door, with my mother's name on it. My mother became very gay and started doing crazy things. One night she dropped a dozen eggs, and she laughed about it! She washed my brothers' pants with the belts still in them. She stripped the gears of our old car. Then she went on a few trips with Luke, and I remember being shuffled off to relatives' houses while she was away. My brothers and I sat back and watched and said, "Oh, ho! *We* understand." We picked up on it fast, and we loved it. We were absolutely enthusiastic about Luke.

One night my mother said to me, "What do you think of Luke?"

I said, "Why don't you marry him?" Just like that. I was eight years old. I've read a lot about how children are violently jealous when their parents take up with other adults, but we were exactly the opposite. We loved Luke from the beginning. This is not the story of the wicked old stepfather. Oh, my brothers might have competed with Luke for a very short time, but when they found out what kind of a person he was, they stopped and went to the other extreme. As for me, I'd always identified with my mother, and I was overjoyed to see her with a new man.

After the wedding we packed into Luke's car and headed for our new hometown. It was a two-day drive, and on the way I began to see that we could be a true family again. Luke was trying very hard, but he wasn't sickening about it. Each day he would buy us a tiny nonsense gift. A penny whistle. A cheap harmonica. He was marvelous with children, and he *should* have been; children were his life's work. He was a social worker, dealing mostly with troubled boys. Now he's in charge of a whole social program, and he makes $11,500 a year, and he's still just as concerned and excited about his boys as he was when he was starting out.

We moved into an apartment in a house occupied mostly by Luke's relatives, with children all over the place, and we hit it off instantly. There was no tough period of adjustment. Within a few months, Luke had legally adopted all four of us. I remember how exciting it was to take out my school book and add my new name to my old.

From then on we were all known as the crazy Smyths, not because we were really crazy, but because we were always doing something together, laughing our heads off about it, and enjoying one another. Once in a while my father would bring a new "brother" into the family, a boy who needed extra help, or an orphan, and we would try to make him feel like one of us. We felt it was like the Smyths against the world. We presented a united front. Everybody talked about us. "There go the Smyths. When you see one, you see them all."

My mother and father both knew that families ran on organization, that if everybody had a job to do and knew he *had* to do it, there would be no beefing and griping. They exploited the fact that we loved them both. For example, we fought to sit next to Luke at dinner, and at first there were arguments about it. Then he and my mother devised a rotating system. You sat next to Luke for one week, and you shifted each Sunday. The person who sat next to him washed the dishes. the next one cleared the table and said grace, and the next person dried. It worked well all through my childhood. We never had another fight about who would sit next to Luke, or who would do the dishes.

My parents had a knack for knowing what was right with children. We'd sometimes take long driving trips in the summer, and like all kids we'd get nervous and restless in the car. So before each meal the whole family did calisthenics. We'd pull up at a Howard Johnson's for lunch, and we'd pile out of the car, stretch out on the lawn and do push-ups and sit-ups and jumping-jacks, and the people inside would look out the window at us, and then we'd calmly get to our feet, go inside, and order lunch.

Financial responsibility was drilled into us early. Even before Luke and mama were married, my brother Bobby lost a quarter, and he went crying to Luke about it, and Luke simply said, "Well, that *is* too bad, Bobby. I'll help you hunt for it." It would have been an easy cop-out for Luke to just reach into his pocket and give Bobby another quarter and dry his tears, but that wouldn't have taught Bobby anything. He and Luke searched for the quarter for a while, and when they couldn't find it, Luke gave Bobby a little two-hour job to do and paid him a quarter for it. You learn from things like that; you don't learn from money that's handed to you.

When we got a little older, my mother and father gave us a better sense of taking part in the home. We played a game where each of us kids would make out a household budget, trying to guess exactly how much each item in the budget would cost in the coming month. At the end of the month we would sit around and tally it up, and whoever had come the closest would get a prize, maybe an extra helping of dessert or something like that. Then we'd have a big round table discussion about running a household. Later on we were given a chance to figure out actual budgets, and my mother and father tried to stick to them, and showed us when we made mistakes. Each of us had regular jobs, and a regular allowance, and savings accounts. We had cardboard money trees that we fitted dimes into, and when the tree was full of dimes, we'd take it off to the bank. I have the same savings account today that I had when I was eight years old.

I think about all this when I hear some of my friends talk about the Protestant ethic and how it's destroyed their parents and made them think of nothing but money. Well, my father was deeply involved in the Protestant ethic, the idea that work is its own reward, and there's nothing wrong with going out and working hard to make money. But he didn't let it ruin his life. He wanted money for our family, he wanted raises, he wanted financial security, and he was willing to work for it, but the dollar wasn't the sole motivating force. He made a joy out of everything he touched, work included. At the end of the day, he'd come home tired, happily tired, with maybe two or three of his young boys hanging around his neck, laughing and happy because they were going to spend the night with us. My father never had to run to the liquor cabinet when he came home. Maybe he'd collapse into a chair out of sheer fatigue, and we'd all jump on him, and we'd see a man who'd managed to make himself tired and happy at the same time.

A child learns by imitating, not by being told, and when I'd been around Luke for a year or two, I was already set in my ways about money. I've worked my way through every year of college, and I'll continue. It just plain makes me feel better. I may not *have to,* but I just feel better if I'm paying my own way. It's deeply ingrained in me. I know how marvelous it feels to work and sacrifice to get something for yourself. I learned that from Luke.

There was no end to our family discussions, or to the respect that my mother and father seemed to have for our own little brains. If we brought home a D or a C on our report cards, the attitude was, "This isn't good, but let's sit down and find out *how* and *why* it happened." Then we'd all sit around and discuss it, we'd be *involved* with each other, and Luke more than anyone, in his role as head of the family. There was never any punishment, any recrimination, for poor grades. We were expected to get good grades, and if we didn't we worked it all out as a family, and we supported and encouraged each other.

I suppose the main thing that Lucius Smyth accomplished was to involve us all, my brothers and my mother and me, in a social approach to the world, the family of man, that sort of thing. I never think of my fellow humans as my opponents, as so many Americans do. They are part of my family. We help each other. We stand together. That's the biggest thing I learned from my father: tolerance of others, regardless of who they are or how they treat me. If I meet someone who gives me a negative impression, I always think, "Now what's in his background that makes him act like that?" I always think, "What happened to him that gave him no choice except to act the way he's acting?" And I always think, "No matter how unpleasant this person treats me, he's my brother, I'm related to him, I'm involved in him." I guess you'd call me a determinist or a behaviorist. I got that all from Luke. He didn't teach me any of it; he *showed* me all of it. Sometimes it's hard to maintain the humanistic attitude when you're being insulted, or ripped off, or reviled, and sometimes my friends tell me to get off it, all men *aren't* brothers, and knock off the sickening Pollyanna approach. But loving my fellow humans isn't something I've assumed or adopted or put on to make an impression or create an effect. It's something deep inside me. Sometimes I would see my stepfather watching the news on television and some little Korean or Vietnamese child would come on, maybe an amputee or blind or something like that, and I'd look up at Luke and there'd be tears in his eyes, or he'd quickly turn off the set and walk out of the room. He was involved. He was *Ulysses*: "I am a part of all that I have met. . . ." He lived that; he still does. He cast this attitude over our whole family, and we're very lucky for it. It's hard for me to think of anybody as *gooks* or *kikes* or *niggers*. I think of them as just people, like you and me.

You might think from this that my father was highly political, but he wasn't political at all. He was so involved in what he was doing with young boys that he never had time for politics or religion or any organized things like that. My mother was active, but my father was too busy with his work. We still joke with him about it. We tell him that he's a political ignoramus. Lately he's beginning to develop a little bit of political consciousness because several of the boys he helped in his program were killed in Vietnam and it turns him purple. I said to him one night, "Why, papa, you're a dove!"

He beamed, and he said, "Why, by gosh, I guess you're right!" And we all laughed, because this was the first political accent we'd ever seen in him.

The first thing I ever wanted to be was an author. When I was in the fourth grade, just after my mother's remarriage, I wrote a book. My mother typed it for me, and it came out to thirty-six typewritten pages. It was about a family, naturally, a family that went through a lot of adventures and moved to Alaska. There was some kind of weird mystery, and one of the members in the family hit his head on the bottom of a pool and suddenly remembered the existence of some gold pieces in a hat, and oh, it was all mixed up. The whole thing hung on a case of amnesia, and after the family found the gold, they lived happily ever after. We were all enthusiastic about the story and we even tried to find a publisher. But the manuscript was rejected. I think I know why. There was one scene where the family was in a plane, and they crash-landed in Alaska, and they stepped out and took a taxi home. Maybe the editors thought that was a slight strain of credibility. Maybe the manuscript needed a little work there!

When I was ten a neighborhood boy took me into the bushes to tell me the facts of life. He was only twelve, but he was big for his age, and when he told me to take off my clothes, I got scared. My mother had advised me not to let anybody see me naked. So he grabbed me and began feeling me, and then he stuck his finger in me, and it scared me, it terrified me! I ran home and I was physically sick. My mother could tell there was something wrong, and we called a family council, and I told them what happened. My father explained very patiently that he knew the boy, that the boy came from a troubled and peculiar family, and that what happened was sick and sad and sorrowful, but not evil or bad. He said the boy was emotionally disturbed and really couldn't help himself, and the best thing for me was to just stay away from him. I appreciated this, but I was left with a funny feeling about sex.

Right after that, mother told me the facts of life herself. First she gave me a book, *Where Babies Come From*, and then she told me the whole story. She made it seem loving and natural and beautiful, and I pretty much accepted what she said, but I still couldn't forget that boy sticking his finger in and out of me, and using terrible words.

I went through several periods; I don't think there was anything special about them. At the beginning of junior high I became obsessed with sex, and so did most of my girl friends. One day Bobby brought home a sackful of illustrated smut books, and I started reading them. There were bad drawings of Elizabeth Taylor making it with a police dog, things like that. I used to read them in the cellar. One time my father walked down and saw what I was reading, but he didn't do anything. He just said, "Hello," and walked right out. I was so embarrassed; I knew that he had seen what I was reading. I heaved that book across the room. I was *so* ashamed. He could have destroyed me by bawling me out, but he was too wise for that.

I suppose it would be too much to expect that such wonderful parents would be completely relaxed and natural about sex, and they weren't. I mean, they didn't fill our heads with ideas of guilt and evil, but they did have the typical morality of their generation, and little by little it rubbed off on me. Like one of my older cousins got a girl pregnant and had to marry her, and I had to find out about it from my brothers because my parents would never tell me. I realized that to them the story was too difficult to relate to a young teen-age girl. I realized that they were uptight and even ashamed about my cousin. And of course this gave me the idea that premarital sex is bad, much too evil to talk about.

Later on my oldest brother began a little swinging of his own, and one day my mother said, "Nat, do you know what it's like to find out that your son is having an active sex life?" She looked distraught, as though she'd failed, as though her whole life was a mistake because one of my brothers had become sexually active. So the computer that we call a brain programmed this into my thinking: that premarital sex was really *out*. I identified strongly with my mother, and anything that troubled her troubled me.

This doesn't mean that my mother and father were prudish about sex, because they weren't. Not a bit. We talked about it a lot, and my mother and I spent hours discussing what I could expect as a married woman. But our sexual conversations were strictly in the context of marriage, and this reinforced my idea that any other sexual activity was wrong. This was the predominant sexual ethic of the generations before mine, and my parents were quite normal in accepting it, and in passing it along to the rest of us.

By the time I went into high school my biggest problem was the fact that I had a small bust. In those years there was so much emphasis on the bustline. *Everybody* talked about it. You'd look through a girl's blouse and if you could see her bra people would say, "She's really *fast!*" And if she was full in the bust you knew that she had it made, socially.

Well, I come from a family of small-busted women. Even in the tenth grade I didn't wear a bra because there simply wasn't anything to put in it. I was ten years ahead of my time! Nobody wears a bra now, or they wear the no-bra bra. But when I was in high school I felt left out.

After a while my mother and I decided to put a little padding in my bras, and it became a family joke because I'd wear a dress and the darts wouldn't look right. Oh, it was so funny! The whole family kidded me about it. I'd go to a dance and gyrate around and end up with my falsies eight inches below my bustline and I'd look like some weird creature with four boobs. My brothers kidded me about it constantly. They made up a little rhyme about my mother and me:

> We fill up with cotton
> What God has forgotten.

Like almost all high school girls I had a time when I wasn't dating much, and I was worried about it. My mother and I would sit down and talk about it. She'd say, "Don't worry, your day's going to come." In high school a few years ago, girls lived and died on whether they dated or not, it was *crucial*. My brothers always had a lot of dates, and they went with very slick girls, and I compared myself to them and found myself terribly wanting. My lack of dates was hard on my head. Nowadays it's different. The kids have better sense. They can take dating or leave it.

Once again my mother came to my rescue. She realized that what was really happening was that I was a late bloomer, and everything would happen in due time. She gave me a lot of support. One night she said, "All those girls that you talk about that are dating all the time, do you really think they're telling the truth? I think if you checked you'd find out it's more talk than anything else." So I checked, and she was right. I found out that most of the girls were upset about not dating, but instead of talking about it they'd strut around and pretend. After that I felt better because I realized the problem was mostly in my head, and it was in the other girls' heads too.

When I did go on a date I was Miss Prissy-prim. I didn't allow necking. I kissed a few times, that was all. I was repressed and nervous about things like that and I didn't know how to handle boys. Later on I learned about the Electra complex, and I could see the relevance of it in my own life. I was always hung up on older men, and terribly protective and jealous of my stepfather, and I think it was because I never had a chance to work my way through the Electra complex with my real father; he died before I could complete the process. This had a profound effect on my relationship with men as I got older. Even in high school I was extremely protective of Luke. If my parents had an argument I'd jump in and say, "Oh, please. stop! Stop or you'll get divorced!" I was always afraid I was going to lose him. If he went away to a convention, I'd be upset the whole week he was gone. My parents could never fly on the same plane together because I'd throw a fit. Well, it's not hard to understand why I acted this way. I was still in the middle of the Electra thing. Men were *terribly* important to me, so important that when a boy did ask me for a date, I'd be uptight and nervous and afraid that I'd blow the whole thing, and usually he'd take me home and never call again. Male-female relationships were *too* important. I was terrified to give my love openly for fear I'd lose the boy. or I'd fail him and let him down in some way; or if I did let him neck, I would do it wrong, and he would reject me. I had too much invested in males, and for a long time I couldn't break out of the pattern and give myself to anyone.

So instead of having a big, happy, active dating life, I got myself a series of part-time jobs to help out the family, and I concentrated on school and work. In my sophomore year I came under the influence of one of the most fascinating men of my life, my high school German teacher. He was a little bit like that other German I'd known in Chicago. He'd been a German soldier during World War II, and as soon as he could, he came to America. He was a Catholic who'd converted to Buddhism as a result of his World War II experiences. He didn't talk much about it, but he made it very plain to us how lucky he thought he was to be in the United States instead of Germany. He conveyed to us a love of this country, and a great sadness over what had happened to his native land. But mostly, he was just a marvelous teacher. I'd taken the regular audio-lingual German course the year before, and it was a terrible class with a terrible teacher, but under Herr Fromm, German was an *experience*. He didn't treat us like a normal class, or like normal students. He made us work like slaves and love it. There was a casual atmosphere, a lot of conversational German, and long raps on German literature. We thought we were having fun, and at the same time we were really learning German because we were inspired by him. He was a strange combination of easygoing and tough. He had a loud voice and he was very authoritarian, but you always had the impression that he was chuckling underneath. He hardly ever smiled, and yet you knew he saw the humor in everything. He was such a *human* person. He had more effect on me than any other teacher, and he's the reason that I decided to enter college as a German major.

But first there was one little problem: money. My father would have put himself into hock for the rest of his life to see that I got a college education, but he was *already* in hock. Remember my brothers? There were three of them, each bursting with college potential, each reaching college age before me. Those were hard times, believe me! My brothers worked, and my father did some moonlighting (pumping gas at a Texaco station, nights and weekends; how silly he looked wiping people's windshields!) and my mother brought in some money working at home as a seamstress—she's a positive genius at anything connected with homemaking. And even with all this going on, my parents had to go to the bank and borrow, and there just wasn't any credit left by the time I reached college age. As usual, we had a family council about it. I told them not to worry.

Luckily, I'd graduated in the middle of the normal high school year, and that gave me six full months before college started. I took three jobs! I worked full time at a McDonald's hamburger place in the daytime. I babysat at night, and I kept my babysitting schedule booked solid. On weekends I worked at the same gas station as my father—they'd installed a car-washing machine ("Free wash with fill-up!") and I ran it.

Those were the happiest six months of my life. Each time I put a dollar in the bank I was that much closer to going to college, and *on my own!* It's always been very important to me to do things on my own, without being a parasite on others. And my poor mother and father had already worked themselves silly. That was four years ago, and they're *still* paying off those old bills.

By the time I enrolled at The College I'd put aside five hundred more than enough to cover the first year's tuition and books. Before I went to a single class I signed up at student placement, and a week after school began I was working a forty-hour week as a short-order cook at a hamburger joint. The place was a little greasy and the clientele was mostly street people, which meant we'd sometimes find somebody zonked out in the men's room with a needle in his arm, but it was a job and I stuck with it.

From the very first day, I loved The College. It fascinated me! I'd walk around the campus with my mouth wide open, taking it all in, like a hick from the country. One night I saw this weird lavender light coming from the Ag building, and I walked in and watched them conducting a crazy experiment, growing mung beans under ultraviolet, or something. Things like that were so exciting to me. You could drift around that campus and never see the same thing twice, and if you ever got bored with the buildings and the fields and all the physical things, you could get turned on just watching the people, all those neat weird people.

The whole thing was just a gas from the beginning. It was such a thrill to reach my first final week and sail right through it with no trouble at all. I wore grubby clothes to class, and I stayed up all night to study, and I even popped a few pills and smoked a few joints. It was exhilarating. I got drunk for the first time. I missed my parents and I went to see them often, but it felt great to be in college on my own, doing my wings. Is that what they say? *Trying out* my wings? Well, anyway, I *was*.

My German teacher was a southerner who taught German with a southern accent. He'd say, *"Wir sprechen D-e-u-t-s-c-h?"* He drew his words out, he always ended on the upgrade. He'd say, *"Machen Sie die Tür z-u-u-u-u-u?"* He used to lecture us with his eyes rolled up in his head and just the whites showing. I'd count how many seconds he'd have his eyes rolled up and it would drive me crazy. I was happy when he transferred to another college and we got a better teacher.

I still didn't date very much. I was working and studying hard, and I didn't have much time for boys. In my spare moments I really began to think about sex and to question my parents' attitudes. I kept a diary, and I wrote on and on about the subject of sex. The theme was always the same: If sex is a natural act, why wait for it? If it's the expression of love and you feel a genuine honest love for someone, why torture yourself? All this was going through my head.

I'd go out on one of my rare dates, and I'd have some of my rare physical feelings, and then I'd come back and ponder it to death and write about it in my diaries. I wrote, "Holding back seems so unnatural. So destructive. The Pope allows vaccines and medicine to prolong life, but doesn't allow medicine that prevents unwanted life. I think he's a bunch of bunk on the matter of birth control."

Mama and I would have interminable conversations on the phone. She brought up traditional points like, "The boy will wonder who else you slept with, if you're not a virgin when you marry." She said there was always a risk that contraceptives wouldn't work. I would always act as though I sort of halfway agreed with her.

One night I had a date with a huge black man from Somalia, and he really tried everything in the book to get me into bed. He didn't go about it very tactfully. He gave me too much at once. He stroked my arm very lightly for a few minutes, and this turned me on slightly, but then he inflicted a very harsh French kiss on me, and it just turned me completely off. I went home and wrote:

> Tonight was the first time I ever really got turned on by a guy—still I chickened out. It is difficult for me to give freely of my emotions to one who I love very much but do not feel that special emotion towards that makes it easy and gratifying to give my affection away. The way he touched my arm about sent me through the ceiling, but his French kiss really missed target. All those huge Negroid lips just engulfed me! My God! I really don't know what to do. Maybe the problem is I'm too thrifty with myself and my affections. I don't want to spend them unless I'm giving to a good cause—unless I'm giving a part of myself along with my physical product. I'm flattered that he desired me, but did he consider me only a product? On the first date how can he really know love towards me? Oh, it's all so silly.

By the end of my sophomore year I still really hadn't dated. I'd necked a little, but I was still a virgin and my body was almost entirely untouched. I was withdrawn and repressed and I lost boys to other girls. I can't say that I blame them.

Then came the big year in my life. I won a full exchange-scholarship in German, and I went off to the University of Tübingen in Bavaria. In that junior year of college I went from adolescence to adulthood or, as one of my boyfriends joked, "All the way from infancy to adultery."

For the first time I was completely away from my family, completely away from my friends. For the first time I was nobody's little girl, nobody's little sister, nobody's little niece. I was completely on my own, and I found to my surprise that I could handle *everything*. I roomed with a German girl who didn't speak English, so I picked up on my German fast. They gave me a language test when I first arrived, and I flunked: three weeks later I took the same test and missed two questions out of fifty. I was so proud. And everything that happened in that junior year only made me prouder. It felt good to be an individual, instead of a member of the incredible Smyth family. I mean, the Smyths are great, and it's great to be a Smyth, but it does have a slight overpowering tendency on your self-confidence. It gave you a sense of being incomplete outside the family setting. Now I was getting over that sense.

I realized that it was still fashionable to hate Germans, but I also realized that that attitude was just plain stupid, as stupid as the Nazi hatred of the Jews. The German students that I met and became friendly with were just plain terrific. They detested Hitler and everything that he stood for, and World War II was the overpowering tragedy of their lives. But while they could hate Hitler and the Nazis and World War II and everything that happened, they couldn't hate their parents, so they were into complex behavioristic explanations of how Germany had gotten itself into a situation where a creep like Hitler could take over. They would trace it all the way back to the Treaty of Versailles and how the German people had been twisted and distorted, and how Hitler moved into a sick, psychotic vacuum. They would say that in the long run the guilt belonged to every German, in the collective sense, but to no German in the individual sense. There was an explanation for each person and his role, no matter what the role, and the explanation was deterministic and behavioristic. Since this is how I'd felt all my life, I enjoyed rapping with my fellow students about it.

But I just couldn't talk to the older generation of Germans. My landlady and I fought the whole time. She was part of the family of man, I guess, and I should love her, but she was anti-Semitic in subtle nasty ways, and still full of alibis for Hitler, and she just sickened me. My younger German friends told me that Germany would never be completely free, completely democratic, until my landlady's generation had died off, and I had to agree.

In my year at Tübingen I bought an old bike, and every chance I got I rode out into the countryside to see how the Germans lived. I visited kindergartens, orphans' homes, hospitals. I really became involved; I really became an adult. I went into monasteries, talked to monks, listened to them sing Gregorian chants—Oh, it was beautiful!

On a short vacation six of us rented a Volkswagen bus and toured East Germany. A profound experience! East Germany gave me the heebie-jeebies in some ways, but it was worth visiting. We saw the Communists in action. There were incredible stupid hassles at borders. The East Germans were building up their industry, but they'd done very little about the devastation of the war. They hadn't torn down all the bombed buildings, and it was like walking through a country at war. In Dresden I got really upset. The firestorm went through there. In 1945, the night the city was bombed, the Dresdeners went into the *Frauenkirche* church thinking they'd be safe there, but all the walls collapsed in the firestorm, and the rubble is still there, and there are still bodies underneath it. I just cried. It was so sad!

Then we saw a huge beautiful lawn in the middle of town, a couple of acres, well-kept and tended, and I said to one of the townspeople, "Oh, how beautiful! It's so *nice* that you keep up this public lawn."

He said, "We keep it up because that's where all the corpses were burned. After the night of the bombing they burned fifty thousand bodies there."

That trip was the only supersobering experience I had in Germany. Mostly my trips were wonderful. The art, the old churches, the beauty, the history that was just breathing around us. Such architecture! Gargoyles, gabled windows, carved walls. Beauty!

Because I was away from home I felt some yearnings for American things, and I took two courses in American literature, and I began to get into the transcendentalists: Emerson and Thoreau became my heroes. They really turned me on. It sharpened my focus to be in Germany reading them and looking back toward my homeland. I loved the way Emerson and Thoreau got down to the basics of life. I could also see this in the German authors and philosophers. To some they seem egocentric, but they're expressing the very essence of life. They're always discussing the questions: What does it *mean* to be human? What is the human condition? What makes humans act the way they do? To me they seem less interested in how they can make more money or have more pleasure than they are in how we can control human behavior, how life impresses itself upon the human instead of the other way around, and the glory of the individual, and the wonder of individuality. I learned so many things about the differences between you and me and all the others, and the respect that we must have for each other, and our sympathy and our love. I learned about cultural differences and cultural similarities; all these things turned me on in Germany. It was like a boiling pot in my head.

Gradually I began to see my own country as a three-dimensional place rather than some phony, flat land-of-the-free where everything was plastic and fake. Before I was in Germany, Kent State happened, *Easy Rider* came out, and the antiwar movement was gaining momentum. Some of the things that happened in the United States made me sick, and for a short time I hated my own country. But of course I've put all that back into perspective. You can hate the American fascists that seem to be popping up in high places—you *can* hate them if you want to waste the time, but it's so much more important to understand them. That's where it's at. That's how I spend my time. I try to understand. I try to love. I try not to become prejudiced. Prejudice cripples you intellectually.

My German year put me deep into behaviorism. I wrote in my diary,

The whole German disaster could have been headed off if they'd listened to their behavioral scientists. The Nazis marched to the most prehistoric impulses, and week by week they fed on their own sadistic successes, until finally they reached the ultimate: the murder of Jews simply because they are Jews. The stupidest thing now is to seek revenge on the Nazis or on the Germans. The stupidest thing now is to be prejudiced against them. The sacred duty is to understand, so that it doesn't happen again. The science of human life is the ultimate science. The nurturing of the human spirit and the lifting up of the oppressed and the injured is the ultimate philanthropy.

One day I took the trolley to a neighboring city to join in an anti-American march, protesting the presence of United States troops in Germany. I was a little late for the demonstration, but I met a Mennonite boy and got to know him. From the beginning, he really loved me. This was a new experience, having someone practically throwing himself at my feet. I took him to be more mature than he was, because he was hitching and working his way through Europe, and I thought that this sounded so grownup. And I liked the way he made all the first moves. He took a job in a shoe factory so that he could be near me, and this was the first time in my life that any boy had ever shown so much interest in little Nathalie.

I suppose you're saying it's about time. Well, it *was*. I was twenty years old, almost twenty-one, and I'd hardly ever even been kissed! Clifford took care of that little problem fast. He kissed me by the hour, but nothing more than that. Remember, he was a Mennonite. His religion did not allow for premarital sex. As for me, I enjoyed the kissing; I enjoyed the feelings that it stirred inside me, but I wasn't sure that I was ready for the all-out act of love, at least with Clifford. He fascinated me and sometimes I thought I was in love with him, but some part of me told me that this was just a stage in my development.

When the semester break came at the end of April, Clifford and I visited Greece, and we checked into a hotel room in the seedy Plaka section of Athens. Our main reason was to save money, but when we walked into the room, we couldn't miss the symbolism. There was a double bed and a crib. I thought, "Oh, wow, here we go!" The hotel proprietor pointed to the bed and then to the crib and laughed a°dirty laugh.

That night it was cold and I went to bed with my clothes on, but after a while Clifford took my sweater off and began to stroke my breasts. This was a first and I thought it was really neat! I just loved it! I'd always wondered how I'd react because I'd had these misgivings about the size of my bust and all, and here I was doing it and loving every second. It was nifty!

The next day we took a bus to the end of the line, and then a ferry to a little island off Athens. There were no cars. just donkeys and carts and a beautiful hostel, surrounded by aquamarine water. So amidst all this starriness I fell in love, or thought I did. The first night in bed, I told Clifford I loved him, and I'd never said those words before. In the back of my mind I was saying, this is really neat, but somehow I'm not one hundred percent positive. Anyway, it's great fun.

But—we didn't have sex. We just couldn't. We slept together naked, and it felt so good to feel our warm naked bodies. He'd get terribly turned on, and he showed me how to play with him, to relieve his tensions, and I did this for about a week, until it began getting a little old, because nothing was happening to my own tensions. After a week or so, we went back to Tübingen and we saw each other for a while; and then the whole affair just faded away and Clifford went home to Michigan.

A few weeks later I met a sensational English guy in my drama group, and I made arrangements to meet him in London on my way home from school in the spring. I stayed in London with his family, and after two nights of being under the same roof with John Sterling-Hanford I did the natural thing. I fell madly in love with him, and I went to bed with him, and for the first time in my life I had sexual intercourse. It was natural and normal and fun. There was a little pain, but the beauty overcame everything. After a few more days together, I went off to the States, and John and I vowed that we would never lose contact with each other. I suppose I should have felt sad, but I loved it all, even the parting. It just seemed like the logical end of my year abroad. I'd evolved completely. I was my own self now. I was me, and this was a fine thing. I'd achieved my majority and lost my virginity, and at last I was a woman.

In some ways The College is a weird place. It's a very heavy social scene, and yet it has something in common with the old style of universities two hundred and three hundred years ago. I mean, there's something for everybody. It isn't a straitlaced place, and it isn't exactly a party place. But there's everything on earth happening, from strict high-level scholarship all the way down to the sorriest use of the worst possible drugs. There's no single type of student or teacher at The College, they come in all shapes and sizes. It's like a big, weird, complicated city. It's not a place of refuge like some of those eastern girls' schools or some of the larger state universities and cow colleges. It's a very complex scene.

I'd never really realized this in my first two years at The College, but when I came back from Germany and my head was on straight for the first time, I could see that there were a lot of possibilities that I'd been missing. For one thing, I'd always lived in dormitories, in a little cocoon where I studied and slept and did very little else. Now that I was an adult, I decided to try one of the many options. With eleven others, I went into a communal co-op, and that's where I opened my senior year.

I guess something like half of our upperclassmen live in co-ops, and the co-ops come in different forms. Ours was a very straight and businesslike one. There were no slimy sex scenes, and there was no communal sharing of LSD or things like that. If someone wanted to smoke a joint he retired to his room and smoked it, so that he wouldn't get the nonsmokers uptight. Everybody had responsibilities, and they either lived up to them or got the hell out. By living this way, we could get our rent down to about forty dollars a month each and our food costs down to about the same, and none of us wanted to risk such a good deal, so we did it *right*. We had cooking schedules and dishwashing schedules, and God help you if you messed up. We got deeply into each other, and we had little informal encounter groups, and saw each other as human beings, as part of a family. We saw life close up, and we lived each other's problems. It wasn't all peaches and cream; some very heavy things happened from time to time. One of the girls had a nervous breakdown and dropped out, and one of the guys got involved in a very sordid homosexual affair. We offered what support we could.

After a while I found that I was doing a lot of talking to a boy named Rob Compson, one of my commune mates. He was a quiet boy from Kansas, with a history of tragedy in his childhood, and he was still *suffering* from his tragedy, whereas I had only grown and learned from my own. After a couple of weeks Rob and I got roaring drunk together and had a great time, and we started necking. From then on, everything clicked with us. We shared the same fantasies, sexually and otherwise, and we were both pretty healthy animals. He'd just broken up with a girl after a long time, and she'd dumped on him pretty badly. So his loneliness and unhappiness from childhood had been aggravated, and I was what he needed, and everything just went plunk-plunk-plunk.

About a week after we necked, we went to bed together, and I knew it was right and so did he. But there was so much more to it than sex. I enjoyed him so much as a person. He's very philosophical; he's into Eastern religions, and so am I. He's a terribly sensitive person, sometimes moody, sometimes withdrawn, always quiet and modest. He was raised on a farm where there was very little verbal communication. His father was killed in a horrible automobile accident when he was ten, and all his brothers were much older, and he felt kind of left out. His mother was a cold, Catholic lady who had had her own troubles, and there was very little time for Rob and the needs of a lonely little boy.

I guess this sounds like I was sickly sorry for him, but if I was, it didn't last long. Rob Compson is the most together man I've ever met. He may have his spells of moodiness and depression, and he may have bitter memories of his childhood, but that doesn't make him a sour, negative human being. Anything but. He takes a full schedule of courses in the School of Education, specializing in the problems of handicapped children, and he works eight hours a day in a laundromat to pay his tuition, and on top of that he's a volunteer at the Collegeville Home for Retarded Children. He's always full of new ideas for working with the kids, projects he can do, new ways to teach them, to reach them, to solve difficult cases.

One night he took me to the home with him to see the kids he was working with. They loved him so much. I'd always thought of retarded children as weird, almost untouchable, but they were loving and dear to me from the very first visit. I wasn't sorry for them; I wasn't maudlin or weepy about it; I just loved them as human beings. They were dancing around and playing and having a nice time, and Rob and I blended right in with them. That night when I went home, I knew that something very important had happened to me. I just didn't know what.

The next day I asked Rob to sit down and explain to me what he got out of working with the kids. He said he did it out of purely selfish reasons. He said that it turned him on. He said that when he left the home to walk back to our commune late at night, he walked on clouds, he felt totally rewarded and happy. I asked him if he felt sorry for the retarded kids, and he said not in the least. He said that that wasn't the point. He said the point was that they could benefit from assistance, that they could reach far higher levels with some personal attention and that the giving of this personal attention was far more rewarding to the giver than to the receiver. I loved this in him, and almost on the spot I made my own decision to switch my major and do what he was doing.

After a month or so Rob and I decided that it would be hypocritical for us not to live in the same room together. But it was too big a step to take all at once. I kept my things in Berneice's room, and I would slip into Rob's room to sleep with him at night. We made love for thirty straight nights, and then we began taking every other night off, and now it's maybe two or three nights a week. I guess that's inevitable. But we still love it, we still love each other's bodies, it's just that the first physical thrill has worn off. They tell me that happens in marriages, too.

We spent a long time trying to figure out how to handle the parental problem. From the beginning we told my parents that we were going steady and, as you might have guessed, they loved Rob as soon as they met him. Of course, we didn't mention that we were sleeping together or that we were planning to live together. And we couldn't say a word to Rob's mother. She'd have died of a heart attack.

After the Christmas break Rob and I decided to work out new living arrangements. We were very friendly with another couple who also worked with retarded children, and the four of us decided to get a house. We figured we'd get the house and move in, and worry about our parents later. We lived in the new house a week or two, and then I got up the courage to tell my mother. She and papa were planning to visit, and I told her on the phone, "Mama, I'm glad you're coming, but please, for the sake of not getting yourself too uptight, *don't* ask where each person sleeps in our new house."

She said, *"What?"*

I said, *"Please,* just don't ask who sleeps where."

She says, "Why?"

I said, "Well, because of my roommate."

She said, "Who's your roommate?"

I said, "Rob."

There was this long, strained silence on the phone, and then she said, "Do you want me to tell Luke?"

I said, "No. not yet."

Well, it really wasn't very hard to tell my mother, but my father would be another story, because he'd always thought of me as his dear sweet little girl, and I knew it would trouble him far more than it troubled my mother. A few weeks later, the two of them showed up in Collegeville, and they stayed in a motel. They called us, but they made it very plain they weren't too interested in coming to our house. Finally I said, "Oh, come on! We're dying to see you, and we don't want to meet in a motel room."

Well, they came over, and they spent several hours in our living room. They made a big point of not looking around the rest of the house, not letting their eyes fall on the beds. I knew what the trouble was. Their basically liberal attitudes were being confounded by reality. My oldest brother had lived with his wife before they were married. and my parents knew it, and they'd learned to accept it, and even to justify it, but now it was happening again, and not to a big strong son, but to a baby daughter. So it was hard on them, and it showed all day. They acted as though they might be struck dumb if they looked into any of the bedrooms. I didn't push it.

They went back home, and Rob and I were nervous for about a week, wondering what the result would be. Then I couldn't stand the tension anymore and I called my father. and we began a long conversation about everything under the sun *except* my living arrangements, and for one of the first times in our relationship he became very irritable with me, and all over nothing. It really hurt me when he mentioned some financial assistance they'd given me, because I was so proud of the fact that I had worked my way through college, and I'd accepted hardly any money from them. This was something brand new, to hear my father berate me for taking money, and I began to cry, and I made up my mind right then and there never to take another penny from them, and I never have. It ended up in a big sobbing scene, and I never got around to mentioning the real reason I'd called: to have a totally frank discussion about my new living arrangements.

Two days went by, and then my father called, and he said, "Nat, I'm really sorry. I'm *truly* sorry. We should never have come to sharp words, me and my little girl. Now let's talk about it."

Well, if there's anything in the world my father understands, it's human relations. That's his whole thing. He may not approve of everything his fellow humans do, but he does try to understand. So he talked for a long time about mutual respect and parent-child relationships and the new attitudes in the world, and how hard it was to be in your forties and to have to accept something that is totally different from your own moral code, etcetera, etcetera.

Eventually he got around to telling me that he knew about Rob and me sleeping together, and he tried to explain that he had spent a whole lifetime believing in one moral code, and he couldn't change now, he couldn't come right out and say that he approved of the way I was living. He said that he would always feel that my moral values were vastly different from his and my mother's, and he said that if it got right down to it, he'd have to say that he felt my moral values were wrong. "But," he said, "I love you very, very much and I completely accept you and respect you. So it's all right."

I started to cry, and he said, "And I want you to know I'll *always* respect you, no matter what." He said, "Nat, one more thing; if you really need money, let me know. I'm always ready to help."

I said, "No, thanks, papa. I think we'll get along now. But it's nice to know."

Several months have gone by, and I've invited my mother and father out to see us again, but they still won't come. Mama says that papa still feels that he can't come into the house. She said he gave her a long explanation one night, and he said that it wasn't only the fact that he disagreed with our moral code, but also that the vibes are very bad for parents on our campus. He said he was well aware that most of the kids in The College are into

an antiparent thing, they don't like parents at all, and
they enjoy nursing terrible grudges and hatreds. Well,
it's true. There's a lot of ridicule of the older generation
around The College, but not by me. There are so many
kids here who just can't understand their parents, and
so they spend their time ridiculing them and laughing
at their ways. I'll *never* do that.

The last time I talked to my father about it, he said he
still wasn't ready to visit us, but he was working on it.
He said, "Honestly, honey, I'd like to, but I just can't.
Maybe I'll come around. But right now I just can't. Do
you understand?"

"Of course I do, papa," I said.

He said, "I just wouldn't be comfortable in that setting,
not for a while. Give me time to work it out for myself."

"Okay, papa."

"And, honey, don't think of it as your fault. Don't
think of it as your problem. Think of it as mine. Okay?"

"No," I said. "I'll think of it as *ours*."

Look how my life has changed since Germany! I was a
child and now I'm a woman, practically married. I'm
learning so much about one-to-one human relationships.
Like I'm much more affectionate than Rob. I love to
hug and squeeze, to talk about love, to kiss. He doesn't.
He's a little like his background: cold and bleak. Sometimes he gets totally into himself, he wants nothing but
his own companionship. At first I didn't understand and
I'd begin to bug him. Now I've learned to back off, to let
him have himself to himself when he wants to.

Rob and I never have violent arguments, but we have
plenty of disagreements. We discuss marriage, but not in
terms of ourselves. His ideas on the subject are very
clear to me. He doesn't believe in marriage unless you
specifically want children. We're different about this, because, frankly, I'd love to be married to him. But he's
leery about committing himself forever to one woman.
He's been dumped on pretty bad, and he once told me,
"Don't love me too much. I'm still pretty freaked out
about love." So whenever we get on that subject, I'm

careful and quiet. The last thing I want to make him think is that I'm pushing him into marriage, because I'm not.

Our agreement is simply to have a steady, monogamous relationship without all the legal trappings. And to me the legalities aren't that big of a hassle, although I'd prefer a legal marriage in the long run. Right now, I figure I can live with him for four or five years before I'll even begin to get uptight about not being legally married. It would help if I could cool things with my parents, and I think that will come in time. They're too bright to cling to the old morality forever.

The main thing I'm learning now is the give and take of the male-female relationship. Sometimes Rob gets into a feeling of claustrophobia, things are closing in on him; and I have to give him a lot of air. I'll get lost for a couple of hours or even for a couple of days, and then he relaxes. But at first it hurt me to see him that way. He'd blurt out, "Please, *leave me alone!*"

I'd say, "I don't *want* to leave you alone. I *love* you." But I soon realized that each of us couldn't treat the other exactly as he wanted to be treated. Concessions had to be made—and we made them.

There was only one time when it got bad. Rob was uptight about his work and his personal emotional problems, his neuroses, or whatever you want to call them, and I was feeling a little insecure over my own problems with my parents and my tight schedule at school —I was taking twenty-one semester hours, and working a six-hour day at the library—and the tension got bad between us, and we even talked about moving into separate rooms.

I went around half-crying for several days, and Rob was all morose; and we were still sleeping in the same bed but not touching each other and hardly even speaking. Then one day I came home from work and Rob came into the room, and he started to talk to me about his childhood; about those cold Kansas mornings when he'd get up and do his chores before the sun came up, and how lonely it was after blizzards would hit and they couldn't leave the house for days at a time, and all they had was the radio, and about his father lying there mangled and bloody. All of a sudden he started to cry. We stood there together, and I began to cry too, and we threw our arms around each other, and that just made all the difference in the world. All the resentments, all the rejections that we'd felt from each other, they just disappeared in that one little time of being together and sharing our griefs, the same way we'd shared our love and happiness. At that moment, Rob Compson was the most real human being to me.

Now that we've established this beautiful relationship, I look around the campus and I feel sorry about some of the other girls. I see so much promiscuity, and it worries me. Sexual jumping around is fine if you can handle it, if you're sexually and emotionally mature, but how many of these little girls are? I think they're playing with fire. Casual sex is very dangerous if your head isn't together, and how many of these seventeen- and eighteen-year-old girls just out of high school are really together? Most of them are still acting out childhood fantasies, childhood resentments, and you don't solve these problems by sleeping with every older man in sight. If you can say, "Sex is fun, I enjoy it, it doesn't bother me emotionally, it's just plain physical fun"—fine. But I don't think that one girl out of a hundred can truly say that. I know that I couldn't have before I met Rob.

But I don't want to get up on a soapbox. It's enough that I take care of myself and bring some meaning into my own life. Maybe I'm just in a stage, but I'm super-enthusiastic about life. I love getting up in the morning. I love walking on this campus. I love to walk through the library and see all those books beaming down on me. The books turn me on. And it's so exciting to know that at last I've found a life's work. At the beginning of the second semester I shifted all my courses into the School of Education with a special emphasis on problem children. That's where it's at for me. I'm working at the home for retarded children every chance I get, and I've already established some good relationships. A month or so ago I started sitting with a retarded girl about ten years old, a cerebral palsy victim, in a wheelchair. She's profoundly, totally deaf; she has no language of communication whatever, and no one had ever begun to work with her. She just sat there in a void, staring. At first I just sat with her, and then I went home and learned the sign language of the deaf, and I went back to the hospital and began to teach it to her.

At first she could barely even move her fingers to shape them into symbols, but now she's beginning to come along. She's extremely retarded, of course, and we'll never be able to communicate very well. But at least I'll be able to teach her to communicate up to her potential. That's the whole idea: to bring your fellow human being to ultimate potential, no matter how slight that potential might be.

Now when I walk into the ward she responds very positively. When she sees me coming she smiles, and since she hasn't learned to repress her emotions like the rest of us sophisticated fools, she sometimes breaks into a loud laugh, just out of sheer happiness at seeing me. Then I come to her side, and we work from goal to goal together. She's already coming out of the void that she'd been in from birth. She's learning. I've taught her how to tell time, and right now we're working with money, how to recognize different coins, how to count a little. I've taken her on a few field trips to the post office, to the department store, the grocery, and we talk about what you buy or how you buy it, how much things cost, what a stamp is. It's simple stuff, but meaningful to her. God, what a challenge! And what a thrill to reach her on *any* level at all. I just love it! I don't stop to analyze it. I just love it, and I can't wait to start working with people like her permanently, every day, for the rest of my life.

REBECCA TAYLOR, 53
Associate Professor,
Department of Sociology

Teaching is the half of learning.

Confucius: Advice to Fu Yueh

Well, no, I'm not the type to talk about myself. I wasn't brought up that way. Come now, I'm really not *that* important, am I? Oh, pooh! But I'd be glad to talk about Collegeville, The College, anything you want, so long as it isn't too personal. My roommate—Lilly Owens, she teaches anthropology—says this is a garden of eunuchs. By that she means that—well, please excuse my language, just quoting her—nobody here has any balls, so to speak. They're set in their ways—they're not after anything— they're contented with just *being* here.

The teachers are consumed with pettiness. I have a slogan for them: Nothing minuscule is petty to me. They don't seem the least bit concerned about political problems, but they'll claw your eyes out over some insignificant matter. Just last week I was at a faculty party, and we were asked to bring our own liquor. Well, fine. This is fairly common; nobody on the faculty is rich. I had a nearly full quart of J&B, and within ten minutes it had disappeared entirely. No, they didn't drink it all up; they drank about half of it and then somebody took the rest out to his car. When I had the nerve to complain politely, this troglodyte of a political science professor had the gall to deny that he had taken it, and pretty soon everybody in the party was having a big fighting session over a few inches of booze. It was *my* Scotch, and I was the least excited about the whole thing. But this is the kind of cause that enlists the faculty's attention. When the fight was over, everybody sulked around in the corners, and got higher and higher on alcohol, and I just wanted to cry. I left about one in the morning, and I wondered why the hell I had ever come here.

It's a strange retarded place, The College. It has a certain amount of prestige among educators simply because of its setting, and therefore it can attract a surprisingly good faculty, and there's a lot of raiding of eastern universities for talent. But when these hotshots get here, they tend to drop out. There's very little intellectual life in this school, and it's so disappointing on that level. The teachers become selfish and self-centered. They hold their students in contempt, many of them, and think of them either as hicks from the country or good-time-Charlies, like themselves, who came here just to have fun in the hills. They approach each student as though he's not quite worthy of a college education, not worth getting interested in or taking a special approach to. The number of committed teachers is really low.

I'm sure you've heard the college described as a play school. Lately there's been a campaign to increase its dignity and its academic reputation, but pooh, it's still the same old play school. Surely you must remember the current events conference they held, and the national columnist came out to speak. And then he wrote an article saying that the only interesting thing that happened to him here was that several coeds offered to sleep with him. It was a very snotty, nasty article. The real point of it was that nobody here cared about current events, and the columnist was absolutely right. I've noticed in the sociology department that nobody ever mentions the news. They stay very remote from reality. And many of the students are the same way.

There are just too many things here to take one's mind off scholarship. Film festivals. Hippies. Freaks. The beautiful countryside. Free love. Half the student body is trying on free love for style. Generally, I don't disapprove, but isn't this the sort of thing that one used to get into *after* graduation, *after* one had earned the right to think more of having a good time and less of burying one's head in a book?

Lately it seems as though the campus is being immersed in freaks. It's changed completely in the three years since I became a professor. The freaks have moved in right around me. I have to plot special routes to get home, so that I don't get insulted as I walk. Just the other day one of them said to me, "Get out of here, old lady. You're not our type. You're not supposed to be here." I don't like that! These freaks are downright dangerous. People have been robbed right in front of my house. I try to put on such a forbidding upper lip that they don't bother me, but they still have their smart comments. I try to look straight ahead without seeing one or the other. A lot of the younger teachers encourage the remarks, but I don't. I've even heard of some of the younger faculty members going out with these freaks. For my part, I think you'd have to be a sadomasochist, or at the very least a neuropsychotic, even to be *seen* with one of these animals!

I walk down the block and these crazy Hare Krishna people corner me and tell me that they want me to help build their temple, and if I would just come around on Sunday afternoon I'd have a wonderful time, and maybe I could contribute a few dollars. I sort of humor them, but I rush away as fast as I can. They look so disoriented, with their saffron robes and their little pigtails.

Before I was at The College, I taught at a down-to-earth state college in the East, and all I saw were working kids who were struggling to get an education, kids whose parents saw no special reason for them to be in college, and yet the kids were there nevertheless, fighting their parents, fighting the world, dying to break out of their lower-class stratum. But here at The College the kids are just the opposite. They're sent here from Scarsdale or Beverly Hills, and the idea is to have a good time. They're apathetic. Education is just *not* important to them. This is a very busy campus, and there are a million things to do, so these kids put in three hours a day in class, and then their real energy and enthusiasm go into other things.

In the faculty, we still live by the old rule: Publish or perish. In order to get tenure, a professor usually has to publish articles or show some kind of scholarly activity beyond teaching. There's one producing scholar in each department, one show horse. We have one in sociology who runs around showing the secretaries reviews of his new book. But there should be many more like him, and there aren't. So many of the other teachers don't contact reality, or even *try*. Lilly is very friendly with one: He's a precious, eccentric little man who knows everything there is to know about the Dark Ages. He speaks so beautifully, and when he talks you have the sense that he's addressing a congregation. But after you know him for a while you realize he's lost touch with reality; he's more oriented to the Huns and the Visigoths than he is to the problems of school busing or racial prejudice or how to get a good man into the White House. He became a full professor a long time ago, so now he doesn't have to do *anything* to prove his worth. And there are lots of others like him, frustrated types from Harvard who have written one book and who love the hills and who stopped thinking ten years ago. People go around blaming kids for dropping out, but we have dozens of dropouts right on our own faculty.

If there's a simple answer, I think it's the fact that Collegeville is a place where you go *after* you have everything else you want. It's a place to go to vegetate and enjoy the scenery. There are no *searchers* here, no people burning for knowledge. My fellow professors tell me that Collegeville is the most wonderful place of all, "the end of the line," one of them said. Well, I agree, but not in the sense that he meant it. Socrates would have been out of place here, but Lanny Budd would have loved it. So would anyone who knows how to have a good time. Not necessarily your great scholars, but then college is becoming less and less about scholarship and more and more about something else—I don't understand exactly what.

Why don't I leave? *Leave here?* What, are you crazy? I'm fifty-three years old, I'm *happy* here, I wouldn't *dream* of leaving. Look at those beautiful hills out the window. Smell that clean, fresh air. Leave here? I'd have to be insane!

ESMERELDA WILSON, 25
Instructor, Department of English

Ingeborg Engemark, assistant professor of English, says:

Esmy's a fine scholar. She knows her subjects, and she does excellent papers. But I have my doubts about her as a teacher. She has absolutely *no* ability to capture the class's attention. Once I saw her read for a part in a campus play. Gadzooks, it was embarrassing! She just stood there and mouthed the lines. No feel'ng wh'tev'r. She lacks oomph! I've never seen her teach, but I'll bet she stands up there and says in that tiny little voice. "Now, *this* is a *beautiful* poem." Which is the *last* thing you want to say to a class. Just give 'em the poem; let 'em judge for themselves if it's good or not. The minute you tell them, "This is a beautiful poem," you've issued a challenge to them. You've given them something to disagree with. And nine times out of ten they *will* disagree. I don't think Esmy has an instinct for subtleties like this. She's just not a born teacher. But as the kid in the Bronx would say, "Well, then, what *is* she a born?" I really don't have the slightest idea.

Ann Stults, an English instructor, says:

Esmy was useful to me when I first got here, but now I'm seeing less and less of her. She's outlived her usefulness to me. When I arrived, she already knew her way around the campus, and she knew about various social scenes, such as charismatic meetings and sensitivity groups. I used her to get into these social things, but then I discovered that her main social thing was religion, and I've had enough of that.

At first she seemed sophisticated, but now I realize that she isn't in the least. I mistook a knowledge of the campus for sophistication, but really she knows nothing about life. And she'll never learn. She's not a strong personality. Others run her. Her mama, for one. There's no independence of thought or action to her. And yet she can be rigid, but only in little, dumb things. Like we're having a beer party up in the hills, but she insists that she'll bring wine. She doesn't think she likes beer and she won't even try it. She's rigid and insistent and *independent* on this dumb point. But on things that really matter you can push her around terribly; so most of us do.

The thing is, Esmy's not real, and she belongs right where she is, in this dizzy English department. Esmy's not existing in a world that you can correlate with the world that the rest of us live in. She's out of touch. She's vague. She dresses like a China doll, mid-1940s style, like Tricia Nixon. Ingeborg says this happens a lot in academic circles, that people become inbred and withdrawn and never grow another inch. People without form or substance, ingesting all the ideas of Robert Browning, but having none of their own.

Bright? I don't know. Certainly she has normal intelligence, she's scholarly, she's a grind. But all her intelligence is centered on reading the right thing and remembering it. Where you and I might have forty things on our minds at once, she has one or two, and she sticks to the one or two and closes her mind to everything else. This can pass for intelligence, but I have other words for it.

Sally Jo Lee says:

Esmy is desperate for a husband, absolutely *desperate!* Underneath her prim and proper exterior, she's just panting for a man. Why, once she was approached by a janitor for a date, and *she almost went!* She said to me, "Do you suppose he's *always* gonna be a janitor?" I said, "No, honey, but he's always gonna be ugly!" Ended up she didn't go, but she *wanted* to in a big way. I guess she just finally decided that thirty years was too much age difference.

Jennifer Scott, a freshman student, says:

Miss Wilson is the best English teacher I've ever had. She doesn't do things by the numbers. Like she's not so rigid on punctuation and grammar; she's far more interested in whether we have a real story to tell and how we tell it. I admire that flexibility in a teacher.

I don't know anything about her personal life, but I have some bad vibrations about it. Like she seems lonely, and sometimes she comes to class and I could swear she's been crying. I think she's unhappy. I think she enjoys teaching, but I don't think there's another thing in her life.

While you're here, I wonder if I might ask you something that's very very important to me. I hope you won't think I'm forward, but it just happens to be on my mind. How in the world do you meet men in Collegeville? Not that it's an overpowering problem, but it's just on my mind. I don't know how other faculty members handle this problem, and I don't dare ask them. The few that I do ask have the same problem.

With me, it's all compounded by the fact that I'm very very shy. One of my friends suggested that I just go to a bar in town and meet men the way certain others do, but all I could think of was, Oh, my, oh, my—I might run into one of my students. I do know that some of my colleagues meet men this way and some of them date their students, but that's just not an attractive proposition as far as I'm concerned.

Well, the truth is that I am dreadfully lonely and alone. I *can't* find men, and I'm competing with women who think nothing of saying to a man, "Hey, let's go to bed!" While I'm even afraid to say, "Why don't you stay for dinner?" I just get terrified when I'm in a situa-

tion where I have to make the advances. The man has
to make all the moves, and then I don't mind cooperating
—I'll cooperate *fully*. There are two men right now that
I would love to know, available and nearby, but I'm
afraid to make the slightest move. One of them came over
the other afternoon and told me in subtle ways how
lonesome he is, how he was having the Sunday afternoon crazies, and I knew that all I had to do was say,
"Well, why don't you stay for dinner?" But I didn't have
the courage, and he finally got bored and left. That's
typical. Later he came over and asked for a glass of iced
tea, and you could see that he was just waiting for a little
sign from me, but I was terrified to give it. Maybe I was
terrified that he would say no.

Another man sent out the same kind of vibrations to
me, and he even came in one evening and showed me
how to turn off the water when I had a slight leak in
the kitchen. He hung around and hung around, but he
was the type of man who has very little to say. He left
it up to me, and all I could talk about was Beowulf and
the leak in the kitchen. Oh, my! And so finally he gets
bored and leaves.

I got so desperate I took the problem to Skip Floyd,
the minister of our church, and he told me that there
were a lot of books on the market that would tell me
what to do. He said I impressed him as someone who
didn't trust herself, but that I *should* be happy with myself because I'm a good person, and go study the books.

But I found myself too embarrassed by those books.
Gracious, they're just awful! And anyway, I think if you
have to buy a book to learn how to be sensuous, there
is something very very wrong. I did peek at a few of
those books in the store, and everything that I read just
made me ill. It all just seemed like one big awful cliché,
and I thought that anybody who told me to read books
like that had a very facile view of reality. There was
something in one of the books about women masturbating in the bathtub, with the water running. Yes, honestly! This was supposed to be helpful, but I just thought
it was one of the silliest things I have ever read. I just

got very very ill when I read it, because I felt it was reducing all of us to bodies.

Sally Jo Lee said that Skip Floyd was stupid to suggest that I read books like that; she said that really Skip must have a terrible crush on me. But I don't believe it.

Ann Stults says:

Esmy covers up her life so completely. I still don't feel that I know her well, and she's my oldest friend on the campus. I don't think she has much social life. A few homosexuals and religious fanatics, that seems to be it. But she keeps her social life to herself, for the most part.

When you see her walking home in the evening with her briefcase, she seems to be the typical aging virgin schoolteacher, lost in a world of her own. I'm sure she'll never get out of it. Her sex life is a total blank. No love, no sex, nothing except Jesus and her students. And the tragic thing is she's not atypical, not at all. Which is one reason I don't intend to stay a teacher. They become wizened little things that come out of dark little caves four times a day to tell their students about life. They know the Bodleian Library backwards, but they don't know who's the mayor of Collegeville.

All this drives the kids crazy. The kids want to know *where it's at right now*. And they'll never find out from teachers like Esmy.

I just don't want to become the schoolteacher stereotype: the frustrated old lady. I am *not* afraid of living a single life, but I would hate to think that the rest of my life would be lived in a funny kind of celibacy imposed from without. I don't think that's healthy. I like sex, I want it, but I can't just walk down the street and pick somebody up and take them home and go to bed with them. I can't approach men, and no men are approaching me. I guess part of the problem is—there's a virginal aura about me, and this is just not a day and age when virgins are very popular on campus. For years I used my sweet little virginal aura as a protection against people I didn't want to sleep with. It was very very convenient. Now it seems as though I spent so many years creating the impression that now my main characteristic *is* my unapproachability. But it's just not true! Goodness, no!

Nowadays I'm just so very very lonely that I could weep. The setting here at The College is so beautiful, so breathtaking, but after a while it just adds to your loneliness. You begin to live against the beauty, rather than within it. If there is no one to care about in your life, no one to drive into the hills and share the countryside with, then the scenery only adds to your misery, and you're just somebody who's adrift in the midst of beauty. Sometimes I think it would be nice to go to one of The College's football games, but I haven't gone to one in the whole three years I have been here. I would love to go; I like the glamour, the colorful confusion of football games, but I've never been invited.

I know I sound like the classical ugly duckling, but you can see I'm not. I'm neat, clean, reasonably happy with my appearance, and *very* happy with it in my better moments. Lately, I've been dressing more—if I can use the word—more *sexy* than I used to. Straight things, fitted things. I went through a shirtwaisty period where everything was high-buttoned, but I'm over that. I'm tending more and more to dress so that clothes enhance me rather than just cover me up. I even wear minilength things—long minilengths, of course—to show off my legs. And I bought a hot-pants suit. I'm different from most of the girls in one way, though, I *always* wear a bra. Some girls look attractive without a bra, but I think the wee little people like me need them. There is a kind of fastidiousness in me that doesn't like to be awry, even when I'm just working around the house. I like to be put together. The other day at a faculty meeting there was a young instructor who wore a tennis suit that zipped up, and obviously she wore no bra and she kept sort of playing with the zipper, and I got so nervous. An older professor was sitting next to her, a good family man, and the whole scene made me *nervous*. Gracious! It was so un-*nice*.

Usually girls have problems with their fathers, but my father was no problem at all—just a menacing, shadowy figure who kept largely in the background. I didn't even see him till I was four, and then I wept my head off when he first came to the house. My mother and father had been separated, and he had been living in Europe, and all I knew about him was a picture on the dresser. When he arrived, I was *so* frightened of him. I was frightened of *all* men. Any time a man came into our apartment I would get very very nervous. I think it was because there was no father around in those early years; there were just a mother and a nurse.

My mother and father got back together again when I was four, and they took a house in Kenilworth, a suburb of Chicago. My first vivid memories of my father are of him blowing up at me. I can remember very very young not wanting to wash my hair and my father spanking me. He was the only one in the family who spanked. At night my mother and father would argue constantly. They both worked, and on weekends mama liked to spend time with me, but father always decided that the weekends belonged to him. There was a bad competition thing between me and my father, and we generally would end up doing what he wanted to do.

My little sister came along, but she didn't help the marriage, and in the second grade, my mother and father separated again. I remember mama sitting there trying to explain it to me, and we both ended up crying. During that time of separation I had a recurring dream in which my mother came downstairs at our house in a lovely-lovely gown, and father was standing at the bottom of the stair and when he saw her they embraced and fell in love again. That was the childhood dream that kept coming back during the years of separation.

After a year my father came home for the second time,

and it seemed as though my dreams were fulfilled. Now I began trying to make a myth out of him. Mama had told me sentimental stories about waiting on the front steps for her father to come home from work, so I started doing the same thing with father. The real feelings were lacking, but I tried. Our house was only a few blocks from the commuter station and I used to run down and meet him when he came from work at night. He would take my hand, and we would walk home hand in hand, neither of us really sure who the other one was, but acting our roles. Usually he smelled of gin. Ever since those early years I have had a thing about trains. Oh, my, it almost makes me weep to see a train pull into a station, and people run into each other's arms, and need each other, and *have* each other.

It was never easy for me to correlate what my mother told me with what I could see happening around the house. When I was in the fourth or fifth grade, she very proudly told me the facts of life, how beautiful it is to sleep with a man. But to me it seemed vaguely threatening. I associated it with all the noise and turmoil around our house. I kept thinking that I would get through my own wedding night the way I'd get through a trip to the dentist.

At school the feeling was only reinforced. In the fifth grade there was a class terror named James who would press me to the school wire fence and try to kiss me at lunchtime. It frightened me to death. In the sixth grade I had my first little sexual adventure, and mama made me feel guilty about it. Several of us began playing post office, and we would end up lying on beds with each other. None of us knew what was really going on, except we knew that lying on beds had some delicious naughtiness to it. Maybe one of the boys would put his arm over my head, but that's about as far as it went.

Mama came home from work early one day and caught us. I never saw her so angry. She *screamed* at me. All we'd been doing was lying on my bed like two sticks, but goodness!—mama was furious and she frightened me to death. She said, "I *know* nothing happened, but something *awful* might happen if you keep on doing things like that!" But all I had done was follow the orders from the "post office," which said, "Go to bedroom and lie on bed." ·

Father and mama separated again and stayed apart till the summer after I was in the seventh grade. Then they decided to give it another try, starting out with a grand tour of Mexico in a station wagon that father bought with money left over from an inheritance. The station wagon was some sort of a symbol that we were all going to make things work.

Father was never a good driver, and he was never a patient man and seldom a sober man. My sister and I huddled in the back of the station wagon while my father cursed the Mexican foods, the wandering cows and pigs, the dirty people, and the whole stupid idea of driving down here with us. Before the trip was two or three days old, he began using words that I had never heard before. The words that were hardest on me were S-H-I-T and F-U-C-K. Oh, my! I hate to even *spell* them. Later mama told me that it had frightened her to death when he started swearing like that when they were first married. It wasn't only the words, but the tone. It seemed to come up out of him like a terrible anger, bursting from his insides.

On about the fourth day of our trip, they had been sitting up in the front seat screaming at each other all day long, and then we pulled into a little town called San Luis Potosi. We were looking for motels, but we couldn't seem to find one, and we let a young Mexican man steer us to a small inn in the center of the old town. There was barely room in the hotel garage for one car, and father managed to scrape both fenders against the narrow sides. Really, the garage was nothing more than a stall; probably horses had been kept there for two hundred years, and now it served the hotel as a one-car garage and a horrible frustration for my father.

Oh, goodness, I have *never* seen anyone so mad! Up in our room he began berating mama, as though *she* had scraped the fenders instead of him. My sister and I began to weep, and father got angry because we were crying. When he told us to shut up, Mama said very softly, "Please don't take it out on the children!"

Father walked over and slapped her as hard as he could on the face. It was very very brutal. It was an awful thing to see. I wept and wept. I went to bed and cried all night. My sister was almost sick from crying. The next morning father said very coldly, "I shouldn't have done that, but you deserved it."

That evening he said that he couldn't stand the tension any more and right there in front of me and my sister he announced that he was divorcing mama. He said there was a conspiracy against him and as soon as the trip was over, the marriage would be over. This was the fifth day of a two-week trip, so you can imagine the tension the rest of the time.

Father filed for divorce and moved out as soon as we got back to Kenilworth, and it was a very sad time. I hate to be reminded of it. I still hear songs that were playing on the radio at that time. The theme from *Moulin Rouge,* "Swedish Rhapsody," "No Other Love Have I," the theme from *Victory at Sea.* The incident seems very far away now, but the songs remind me.

Maybe it's because Father left home so many times and finally left home for good, but I *always* expect men to leave me. And it never surprises me when something breaks up, because that's just part of life: *The man doesn't stay.* And it's not a trauma for me when they go. I had my trauma already, years ago.

But my father is not a major character in my life. You mustn't see him that way. It's very sad, but he just doesn't matter. I dated someone last summer who announced to me that obviously my father had given me a hard time, and that it affected everything I did; and I could never figure why he said that because I don't even think of my father as someone who has influenced me at all. Somebody else warned me that women tend to look for their fathers when they seek a husband. I said, "Oh, my, oh, my, please don't tell *me* that, of all people!"

Those were not very happy years after father left. Mama was very depressed. She said to me one night, "I wish I could go to sleep and never wake up." That *terrified* me. The only way I could go to sleep was to keep humming the hymn, "What a friend we have in Jesus," comforting myself.

Father went to live nearby in Chicago, but he would come up to visit my sister and me on weekends. By two thirty in the afternoon he'd be almost dead drunk, and he'd take us to lunch and it would just be very very embarrassing, and we wouldn't know how to handle it. One Sunday he was supposed to take us to a restaurant at one o'clock. He showed up at four incredibly drunk, and I was terrified by his driving. Then he had more drinks before eating, and it was even worse driving home. He was slobbering, inarticulate. He would always get very affectionate, particularly with me, when he was drunk—but that was the only time that he really was affectionate. Going home, he pawed at me, and I couldn't believe his driving. He drank more at the house, and when mama got home from work he was almost unconscious. She gave him some coffee and he slept in his car for a while and left.

Sometimes my sister and I would go to Chicago to see him at his apartment and spend the weekend, and I remember always being so nervous about that and embarrassed when he would hold hands with me at a movie, because I don't like the concept of your father holding hands with you—I don't know, I just never had the feeling that I wanted physical contact with him.

School saved me. I loved my books and my studies. If I didn't get straight A's, I was disappointed. In the ninth a group of us started a writing club called The James Gang named after Henry and William James. We wrote stories and read them to each other. I remember a very romantic story I wrote called "The Hunting Season." A little girl was very lonely, walking in the woods. She heard a shot, and found a terribly handsome man who had just shot a squirrel. She bawled him out for doing it and eventually they fell in love and it was all very charming. That story was my magnum opus. But I wrote many others, mostly romances. It was a fantasy thing. Nothing was going on in my life, so I had to write.

For a while I had a crush on our advisor, a man of thirty-eight or forty, unmarried. My fantasy was that in ten years I would come back to school, and I would be grown up, and he would meet me on the street and he would look very lovely, and we would have a romance. I was always trying to figure out if there was too much age gap—twenty-four years. I didn't think so. But mama told me not to spend time thinking about the man, that he was obviously a homosexual. Looking back on it, he *was* a very tidy and fastidious man, and mama might have been right. But I enjoyed it when he was vaguely affectionate to me, sort of patting my shoulder. At that point any bit of affection was very very meaningful to me.

One of the girls in the James Gang came from a fundamentalist background—The Christian Missionary Alliance—and her parents took us all to the Billy Graham crusade in Chicago. How can I ever forget it! There were thousands and thousands of chairs, and a huge streamer across the front with the Bible verse, "I Am The Way The Truth and The Light, Jesus Said." From the instant I walked into the place there was a kind of spirit around that just filled me with something very very happy. Goodness, it was inspiring! I said to a girl friend, "Nancy, I think we're going to find something very very special tonight." Dr. Graham preached on the blind beggar in Mark, and I was sitting on the edge of my seat, it was all so overpowering. Dr. Graham said, "A lot of you here have eyes, but your spirits are virtually blind!" It sounds simple and trite now, but at the time it said a lot to me. He also said, "You need to know Jesus and let him open your eyes."

When he was finished, he asked us all to come forward and accept Jesus as our personal savior. It was a real step for me. I stood there getting up my courage. A hymn was playing, "Turn your eyes on Jesus, look full in His wonderful face, and the things of earth will grow strangely dim, in the light of His glory and grace." I went down to the front, and Dr. Graham prayed with all of us. We repeated after him, "Dear Father, I know I have sinned and come short of Your glory, but I accept Jesus into my heart as my personal savior," and I felt that I was beginning a whole new life. That night I wrote in my journal, "I've finally found God!" The next morning it meant so much to me to wake up and feel a *need* to read the Bible.

When I told mama, she immediately started using my Christianity as a club. "If you're a Christian, you'll do the dishes." "If you're a Christian, you'll do this and that." She also told me that Christianity could be as selfish as anything else.

My religion gave a wholeness to my life that wouldn't have been there otherwise. It permeated everything that I did and it integrated my life by centering it on one focal point. Troubled children do this. They have to go out and find the center of the universe for themselves, or else they're lost. Bonhoeffer says that often religion becomes a *deus ex machina,* and in some ways that's what it was to me as a child. The one thing that provided something soft and rosy and sweet and good was Jesus. God comes into your life and picks up the pieces, when all human effort has failed. It's magic. But it's *good* magic. I would be lost without it.

After that wonderful experience, a little group of us would meet in a prayer group in the morning in the cafeteria of the school, and we would exchange Bible verses when we passed each other in the hall. I carried the Bible everywhere I went, and I started going to a little Baptist church because it was very fundamentalist. It taught the kind of Bible Christianity that I wanted. Mama continued to fight all of this. One night when I was at the evening service, she came right in and announced that I had to go home and do my homework.

I think she felt that Christianity was getting the loyalty from me that she wasn't.

I had an arrogance about my religion, no doubt about it. There is a Charles Schultz "Peanuts" cartoon in which Linus says to Lucy, with wrinkled brow, "Do you ever worry that God is upset with you?" and Lucy says, "Oh, no! God *has* to be pleased with *me!*" That's the same feeling I had in high school, the attitude of someone who has found Christ and deep down inside thinks this makes him superior to all the poor sinners around him.

In many ways I was a perfect little Christian.* I did not date at all. I refused to go to my senior prom. Girls would try to fix me up with boys, but I would not go out with them. Dancing was forbidden. Sunday movies were out. Once during high school I had to go see a movie with father on a Sunday afternoon, and I had this terrible fear that Jesus might come back, the Second Coming might happen, and what would I do if Jesus returned on this terrible day when I was in the movies? It would have disappointed Him so much.

At the same time, I had crushes on people who were far away and unapproachable. I remember a boy at my Christian camp playing Mendelssohn's *Rondo Capricioso* on the piano. I built up fantasies about boys, and often I had crushes on tennis instructors, people like that. But most of my crushes were on real Christians. My idea was to marry some beautiful Christian man and be all enveloped in clouds and we'd go off and do God's work together. I was no longer worried about what would happen on my wedding night, because I *knew* what would happen. We would pray together all night. That would be perfect.

I graduated almost at the top of my class, and only a little problem with geometry kept me from graduating *summa cum laude*. Mama had some kind of idea that

---

* "Christian," as used by Esmerelda Wilson in the rest of her narrative, means those who have gone beyond the usual traditions of churchgoing and accepted Jesus Christ as a special sort of personal savior. To Esmy and her colleagues in various extreme Christian movements, a person who worships Jesus Christ, who believes in God, and who attends church regularly, is not necessarily a "Christian."

she wanted me to go to college and study English because she thought I had a flair for it, but by now I had become consumed with interest in religion and it seemed to me that it would be heaven on earth to become an archeologist and go puttering around the Holy Land finding Dead Sea Scrolls and things that prove God's existence beyond any question of a doubt. So I decided to study both English and archeology and see where Jesus led me.

My Baptist minister and his wife used their influence and got me into the finest school imaginable, Christian Union. I realize that some people deride Christian Union, but it has a very high academic standard. It's not Harvard or Swarthmore, but it's not far behind, and it had a very good religion department and some good courses in archeology.

Christian Union gave me the environment that I had wanted at home and hadn't been getting. There were no overnight passes. There was no intersexual visiting: One night a year the boys could go into the girls' dorms, but only for open house. There was compulsory chapel. Each student had to have sixteen hours of Bible to graduate. In the second year, we studied New Testament and basic Christian Apologetics, and Old Testament and some biblical archeology. In the third year, we studied Christian Doctrine, and in the fourth year, advanced Christian Apologetics. All of us carried our Bibles wherever we went, and at lunchtime it was nothing to see hundreds of students lying about the grass exchanging quotations. Oh, my, it was breathtaking, it was wonderful!

Christian Union worried a great deal about getting people too sexually aroused. You would get couples going together and not being able to do anything. I can still see them sitting in the dormitory lounge just looking at each other in agonized ways. About all they could do was hold hands. Most of them would either decide not to touch each other at all or to get married in college. At Christian, there were a lot of marriages.

Looking back, I suppose you would say that we were repressed. I had a few boyfriends, but the most we did was a very small amount of kissing. We were *Christians,* and we believed very much that there should be no sex before marriage, but we were also physical human beings. One night my roommate confessed that she masturbated, and she was so embarrassed. She said, "Oh, Esmy, I have to tell you a terrible thing that's been preying on my mind." When I told her that I did this too, she couldn't believe it. So she went to one of the deans to talk about it, and the dean told her not to do it. The dean told her that if she became sexually tense and absolutely *had* to masturbate, well, that was one way to release tension. But don't do it if you can possibly avoid it.

It was in my junior year at Christian when I had my first visit from Jesus. My first real visit. I had had an appendectomy, and I was just coming out of the ether, and I felt Jesus come to my hospital bed and just be there. I know it sounds like seeing visions, but the experience was meaningful to me. I didn't actually see Him, but I had a sense that His presence was in that room. At first I heard angel choirs, then I sensed this outline that was standing there by my bed. All through my senior year I kept hoping that that experience would repeat itself, and once when I was very lonely, I wrote in my journal, "Oh, how I long for the night when it seemed like heavenly choirs echoed heart strains of 'My Jesus, I Love Thee,' and I long again for that sense of Him that is so easily obscured by the everyday world."

Graduation was like being thrown from the womb. Christian had given me wonderful years, a beautiful environment. The night before commencement, I wrote,

Tomorrow Christian will no longer be quite my own. It slipped away so much more quickly than I would have hoped. Christian as my home is gone, and I can never again bury myself in a library carrel, hidden behind long shelves of books, and I can never again walk home from the library, breathing the lonely ecstasy. These have been such rich years, such special years—and today Professor Evans softly hugged me, and when he left I cried. A week from today Christian will be irretrievably behind me, summer will no longer be a parenthesis but a strange and somehow unknown beginning.

To my absolute amazement, a wealthy aunt who had seen me maybe three or four times in my life gave me an unbelievable graduation gift: a summer in London. And how I loved it! London was everything to me. It was a city steeped in my two majors, archeology and English, with museums that could occupy me for days and days. I soaked everything up. I wrote, "How to describe the curious spell that history has cast over this city of damp and heat, of green trees and subway tubes." I was hypnotized. At City Temple I engaged in a long discussion about Jesus with some young London women, and they asked me if I would join them at a meeting later that night. I asked them what the meeting would be about and they said, "The charismatic movement." I had heard a little about the movement, but I had no idea what was in store.

The setting of the meeting was very working class. We took the Houston Street tube and went to an upstairs flat that was very very dreary. It was a gray, foggy London night, a Sunday, and the members of the meeting sat around a tiny, sputtering fireplace as shadows flickered on their faces. My first reaction was fright. The two girls who had brought me seemed bright and levelheaded, but there was an older woman who began speaking excitedly about the vision of God coming to her and she had dirty fingernails and I was repulsed by them. Another woman turned out to be retarded, and kept running her fingers through long blond stringy hair.

They began explaining the charismatic movement to me. They said it begins with the Pentecostal idea that when you're instilled by the Holy Spirit, that is a separate and distinct experience from conversion to Christ. The Holy Spirit is the third person of the Trinity, it's Jesus in you on earth. The charismatic movement emphasizes speaking in tongues. Involuntarily, without your even trying, Jesus comes into your body and speaks through your own mouth and tongue, in words that must be interpreted by others in the movement.

I was horrified when I heard this. I didn't understand it at all. Then—good grief—in that dreary little flat, they served a stew, supposed to be a symbolic Last Supper kind of thing, and you couldn't talk during the meal. That is, you couldn't talk naturally. You had to do the literal thing that they talk about in the Bible: each person contributing a verse from the Bible or some religious story. I told them a story from the book of Eliade, about a rabbi of Cracow and his dream that a lovely treasure was buried under the palace gate of Prague, and all the time that he is dreaming that dream, a palace guard at Cracow is dreaming that there is a treasure under the rabbi's own hearth. My point in telling this story was that I had come to England to find something and I was realizing that there was treasure to be found back at home, too.

After I told this story the woman with dirty fingernails said, "I never travel for pleasure, I only travel in God's service." She sounded very pompous about it, and the rest of them sort of scowled at me, like witches.

Now the women began preaching the baptism of the Holy Spirit. They said not only should I become a Christian, which is available to anybody, but there is also the experience of being baptized in the Holy Spirit and beginning to speak in tongues. The speaking in tongues is the sign that you have been baptized in the Holy Spirit and accepted.

After the women preached at me for a while, they began speaking in tongues themselves. It totally repulsed me. Someone would speak, and someone else would interpret it. The interpretation always seemed to be rather uninspired words of comfort, like "I am the Lord and I am with you, and I know your trials." The actual speaking in tongues didn't sound like any particular language. Later I learned that sometimes it is old Yiddish languages that are gone now. There are authenticated cases of rabbis hearing people speaking in tongues and recognizing the language as ancient Hebrew.

But it all seemed absolutely spooky to me. I didn't like it one bit. Each person got up and told how he had become a Christian. The woman with dirty fingernails had had an accident and had found Jesus, and I wondered if it had deranged her. The retarded girl just didn't say much. She smiled all the time, and they would say to her, "Hasn't Jesus done wonderful things for you?" And she would smile back. The woman who had brought me to the meeting got up and said that she had lived a totally pagan life before, but now she had given herself to God and had even stopped wearing glasses because she believed that God was her healer and she could trust Him for everything.

The meeting disturbed me for several days; it even seemed to take some of the brightness out of my wonderful London. I told you I had a thing about trains, that I always associated them with my father, and I had made a myth out of meeting him at the station, so I packed a small bag and went to the railroad station in London, seeking solace, willing to go wherever the first train took me. It took me to Edinburgh, and thence to Inverness and thence to a very very wonderful experience. I walked around Inverness all afternoon and was captivated by it. That night I began reading Virginia Woolf, and I went to sleep strongly under her influence. The next morning I decided to go back to Edinburgh, and I booked an overnight train that left at eleven.

Walking to the station that night, I noticed some young boys following, making clucking noises like construction workers. They acted like they had never seen a young woman alone in the Inverness Station. When I climbed onto the train, a handsome man wearing kilts was right behind me and he said, "They've got a lot of ruddy cheek, don't they, Miss?" I turned around and looked at him and nodded and I was very impressed with his handsomeness. Standing there in his plaid kilt and tweed jacket and brown curly hair, he looked like a vision. A song began to run through my head: "Oh, Where, Oh, Where Has My Highland Laddie Gone," and now here he was!

When we boarded the train I went into my compartment and he went into his, but soon he knocked on my door and asked if we could chat for a while. I don't exactly know how it happened. I'd been reading *The Waves,* and something in that wonderful story connected with my *wanting* something to happen, something to just burst out of the blue. My new friend told me he was married, that he was a businessman, and that he was going to Edinburgh to meet a friend. And somewhere in the middle of all the talk, he turned out the light and began to make love to me.

It all seemed inevitable, dreamlike, completely out of time. In the middle of a sentence he walked to the window, pulled the shade down and said, "I would like to give you a little kiss." Before he was finished kissing me, I thought I would burst out of my skin. And suddenly it was *all* happening. I had enough presence of mind to stop in the middle of the sex act and say, "I don't do this with everyone."

"I'm sure you don't, my darling," he said, and continued.

I said, "You know, all American girls aren't like this. I hope you don't think that I do this all the time."

But still I wanted it all to happen, and there was no question about that. And it wasn't one of those grim things that happen to some girls, where they are sort of forced down on a bed in a grimy hotel room. True, there was an instant when I was the girl who wouldn't dance in school, the prig. I felt guilty and strange, but I asserted my will and I said to myself, "No, this is not dirty, this is wonderful, this is good," and something in me affirmed that.

My Scot was a gentleman, and everything we did was conventional. I was *so* lucky; another friend of mine had her first sexual experience with an awful man who just went through all kinds of advanced sexual things with her, and she, not knowing anything about sex at that point, found it very traumatic. I have since done these advanced sexual things myself, and I take them in stride, and I believe that everything that a man and woman do together is natural and good, but just the same I'm glad that I didn't find it all out on my first night.

When it was over I realized that I had not had an orgasm, whatever that was, but I could see in my Scot's face that he had. He rolled to one side and said, "That was luvly!" Oh, it was so sweet, so right!

After a bit he returned to his compartment. Something told me that I must not sleep on those same sheets, so some part of me must have felt that I had done wrong. I got out of the bunk we'd made love in and got in the other one to sleep. For a long time I tried to piece together what had happened, to reconcile my attitudes about the church and about Jesus, and strangely enough I did not find them difficult to reconcile. I decided that the experience itself was proof that it was right. Jesus had sent this man to me and I had accepted him for what he was. I am still that way today. I have my small guilts about carnal activities on those rare occasions when I am permitted to enjoy carnal activities, but mostly I accept whatever Jesus sends me.

Days later when I had returned to London I wrote in my journal:

I will always remember the Highland Lad who happened to me in his lovely kilts on the night train from Inverness, and I will not regret the night given up to the most ephemeral of romances—even if I still do not know how it happened or why I let it happen—for it had a kind of beauty simply because it was a Brigadoon that could not be recaptured, and *should* not be—I will forget his face long before I forget the way in which he made me be a woman, and although introspection comes not without some uneasiness, I will not be ashamed of saying that even in this I found more of myself—the part that I needed desperately to find—even thus in Scotland.

I didn't enter his name in my journal because I didn't know his name. In my memory he was not so much a man as he was an experience, and experiences don't require proper names.

Sally Jo Lee says:

Oh, I just think Esmy's a tremendous female! She's great! She's so *goooood!* But the big love of her life is a homosex-u-al! Phil Hanley! Can you imagine? I didn't know it till we took a course together. When I found out, I nearly dropped dead! Her long-lost love is a fruit! Oh, she's so smart, she's so good! But she doesn't have one shred of common sense. Not one shray-ed!

The first time I ever ate dinner with her, she told me about Phil and how he came here because she was here. Imagine a fruit chasing a girl all the way across the country! But he *fooled* her. He said, "Esmy, I want to marry you, I've come out here to marry you." And then he said, "Oh, by the way, I'm a homosex-u-al, but I think I can overcome it!" And she believed it! When she told me that, I said, "Are you kidding? I'd have just *died* right there on the spot." I said, "Esmy, what's the deal? *What's the de-al?*"

You'd think something inside her would have told her Phil was a fruit a long time ago. But no. She's *out* of it. She's from another planet. She's so busy hearing voices and going to black masses that she doesn't catch the obvious when it's dished right into her lap. Why, I'd have smelled a rat the minute that fruit opened his fruity mouth! *The instant!* And I'd have said, "Now, come on, Phil, what's the deal?" I'd have gotten to the bottom of the whole thing fast!

Back home in Chicago I enrolled in some courses at the university, took a daytime job as a librarian, and moved into a little apartment on the Near North Side. I resumed my activities in the church, and I began reading about the charismatic movement. I knew I was not ready for it, but I was still intrigued by that peculiar meeting in London. One night, at a devotional group,

I met Phil Hanley, a very handsome designer, a man of about thirty-six, who seemed just as devoted to Christ as I was. We had coffee that night in the Loop, and we walked over to Ohio Street, where his apartment was, and then I took the bus home from there. Later I thought how funny it was that *I* had taken *him* home, not he me. But I also found myself with strong feelings about him. At one point in the evening he had said, "I feel as though we have been talking for years." I felt exactly the same.

After that I saw him at several meetings, but he made no attempt to become personal. Finally I invented an excuse for us to have lunch, and we did, and then we started meeting more often. We would have dinner at his apartment and then we would pray together at the table. We were soulmates, we could talk. There was an incredible connection. We used the same images. For example, it seemed to both of us that the snow came up from the ground instead of down from the sky. Little things like that made me feel that he had been sent especially for me. But after ten or twelve evenings together, I began to wonder why nothing physical was happening. Oh, my word, did I have physical impulses after those evenings in his apartment! But he never made a move. It was confusing. No kissing, no hand holding, nothing! Only prayer. I began to wonder why we never dated weekends. It was always Wednesday night at his apartment. I found later he was doing the same thing with another girl, praying with her on the weekends, and praying with me on Wednesday night. He never laid a hand on her, either.

We had been seeing each other for a few months when we finally went to a Saturday night movie together, and I could tell that it was very hard on him; the whole evening was just awkward and uncomfortable and tense. I suppose it was out of pattern: He had me categorized as his little Christian friend, and you didn't go out on dates with your Christian friends. After that date I didn't see him for weeks, and in fact he stopped showing up at the regular devotional services. Then one night I bumped into him on the street and we went for coffee and he told me that he had gone through a remarkable experience. I got him back to my apartment and made him some food, and told him to tell me about it, but he said it was too personal. I remember praying over the salad with him, and asking God to give him strength to tell me what was going on.

Finally he said, "Esmy, I need to tell you something for your own protection." He looked down at the floor. "I'm a homosexual." It came as a huge shock to me because I had already begun thinking of him as a lifetime partner, as the Christian that I had always longed for, the one with whom I would go out into the world and perform Christian works.

Once the secret was out, I couldn't shut him up. He told me about the different men he had been sleeping with, about picking up men in Lincoln Park, and allowing himself to be picked up at concerts and recitals. He told me that he had a strong desire for men and that sometimes it would overcome him and he would go to the Art Institute just looking for a male pickup. He didn't explicitly tell me what they did together, but then he didn't have to. He told me that he had made pilgrimages all over the midwest to people who would pray for him and help to heal him of his homosexuality. He said he would dream that he was healed, but the next night he would feel the same urges. Then, he said, something had happened to give him hope. "I found out about the charismatic movement," he said, "and I began to speak in tongues. Now I think I'm on my way to being healed."

I was stunned. I told him about my own experience with the charismatic movement in London and how it had piqued my interest but at the same time turned me off. "There are strange people in every movement, even in the most exalted movements on earth," he said, and I realized that he was right. I could not judge the charismatic movement by a few strange people, in a strange London flat.

Phil talked for another hour or so about his experience

as a convert to the charismatic movement, and I told him how grateful I was that he had confided in me, and I confessed that I had deep longings for him. Perhaps to comfort me, he took me in his arms and kissed me goodnight, but it was an extremely avuncular kiss. If he he was on the way to a cure he still had a long way to travel. That night I wrote in my journal,

> My body aches for the realization of my woman-hood, while there is only silence. Patience, little one (but how hard is patience when my physical needs are *now*). I must try to bear them. I must wait. Phil will change. I am desirable and lovable, and I *will* be loved—only *patience*———.

I consoled myself with masturbation.

When I didn't see Phil for another few weeks, I began reading everything I could about the charismatic movement, as though to have something to share with him if he returned. I read the book *They Speak With Other Tongues* by John Sherrill, and started going to a Pentecostal church on the North Side. Suddenly it became very important to be baptized in the Holy Spirit, whatever it meant. I prayed and prayed that God would bring it to pass. I went to a couple of meetings of the charismatic group that Phil had been going to, and I found the people very strange. There were some musical comedy dancers, and one girl whose wristwatch had stopped and she prayed for it to start. It did. This made me a little nervous at the time. Then some great muscular boy prayed that he would have the courage to go to the dentist, and I was impressed by this, that such a strong-looking character had to pray for strength to go to the dentist.

Very early I could see that the experiences of these people at the charismatic meetings was close to sexual experience. They would build up to kind of an emotional pitch and they would worship towards the same kind of ecstasy that you go through in an orgasm. Some critics bring this up about the movement, as though it's evil and bad. But in my opinion it's too facile to call every release sexual.

After a few more meetings I began to find the charismatic movement extremely attractive. One Sunday night I stayed up half the night reading the New Testament about the Holy Spirit and praying that God would do this thing to me, whatever it was. The following night, Monday, I was going to go to the group and ask them to lay their hands on me and pray for me to receive the baptism of the Holy Spirit and enable me to speak in tongues.

But God moves in his own wondrous ways. The next day I had lunch with a divorcee, a woman who'd also been converted by the Billy Graham crusade and then moved into the charismatic movement. I told her I was going to a meeting that night to be prayed for, and she said that she could tell that I had *already* received the Holy Spirit. I hadn't acted it out yet by speaking in tongues, she said, but why didn't we go right around the corner to a little church, and she would pray for me, and we would make it happen.

So we went into a chapel and she laid her hands on my head and prayed that I might receive the Holy Spirit and that I might receive the gift of speaking in tongues. Then she left me alone and said, *"You* pray now." The little chapel was dark and I was alone. It was raining, drizzly. I was sitting in a pew, my head bowed, praying. I prayed and prayed, and suddenly I began to speak in tongues. It began with about six syllables that I kept repeating over and over. I can't remember them now, but I remember clearly that I was flooded with a joy—a deep deep joy—and the rest of the afternoon those syllables just kept ringing through my mind. They were the words of Jesus. They were the comfort of Jesus. I walked around with a smile all day. Nobody else knew what was in my mind. Oh, my! I was *so* joyful.

That night I went to the meeting and told them the whole story, and I walked home through the rain in a joyous joyous mood, and then I got a telephone call from a relative. My father had been in a terrible automobile accident and was in critical condition. He died later that night. It seemed to me to give the lie to my joy, and I didn't understand. Why would these two things happen on the same day? I said to myself: "How do you stay joyous in a world where fathers are killed and mothers do not understand?"

As the weeks went by I became accustomed to speaking in tongues, to praying in tongues, to the new fullness of the Holy Spirit that was mine. I wrote, "I don't exactly understand all this except that *something* has happened, something that makes available the power of the supernatural in a new way, because of Jesus."

I would bow my head at night and begin to pray and after a few minutes the words of Jesus would roll from my mouth in a strange tongue that I could not understand. The texture of the language was almost guttural, with heavily rolled Rs, and I thought it might be the way that the ancient Hebrews had spoken. I would pray, "Father, I give this to You, just You. Worship is due Your name. Worship and praise to You who live and reign, Our God and Lord and Father, worship and praise to You who live and reign in our Lord and Savior. Worship and praise to You who live and reign as our Holy Spirit. Father, I just worship You, praise You, in the sanctuary which is this room and which is this world and which is creation. Father, I worship You, I praise You. Hallelujah, Father!" And then strange tongues would begin to roll out, and for five or ten minutes I would speak in a language I did not understand, on an impulse that I did not create myself. And then just as suddenly I would find myself back in English, and I would be saying, "Father, these are Your words. Father, these are Your words, to glorify you. Father, I thank You. In the name of Jesus."

I went around singing to myself, praying to myself, writing little notebooks of things that God was saying to me. I lived an almost completely interior life. My face was a perpetual smile; I was one with the Holy Spirit. But if there is one thing I have learned, it is that we are always physical beings, no matter the extent of our spiritual awareness. I asked Jesus for help. I wrote in my journal:

> My needs now are: 1. That I let go of female sexual needs that I try to meet myself, and let Jesus be my completion sexually. 2. That I marry Phil. 3. That the rest of my house (Acts 16:31?) come to know Jesus Christ. 4. That the *next* step be made clear—and the new sensitivity of my own sin and un-Christ-likeness, that God might be glorified—more confession—more praise to this Jesus that I am meeting in a new way. Amen.

But unfortunately Jesus *wasn't* my completion in the sexual area. It had been an unreal hope that Jesus would provide sexual satisfaction for me. In the end, the physical is always the physical. I had hoped when I was baptized in the Holy Spirit that I could just forget that I had a body, and for a while I could, but not forever—I really don't think you're supposed to. It was like Phil deciding that the baptism of the Holy Spirit cured him of being a homosexual, but it didn't. We're physical creatures and God doesn't deny it. Phil went on seeing his men, and I went on masturbating. We saw each other a few more times, and I loved him as much as ever. And I said to myself that if God wanted us married he would perform a miracle. But the only miracle that took place was an opening for a teaching assistantship in English in Collegeville. I knew the position was right for me because it came out of the blue, like a gift from God, and because it was separating Phil and me from a romance that could go nowhere.

When I left Chicago, Phil took me to the airport, and on the plane I wrote in my journal on tear-spattered pages:

> I have said goodbye to Phil, and after a few tears I have felt only a strong sense of God's hand in our lives, and the stern upholding of the Holy Spirit. I

want only to give Phil to God in love and to let God have his way, and at least tonight no longer need to love him and yearn for him, for he is God's. Thank you, Jesus, for weaning me so gently and yet so firmly from a strong but imperfect love—and be with Phil, and be with me—and thank you, and thank you.

Ingeborg Engemark says:

This lack of sex life around Collegeville isn't as bad for me as it is for the younger girls like Esmy Wilson. At least I can go back to the Gertrude Lawrence line, "I've had a love of my own." Or two or three. I didn't sit around in the virginal state till I was twenty-seven or twenty-eight, like Esmy. No, sir! I have memories to fall back on, even if things are disgustingly quiet right now. But Esmy has nothing! And it comes out as soon as she has a few drinks in her. Then the sob-sister act begins. Alas, alack, sob, sob, sob!

Most women manage to snap out of it, to find a man sooner or later, but I'm not so sure in Esmy's case. I *can* see her as an old maid, early phase. There's an air of quiet desperation about her, as Thoreau would have put it. She's like that old song, "Born to Lose." It would do her *so* much good if somebody'd just fling her down on a bed and knock that virginal halo off her head. But don't hold your breath. . . .

Almost from the beginning, Collegeville was a lonely place for me. Weeks went by before I had a single date. I wrote, "I am tired of weekends cooped in my suburban apartment above a drugstore, and I am painfully tired of knowing no man. I have found a hard silence here: it is the hours between those spent in the classroom that are the hardest . . . And yet I do know and I *must* know that God is working here and He will bring His own thing to pass (not necessarily *my* thing)."

I went to a few faculty parties, but I did not like what

I saw. At the very first one the hostess got so drunk that she passed out and various men kept going into the bedroom presumably to arouse her, and this made me a little nervous. I imagined all sorts of evil things were going on in that bedroom. Maybe they were.

Out of my desperation I had a few romances, some more tawdry than others. The first was a big, overweight Irish tenor who took me to an Irish bar and sang Irish folk songs, and then back to his apartment where he nearly assaulted me while I kept trying to tell him that I acquiesced and that it was not necessary for him to commit rape. I stayed the night with him, and I felt so funny about the whole thing that the very next morning, having had no sleep, I went to have my hair done, as though *that* would make it all right. A fairy did my hair and it was so reassuring, after that long night, to know that he *was* a fairy. The next night I slept in my own bed, and I remember being so pleased that I had my own bed and yet not all disappointed that at least *something* had happened in my life.

More months went by, and more loneliness, and then I met a twenty-eight-year-old freshman comp teacher, virginal and shy and very much like me. From the beginning I desired him physically. But for a long time he seemed to feel that kissing and hugging were enough, and that intercourse should be saved for marriage. I didn't argue.

One night the whole scene became too much for him, and we had our first relations. It was very obvious that he was a virgin. When he finally did it, he said this beautiful thing, "Oh," he said, "so *this* is how it's done!" I wrote in my notebook, "The end of one kind of aloneness has come, and I am almost in tears of joy—words will not say anything but I love—and am in love—with George Vitaci." Every day there was a new entry. "I may someday be Mrs. George Vitaci, but today I am still Esmy Wilson and there are papers to grade and a job to do." "A week has passed and still I love George Vitaci, whatever that means. There is a quiet joy in both of our lives now. How good these days, even as being in love becomes routine. . . ."

Neither George nor I realized that from the beginning we didn't have much to say to each other. He was religious, but certainly not a Christian. He had annoying little characteristics, such as cheapness and chintziness. When a dinner bill went beyond eight dollars he would have a nervous breakdown at the table; and when we went to visit friends, it always seemed to him that a bottle of New York State champagne was adequate. At first it seemed that we were truly united in bed, but even that proved to be an illusion. We played the different roles, tried different positions, like two children in a playground, wondering always what might be possible for a change. We never felt dirty or perverse about it. It was a wonderful, physical pleasure. He took me in every way imaginable and I encouraged him to. One night we were trying out different positions and somehow or other I realized that he was trying—oh, my, how shall I say it?—he was trying to use another entrance. And *I didn't mind!* It all seemed so natural, and it felt very very very good. There was something about being *full* of George Vitaci that pleased me. After that, we would try the new way more and more, and it always felt as good or better than the so-called normal way. I refuse to look back on it as bad or immoral. It just *was,* that's all. I only hope that God will accept *all* of me, everything I do, as an offering to him. I don't feel at all ashamed of the ways George and I made love. To me it's all love.

For a long time George had a thing about not having sex during the week, reserving it for weekends, and I would revel in getting him into my apartment and egging him on, on a week night, and finally getting him so aroused that he had to put his books aside and do it. I preferred our sex to happen at my place. He had a huge double bed in his apartment, there was a horrible crease right down the middle where it sagged, and I would get lost in that crease and not be able to perform right, and then he would get annoyed and make me run into the bathroom to get more Vaseline, but it wasn't more Vaseline that we needed, it was simply that the bed wouldn't work right. So more and more we would end up at my apartment, where the bed worked perfectly, and so did the chairs, and the floor, and the kitchen table. For a long time it was beautiful, savage, fun. In the middle of the act I would be praying and thanking God for it, hoping that the giving to George might be a giving to God, and I was also enjoying the plain physical sensations.

But as our relationship went on, we began to have the same problems as married couples. Sometimes I would still be aroused after George left. It began to be the classic example of the man getting his satisfaction and then thinking it's all over. He wasn't experienced, and he didn't know how to gauge what was happening on the female end. So I'd be left to satisfy myself alone. Soon I began to realize that the troubles in bed only magnified the troubles out of bed, and the little annoying things that he did began to bother me all the more. But there was worse to come. *He* dumped *me!* I wrote about it in my journal:

Tonight George Vitaci said he didn't want to marry me, and he suggested that we might be at the end of things. I am weeping real tears now, and I am the one who is being hurt. It serves me right for being so smug, for George is ultimately the honest one, and I am the one who will hurt now. He sounded like a bad French movie when he tried to tell me how he felt, and he kept anticipating teary response long before the tears came—and no matter how humorous it all sounds on the one hand, still there are tears. I need church tomorrow: a selfish thing. I am crying into my pillow—better somehow to cry.

Someone else will have to explain why we mourn over those who annoyed us the day before, how a purely physical relationship suddenly flames into love the instant it is over. It has something to do with the losses of childhood. We are not in love with love; we are in love with loss, and every loss of our lives duplicates the losses of our childhood, and makes us little babies screaming in our cribs. But I have always entertained the fantasy of God the Scriptwriter, never allowing life to wind down and become trivial. Something will *always* happen; His ends will always be served. And so it was this time. One week after I said my last goodbye to George Vitaci, I opened the door to my little apartment to see Phil Hanley, the great love of my life, standing there shyly, twisting his hat into shapelessness, like a twelve-year-old calling on his date. I threw my arms around him, and he threw his arms around me, but I noticed that he made no attempt to kiss me. His words came out like a burst dam. He told me that his homosexuality was cured, that he was going to charismatic meetings and now felt that he was a whole man. He said he wanted to marry me, that it had taken him much too long to realize it, and he asked if I would consider seeing him on a regular basis because this would be a huge step for both of us. I was thrilled, but I was also nervous. Long after midnight he kissed me lightly and kind of apologized for how he did it. He said, "I'm just learning how to be physical."

"Phil," I said, "the only way to be physical is to go ahead and do it. Be physical!"

He said, "Well, it's too soon. I'm not sure that it would work. Maybe the best thing to do would be to spend the weekend in some motel room. Maybe that would put us in the mood." Then he blew me a kiss and left.

I wrote in my journal:

Is it possible that Phil Hanley told me tonight that he was in love with me, that he wanted to spend the weekend in some anonymous motel room, that he wanted to make a life together? Is it possible that he somehow took back all those things that hurt so, all those barriers that were between us? I am happy and dazed and confused and tired, and I need God's clarity, and this cannot be but some mad dream. How hard, hard to grasp—but I could yet be in love with a new wonderful man—a Phil Hanley very different—so different—from the one who left me at the plane in Chicago. Is it possible? Is it possible? I am still overwhelmed.

No, it wasn't possible. Oh, my, how we human beings deceive ourselves! Phil had given up his career as a designer in Chicago and come all the way to Collegeville to be near me, to make a life with me, and to throw over the homosexuality that had consumed him for twenty years of his life. But nothing had changed. I found it out on our first date together after he returned. We went to a movie, came back to my apartment, prayed together, and then as I waited with trembling anticipation, he rushed off into the night like a terrified fawn. I remembered that my Irish tenor, my brutal lover, had told me that once a girl had quite literally taken his pants off and he just loved it. I thought that perhaps I should try that with Phil. But if I ripped his clothes off what would happen? The mind boggles. And anyway, it wouldn't be like me, it would be somebody else, and he would be entitled to despise me. I had already said to him, "Maybe the answer is just to fall into bed and see what happens," and his response had been: "Esmy, I think that would destroy the relationship." So I was painted into a corner. I could have him so long as I didn't have him. After a while I began to see elements of humor in it. At one point we wound up at a vacation spot with some people from the charismatic group, and Phil and I had one whole big room to ourselves, and the entire night was totally chaste. I thought of the ironies. All through dinner, there was Phil, the doting lover, and now he was the bored companion in bed. It was a farce, and I was the victim of the farce.

One night he told me about a dream. He and another man and I woke up in his bed, and I was rubbing his stomach. Later it seemed to me that maybe his dream was a way of asking me to arouse him. But I couldn't because I was so frightened of being rejected, because that had been the whole pattern: him rejecting me and putting me off. It was all so puzzling! I wrote:

I have brought deep confusion and fear and bondage into Phil's life—and I have no answers except the love that is willing: not painfully physical, as it once was, but somehow weighted down by his initial inability to carry on where we left off. Why is it so hard to say what is really true—what I really feel—and why I am so easily hurt (damndamndamn). I love you, Phil Hanley, and I am tired of all this fool'shness. I wish I were not so vulnerable, and I wish I could cry.

We saw each other less and less, and it all ended one night when I went to a movie and saw two men huddled close together in the back row, and realized that one of them was Phil. I thought none the less of the charismatic movement, none the less of the baptism of the Holy Spirit, but I also realized that it was foolish to look for miracles. I tried to pick up the pieces, and the next night I went to a meeting of the group. Someone stood up and began praying in tongues, and then someone interpreted, and I was so thrilled to hear the interpretation. "Be glad in the city that you're in," Jesus was saying through the other person's voice. "In this city you will shine as a light. Be a light to your neighbor, and be glad in the city you're in." This all connected me with the lights of Collegeville, and it encouraged me just when I desperately needed it.

By now I had taken my master's, and I decided to go on for a Ph.D. In my better moments I had learned to love teaching, and with a Ph.D. there's more freedom, better teaching assignments, and a great flexibility. You don't have the seven thirty to four thirty job and the boss breathing down your neck every second. And there has always been something comfortable about the rhythms of the school year. The pattern of beginning in the fall and ending in the spring—there's something wonderful and positive for me about the new school year, the new people, a new way of teaching a course. Perhaps it's just an easy and comfortable way of organizing your existence, but I have come to enjoy it. Still, there are moments of doubt. Sometimes teaching is not enough for me, and students are not enough. Sometimes it feels silly after you've taught Sir Gawain and the Green Knight three times to so easily walk into the classroom feeling not prepared enough and still be able to act like somebody who knows the subject. So there is a tremendous self-discipline required, or else it becomes boring.

Since Phil dropped out of my life, I have been more active than ever in the charismatic movement. If I have an objection to it, it is simply that some of the charismatic movement people have nothing else in their lives, and the whole thing becomes navel-gazing and introspective to the point of silliness. It becomes a religious ego-trip. Some of the movement's biblical ideas are very very fundamentalist. They see clouds of glory on people's heads and things like that. Those things I just can't do, I'm just not there. There are people who give up their jobs just to work for the Lord, and I'm not *there* either. And I still find myself being bothered by the freaks (there is just no other word for them) who turn to the charismatic movement. I cringe when people stand up at the meetings and beg God to fix their stammer, or cure them of thumbsucking.

Maybe it was my disenchantment with people like this that caused me suddenly to lose my religion—the most important thing in my life. Oh, my! My, my! It was a *terrible* experience, it left me shaken. One spring night, after several strange persons had spoken their pieces at a charismatic meeting, I suddenly realized that I didn't believe. I mean, I didn't believe in *anything,* Jesus Christ, God, the Holy Spirit, *anything.* I didn't know what to do about it. I went around in a horrible state of confusion for days. Then I remembered what a centurion says to Jesus in the Bible.

"My son is sick," the centurion said. "What can you do?"

And Jesus said, "If you believe, I can do all things for you."

And the centurion said, "Lord, I believe. Help my unbelief."

So that night I rushed home and read Dante, and it excited me that Dante was lost in the woods and had lost the right way. And I prayed to God to help my unbelief. Two days later at a seminar one of the professors said the trouble with this age is that nobody believes in God anymore, and I jumped up and said spontaneously, in front of all those atheists and agnostics, "I believe!" And I realized later that I *did* believe, and that the Lord had helped my unbelief. But I still feel that I had a close call, that I almost lost the whole basis of my life: the movement, God, and His Son Jesus Christ.

Now my life seems to be well ordered, with the single exception that there are no men, none whatever. This is my only worry, my only concern. I don't worry about my own death, or what will happen in the future. It's the Thomas Wolfe thing, we are twenty-one and we will never die; *that* concept. I see one more year here at the college, finishing exams for my Ph.D. Then my dream is to go to England and teach in a private school for a year, because I love England, and maybe I'll go back to Scotland and not only because of that one lovely encounter. My life pattern is that I can't have what I want most, so I am conditioned to believe that my dreams are not going to come true. What will happen to me? I don't know, and I love not knowing, because I am always in a state of expectancy then. It would bore me to know what's going to happen.

In all her letters and on all her visits, mama talks about nothing but marriage, as though it were going to happen next Saturday, and we are out shopping for bridal gowns. Whenever a man comes into my life, however fleetingly, she sees him as a potential husband, and we discuss it for hours. I don't know whether I am humoring her or humoring myself. But men are coming into my life so seldom that I wonder if I am cut out to be an old maid schoolteacher. I don't know. I hope I'm not sending those sorts of signals yet. I hope *some* man will find me.

Sometimes I worry that my male students seem *too* attracted to me, and they are the only ones who do. Sometimes they call me for dates. They announce that they are as old as I am, because some of them are twenty-three. But I don't date people in my class. It's not good policy. I was thinking in class today that I could tell by the way the boys were looking at me that it wasn't just "looking at teacher," there was a *sexual* thing going on, and remember, these are liberated boys. But I couldn't imagine one of them becoming involved with me. Most of them are eighteen and nineteen years old, and they don't have enough to give me to interest me. They are too shy. Yes, I confess, I did become very interested in a student named Matt Gould, but luckily I got hold of myself in time. He and a few of his friends took me out for dinner, and I found myself drawn to him. He was very bright, interesting, attractive, and at the end of the evening, when he took me home, I was terribly sexually restless. He came into my apartment and whenever we'd look each other in the eye there was something I found very hard to control. So I sent him home. Later I realized that this sort of thing was happening only because *there's nobody else around*. And women who are not having a normal sexual relationship with a husband or a mate become interested in *every* man as a sort of target. This worries me. This is why I worry about being promiscuous.

Later on Matt Gould invited me to his parents' home in the mountains for a summer weekend and on the way there I prayed that nothing would happen that I would regret later. But I realized there was an attraction and I was acting on it. Luckily he turned out to be very very boyish when I really talked to him—it was clear that there was no relationship possible because he was still such a child. I doubt if he's ever slept with anybody.

I went back home after the weekend and satisfied myself in my own way.

More and more this incessant masturbation worries me, but sometimes I have sexual tension that is so extreme I can't even sleep. I pace back and forth, I stand in front of my mirror brushing my teeth for hours, working out the next day's classes, trying not to masturbate. It gives me such emotional problems. It gives me far more emotional problems than normal or abnormal sexual intercourse would give me, or ever *did* give me. I always remember: the Bible talks about abusers of men's selves. Oh, my, it's so hard to be trapped in this human shell and to do what's right.

I go through periods where I just pray that I won't masturbate, that I won't need to, that God will take care of my sexual needs. But I am a physical person, there's no question about that. I've even thought of going to a gynecologist and asking about it. It's funny that masturbation should be such an issue. Even though I'm reconciled that this is something that I *do,* and something that I will keep on doing, I still feel that I would be a better Christian if I didn't. I sometimes have feelings of guilt about desiring the bodies of men, but I get over these feelings, because somehow I feel that sexual intercourse is always justifiable. But not masturbation. Maybe because masturbation is something that I live with. I reconcile intercourse as a beautiful thing, a thing of God, an offering to God, but I don't think of masturbation as something that's of God, because it's not happening between two people, and when one person is doing it, no matter what the release is, it's sad and weak, and somehow I feel that if I were a stronger person, I wouldn't have to resort to it.

Marriage is the only solution, of course. My married friend Margot said that for the first time in her life she has been able to stop thinking about sex, because sex is there and it's comfy and it's good. She said that there was a time in her life, just before her marriage, when somebody would walk up to her desk at the athletic director's office and she would start undressing him mentally. I've become the same way. In my fantasy life I spend a lot of time thinking about men and being in bed with them. Luckily, I've never felt any physical attraction toward women, but I'm even aware of *their* bodies. I envy women with very very well developed bodies, but I don't desire them. Thank goodness!

Sally Jo Lee says:

Esmy and I have one thing in common: We have the same philosophy about love, or sex, or whatever you want to call it. Our philosophy is simple: We neither one of us believe in free love. That makes us rare on this campus, you better believe it! Esmy's very much a virginal type, just like me. I'm sure she doesn't do any sleeping around. I've got extra antennas for that kind of thing.

You don't have to point out to me that there's a contradiction between my religious attitudes and my attitudes about sexual intercourse and free love. Plainly, I believe in free love. Not free promiscuity, but free *love*. And I realize that the Bible is very explicit against this. It's just a contradiction in my life, the central one, and I'm not sure I reconcile it. If some of the people in my charismatic groups knew about my sex life—oh, my! People like Phil don't know that I've ever had any kind of sex with anyone. If they did know, they would keep telling me what a contradiction it is. Well, of course, it's a paradox. I'm a great fan of Kierkegaard, and Kierkegaard is big on the paradox, and that's where I leave it: It's just a paradox, and it presents no problems.

I recognize the possibility that I have accommodated my sexual activities to my theology out of sheer need, and that's why I have no guilt. I've never been a martyr or an ascetic in my religion. Despite the Ten Commandments, I keep taking these little existential leaps. I guess I feel like Lucy in that cartoon—God *couldn't* be upset with me, no matter what I do. I'm not worried about God damning me. I'm happy with what I've done, sexually and otherwise. I read the book of Paul—of course, Paul isn't Jesus—and Paul finally says, "Well, I really don't think you all should get married in these hard times. It's much better if you're not married, because then you can please God and not worry about marriage. But if you *have* to get married, let each man have his own wife and each woman her own husband. It's better to marry than burn."

So then I get angry because I think, What options has God given me? I can get married or I can burn, which I interpret to mean going crazy without a physical relationship. Well, I don't have the option of getting married in Collegeville, because there doesn't seem to be anyone here to marry me, so my only option seems to be to do without all sexual activity, to burn, and I just *can't* do that.

So I just pray, "Jesus, this is who I am, with all my faults and imperfections, and I offer myself to You." And I somehow feel that I please Him. And I feel that if somebody were to walk in the front door right now, and I felt an attraction for him, I would go to bed with him, and it would be part of the Esmerelda Wilson that I offer Jesus, and He would accept it eagerly. I have no money and no jewels, and I myself am the only offering that I can make.

Postscript: Several Months Later

This summer a young man, a banking genius, Thomas P. Hamilton by name, arrived from Seattle, and at the beginning he bored me to tears. I met him at one of the charismatic meetings, and after that he kept knocking at my door, dropping in, and I don't like that. It seems like an invasion of privacy. I want a phone call first; I want fair warning.

He would come in and sit on my couch and run his fingers through his thinning unruly red hair, and sit, and sit, and sit. It would be up to me to make what little conversation there was. Besides that, I found him very clumsy and unappetizing. At thirty years old he still suffered from acne, and his posture was horrible. When he sat down he looked like an eel, slumped all over the house.

For several weeks he kept dropping over and asking me if I wanted to go out for a hamburger. Or sometimes he would ask me to come to his apartment for carrot juice. He had a fifty-dollar juicer that he said he'd bought on the theory that a life without carrot juice was unhealthy. Sometimes I went; he was harmless enough, and even though I didn't like him, he was—as the book title says—the only game in town. But I said to myself that I simply would not get involved with such a creep except superficially.

One night we came back to my apartment after a charismatic meeting where he had told the group in a very sincere and impassioned manner how thrilled he was to be involved with them. At the meeting I prayed aloud for him and asked God that in the midst of adjusting to a new town that God would be with him because it's so lonely to come to a new place. This made me feel a little better about him, and on the way home he kept telling me how much he appreciated the prayer.

Once again he slouched down on my couch, but this time he seemed to want to talk. He told me that he was half Scotch, and that he felt himself to be far more Scotch than American. This pleased me, since I have always been captivated by Scotland. He told me about his difficult childhood, his irreligious parents, and how he had found spiritualism through a book by Jeanne Dixon, and then soured on that and got a copy of the New Testament and opened up a whole new life for himself. I was moved by his individual search and his individual acceptance of the Gospel in the face of a difficult situation at home, and I began to see him as more of a human being. My friend Ingeborg Engemark dropped in, and he even won that tough cookie over with his sincerity, his honesty. She told me later that there would be a lot of adjusting to do if I married him, but that he *was* a very special person. "The only thing, I wonder, Esmy," she said, "is could you spend the rest of your life praying and drinking carrot juice?" I still didn't know.

For weeks and weeks nothing more happened except that he continued to make me nervous and he continued to make me do all the talking. One night he took me grocery shopping in his Volvo and we went to his place for carrot juice, and I remember sitting on the couch being a nervous wreck because he sat there sort of staring at me and once in awhile quoting Adam Smith. I didn't know what in the *world* he was up to and at ten thirty I said I had to go home. The truth is, I had begun to feel an attraction for this strange wraith, but I just didn't want to cope with it. When I came home I was very nervous and restless, and for a long time I lay in bed fighting an urge to masturbate.

Then an alarming thing happened. A woman of about thirty or thirty-five came to visit him, and actually moved in with him for two weeks. Ingeborg told me that she found out that the woman was an old girl friend and she and Thomas were very thick, and I found myself in a great state of annoyance. I had never dreamed that *anyone* would become interested in him, let alone travel all the way from Seattle and live with him in his apartment almost as though they were man and wife. This gave him a new charisma, and fascinated me altogether.

When the woman went back to Seattle, Thomas began dropping in on me again, bringing me carrot juice, taking me out for hamburgers, and one night he said, "I wouldn't want you to get the wrong idea about Marilyn. We're just old friends." One night he asked me to his apartment for carrot juice, and as we sat on the couch, in nearly total silence, as usual, I began to feel my customary attack of nerves. Finally he said, "You know, it would be nice if you and I prayed together."

I said, "Yes, that *would* be nice."

He said, "Well, how about right now?"

So we bowed our heads, and each of us prayed individually, "God, thank you for this. God, be with this person or that. . . ." Prayers of thanks and supplication and adoration. This went on for about ten minutes.

At the end of the prayer session he gave me a little brief kiss. He said, "Well, at least that's a beginning." I thought this was very sweet. But I wondered: What was it the beginning of—more praying or more kissing? He left it ambiguous. But I chose to think it was the beginning of something real. I had long since decided that Christians were very very contradictory and that I never wanted to become drawn into a romantic relationship with a Christian, but now I was on the verge of a new relationship in my life and it was very beautiful and I went home and just wept, it was just so very very special. I felt that I could love him. He had seemed like such a total oaf, but now he seemed so very very wonderful.

The next weekend he was at my apartment, and he has this thing of opening the Bible to just any place and putting his finger on the page haphazardly and deciding it's God speaking, and this makes me very nervous, but he was sort of into that system that evening. I have a Bible that has the Apocrypha in it and he opened it to the Apocrypha, which I thought was very funny at the time, because I didn't regard the Apocrypha as scripture. And he was trying so hard to find something meaningful in Second Esdras, and I just knew that *nothing* meaningful was there. The Apocrypha are all superstitions.

But then he asked me to do the same thing, to look for something meaningful, but what he ended up doing was getting very close to me physically while we both concentrated on the Apocrypha. That got me very nervous. How do you concentrate on the Bible when someone is sort of edging up to you? And, anyway, I just didn't believe in this way of getting truth from the Bible. So I told him it seemed to me that God was telling us we didn't need a scripture, that whatever was in our hearts was all right. Thomas acted as though he had failed, that he hadn't come up with any great revelation, that his system hadn't worked. So he left around midnight, and I was very worked up physically. It just made me very very angry that he hadn't even kissed me. It was like a romance in church camp. It all left me very angry at myself because I don't like using religion for this kind of male-female game. I'm not sure that Thomas even knows he does it, but I think he uses religion for social reasons, and I felt that something very dishonest was going on. It would have been so much more honest for him to just push me down and make love to me. But it was dishonest to edge close and get me all excited and then leave.

I saw him a few nights later, and it turned out that he was as disturbed by the evening as I was. He took me to dinner and didn't say a word all through the meal. Then we went to a charismatic meeting and prayed together, but he kept on acting strangely. On the way home he walked ten paces ahead of me, as though he didn't want to be seen with me, and I finally had to say, "Will you please drop back and take my arm?" He really infuriated me! But then he came back the next day and he said, "I don't know many things for sure, but I do know that I like you." This was a major address for him, so I was happy for another week, and I was very very interested in him by now.

For several weeks we went to religious meetings together and prayed together and went back to his place for carrot juice, but nothing else happened. Sometimes after praying he would hug me and squeeze me or stroke my hair, but clearly it was only going to reach a certain point. I got my hopes up a little bit one night when he lay down on his couch and put his head in my lap and asked me if I would stroke his hair. So here I am stroking his hair and he begins to touch me and get very affectionate and do everything but kiss me, and then he jumps up and leaves! And I'm wondering what's going on, what's the problem, and feeling very frustrated.

We had been seeing each other for two or three months when he finally gave a sexy kiss, after we had prayed together at his apartment, and then just as suddenly he began saying, "A beautiful woman is like a flute. You can play a flute, but we both know that we can't get involved." Then he said, "I have very strong feelings about you, but I don't want to infringe on your friendship, and I don't want to make too many demands on you. So we just *can't* get involved." I told him that I couldn't see the problem and he said that he had been struggling about whether to give up his Christianity and seduce me. I finally said, "I don't see that there is a contradiction. Why can't you have both Christianity and me?" So we prayed about it, and it was all inconclusive.

But on the very next night, the pressure seemed too much for him. We prayed together and sat around and talked together, and around midnight he put on his coat and sort of hugged me goodnight, and suddenly he said, "Well, I can hug you better with my coat off." So he takes his coat off and we sit down on the couch and he hugs me again. I made some comment that this was certainly good for the soul, and before I knew it he was kissing me, which was fine, and then before I knew it I was being carried into the bedroom.

It all happened very very very fast. I literally didn't expect it, but I was delighted. After he made love to me the first time, he said, "Are you relaxed, or do you feel frustrated?" Frustration wasn't even on my mind at the time. It didn't occur to me to feel satisfied or dissatisfied. From the couch to his orgasm, it hadn't taken five minutes, and there was very little time for me to ponder deep, philosophical questions. When you haven't been trafficking in this kind of emotion for months and months, it comes as such a pleasant surprise that the last thing you're worried about is whether you're satisfied. It's just overwhelming, in a good way.

Then it happened a second time and he was clearly clearly clearly trying to give me a climax. And then he wanted to know if I had had one, and I was just very sorry he asked the question. He missed the whole point. I wasn't interested in the mechanical part of sex, but just in the fact that *it had happened*. The point was *closeness*, being together, not whether certain secretions flowed and flowed. So his question was irrelevant.

So I told him, "I don't *know* if I had a climax," and

he said, "Oh, I'm sorry!" He was ready to take on the instant pose of the inadequate male. There was very little said after that, but he quickly decided that he had to go home.

As he picked up his clothes, he said, "Do you do this often?"

I thought this was humorous and I said, "Only with friends," and he laughed. I said, "Do you think it's all right that it happened?"

He said, "I should be asking *you* that question. I have to admit that I feel a little guilty now that the desire has passed."

So I said, "Well, I hope you realize that this doesn't impose any claim on anyone. I just hope it'll all be a part of growing together."

The next night we went to a charismatic meeting, and it was clear from the beginning that there was something very very wrong. When we got back to my apartment, he wanted to leave right away, and I literally insisted that he sit down and talk about what had happened. He didn't want to, but I felt it had to be clarified in my own mind.

At first all he would say was, "Well, you know those furnaces can get pretty hot at times." That was his explanation for the whole evening, that it was just a biological impulse that had possessed him.

When I insisted that he give me a better explanation, he stayed on for an hour, telling me over and over that he didn't want to talk about it, and getting angrier and angrier and angrier. He told me that Marilyn, the girl who had come to visit him, was not just a friend, but someone he planned to marry some day. He said, "She's not the prettiest girl or the sexiest girl I have ever known, but I think a lot of her, and I think she's someone who would accept me whatever I did."

I said, "Well, if you feel that way, why didn't you marry her before?"

"Well, she has two children. That's a problem. We've known each other for a long time and I'm waiting for

God to give me a revelation about whether or not I should marry her."

He said he was terribly attracted to me physically, but he didn't want to be running up here all the time to go to bed, and he didn't like the idea of sex coming before anything else. He said he respected me and thought I was a fine person. He said there was a lot of passion with us, but there was no real love, and he just couldn't handle the relationship on a purely physical level.

That really sort of hurt me, and I dealt with it in a very very dishonest way, and I knew I was doing it, but I didn't care. I said, "Could we just pray about this, because it would help me?"

So I did what he does all the time in prayer: Say things that I wouldn't have the courage to say otherwise. It was cowardly of me. I started praying for him and for Marilyn, and praying that God would give him the courage to marry her if that's what he wanted. I prayed that God would give him some sort of revelation and that God would just use me to be whatever Thomas needed, at the time, if I could just be of some help in his life, if I could just help him to reconcile his own problems. I prayed that my own role in his life would not have been in vain, and I offered myself up as a sacrifice to God so that Thomas would be happy. It was all sort of goopy.

Then I realized that Thomas was neither reacting nor praying. He was ominously silent. He looked terrible. I said, "Well, I feel much better now, but you look pained." Then he just burst out and said he was very very angry. He said he felt as though his and Marilyn's privacy had been invaded, that he and I had had a pleasant evening the night before, but there was no reason why I should make him stay and talk. "I don't need this!" he screamed. "You've just ruined things. There was no reason why I needed your prayers for me and Marilyn. That problem will work out of its own accord, thank you, and *you* don't have to feel so responsible for *me*, because *other* people minister to me, and I don't need your ministration. The whole problem with the Collegeville Christians is that they're always on the phone talking with each other, doing social work with each other, and I just can't cope with that kind of thing, and I *won't* be drawn into it!" It was tremendous anger coming out, loud, terrible, but on the other hand, I think it was very good for him because he usually doesn't talk, he's usually so quiet and inexpressive. So while I was terrified of his anger, I felt that all this was a wonderful catharsis for him and might do him some good. Finally he said, almost plaintively, *"Why* did you have to pray like that?"

I said, "Well, I had to pray or cry, and I chose to pray."

He said, "Why can't boys and girls be friends?"

I said, "Well, you can say that, but your actions belie your words."

He said, "Well, you'll just have to beware of me, because this is the way I am. Passion is one of my weaknesses. I come on this way without meaning anything by it."

So I said, "Well, you'd better beware of me, too." Right after that, he left.

Where's the happy ending? Well, that's just one more thing I've had to learn about myself and my life. *There are no happy endings.* I didn't see him for weeks, and then one day I ran into him in the street, and he walked me home. He said almost literally nothing on the ten-minute walk, and when we got to my door I opened it and invited him in, but before I could even finish extending my invitation, I discovered I was talking to his back. His final words just hung in the air. "Goodbye, kiddo," he said.

I haven't seen him since, except at an occasional charismatic meeting, where he manages to stay as far from me as possible. I realized as I thought about it that as usual I had created my own myth of a person. I saw some very beautiful qualities in him, a way that he had of making me feel important. I thought that something lovely was going to happen, but I always think this too soon. For a while I thought I could marry him and take on his life-style, but now I realize we are very different. There are times when it's good to drink brandy in the wee hours, rather than carrot juice, and there are times when it's better to make love than to pray.

So I'm very confused, and it troubles me that he may have me marked down as some kind of sexpot, and not a good person, and that *I* somehow enticed *him* into bed. It just seems to me that he *wanted* a physical happening as much as I did, but he denied it, which is dishonest. I wanted it and I *didn't* deny it, and now he puts me down as some kind of wanton. I know that's what he is really thinking, and I am so ashamed.

The other day, my good friend Ann Stults told me that he had asked her out, and that they had gone back to his apartment and prayed and drunk carrot juice. I told her that I hoped she would enjoy her friendship with him, but to be very careful when they reached the Apocrypha. She said that she wasn't sure that she understood, and I told her to enjoy herself, she would understand soon enough.

ANN STULTS, 23
Instructor, Department of English

Esmerelda Wilson says:

Ann Stults is a very very moody girl, a strange, ingrown person. She sees the world entirely in terms of how it treats *her,* and she isn't gracious or grateful at all. For example, I got her a job teaching, but she's never expressed any appreciation, and she never mentions to anyone else how I got her the job. She'll proudly tell you how *she* applied for the job, and *she* got it. Oh, my, that's just *not* the way it happened.

When Ann first started teaching, she was over here every five minutes asking questions, getting advice. She'd think nothing of calling me at midnight. She has no respect for the fact that other people want their sleep, their privacy. She'd call at eleven P.M. and ask if I had a newspaper so she could see what was on TV, or I'd be writing or grading papers, and she'd know it, and still she'd call and ask me if I could direct her to a good fortune-teller or someone who knew ESP. It didn't matter that I was inconvenienced; she is not troubled by the inconvenience of others. If she wakes up at six A.M. and decides she'd like to take a walk, she'll call and wake me up and say, "Come on! Let's take a walk!"

And she's rude. My goodness, she just doesn't understand courtesy! I'll have people in for dinner and she'll say, "Oh, Esmy, you need to do something about your furniture. It's so tacky!" Or she'll complain that my telephone has a disagreeable ring. Funny little undercutting things like that. I don't understand it. I'm not dating any more than she is, so it can't be jealousy. I think maybe she had too sheltered a childhood, in all those parochial schools, and she's still learning how to be a grown-up person.

Ingeborg Engemark says:

Ann's just plain moody. When she's happy, she's like a merry little elf. And when she's sad, God, it's awful. "You bonnie bird, how can you sing?" She went to Catholic schools, and in the Catholic schools you pick up the Irish culture, and the Irish are moody buggers.

Some of my close friends shudder when they hear that I had a completely Catholic girlhood, but I don't look back on it with loathing or trauma at all. Maybe I am not one big happy bundle of fond memories, but I don't think that early Catholicism seared me the way it seems to have seared certain other people. Mary McCarthy, for instance.

Maybe this is because I always had my own ideas, and I don't think there was *ever* a time when I was totally taken in by everything that I was being told. I remember when they were teaching me the "Hail Mary," and I couldn't have been much older than two—this is the age when Catholic families, if they mean business, start their kids on prayers—and I deliberately tried not to learn it. I can't tell you why, but there was always that kind of resistance in me. I just didn't want to learn prayers at the age of two.

I wasn't all that thrilled about making my first communion in the second grade, or my first confession either. As a young child I used to have a terrible time thinking of things to confess. I mean, there aren't a lot of sins open to a second grader. "Disobedience" was a popular one, or "lack of charity," which meant that you had been angry with a friend. The nuns used to push "I did not pay attention in school," but we couldn't find that sin in the Bible, so we didn't often use it. Mostly I just went in and told the priest that I had been disobedient. I felt silly going in there empty-handed. I wanted to give the poor man *something* for his trouble.

Confession was once a month on first Fridays just before communion, and if you made nine of the communion services you were guaranteed a trip to heaven. Sister said that was a promise that an apparition of the Blessed Mother had made to somebody. I quickly got through my first nine communions so I wouldn't have to worry about going to hell, and this set my mind at ease. Monthly confession and communion weren't so onerous, but daily masses were another story. I *hated* them.

The public school kids didn't have to go to school till nine, but we had to be there an hour earlier for that silly mass. We all resented it. It bored me stiff. At first I was kind of intrigued by the Latin, but then the Gregorian chants became boring, too. They were kind of wailing—*yah, yah, yah.* The mass was always the same, and it didn't take long to get bored by it. I used to read a lot during mass. I would hold up my hymnal and read behind it. *Jane Eyre. The Yearling. Girl's Love.* I was always reading.

Our main pleasure was funerals because we got to sing different things, and we got out of school for a while. The funeral would be going on and everybody would be so sad, and we kids would be laughing and running around in the choir loft. I don't know what the mourners thought. We just *had* to laugh because the hymns and chants and the *Dies Irae* were so ridiculous and depressing. Father had a funeral sermon that was always the same. He never mentioned the person who was dead. He just recited the same words and flang a little holy water around. We didn't get it, but it was amusing. A break in the action.

Our grade school teachers came from a dingbat order of southern hillbillies. They had a reputation for being dumb, and they *were* dumb. This particular order took women from the eighth grade on, even though the church says that's too young for nuns, so usually they got backward, backwoods women. They taught us out of old-time books that said things like, "Use oil on your mop when you clean your floor, unless you happen to be one of the few families that own a vacuum cleaner." That was actually in our health and hygiene text. There were illustrations of women with dresses down to their ankles, and men in spats and derbys. Very relevant.

Esmerelda Wilson says:

Ann told me that the nuns put horrible ideas into their minds about sex, that boys were put on earth to take advantage of them, things like that. She told me that she can only think of boys as attackers that she must fend off and repel. This consigns her to the permanent role of teen-age girl trying to become a woman, trying to learn a new and totally different approach. I think a Catholic education does this very very often.

In our catechism classes, the nuns used to teach us about sin. None of them had a degree or any practical experience in this subject, but they seemed to think they could tell us about it. When we were little, they used milk bottles to get the point across. The white bottle was the pure child, totally lacking in sin. Then there was the white bottle with spots in it, and that was somebody who'd committed venial sins. Then there was the black milk bottle for the rotter who'd committed mortal sins. The nuns told us that our souls would look just like these bottles. Thank God we didn't have any black students; I think they'd have been even more confused by this bottle number than we were.

In the sixth grade, Sister took us out in the hall, first the girls and then the boys, and said in a panicky voice, "Do you know that some of our girls have been calling up boys? Do you know what that could lead to?"

We all looked at her funny. She said, "Well, I just want it stopped!" Then she led us all back into class, her face red, as though she had just said something horrible and embarrassing. That little session in the hall turned out to be our sex education class. It was the only sex education we ever got.

Later on, in junior high, the nuns would do the little number about the patent leather shoes and the white tablecloth. *That* old cliché. You never heard it? Why, it's a standing joke among people who've gone to Catholic schools. Sister told us that patent leather shoes reflect up your skirt, and therefore we should never wear them. She said some men made a profession out of studying female anatomy through patent leather shoes. We were stunned! Some of us girls tried looking into each other's patent leather shoes, and we found we couldn't see a thing. The curved surface diffused the image. We even got down on the floor and stared straight into the leather, but we *still* couldn't see anything. It just didn't work the way Sister had said—unless you wore patent-leather shoe boxes. We put her down as weird.

The other cliché was never to use white tablecloths when serving food to a man. One of the girls was silly enough to ask, "Why, Sister?"

"Never mind!" Sister said.

When the girl insisted, the nun said shyly and demurely, "Well, white tablecloths suggest bedsheets, and this might get the man thinking in the wrong way."

In high school the nuns were always behind the times. Five years after spaghetti-strap shoulder straps had been completely out, Sister was still telling us not to wear them, that they were too suggestive. She finally banned them at our proms, even though nobody would have worn them anyway. Our prom dresses had to go up to the neck and have collars on them. There was something dreadful underneath, and the sisters wanted it concealed. We got the idea.

In ways like this we were given a constant view of ourselves as defenders. It was made plain to us that hideous things would follow if we were seen holding hands with a boy. By high school these teachings became so ridiculous that most of us just ignored them. But I don't think that some of the more disturbed girls were helped very much by a picture of men as dragons and girls as defenders of a holy treasure under their dresses.

We learned absolutely nothing about how to handle

men as adults. Almost all my classes were girls only, and then I went to an all-girl Catholic college, and as a result I never learned to accept men as an everyday occurrence. Men became an *event,* and I found myself overreacting to them. I'm only now getting over it, and the problem still comes up. When you are always admonished to keep men away, to make them keep their distance, not to touch them or let them kiss you, it's hard to change overnight. As one of my girl friends said, "If you get in the habit of turning men off all the time, if this becomes an instinct, what happens when you get married and you have to do exactly the opposite of what you've been doing all your life?" I still don't know.

All the way through high school I felt that I was pretty cool about the church, that I could take it or leave it alone, and throw out the obviously stupid superstitious aspects. But in my senior year I went on a retreat and listened to a Jesuit priest talk about hell for three or four days, and he scared me to death. He went on and on about the mental suffering, how horrible you'd feel in hell, and the physical torture. He worked his way up to people who'd committed their first mortal sin and then were killed in an automobile accident immediately afterward. By the time he got through I was afraid to drive home. I hadn't been to confession for a couple of years, because I'd quit going after the eighth grade. In high school the nuns let us out on Friday nights to go to confession, and we'd go out and walk around the block and say, "I've been to confession." But now I went to confession right away. The priest assigned me a Rosary a day for a week. This was stern. Usually it was two "Our Fathers" and two "Hail Marys" and a good "Act of Contrition." My reformation only lasted a week or so.

Going to an all-female Catholic college is almost like being in a convent. The sisters had a list of things we had to do. Everything began with "We do" so as to emphasize the positive. *"We do* avoid Jonas Street." We always wondered if there was a house of ill-repute on Jonas Street, but it developed that lower-class Protestant families lived there, and the sisters thought we might become contaminated. *"We do* wear nylons to class." *"We do* wear feminine attire." This meant no shorts or slacks. It was all very oppressive and silly, because this was an all-girl school, and who was going to see us?

As anyone could have foretold, the main subject of discussion was sex, implicitly or explicitly. With no boys around, we thought about nothing else. Some of the nuns seemed to be in the same condition.

There was one called Sister Loretta Lorivius, whom we quickly learned to call Sister Loretta Lascivious. Her sexual hangups were on permanent display. She'd weave sex into everything. Once we were reading *Notes from the Underground,* and there's a section where one of the characters preaches to a prostitute. Well, we stayed on that part for weeks. Sister Loretta Lascivious would not pass beyond that point, and she kept going into the Lisa episode, and what did that mean to him? This led her into asking questions like, "Where's the redlight district in St. Louis?"

The confused student said, "I don't know, Sister," and Sister said, "Well, you'd better find out, so you don't wind up there someday!"

If she came across two men in a novel, she would somehow find a sexual relationship between them, and that's all we would discuss. She would chart out the short stories we wrote, and then call us in and tell us how much we'd revealed about ourselves sexually. She spent weeks on "The Wife of Bath," saying things like, "Do you know what gap-toothed means? Heh, heh, heh!" She could turn the Boy Scout Handbook into a sex manual.

All the nuns were paranoid about lesbianism. At one time there must have been at least one horrible case, but there were none when I was there. The sisters had a hard rule about never locking the door to your room in the dorms. Once in a while a nun would burst in without knocking, and we assumed she was looking for lesbians in *flagrante delicto.* She couldn't have been looking for men—it was just plain impossible to get a man into your room. It would have been easier to smuggle an elephant in.

Three years have gone by since I went to that college, but I've only lately begun to realize that once you're a Catholic you're always one. When I first came to Collegeville, I went through the I-don't-believe-in-anything stage and the it's-all-silly stage. But now I'm getting into my own kind of thinking; I don't totally believe in Catholicism or the God of the Catholic Church, but I do believe that it's very likely there is a God. I also believe that much of what is taught about him is bunk.

But during the year that I was working on my master's degree at The College, I found it hard to believe in anything. I had moved in with three other girls from Catholic colleges, and they went to church regularly and tried to get me to go, and one day they had a mass in our apartment. That was very big in the avant-garde circles we all traveled in, to have a home mass, and as hostesses we were supposed to select the scripture readings for the service. I did a reading from Bertrand Russell, *Why I Am Not a Christian*. There were several nuns there, and they didn't appreciate it one bit. I hadn't known there were nuns there, but they were sort of undercover nuns. They ran around in Bermudas and you didn't know they were real live nunny nuns until they told you. After the mass, one woman was livid and made a big attack on me and Bertrand Russell. I didn't care one way or another. But after that one act of rebellion, I seemed to find a balance about God and religion and the church.

As soon as I took my master's I applied for a teaching assignment, and they told me that they thought I could teach a class in composition. Two days before the school year started, the dean called me in and said they had changed my assignment to Introduction to Poetry. I panicked. I thought, *"Poetry! What's that?"* My reaction was stark terror. I had spent the whole summer preparing to teach composition, and I hadn't read any poetry in months. Now I had forty-eight hours to get ready.

The first day that I was to teach, I was up at six A.M.

I walked around my apartment trying to breathe deeply, because I was afraid that I would appear in my classroom and be out of breath from sheer fright. I didn't know yet that students are mostly asleep at their eight o'clock classes, and I could have read them the Collegeville phone book and they would have thought it was Robert Lowell. I went to the building and hid in my office, and at eight o'clock sharp, when I heard the bell, I headed down the hall toward the room, like somebody walking the last mile. There they were, all those half-closed eyes, sixty or seventy of them. They looked cold, unenthusiastic, and annoyed, and there was some snoring.

I decided not to try to teach them anything that first day. I spent the session asking incredibly stupid questions about things that I had no business asking. One of my questions was, "Are you likely to have any sort of physical attack in my class, and what kind of treatment would you require?" When I got back the written replies, I found that hardly anyone had answered that question. It was a big blooper; it was too personal. Most answered, "None of your business," or didn't answer at all. I was off to a *great* start.

The second time I saw them, I opened with e.e. cummings, to get their attention. I read "the balloon man," and they seemed to perk up a little, and then I gave them, "anyone lived in a little how town," and that other great poem that ends with the line, "how do you like your blueeyed boy, mr. death?" This seemed to get their attention for a while, and we ended up with a fairly good session.

Ingeborg Engemark says:

My impression is that Ann has a lot to learn as a teacher. She's too recessive, too intimidated by the whole thing. She has this tiny little voice, and the only way you can hold freshman English students is by screaming at them once in a while. She won't do that, so they drift off into sleep. Gadzooks, they don't drift off into sleep when I'm teaching! I'll break their eardrums and their pointy little heads to get their attention, and they know it. But Ann just stands up there and takes it, and then she goes home and gets depressed and tells the birds to quit singing.

I've been teaching for a full year now, and every day I have deeper reservations. Not only about what I'm teaching and how I'm teaching it, but just general reservations about these kids that come into my class all bored and stiff and miserable. Most of my students go through their classes like automatons. This morning, I was trying to teach *Metamorphosis,* by Frank Kafka, the story about the guy that wakes up and he's a cockroach. I thought the kids would really be into the idea of isolation, of alienation. But the whole subject died. I don't know when I've ever seen students so bored. I did everything but stand on my head to get them interested. I tried to be funny. I tried to be informal and friendly. But all I got was some loud yawns.

Finally I said, "Well, what do *you* think about this work?" One girl stood up, cleared her throat, and said, "Well, I don't know."

Now if these students can't get interested in *Metamorphosis,* what *can* they get interested in? It's the *perfect* story for them. The hero wakes up and finds out he's a cockroach. His family can't deal with him as a cockroach, they have to deal with what they've made him. He dies at the end, because the family simply cannot tolerate him in their lives. When the cockroach is dead, the rest of the family is free. Those freshman students should have loved this. But they just didn't get it.

I find that this is more the rule than the exception. They come to class with no reaction. They're just blank. And they look so terrible when they come to my eight o'clock classes. They look like they've been bludgeoned, as though they've had it. Don't ask me to explain why. They seem to just exist, sitting there like zombies. I got up the nerve to ask a girl about this one day, and she said, "Well, an eight o'clock class is too early. By nine o'clock, I'm starting to wake up. Ten o'clock's all right, but by eleven o'clock I'm hungry, and at the one o'clock classes, I've just eaten and I'm sleepy, and by two the day's over." You wonder why they go to class at all.

Somebody said, "Well, students aren't interested in their classes anymore, because they've got so many things going on on the outside that they're *really* interested in." But I don't even think *that's* true. I don't think they're interested in anything except dope and sex. I was very into the idea of student activities when I first came to Collegeville. And I thought that the younger kids were really into it in an intelligent way, mainly because I'd see them gathering and I'd read their placards and it all seemed to make sense. But since I've been teaching here, I realize I was wrong. The main demonstrators are the street people, not the college people. The college people go along, yes, because they get a couple of days off and a little excitement. But they don't show the real dedication to causes that I expected. At the time of the Cambodia bombing the students had a big strike, and they made a lot of noise, and the university wound up canceling all classes for the rest of the year and giving everybody credit. I kind of got disillusioned watching all those self-satisfied students packing up their swimsuits and going away, calling it a strike and yet getting credit for the whole semester. What kind of a gesture is that? But that's the kind of activism they're into. The painless kind. The meaningless kind.

I really don't know why they're here in the first place. We're educating huge crowds of kids, and they don't seem to be moved by the college experience at all. They come into class and immediately renounce the past. They'll say, "Don't give us any classics. We don't want *that* old stuff." They throw out all recorded history, but you just can't do that. Knowledge and understanding did not begin with Abbie Hoffman.

Esmerelda Wilson says:

I think there have been very few men in Ann's life. There was a little dating in St. Louis, but only a little.

And there's been very very little dating here in Collegeville. But that's not so surprising. None of the girls in my age group seem to be dating much.

Once I introduced her to a grad student of her own age, and they went out a few times, and she was horrified because he kissed her rather passionately, and that passionate kiss became a big issue with her. It was something the nuns hadn't told her about, where the tongue comes into use, and she thought it was naughty and sinful. Her only other love life is a fantasy crush on a professor in the classics department, and I don't understand this at all. The man is an obvious homosexual, and we all know it, but she still fawns on him.

One of my friends, a psychology major, said that my apartment looks very open and ready to change, but that Ann's looks closed and old-maidish, a place for everything, as if it's all screwed down and permanent. My friend says this might indicate that Ann's life is already subconsciously closed, that even though she makes a big thing out of the shortage of men and how very very frustrating it all is, that she really doesn't want relationships with men at all.

I've never had as much trouble developing a social life as I've had here in Collegeville. I realize that I'm no Elizabeth Taylor, but I'm not a gargoyle either. I'm tall, I have a nice figure, I have a nice face with good skin, and I don't think that I'm the klutziest woman around. But I've never been willing to chase men, and on this campus men are simply not willing to chase *me*. At twenty-three, I'm afraid I'm getting into the senile age group. Everyone else seems so young, and there are so *many* of them. As for eligible men of my own age, they hardly exist. I don't know where they are. When I came out here, I thought I was going to have a neat social life, but I never have. Men here are so complacent, so self-satisfied, and they seem to have their regular stables of girl friends, which don't include me. The male teachers all date teenyboppers. The professors and the instructors whom I *should* be dating—they look like Greek gods to the young girls in their classes, and so it's very easy for affairs to get started. The young male students in my own classes seem to like me, and they often flirt, but this is an option that isn't open to me. No matter how many goo-goo eyes I get from the males in my classes, I'm not about to start dating them. I would be *ostracized* by all my peers. No, I don't understand this double standard, but there it is. It's perfectly okay for a male teacher to date a female student, but not for a female teacher to date a male student. I've never known a female teacher to break that taboo. It's as rigid on campus as the taboo again incest.

Sometimes I think I may have educated myself right out of the social scene. When men find out that I teach, they just disappear out the door. Or a coldness will come over them. Secure men wouldn't be bothered by my intellect, but the secure men of my age group are already married. The insecure men get all sweaty and nervous when they find out I have a master's degree. So I try to keep it quiet, and I guide the conversation so it won't come up. But when men do find out, they seem to gravitate away. It's not just me, either. The other young female teachers have the same problem.

Ingeborg Engemark says:

Ann complains a lot that the immoral girls around the campus constitute unfair competition to the decent girls, but that's just an excuse. I think she's too insecure to compete, but she won't admit it. It takes a few drinks for her even to admit that there's a problem. One day we got drunk together, and she told me she was up the wall about men, the shortage of them. And she said, "Inge, how in the world do you attract them? I've just *got* to learn." I don't remember what I told her—I was too drunk—and anyway, since I've come to Collegeville I'm no authority on *that* subject. I used to have to beat men off with a club, but not in this boring town.

Once she embarrassed me to death at a department

picnic. She and Esmy Wilson had had a few snorts, and they cornered the department chairman and began berating him for not hiring single men around their own age. This mortified me! They were so insistent. Stults was doing most of the talking—you know Esmerelda, she wouldn't *dare* say too much, except, "Yes yes yes! That's very very true!" Agreeing with Ann, but not having the guts to add anything herself, the little mouse. Anyway, "Liquor is quicker," and it certainly was in this case. They *wouldn't* let up on the subject, and I was embarrassed because the chairman was embarrassed. He just didn't know how to extricate himself from this ridiculous predicament because he was a little drunk himself. I was hoping he'd blow his top and tell them that he had a big enough job, Goddamn it, without worrying about the sex lives of all his junior assistants. But he didn't. He just told them he'd see what he could do. And did nothing.

There's simply no competing with the teenyboppers. They're all emancipated, and they'll do anything a man wants. They'll smoke pot, they're not inhibited sexually, and there's nothing off limits to them. So why should a man take up with me? There are things I'll do and things I won't do, certain ⁻moral codes that I obey, so why bother? Men can get everything they want, fresh and new and young, among the freshmen and sophomores, the wild swinging liberated group. These kids come right out of high school *ready*. The word "no" is not in their vocabulary. They're rioting and getting arrested, flushing all kinds of dangerous chemicals through their systems, doing advanced research on the number of positions of sexual intercourse. So where do I fit in? The strange thing about those of us in our midtwenties is that we're far more like our forty- and fifty-year-old mothers than we are like our eighteen- and twenty-year-old sisters. The social explosion has come that *fast*.

The result is distorted love lives for us elderly teachers in our midtwenties. An eligible male is *solid gold*. There are regular cat fights when one comes on the scene. The department hired a new bachelor professor recently, and we all sharpened our claws. He was exactly the right age, unmarried. We all went ape over the prospect! He was here about two days when his girl friend transferred in from Columbia. How typical!

Some of our young teachers get involved in tragic affairs, probably on the theory that a tragic affair is better than none at all. Not long ago one of our professors, a precocious intellectual of about thirty-five, broke up with his wife. He was terribly upset for two weeks, and' then he started dating one of the young instructors, a good friend of mine. They announced their engagement about two weeks after that and decided to do a trial marriage, and he moved in with her, and they were holding hands at campus parties. When the professor's wife said she was going to have a nervous breakdown, he dumped the instructor and went right back home. I don't know how she *stood* it.

I was talking to my friend Esmy Wilson about this, and the thing that struck both of us was how easily this could happen to us. You spend so much time on this campus thinking, "How can I get *anybody* interested in me?" and finally deciding that no one ever *will* be. And you're ripe for a relationship with *anyone*, and then you find yourself in a stupid situation, crying your eyes out. Our poor friend had to leave the campus after the professor dumped'her. She had desperately wanted to teach here, but now she can't. If she asked for a teaching assignment, they'd laugh. The professor's wife wouldn't have it. That sort of thing happens around here quite often.

Well, so far I've managed to avoid any such entanglements, but it could be in the cards. I sit in my apartment, night after night, my virginity intact, and I don't even get an opportunity to lose it. My mother's generation thought of virginity as a moral value, but I don't regard it as important. I don't think that even in Catholic circles they're going in for virginity anymore. I certainly don't consider it something vital to take into marriage. On the other hand, I don't like the idea of meeting someone and a half hour later falling into bed with him. I know my attitude is gauche and outmoded. I do believe in free love, but with the accent on the *love*. I don't believe in sleeping around, but then I'm not getting the chance anyway. Some of these teenyboppers, they date a man once and the next day they're *living* together. I find this shocking. It's far too speedy for me.

And yet. . . .When I had my astrological chart done, the astrologist told me that I had the same horoscope as the wife of Bath, except it was slightly transposed. All I could say was, "Well, somebody slipped up somewhere. I am the *opposite* of the wife of Bath." But she said I was wrong.

Esmerelda Wilson says:

Last year Ann began taking the supernatural very seriously. She went to a fortune-teller and paid five or ten dollars an hour. She put hex signs on her car, silly things like that. When the fortune-teller told her that she would be taking a trip to Europe that summer, Ann actually began going to travel agencies to work out the best trip. And when the fortune-teller told her she would be married in six weeks, oh, my—she was *so* excited! She practically went out and bought a trousseau. When I told her that she was taking it all far too seriously,. she told me that religion was just as superstitious as fortune-telling. Imagine! I told her that fortune-telling and card reading are not founded in historical fact, whereas religion very definitely is. At least the Protestant religion is. She had no answer for *that*. Soon afterward, she told me that she'd lost her Catholicism, but I think there's a lot more left than she'd be willing to admit. She began fooling around a lot with ouija boards and tarot cards; so maybe she's lost her Catholicism and found the ouija board. One superstition has moved in to take the place of another.

Lately I've become very interested in astrology and the supernatural. A lot of my reading is science fiction. I read the Bridey Murphy book, and I also read the Joan Grant books, a whole series about her previous incarnations. One told about how she'd been taken backwards into her earlier lives by hypnosis. I thought that was fascinating, and I'd like to try it. I saw *Rosemary's Baby,* and I was transfixed. Now I'm reading Edgar Cayce.

I know a fortune-teller up in the hills who is really good. At first I was dubious, but I took a five-dollar bill up there and listened to her describe my life perfectly for about thirty minutes. It was really spooky. When I walked in the door, she didn't know a thing about me except that my name was Ann. She dealt out the cards, and she didn't ask me anything about myself. She started right in, "You're from St. Louis. You have one brother. Your father owns a store." It's a little hazy in my mind now, but she knew all sorts of things about me and my family. She said my father dominated the family, and he does. She said he was a chunky man, and he is. She said I looked like my mother, which is really odd, because I do. She very seldom said anything wrong. There wasn't any doubt about it whatever: *she was reading my mind.*

Then she did a future reading. I would have felt terrible if she had been able to read the future because I don't want *anybody* to read my future. Luckily, she blew it. She had me getting married in six months, and she said I'd be going to Europe in the summer. Well, Europe *was* on my mind, but I wound up not going. I took her predictions very seriously because she had been so right on the other things. I was shook! And I was glad when she was wrong about the future.

I found out later that she had done some very good work with a young friend of mine, a boy named Roy. He had begun seeing ghosts and I loaned him a Bible because I thought it might help him. But it didn't. We took him to an astrologer, and the astrologer did his chart, and he said there was no reason for Roy to be seeing ghosts. But the next night he woke up and there was a ghost standing there looking at him.

The fortune-teller in the hills gave him a hex sign to put on his watch, and he saw no ghosts after that. Later I had these hex signs put all over my car, to protect me. They looked like little circular reflectors, with adhesive on the back, and black patterns of stars and Xs and crosses on the front. I have six or seven on the car. I guess they're working, because my car's been creamed several times, and each time I've been out of it. A dump truck backed into it once when it was parked, and a friend borrowed it and totaled it in an accident. But I was home in bed, safe.

One night my friend Esmy took me to a meeting of a strange religious group. I had seen the book *They Speak In Tongues** in her apartment, and she had given me a copy, because she had about twenty of them stacked up. Then she said she wanted to take me to a meeting of some religious friends, and I'm always a sucker for the first visit, dying to meet people and find out what's going on. We went to a private home, and there were fifteen or twenty of us, and we all sat in a circle. They started with prayers of thanksgiving, very repetitious. Somebody would say, "Thank you, Jesus, for our good health," and then everybody else would say, "Thank you, Jesus, thank you, thank you," and they'd keep coming up with things to say thank you for. "Thank you for getting rid of my halitosis and my husband." My first thought was, This is pathetic, we all have our problems, but who wants them hanging out in public like this? I was sitting next to a teacher, thirty-five or forty, who said she feuds with her neighbors and then broods about it because Christians don't do that. The wallpaper store had cheated her and she wanted to know if it would be Christian to go and make a complaint. I looked at her during the prayers, and she seemed to be almost in a trance. I noticed very quickly that everyone in the group spoke of himself as a "Christian" and of all others outside the group as "non-Christians," and this began to irritate me. It seemed to me that there was a

* *They Speak With Other Tongues* by John Sherrill.

lot of arrogance in it. I was not really a member of the group, and I wondered what that made me in their eyes. Jewish?

Things became curiouser and curiouser. With no noticeable transition, somebody started a hymn, and then somebody else started a different one, and then they were all singing different hymns at the same time. It was eerie. Later I found out they called it "singing in the spirit." Singing what comes into your mind. Some of them were just saying, "Hallelujah," over and over. Then it all ended at the same time, which I thought was very mysterious.

After more hymn singing, this time in unison, an obvious homosexual named Phil Hanley stood up and started talking a language that sounded like Russian, and this did not sound like random garble. The way it went, it really did sound like a language, with rhythms and patterns and phrases, like someone talking Russian or Hebrew or a dead tongue. There were a lot of gutturals, and a Slavonic texture to the language.

When Hanley was finished there was a pause. I wondered what was coming next. A middle-aged woman raised both her arms above her head, as though they were levitated, and began speaking in English, saying things like, "I'm here to comfort thee, to guide thee and to make thee strong. Whatever thou doest, be comforted that I am with thee. I offer my hand and my strength to thee, and give thee peace." That sort of thing. I noticed that her speech seemed approximately the same length as the homosexual's. Esmy whispered to me that the woman was interpreting what her friend Phil had said. "He has the gift of tongues," she said, "and she has the gift of interpreting it. What you heard was the voice of Jesus, coming through Phil and Ethel."

So I realized that these people and their "charismatic movement" were really a bunch of Jesus freaks. They treated themselves like something special, as if they had a direct hotline to Jesus, and only they could save the heathens. The more I heard them use their narrow definition of "Christian" the more annoyed I got. At the same time I was impressed by the fact that they did

seem to care about one another, and there's little enough
of that in our society. You seldom see people who genuinely care for each other. The service was ridiculous,
yes, but I can't put it down entirely, because they did
seem to believe in Christian love, and Christian love
can't be *all* bad.

A few weeks later Esmy talked me into going to a
second meeting of the charismatic group, but this time
it turned me completely off. Several people got up and
spoke in tongues, and it just sounded weird. I can't
imagine anyone speaking through me. Come on! I can
do my own talking. I asked Esmy why the middle step
was necessary, why we first had to hear somebody speaking in this strange babble? I said, "Why can't Jesus speak
to you through your own language, and then you wouldn't
need another person to interpret?"

She said, "Well, that's how it's done. It happens that
way. We Christians just accept it." I bristled at that.

I also noticed that at this meeting there seemed to be
a couple of people who had flipped their lids. There
was one handsome young man about my age who
seemed to have the maturity of a thirteen-year-old.
He kept asking me, was I spirit-filled yet? Over and
over again, "Are you spirit-filled?" I was tempted to ask
him if he thought I was a cigarette lighter, but I held
my tongue. A few nights later, Esmy asked me to dinner, and there was the same young man, bearing a copy
of Katherine Marshall's *Beyond Ourselves* for me. I've
yet to read it. It's right over there in my bookshelf with
They Speak In Other Tongues. All through the dinner
he kept nudging me and asking me, "Are you spirit-filled
yet?" When he left, he said, "I hope you'll be spirit-filled
the next time we see each other." I made sure that there
was no next time.

Esmerelda Wilson says:

One night Ann was telling me how insecure she felt,
how she didn't like herself as a person. So I told her that

I was going to a sensitivity group, and that it might be meaningful to her. Well, at our first meeting she stood right up and revealed incredible things about herself that I never would have *dreamed* of revealing. She said she'd always thought of herself as ugly and that she'd been especially repulsive as a child, and she'd always had this negative feeling about herself, that she was dirt. My goodness, she'd never said *anything* like this to me, and now she was saying it to all these strangers! Well, I was embarrassed for her. But then things became so ridiculous at a later meeting that I just dropped out of the group. They played Artie Shaw's music, and told us to hold each other—perfect strangers almost!—while the music played. I guess this thirty-year-old music was supposed to turn us on, but it had the opposite effect on Ann and me. Then there was this weird dialogue, where somebody asked how I felt, and I said, "Slightly tense," and somebody else said, "Where does it feel tense?" I said, "In my stomach." Then somebody said, "Well, I don't *care* about Esmy's stomach. I've got much more serious problems to worry about," and then somebody else said, "I take issue with you, because I really *care* about Esmy's stomach, and I *want* to hear about it." It just got so laughable, Ann and I never went back.

If you're like me, you find yourself going to bizarre gatherings because there's so little normal social activity in town. I didn't learn from my experience with the "Christians," and when Esmy asked me if I would like to attend a sensitivity group at her supermodern church in Collegeville, I said okay. Once again, we all sat on the floor, except for Old Weird Harold, the minister of the church, who was running the show. Old Weird Harold, alias Skip Floyd, alias The Reverend Stevenson L. Floyd, thinks he's *very* hip. He was being assisted by his ever popular wife, Bobbi, an aging teenybopper in a blond wig. They were the caricature of the supermodern minister and his understanding, liberal wife. Esmy had told me I'd love them, but I didn't. When I hear Jesus Christ described as "the coolest cat in history," I want to throw up.

We went around the circle and told our hairy little life histories. Anything that you thought was relevant about yourself. I forget what I put down for them. I think it was just that I had been brought up a Catholic, and that I was teaching now.

In the middle of the session, one woman got up and went to the kitchen and began crying. Skip and Bobbi steadfastly ignored her. They said they had a theory that if you felt like crying, it was best for you to cry alone. This woman was feeling worse and worse because we were supposed to be a sensitivity group and we were ignoring her. I think she was right to cry. If I went out to the kitchen and began to cry, I'd expect somebody to at least ask what was the matter. What this really was was an insensitivity group.

After a while, Bobbi made a little speech about her own life, all bubbly and bouncy. She said she liked to sing as she strolled through the grocery stores; "That just *sends* me! Far out!" She said she liked to buy artichokes, "the sexiest vegetable around," and so on. I hope this gives you an idea of the intellectual level of the sensitivity group.

But before we had gone to that first meeting, Esmy had made me promise that I would attend at least two. At the second meeting, the lady who'd cried in the kitchen got herself all tanked up, and told us a tragic story, really ghastly, from childhood on. She had almost been electrocuted, she had been in three bad automobile accidents, two husbands had left her, and she didn't know what she was going to do. When she finished, she ran off into the kitchen and cried.

Old weird Skip told us to get down on the floor with a partner. There was an overabundance of women, but I decided that whatever this game was going to be, I was not going to play it with a female. I wound up with somebody's bearded husband, and he was also acting very hip and modern. Skip told us to look at our partners for a long time, look deep into their eyes. I thought it was very funny and tried hard not to laugh, but I began to giggle a little, and my partner looked disgusted. Then Skip told us to put our arms around the back of our partners' necks, to see what the reaction was. I did it, but my partner didn't seem any more appealing that way.

The third step *really* set me off. Old weird Skip put on this music, like 1940 schmaltz, Artie Shaw, *really* strange. Then he told us to have a fantasy about the person we were staring at. Well, from that time on I was in stitches because that music was so weird. Dance music, for God's sake! Music to meditate by. So naturally I couldn't come up with a fantasy about my partner because by the time I could even begin to fantasize, "Frenesi" was over.

Now we were supposed to tell the other person what our fantasy was about, and I said, "Well, I'm sorry but I didn't make it."

He said, "Well, I fantasized you going out on a date, and I saw you being picked up by your boyfriend, and then dancing around." I thought, "Bullshit!" He'd fantasized himself right out of the picture. I would have been insulted if I hadn't already developed a dislike for him. I think he made it all up, and didn't want to tell his true fantasy.

There was another minister there, and his partner had been a married woman, and they hadn't had time to finish discussing their fantasies, so he said he would like to leave the room with her and finish their discussion privately. She agreed, but they left it up to the group. Everything was, "How do you feel? How do you feel?" We decided we felt they could go, so they went down to the basement and imparted whatever shattering things were on their minds.

After the meeting we had a little social session, and the sobbing woman came out of the kitchen and wiped her eyes and said, "I think we're gonna be a good group this year. We're really getting to know each other. Boo hoo. Once we get to know each other it's fun. Boo hoo.

You can have tantrums, you can cry, you can even get hysterical!" It all was so stupid that I didn't go back.

Postscript: Several Months Later

When I met Thomas P. Hamilton, I figured he would be perfect for Esmy. He and I went out to dinner when he first arrived in Collegeville, and we were just sitting there, saying nothing, and I happened to make a comment on the charismatic group that I had visited. Thomas P. Hamilton sat straight upright and his eyes opened wide and he said, *"What* did you say?" He wanted to know all about it.

I described the meeting, and then he told me about a Pentecostal group he'd belonged to in Seattle. He said that most of the members were Catholic, and I said, "I don't see how a Pentecostal group could be very Catholic," and he said, "Why not? It's right there in the Bible. The apostles spoke in tongues."

Well, up until then, the evening had been lagging horribly. Thomas was supposed to be a young banking genius, but you'd never know it by being with him. He seemed to think it was a rip-roaring social occasion if you just looked at each other and ate your meatloaf. But when the subject of speaking in tongues came up, he changed around completely. He started talking about it at eight o'clock that night, and when he got me home at eleven, after a little drive around the campus, he was still going. It just *poured* out of him. I'd never heard anything like it: how he had first spoken in tongues at a revival meeting, and on and on and on. He sounded like Esmy. I finally had to tell him that I had an early class and I was tired, and that I had a friend he would like very much. I gave him Esmy's phone number and address, and I told him she never missed a meeting of the Collegeville charismatic group.

When I came back from vacation I saw Esmy and she told me she didn't care for Thomas a bit. She said she couldn't stand the long silences when she went out with

him and she hated the way that he would drop in on her
without warning, as though he owned her, and the way
he would sit on her couch for hours without opening his
mouth. After that, the subject of Thomas became moot
because a girl friend from Seattle moved right in with him
and we hardly saw him.

A few weeks went by, and then I was having lunch
with Esmy, and I was telling her what a jerk Thomas
was, and she said, "I want to tell you this, Ann, because
I think you ought to know. I'm getting interested in Thomas. I don't know how it happened, but after that girl
moved in with him, I began thinking about him all the
time."

I said, "Well, in Collegeville any man is better than
none. Though in this case I'm not sure."

I did warn her that she could be hurt, and I
reminded her about our friend who had fallen for the
professor and gotten thrown out on her ear as a reward. "Keep it in mind," I said, and she said she would.
Then she told me that the girl friend had gone back to the
coast and Thomas and she had begun dating and praying together. This fascinated me. I'd never heard of couples praying together before. I wanted to ask her, "How
in the world do you do it?" But I didn't have the courage. She also told me that Thomas was insane about carrot juice, that he had a fifty dollar juicer, and that they
frequently ended their dates in his apartment, drinking
carrot juice and praying.

After that I began to date Thomas occasionally myself, and sometimes we would have carrot juice or
hamburgers. I thought I came to know him quite well,
and I found him a completely confusing sort of person. He was utterly and completely unpredictable. In
his apartment, he had a set of carpenter tools, and he
said to me one night, "Any time you need something
fixed, just ask me and I'll be very happy to do it." So
about a month later I asked him to tighten a screw on
a bathroom fixture, and you'd have thought I'd asked
him to rebuild the Taj Mahal, the irritable way he
acted about it. But just when you thought he was ter-

ribly moody and completely out of reach, he would knock at your door at eleven o'clock at night and ask if you wanted to go out for a hamburger. He seemed to be taken by urges. Sometimes he came on as a very sweet person, shy, gentle, kind, nice, giving off a very positive impression. But then you began to realize that he was a klutz, he just lumped along. He didn't know about anything that happened outside the financial world. He was a dork, he was so *slow*. He thought a lot before he said anything. He made chatterers out of people like me, because we just couldn't stand the silence. It was like dating in a mausoleum. I'd ask him if he liked rutabagas, and fifteen minutes later, he'd say, "A little, I guess." He had the reactions of a very elderly sloth.

From the beginning, I noticed something else strange about him. He *never* failed to notice what I was wearing and to comment on it. Certain styles drove him up the wall. He didn't like dresses, he didn't like extremely feminine things. One time I showed up in a new pantsuit and he was raving about it. He said if it was food he'd eat it. "It's such a yummy color." All this interest in feminine attire seemed to me to be a feminine characteristic. I'd never known another man so interested in female clothes.

One night we double dated, Esmy and Thomas and me and a funny guy named Jim, and as soon as we got to Esmy's for dinner, Thomas just slid into a corner and hardly opened his mouth. He seemed totally nonplussed by the appearance of another man. He acted like a hermit ripped out of his hermitage. It was really ridiculous. Esmy said to me later, "He's insecure around men, and he can't seem to stand the competition, so he withdraws."

Later that night we all trucked off to the charismatic group. Wow! All I could see were unattractive people. Jim and I spent the evening in the corner looking for salacious passages in the Bible, and giggling. The sermon was a pat-yourself-on-the-back thing where they use Biblical references to show how wonderful it is that they all love Jesus and can speak in tongues, and over and over again I'd hear, "We are Christians, and we're unleavened, and isn't that great, and aren't we pleased to be that way?" A sloppy, paunchy man of about fifty did the sermon. Jim whispered to me that he looked like a homosexual. The charismatic movement seems *full* of homosexuals, I don't know why. This "preacher" was sloppy and shapeless, soft and bloodless. We found out that the service was to be communion, but the fat old slob warned everybody beforehand, "If you're not ready to make the *total* commitment to Jesus, then don't eat the bread!" Big deal! I said to Jim, "Let's tell him what to do with his bread!" But we didn't. Instead we sat there and giggled.

Along about eleven o'clock, a teen-age kid with a bad complexion and horrible breath came over and put his hands on Jim's shoulders, unasked and uninvited, and began praying for him. Then somebody began speaking in tongues, and there was nothing but confusion. Poor Jim looked like he would die of embarrassment. I could feel hysterical laughter coming over me, but I contained myself. Then a beautiful young girl went out in the middle and danced, and everybody began clapping and clapping, and shouting, "Oh, yes, Jesus! Ha, ha, ha!" A woman of about sixty, built like a sausage, in a blue jersey dress that clung to her like a sausage skin, got up and began to dance and sing about Jesus, and then she began speaking in tongues. She reminded me of Tiger Lily in Peter Pan. She had these great big arm gestures, guttural sounds, yelling and screaming, and then repeating certain syllables over and over.

Another girl stood up to interpret. "I am coming now. I've said I'd be with you, and I'm coming now. The last days are here, my children." Then they all thanked God for the privilege of being able to speak in tongues, as though they were God's chosen people. Esmy stood up and prophesied, "You are all well, and I love you as you are now." We asked her later what that meant, and she said it was the voice of Jesus, speaking through her, and it meant *everybody*. She said, "It meant, 'Don't change yourself, you *are* loved.' "

The next afternoon Thomas knocked on my door and asked if I wanted to go out for a hamburger. I said okay, and I changed from grubby jeans into a dress. He didn't like that. He said I shouldn't have changed, and he kept talking about it, which I think showed a lack of cool. My feeling was. Okay, you didn't like it, you mentioned it, now shut up. I figured it was up to me what I felt the most comfortable in. But he went on and on—he does things like that—inexplicable, unpredictable.

Then he invited me back to his place for carrot juice, and when we got there, he opened the Bible and started showing me different passages. He said that he could prove that Moses was married to a black woman, and he worried that subject to death, turning the pages and saying, "See? See?" and edging closer to me on the couch.

Then he put the Bible away, and the conversation lagged. He would just sit there looking off into space. I timed it on my watch—three minutes went by without a word. Finally I couldn't stand it. "Are you thinking about something?" I said.

He said, "I was thinking, I'd like you to see some religious papers I've written."

"Fine," I said.

"I feel like running a little bit," he said. "You read the papers, and I'll run around the block for an hour or so and come back."

I couldn't believe all this, so I said yes. An hour or so later he came back, all sweaty and tired, and began making more carrot juice. I told him no thanks. I've decided that carrot juice has a weird taste. I looked it up and found that it's about 50 percent carbohydrates, and I thought how ridiculous to get fat on something you hate, how silly! If you have to get fat, get fat on a hot fudge sundae, not on a glass of carrot juice.

After another long, shattering silence, he began reading from Kahlil Gibran on teaching, but Thomas doesn't read too well, and he asked me to read aloud. So I did, and then he asked me to read some other Gibran. That immatu e saccharine stuff! Early day Rod McKuen! Then he told me the whole history of Kahlil Gibran, and I listened, and I kept wondering where this was leading. My main motivation is I have an awful lot of curiosity, and I'm always hanging around trying to see what's going to happen. And also—I hate to admit it—since Esmy saw something in him, I was trying to figure out if I had missed anything. Had I passed up something I shouldn't have?

Then we went back to the Bible playing a sort of trivia game. saying things like, "Who was Micah?" and "why did they say they were going *up?*"

"Because there are mountains there!" Thomas said. "That explains it!" I began to realize that this was a very peculiar date.

Around twelve thirty, I began to get too bored to put up with this any more, and I started to go. Thomas suddenly said, "You know, praying together is an exciting experience."

I edged toward the door and I said, "Oh, is it?"

He said, "I think we ought to try it sometime."

I said, "Well, maybe that's a nice idea." In the back of my mind, I said to myself, Well, at least you'd find out what it's all about, what this praying together means. You'd *know* then.

He said, "How would you like to pray a little tonight?"

I said, "Okay."

He said, "Well, we just sit down here on the couch, real relaxed. Nothing to be tense about." He picked up his Bible. "I can't pray unless I'm holding the Bible," he said. "Now lean back and close your eyes."

Horrors! Nothing came to my mind to pray! I was just thinking, How awkward! There was overwhelming silence. Finally he began to pray. He thanked God for the day and everything in his life, and then he moved right into thanking God for the relationship between me and him—really speaking to *me* but pretending to be praying to God—*and there wasn't any relationship between us anyway!* He was saying things like, "Bless us,

and let the love between Ann and me grow," and I
sort of jumped when he said that. *What* love between
Ann and him? This went on, and I didn't pray anything,
I just sat there with my eyes closed. There were huge silences in between, and then he'd pray something else
about "our relationship."

The silences began to get me. I was tongue-tied, I
couldn't think of a thing to pray. Then I began to feel
this hand moving over, and it grabbed mine, and we
held hands. This seemed to stimulate his praying. When
I thought he'd finished, he kind of slumped with his head
on my shoulder, and I thought, "What in the world is he
going to do?" And he said, "I'm sure you'll have a husband and children one of these days." *Non sequitur!*

I thought, Well I've had enough of *this*. I quickly
made my goodnights and walked the two blocks home,
and just sat there for thirty minutes thinking, How
weird! I can't figure it out. What's he doing? Why did I
do it? What a totally unrewarding experience. Was he
trying to convert me? To seduce me? Or what? What a
creepy crawly experience!

It just seemed to me, after I'd really thought it out, that
this man was accumulating some kind of religious harem,
trying to turn us all into "Christians" one by one. At
least that's my theory. So I confided all this to Esmy,
because I thought she might be in a position to get
hurt. I told her it sounded to me like he was playing exactly the same kind of game with her. She said she
would keep that in mind. I told her there was something
very strange about a man who had the impulse to pray
with all the women in the world, to speak to them
through prayers instead of directly, and to be so terribly
insecure around men. She said, yes, that was interesting.
I told her I really didn't like him at all, that I thought
he was a first-class creep. She said she was sorry to hear
that, because at least he *was* a Christian.

Weeks have gone by, and I'm certain he's playing
the same couch-and-Bible seduction game with Esmy.
And I can't believe he's not aware of what he's doing. I'm
certain he'll hurt her. I don't think it's necessarily seduc-

tion that's on his mind. I think it's some kind of power game, to have power over women. He told me once that he's an intensely sexual creature, but he said he was carefully keeping his sexual drives in check. He told me that sexual intercourse outside of marriage was definitely not Christian, and he would never be guilty of it.

I haven't had the nerve to talk to Esmy about it anymore, but I did find out that she's been calling up the head of the Collegeville charismatic group and praying with her about some deep problem over the phone. Isn't that wild? Esmy's mother finds it fascinating. She came out here on a visit, and she said to me, "A daughter of mine! *My own daughter!* Praying on the phone!" Esmy's own mother was also horrified that Esmy was praying with Thomas. She said she could not understand how any daughter of hers could go to a man's apartment and sit there and drink carrot juice and pray. She said to me, "It's certainly not the sexiest way to begin an evening."

I told her, *"Begin* an evening? That's the way they *end* the evening!"

She just groaned. "Yes," I said. "It gradually builds up to that climax."

I've seen Thomas a few times in the last week, and he's been looking terrible. I don't know what's bothering him. And Esmy looks so troubled, too. I started to tell her the other day that I thought she should stop seeing him, that he would eventually harm her. But then I realized something. He already has.

INGEBORG ENGEMARK, 42
Assistant Professor,
Department of English

Esmerelda Wilson says:

Inge is a classic character, an extraordinary character. I met her at a faculty club meeting, and she sort of took over by sheer power. Her thick mane of gray hair was done in a weird 1920-style pageboy effect. She looked Russian, but she turned out to be descended from a Norwegian family that'd been here for a couple of hundred years. My goodness, she was *loud*!

Then I started having coffee with her between classes, and she impressed me. Not necessarily by her intellect, no. She has this terrible tendency to throw her erudition around, but there's something missing there. Ann Stults says that the only difference between Inge and somebody who doesn't have a Ph.D. is this: They both know the expression, "A stitch in time saves nine," but Inge knows who said it first. That has been the value of her Ph.D.—to assign origins to the clichés she uses. I sometimes feel that she perverts her education—I mean who really *needs* the original source of "All's fair in love and war"?

No, what impressed me about Ingeborg Engemark was her amazing élan and spontaneity. I've always been attracted to people who can be so free and spontaneous and open—exactly the opposite of me. I'd like to be able to burst into a classroom like Inge and shout, "Hello, folks! I'm here, and let's get started learning something!" The way she does—just burst in and take them all by storm. I envied this in her, and I decided to get to know her.

Well, I found out that knowing Inge entails certain

sacrifices. One morning she burst into my apartment and sat down and lighted a cigarette before anybody had even asked her in. Mama was visiting me, and she was horrified! There was just something so very very rude about it. Mama called her "the apparition" after that, because of the way she would just burst in, out of nowhere. I also was amused by the way she'd tell us about Bruce and Tom and Nancy and Bill, without ever offering any last names or descriptions, and I realized that she was just someone who assumed that you would enter into her own mythology, as though *her* life and *her* friends were of such overriding importance that of course everyone would automatically know all about them. There are a lot of teachers like that.

After I'd known Inge for a month or so and had coffee with her maybe three times, she moved right into my apartment building! She said, "I just wanted to be in the same building with such a nice person." I was panicked! There was something very very strange about it.

Oh, my, she drove me crazy! She'd telephone at funny times—when I was in the middle of cooking, or late at night, and she'd drop in at odd hours, and since Ann Stults was busy doing the same thing, I was beside myself. One Friday evening around six Inge showed up just when I was putting something into the oven, and she said, "Esmy, I wonder if I could possibly buy a glass of wine from you?"

What she really wanted was company—I could see that —so I said, "Why, that's ridiculous, Inge, I'll *give* you a glass of wine. Come in!" She stayed for a good two hours and drank half my sherry.

From that evening on, she kept doing the same thing over and over. She'd always say, "I have to go to Raymond's Liquor Store and get you something," but she never did. I just had to get used to the fact that whenever she dropped in, the entire bottle would be drained before she left. Is it alcoholism? I don't know. Maybe more loneliness than anything.

It all reached the point where she became so neurotically dependent on me that she'd throw a fit if I wasn't in the apartment when she wanted me. She'd go pestering all the other tenants, and ask them where I was, and when I'd be back. Gracious, I'm a little neurotic myself, at least about privacy, and this was driving me crazy. I don't like the concept of somebody knocking on my door at all hours and inviting herself in. So I moved. But not far enough away. She kept dropping in, and she *still* keeps dropping in, and poor little me—I'm too courteous to say anything about it. One of these days, though. . . .

Ann Stults says:

Inge will come to my apartment at ten in the morning and she'll be a little high. You'll meet her on the way to an eight o'clock class, and there'll be wine on her breath. I think she must drink a half-gallon of wine a day.

I know they talk about me, it's the favorite campus pastime. Well, to hell with them! There's no place pettier than a university campus and this is one of the pettiest. Just the other night, Wanda was telling me that Jimmy Helder said I shouldn't be allowed to teach, that I come to class drunk, and things like that. Well, Goddamn him! Everybody knows Jimmy comes to class with three or four martinis in him and starts quoting Ben Jonson and attributing it to Andrew Marvell. Alice said the other day that I might be falling down drunk, but, gadzooks, I'd never make *that* mistake.

I've been here since 1960 and I've certainly livened things up, right? You've already heard that about me? Well, I don't deny it. They all think I'm the campus lush. I like bubble water, it brings me out, makes me talk, but I can hold it better than most of the people on the campus. Teachers like Ginny Yarmouth are far lushier than I am; one sniff of the cork and she's out. And the rest of the time she's so snooty, so la-de-da. Jimmy's not much different. No, bubble water is not my problem. Alas, alack, my problem is different. These ten years at The College have been almost completely celibate, and nobody's sorrier than I am. I used to think it's my age, but then I began talking to Esmerelda Wilson and Ann Stults and I've found out they're not finding anybody either, and they're young girls. What's *wrong* with this place? What's *wrong* with Collegeville? Because you don't have to go very far from Collegeville and the men start popping up every place. One old timer told me that Collegeville has always been like this. No men. I'm damned if I know why. It's *always* been a federal case to find a man in Collegeville.

I'd have a complex about this, except that as soon as I leave here, the men start chasing me. They come right out of the woodwork, all gung-ho. Last summer, on my vacation, I drove into a rest stop near Amarillo and right away I met a very nice fellow, an Omaha policeman, and we had a drink of whiskey together, and we could have had more, but he had people with him. I drove on to Wichita Falls and went swimming in the motel pool, just for something to do, and two guys tried to pick me up. One of them was rather insistent—he left his watch in my apartment, and Dr. Freud says that that means he wants to come back, and did he ever!

When I came home to Collegeville, it was the same old story: no men. I go to parties and various functions and I drop the broadest hints, but I don't get any takers. Too bad. One night there were some leftover men at a party and I started telling them that they ought to see how I look in my red nightgown. I told them how you can see right through it and how sexy it is. But they must not have thought I meant it.

Esmerelda Wilson says:

Inge's self-concept is of a young wood nymph. She must not own a mirror. She thinks of herself as a femme fatale, irresistible to males in general, and she can't understand what's happening to her in Collegeville. Well, she's like the rest of us—she just *doesn't* have dates.

But she can't imagine that it has anything to do with her. Her self-image is impenetrable, invulnerable to any outside assaults. She once told me how a young man came to visit her, and when he decided to leave after a little while, she said, "What do I have to do to keep you here, throw my naked body against the door?" He fled in horror and she couldn't understand why.

What kind of sex life does she have, really? Did she ever go to bed with John Aldrich? I think not. She talks about sex so much, but I wonder if she really has any, or if it's all mythology like the affair with Aldrich.

She's very very bitter about Collegeville because there's so little sex here, except that she mentions some married man who was coming to see her this summer at the wrong times. She feels sorry for herself because that's the only real sex she has. But she loves to be a campus caricature of sexuality. She feels proud of the fact that people are always talking about her and her sex life. Her red nightgown, things like that. She has a terrible need to be a sexpot, and it's rather pathetic, because I doubt if she ever *was,* even in her youngest and most attractive days. Why does she have this need? Goodness, she's in her mid-forties; you'd think she'd be over this silly adolescent attitude by now.

What is it that repulses men about her? She turns men off terribly! Is it that she's so aggressive? Or that she takes so much for granted? Goodness, if a man looks at her twice she fancies he's got a wild crush on her, and she takes right after him. Of course, we all fantasize to some extent, and if there isn't a man right at hand we dream dreams to satisfy ourselves. But when the dreams become living, walking things, and you begin to believe them—oh, how very very baleful.

Ann Stults says:

Ingeborg has no sense of how she appears to others. Most of us don't see ourselves as others see us, but there's at least *some* correlation. But Inge has *no* idea that she's a frowsy old woman of forty-two. She still thinks she's young and beautiful and vivacious. In any situation, she perceives herself as a coquette, and sometimes she even comes on as a nymphomaniac.

I'm not sure that she really means it—it's just a role she seems to enjoy. Friday at the faculty club we were having a discussion and drinking a lot of wine, and one of the professors passed out with his hand in the cheese dip. So we decided that the discussion was over. I looked at Inge and she was falling down drunk; she couldn't even walk. I scraped her off the couch and said, "Don't you think it's time we were leaving?"

While I was getting our coats, she began a rambling routine, asking a group of teachers one by one if they'd go home with her. Repulsive! She kept mentioning her red nightgown and how slinky she looked in it. It was very chilling, and thank God none of the men took her up on it. It was so terribly unfeminine. I finally dragged her outside, and a young instructor offered to drive us home, and she asked *him* in for a little drinkypoo, as she put it so cutely, and he said, "No, thank you," and almost ran away. Then she tried to get me to come in and have a nightcap drinkypoo and I said "No, thanks." I helped her with her key and went home. The next morning at the cafeteria she said she was sorry we'd left the club so early because it was just getting to be interesting. She said she guessed she must have been the life of the party, because several of the men had tried to take her home. What *is* that? Is it insanity? Or just drink?

Her friends tell me that she always acts like this, and they've had to stop inviting her. She gets all drunked up and starts climbing on the men, and they just won't take it. That's her pattern. Then she fantasizes later that she was the belle of the ball. I figure it must have something to do with her childhood. She must have been a precocious little kid and *really* the cynosure of all eyes.

In the whole damned ten years here, there's really only been one man, and he is strictly a case of Goethe's expression: "When there is nothing better, the devil eats flies." His name is Ted Baynes, and he's a dull, boring business man in Collegeville. I met him four years ago, and he must have thought I was mighty hard up for sex. Well, I *was* mighty hard up for sex, but I don't like his kind of sex. His idea of sex is to come in the front door unbuttoning his fly. Bam, slam, thank you, ma'am, as they say. The usual inept male. He didn't even bring liquor; he didn't believe Ogden Nash,* he brought *nothing!* Well, it's just as well that he didn't bring candy. Don't ever bring me candy with nuts in it. I'm allergic to them and I don't like them. I like human nuts, crazy people, but I don't like the other kind.

I'd say to that stupid Ted Baynes, "Couldn't we go out someplace and at least have a drink?"

He'd say, "I'm too well known."

I didn't see him for a long time, and then one day he came back and said, "Hurry up and undress! I'm aching for you."

I said, "Listen, Ted, what's in it for me? Your wife could find out and then it's trouble for both of us." He didn't say anything, he just kept unbuttoning his fly.

Ted's about the only one that's buzzed around here in the past few years. Well, he's better than nothing, but not much. Oh, there were a couple of more, but they're hardly worth mentioning. I don't see them for months at a time. There was a Latin professor from California. He used to come to town maybe once a year, and take me to a motel. I guess that's the total. So sexually, there's really been nothing for me since I came here. I could count on the fingers of one hand each year. That's lousy. Lousy! A friend said, "Well, maybe you're just too old." But I know better; it's not my age; it's this God-awful town.

Of course, I never go the rounds of the bars, or down to the city. That's not my style. Sure, I could go to

* "Candy is dandy, but liquor is quicker."

some bar and I could pick up *anybody*. But that sounds rotten to me. Sure, I can attract men. I can remember trying *not* to attract them, trying to get rid of them. I can remember one guy who fell for me and just sat on my front steps for the whole Fourth of July weekend, just waiting for me. That was a few years ago. Another guy came knocking on my bedroom window and wanted to take me to the racetrack. Actually rapping on my window! Why, I almost had to call the police!

When you do meet a man in this town, he turns out to be effeminate, if not an out-and-out nance. Somebody told me a terrifying theory, and I defy you to disprove it. For twenty or twenty-five years now all the cattle in this country have been fed on female hormones. It increases their size and weight. My friend says we are now dealing with the first generation that ever was brought up on a steady diet of female hormones. This is why the girls are so horny and willing to go with anybody at any time, and why there are so few men around who are interested in normal sex. Ironic! But I dare you to disprove it. My friend says that every time you go to a hamburger stand you're putting a dose of female hormones through your body. Think about it! It explains a lot.

I happen to know that these liberated teenyboppers aren't quite as copacetic and happy as they let on. I know; I've talked to them. They're not really liberated. How can you be liberated if you keep running around breaking your heart? You know, nobody's ever nonchalant about physical relationships, even if they pretend to be. These girls are guilt ridden, wracked with worry and pain. "The wicked flee when no men pursue." It doesn't matter whether it's wickedness or just plain guilt. I don't think this younger generation is nearly as satisfied about physical relationships as it pretends. I think the kids fake it a lot. I think it's a facade. They have group sex scenes together, but I think that's just to impress one another. What normal person would want group sex? Ods bodkins, sex is kind of like going to the toilet; you want to shut the door!

Esmerelda Wilson says:

As a teacher, Inge's very very good. Her students are fascinated. Teaching is perfect for her because it gives her a chance to objectify some of her need to be the center of attention. I don't think she necessarily develops close relationships with her students or gets to know them as human beings, but she's excellent as a lecturer. She's a buffoon, a clown, and a Helen Hayes at the same time. The classroom is her stage, and she's exactly the kind of teacher it takes to reach these freshmen we're getting nowadays.

Ann Stults says:

Inge took over one of my classes when I got sick, and the students talked about her for the rest of the semester. They told me she'd come bouncing into the classroom making comments, and some of them thought they were on a weird trip left over from the night before. Well, trip or not, there isn't a kid in that class who isn't into James Fenimore Cooper now, and *that's* teaching. I wish I could inspire them the same way, but I just can't. Why, Inge would roll on the floor to get their attention.

I can't do anything but teach. My father had a famous remark. He used to say, "Ingeborg can't even boil water." With me, it was teaching or acting. I'm a ham. People always notice me, and if they don't, I see to it that they do. It may sound egotistical, but by God I'm a good teacher. I make them pay attention. If you can't make students pay attention, what the hell are you doing there? I pretend I'm on stage. I go out there and play my role. I practically have them hollering "Hubba hubba" when I get through with them.

Once Ann Stults called me and said she just couldn't teach her eight o'clock the next morning; she had laryngitis. I said I'd be glad to take over the class. She said, "I want to warn you, these kids won't wake up, they're kind of dull."

I said, "Have no fear. Inge's here."

The next morning I got their attention; you bet I did! I *always* do. When they were all in their seats, I made my grand entrance. I yanked the door open with a bang. Then I shouted, "Shut, damn you! You always used to shut!" Then I looked around, peered through my glasses, and said, "Now, where's that damn lectern? Ah, there you are! Come up here, lectern, and let's get started!"

Those sleepy kids woke up fast. They'd never seen anybody make such a production out of walking into a room, and that's exactly what I'd intended.

Ann had told me that most of the students were behind on their journals, and I told them, "I know you're all behind, you're all waiting for some divine inspiration but you get right home and start on those journals tonight!" I told them how to write their journals, how to lie efficiently and yet tell the truth, because the truth is not the important thing, but how you *feel* at a certain moment. Then I told them about trees, to show them how you can weave feeling into any subject, and I went to the window and talked to a tree for a few minutes. It's very difficult at eight o'clock in the morning to carry on a conversation with a tree, but that got us into the day's lecture: James Fenimore Cooper. That was the whole point, right?

I don't care how much of an ass I make out of myself, I'm there to teach. Whatever they say about me, they can't say that I don't know how to teach. The dean gives me the tough jobs. Once he gave me sixty-five men in a black studies course, most of them athletes, most of them highly unscholarly. I had watched them throw the other teacher out. It turned out they'd demolished three teachers in two weeks. I was standing outside the door and the last one came out bodily. These double French doors burst open, and this woman ran out screaming, "Oh, my God! My God!" Behind her I could hear these voices, "Get out, you son of a bitch! Run, you old whore!"

The president was very apologetic when he gave me the class. He said, "I hate to do this to you, but you're the only one left. It's a black studies course and we've lost three people in two weeks and the last teacher is under a doctor's care. Will you take it tomorrow?"

The next morning, I went in and I banged my books down on the desk. I said, "My name is Engemark. *Miss* Engemark. I'm taking over the class. Now, men, it's dark and smoggy and smoky in here. From now on, there'll be no cigarettes in this class! Tromp on your cigarettes and make sure they're out! Now! You're too far from me, I can't reach you, I want all of you guys up twenty paces. Come on! *Move it!*" They got up and they *moved* it.

Everything went fine for a few days, but then a few problem men began to surface. I settled down two or three of them over a drink of whiskey, but one was still troublesome. He was a bright kid, and he liked to make smart remarks. One day he was standing up pretending to recite, but actually cracking wise, and he was kind of leaning on his desk, half balancing that way, and it occurred to me that if I caught him just right I could knock him flat. So I strolled down the aisle with the textbook, as though to show him a point, and just as I came alongside him I slowed down and said, "Look here," and as he leaned over I went bam! with my foot and knocked him flat.

I said, "My goodness, you've lost your balance!" He got up, and there was no more trouble. A year later he came back to visit, and he told me how I'd straightened him out. Of course, that's instinct with me. My mother was a schoolteacher, an old-time schoolteacher, and she'd have done exactly the same thing. When they're cruisin' for a bruisin', you just have to oblige.

That black studies course turned out to be one of my favorites. You never knew what was going to happen. One day a kid got up and said, "What's your basic attitude about blacks?"

I said, "The same as my attitude about whites and purples and pinks. What's yours?"

He said, "I don't particularly like whitey."

I said, "Well, then sit down, Mr. Jones. You are a racist, and you don't belong here, but stick around, and maybe you'll learn something."

I quickly learned that the main attitude you're going to get is, "I'm black, and you hate me because I'm black." When I hear that, I just say, "Please sit down, sir! I won't hate you unless you *make* me hate you, and you've just made a good start!" After that they soon straighten out.

You have to treat students as they treat you. I was subbing for Dr. Osborn the other day and a kid walks in and he says, "I think I'm in the wrong class." I continued calling the roll, and he came back in and said, "Where's Dr. Osborn? I'm supposed to be in Dr. Osborn's class."

I said, "I'll explain that after I call the roll. You're *in* Dr. Osborn's class. Sit down, please!"

He said, "I want Dr. Osborn, not you."

I said, "Will you shut up, sir, and sit!"

He starts to yell, "I'm not gonna stay here! I don't have to do this! You can't talk to me that way!"

"Then get the hell out!" I said, and walked him to the door.

He says, "You can't talk to me that way."

I says, "Oh, but *you* can't talk to *me* that way."

He says, "You're not very polite, are you?"

I says, "Neither are you. Now get the hell out of here and stay the hell out."

About five minutes later, he came back and said sweetly, "I beg your pardon," took his seat and I never heard another word out of him. Of course, I never swear *at* a student. I'll say, "We'll have none of this damn noise!" But I *won't* say, "You son of a bitch, Goddamn you!" There's a big difference.

You also have to learn to speak the same language as your students. In other words, you can't necessarily teach English by speaking English. Like the other day I was teaching the Iliad, and I said, "Achilles gets mad, so he cuts out of the scene. Why is he mad? Why, *any* man would get mad! It was the all important question of sex. He's got this chick, see."

Later, I said, "By the way, who's the wife of Agamemnon?"

Somebody said, "The blond broad."

"No, no!" I said. "You've got the wrong broad. Helen's the blond. And you know, you can't trust a blond. They're deceitful."

Somebody wanted to know who Agamemnon was really married to. I said, "The wife of Agamemnon is a dame named Clytemnestra. She fools around a lot, including with her brother-in-law, while her husband's fighting a war, see? And when Agamemnon gets home they roll out that red carpet for him. It *better* be red, because they're gonna knife him to death and then they won't have to send the rug to the cleaners." So I had them in the palm of my hand after this. One of them came up after the class and said, "Miss Engemark, how in the world do you make a subject like this so interesting?"

I said modestly, "Well, I'm just doing my bag."

It's reached the point where they don't even jump when it's time to leave. They want to keep talking. I have to say, "Ladies and gentlemen, it's time to go!"

I learned a long time ago that one of the first questions they'll ask in any freshman course, is, "Is there a God?" I always say, "Yes, there's a God, and he has a sense of humor. He lets funny things go on existing, even though he should have killed them off years ago," I tell them; and I say, "If you don't believe that, look to your left and look to your right, and if you're still not convinced, then look straight ahead at me!" And I watch their faces, and then I know who my intelligent people are just by watching how rapidly their eyes flash. I did this the other day, and one of the men got up and said, "Well, if God were a woman, that would explain this hell of a mess we're in."

And I said, "Yes, but suppose God is an insect.

Wouldn't that blow all of your Homo sapiens' minds out of joint?"

When I told Esmy Wilson what I'd said, she said, "You'll get called in, Inge. The trustees will never let you talk that way to the students." Well, that's just like Esmy, she's so timid. She mouths every word from one side of her mouth to the other and back again before she dares to let it come out. Gadzooks, I don't believe in that. I believe in keeping them jumping. And there's no better way than a lively discussion about God.

If you want to know what I really believe, I never could go along with Clarence Darrow that there's no God. He's there, but we just don't know what he's like. The real question is, "Where *are* we?" My grandfather always said that this was hell and we were just too damned dumb to know it.

I think there's a God, all right, and I think he has a marvelous sense of humor—exactly like mine. If he didn't, he'd have ditched the whole thing years ago. I'm a Saggitarius and so is God, and that's no accident. Jesus Christ is a Capricorn, and his behavior shows it. But I definitely believe there's a God. I'm with John Stuart Mill; I believe that there must be an intelligence that runs the universe. But as to what God's attributes are, who knows? But then who *ever* knows about a Saggitarius?

Sometimes I get to teach the Bible as literature, and it can be fun and it can be awful. I'm really not religious enough to teach a course like that. But I'm the old pro, and I can teach anything. I can teach the gospel according to St. John and then walk right into the next classroom and get them all hot and bothered about Marx and Engels. A pro's a pro. I know all this sounds egotistical, and I don't mean it that way. I think it's just a gift. And of course I wasn't always the old pro. I had to learn many things, but I never had to learn how to get their attention. That came naturally.

Sometimes when you're up there, you get the feeling that you're casting your pearls before swine, as the Bible says. But a teacher lives for that one flash, that one moment, when a kid suddenly says, "I see"; for the day they forget the bell when it rings. Or the day the course ends, and they come up to thank you. Good-bye Mrs. Chips. They walk up on the stage after your final performance, and you realize they liked it all the time. Even when they were shooting the paper clips and jabbering their heads off. They liked it all the time.

Esmerelda Wilson says:

Ingeborg has been having a fantasy romance with a professor in his midfifties, and it's reached the point where I'm not sure she's all there. I think there may have been something to the affair at one point, but now it's in the realm of pure imagination.

His name is John Aldrich, and he's a prissy-prim, handsome, dapper fuddy-duddy. Personally, I can't even think of him as a sexual being—he's so *strange*—but he just *floors* Inge. She used to tell a grisly story that when she took her Ph.D. examination, he came in to try to settle her down and ran his hands up and down her arms, and made her so nervous she nearly failed the examination. He was actually *pawing* her—that's her story, anyway. I don't think even *she* believes it anymore, and I notice she's stopped telling it.

For a while, Professor Aldrich would go to lunch with her day after day, and he'd tell her how very very lonely it was to be a bachelor and eat dinner alone every night, and then she'd get all excited. He'd say he couldn't talk to anyone else the way he could talk to her, and she'd shake all over. Why was he doing this? Well, John Aldrich is a terribly self-centered man, with a reputation for taking care of Number One. He'll do anything for his own pleasure, and never mind the people he hurts. He has a reputation for letting his graduate students down, letting his secretaries down, not sticking up for people, deserting them and leaving them to fight alone. He has *no* courage. Gracious, he doesn't even have the courage to stand behind his own flirtations.

He seemed to love to egg her on. It would be a rainy day, and she would come into the department office and he'd say, "Why aren't you out walking nude in the rain?"

She'd say, "Well, who'd want to see *me* walking nude in the rain?"

"Well, *I* would," he'd say.

"Well, why don't you come out in the rain and walk nude with me?" she'd say, and that's the way it would go and she'd take it all seriously. It was reality for her; it was banter for him.

Then one day another teacher called on Aldrich and, the way I get the story, he said, "Dr. Aldrich, you may not know it, but Dr. Engemark is deeply troubled about you, and the rest of us are of the opinion that she's become psychotic. She shouldn't be allowed to teach here anymore. And you should have *nothing* to do with her."

From that second on, Aldrich started acting absolutely sadistic to her. He knows he can't just throw her out, but he's done everything on earth to make it impossible for her. And she—poor thing—she still has no idea what's going on. First he started snubbing her, walking right by her in the halls without even saying hello. After that, he just acted as though she repelled him, as though he couldn't stand to look at her. Oh I hate him for it! It's so cruel, because she may *be* mentally ill, she may *need* help, and he's giving her nothing but scorn and cruelty.

She's so upset that she comes over here and talks till three A.M. about him, tracing the whole affair, trying to figure it out. She can tell you the exact date hour, and minute of every conversation they've ever had, everything that's ever gone on between them. She'll say. "I don't understand it, Esmy. He was *so* attentive to me. One day in 1969—it was a Friday, raining outside, October 16 my comp class had just ended, it was nine thirty, and he walked up and he said. . . ." Date, hour, and *minute!*

She tells you all those times and dates with exactly the same authority that she tells you who said "For fools rush in where angels fear to tread." Her mind seems to work that way. She's a human trivia game.

She sits in my living room, slobbering over wine, her fingers yellowed from cigarettes, and she says over and over, "Esmy, I need your advice. Should I confront him about this? But if I do, won't I risk losing' him?" *Losing him!* Can you imagine? I think she's very very sick. Dear me, she never had him to lose!

This summer when Mama and I went to Hawaii, Inge sent me a six thousand-word letter, and it was almost entirely about John Aldrich. The letter said, "Be *sure* to show this to your mother," as though my mother cares, as though we're all swept up in the mythology of Ingeborg Engemark and have nothing else to do with our time. When I got back to Collegeville, I found out she'd written another friend that everything was fine between her and Aldrich, that they were going to have a tryst in Yellowstone Park. Why, that's the last thing in the world he'd *dream* of doing. It's crazy, it's ridiculous.

I met John Aldrich June 18, 1960. He was a bachelor, and damned good looking. He's *still* damned good looking, at fifty-nine. He was so much older than I was that it was almost a student-teacher relationship at the beginning. We talked a lot and he always understood my ironies. I took one class under him, and a few times he joined me in the cafeteria when I was having lunch with my friends. On the last day of the course, he came over to me and said, "Well, it's all over now."

I looked at him and I said slowly, "Yes, there are a lot of things over now." I was already in love with him, and he looked at me and he knew exactly what I meant. There was always *something* going between us, but he would never admit it. One time another teacher said to me, "Gee, he certainly gets a kick out of you, doesn't he?" We were always terribly *sympathique*. A teacher said to me, "You're crazy if you don't set your cap for him." I told her not to worry; I'd set my cap for him the minute I laid eyes on him.

For a long time, John flirted with me on the campus, at faculty parties, and we'd have these verbal tennis matches. He was always showing me things- asking my opinion. One day at lunch I got up to go and he grabbed my hand across the table and said, "Oh, do you *have* to go yet? Let me get you more coffee." It sent chills down my spine. If he didn't have feelings for me, why would he do that? At faculty parties he wou'd light my cigarette, share his book with me, get me drinks. and sometimes I would feel his arm brush against my shoulder, and I would say to myself, "John, John what are you doing? You are driving me crazy!" Because I knew he was in love with me. Aye, marry, *he was*!

But it never moved beyond the teasing stage. He loves to tease me. I know he has feelings about me because of the way he acts. I fascinate him. that's obvious, but why won't he follow through? I've been waiting all these years, sitting and waiting, sitting and waiting. crying, hoping, sometimes praying. Ann Stults told me to stop waiting. She said "I wouldn't wait two minutes for *any* of the men in this department. They're all fairies." Well, she's wrong about John Aldrich.

But he *is* strange. He does little things that drive me crazy. I was at a party at his house once. November 17, 1968, and when he put my coat on at the end of the evening he sort of hugged me, tightened his arms around me and said, "Well, we're good friends, aren't we?" I didn't sleep all night. thinking about it.

But after that he began getting in little digs, and I didn't understand. One night at a faculty party I heard him tell another teacher, "You should hear what Ingeborg did at the teachers' convention in Chicago."

I walked over. and I said, "Do you want to hear more?"

John said, "No. no, Ingeborg, don't tell us!"

Why, hell, there was nothing to tell. We'd had a two-week convention and we'd done a lot of drinking and telling dirty jokes and I'd met some guy from Oberlin and had a nice time with him and a very nice time with a couple of other teachers, too. But that was years before! *Years before!* I don't know why he brought it up. I said, "Well, you just go ahead and tell everybody! I don't care." And he said, "Oh, no, Ingeborg, I wouldn't tell on you."

Sometime after that I was with him at a faculty picnic and one of the younger professors said, "Come on, Inge, let's take a walk in the woods," and I quoted Molly Bloom back to him. I said, "Yes I said yes I will yes." I mean, if you can't quote James Joyce at an English teachers' picnic without their understanding you instantly, where can you quote him? John overheard and he said loudly, so everybody could hear it, "Inge will say yes to any man." Can you imagine? "*Inge will say yes to any man.*" In front of the chairman and his wife and everybody else! God knows how many people heard him! There was no provocation!

I said, "Why, professor, surely you must realize I was just quoting Molly Bloom." There was a dead silence.

Then he said it again, "Inge will say yes to any man. Won't you, Inge?"

I said, "Well, that depends, sir. Only to *certain* men."

He brought it up several more times. Maybe he was drunk, I don't know. Somebody told me he'd had two double martinis, and that's a lot for him.

Lately he seems to be doing more and more cruel things like that. My friends will invite him to dinner and when he finds out I'm coming he begs off. He's done that a dozen times. Or he'll come right out and ask them if I'm going to be there, and then make an excuse for not showing up. When we both go to the same poetry reading or drama reading, he bolts out the door the minute it's over. He acts as if he doesn't want anybody to know about us. Just before he left for his sabbatical, I ran into him in the hall, and I said, "Well, I guess this is good-bye."

He looked terribly emotional. He said, "Why, I'm not going yet, not for a few days." As though he could barely get the words out.

As we started down the stairs together, he said. "Let's not say good-bye yet. We'll be seeing each other again before I leave."

At the bottom of the stairs, he said, "Now no more good-byes. Promise me we'll see each other at least once more before I leave."

"I promise," I said.

But I didn't see him any more that day, and the next day his office was empty. That night I walked over by his house. and the light was on, and he was there! I was furious! But what do you say, what do you do? *There he was, right in the picture window!* And he was having some kind of gathering, and I could hear the noise, joking, and laughing. I said to myself, "What the hell's going on?"

Later I figured it out. He *knew* I'd come to his house and check on whether he'd left or not. And he wanted me to come over and take the initiative and say, "Darling, kiss me good-bye!" But I don't do things like that. I will *not* take the initiative. That is up to the male, and John will just have to get up his courage and make the first move.

Well. I don't want to belabor the whole thing, but it colors my life. That love affair is the only thing that's made my life interesting. What would my life be like without it? There's only been one other man in the last few years, the man who came around, Ted Baynes. Bam—zam—thank you, ma'am.

I realize that I spend a terrible lot of time thinking about John Aldrich. He's on my mind always. The fun we've had. The fooling around. The verbal sparring. We've had a ball, talking and laughing and telling jokes. And then suddenly for some offense I'm not even aware of, it's over. He won't even look at me! And I remember all the faculty parties where he couldn't keep his hands off me! In front of everybody! And all I can think of that I might have done was give him a carton of cigarettes for his birthday and suddenly—*his retreat is so pathetic!* You would think I did a striptease and jumped on top of him and said, "Come on, let's do it!" But all I did was quote to him on a little card something he'd quoted to me: "You're the only one who knows my ironies." And after that he wouldn't even meet my eyes in the hall. And the quote was *his*, not mine. I was just quoting it back to him. Ods bodkins, what was wrong about that?

When I try to figure it out, sometimes I come to the conclusion that he's impotent, and therefore he doesn't want to start something he can't finish. I've thought a lot about that possibility. There isn't *any* possibility I haven't thought about. If he's impotent he has to keep me at arms' length, so to speak. I've thought that maybe he's another Lieutenant Henry, that something could have happened to him during the war, but why doesn't he come out and tell me? I would understand. I swear he's not a homo. I would know if he was. Any time a real homo comes near me I can feel it; my flesh creeps. But I've never felt that way around John. I don't know, I don't get it. I don't mean to belabor it, but it's the major thing in my life.

One of his close friends told me that a girl broke his heart during World War II and that he's never married because of that. It was South Pacific all over again, "Some Enchanted Evening," and he intended to ask her hand in marriage, but his best friend beat him to it. "The Tennessce Waltz." And they say he's been getting even with females ever since. Maybe that's it. Maybe that's why he's such a tease. I'm always glad to hear that theory, because I've begun to think I might be nutty. God knows, I've never given any man the come-on I've given John Aldrich, and with no response. There's something strange. He must know he could have me any time, on a minute's notice. I've made it so obvious, short of going into his house and doing a striptease. My friends tell me I'm too old to let this kind of thing bug me and to forget about him. As Shakespeare said, "It was much ado about nothing." I thought, we're a pair of idiots. This is all happening twenty years too late.

But I can't take it lightly. It hurts me so. One of his best friends told me that he was having an affair with a woman in the physics department. I couldn't sleep. For a while I was going to confront him with it—why was he having an affair with another woman while he was making goo-goo eyes at me? But I didn't. Thank God! I have a horror of making a fool of myself.

The other day, Ann Stults said to me, "Now, Inge, you must get over this. Why, the man has never even taken you out. There's nothing there, you're *dreaming*."

I said, "I know better. When you're around a man a lot, and when they call you into their office, and fool around and talk, and *fool* around and *talk*, and watch you *all* the time, never take their eyes off you, and always ask your advice, well, you're entitled to draw a conclusion."

Alas, alack, I love him so much. Unfortunately! I wish I knew how to grapple him to my soul, as Shakespeare said. For a while I thought of having an affair with someone else, to make him jealous. The department chairman likes me, I can tell by the way he looks at me. But he's married and he's an honorable man, so he just makes eyes at me. I'm glad we're both so honorable. Or are we? It would be a delight, wouldn't it? And it would make Aldrich so jealous and maybe force his hand. There's not that much time left. Soon he'll be sixty.

Well, as Spenser said, "There's no fool like an old fool." Will I get over it? I don't know. I'm curious; I want to know how it'll all come out. I thought I knew men, and I thought I knew Aldrich, but I guess I didn't. There was a time two years ago when he was a-comin' slowly, I was reeling him in, and victory was in sight. All my friends said, "Be careful, don't lose him," and I said to myself, "Yes, I, *will* get him, I *want* this one, so I'll be careful. I'm not going to come on too strong. I'm not going to be the woman who goes out with a man twice and then walks him past the jewelry store." But I must have been too careful. I should have been more aggressive. I should have flung myself naked against his bedroom door. When I didn't make a move, he just seemed to panic. I don't know why. I'll never know. I'll never figure it out.

Ann Stults says:

At a faculty party a few months ago the group thinned out and Dr. Aldrich came over to me and said, "I'm kind of worried about Dr. Engemark. Would you sort of take charge of her and try to steer her away from me?"

My feeling was he's a big grown man and he should handle his own problems. I felt like saying, "Why, you big baby! She's not gonna knock you down or injure you in front of your peers."

But a few minutes later he started playing up to her! The two of them got into a loud, centerpiece conversation, with everybody else ringed around them like spectators at a cockfight. The colloquy got more and more brilliant. At one point they were asking and answering entire questions in Shakespearian quotes. And all relevant! It was an amazing display. Then they did the same thing with Renaissance drama, and then in lines of iambic pentameter from Pope and Milton and Dryden and people like that. Fantastic! It was like a Ping-Pong match with words, and I could see that Inge was exhilarated out of her skull.

But then Aldrich began flashing me signals to extricate him, like he was going down for the third time and desperately needed help. Whenever Inge would turn her back, he'd make these panicky gestures, and I thought, How degrading, how insulting, with all the others watching him and knowing what he was doing. It was his way of telling the crowd that he was just playing, that he realized he was involved with a grotesque, but he really didn't mean it, and he wanted out. Cruel! Vicious!

And what is poor Inge to think? He persists in giving her these attentions, and she persists in taking them seriously. She doesn't know that she's being used.

No matter what we tell her, she refuses to believe that there's no chance. She sees a secret meaning in every little thing he does. If he drives by our apartment house it's because he's yearning for a look at his beloved Inge. If he sends her a note, strictly business, she studies it for codes and invariably finds *something*.

Well, it may be that she's completely around the bend, as some insist. Personally, I doubt it. But she *will* be completely bananas if she stays in this faculty for another year or two. There's something basically unhealthy about this place and this English department and this stupid, sterile Collegeville. The campus is an insane, disorienting place, run by insane, disoriented people. They live in their own little Renaissance worlds, and they're totally out of touch with reality. No wonder the kids can't relate to them, but then the kids solve the problem by going off into their own drug-soaked worlds, and the result is that nobody knows anybody, and the whole college seems to be working at cross-purposes, just spewing out irrelevance. It's entirely possible that Inge is not insane, that she's the only sane one. It's hard to tell here in the kingdom of the blind.

Well, I'll just keep on living for the philosophy, "Live for the day. Drink and be merry, for tomorrow we die." Nothing will change, nothing! I'll keep on teaching, I love to teach. The rest of life I just endure. The rest of my life will just spin out about the way it's been going. I'll take it a little easier. Occasionally, I'll pick up a man or two, but most of them will let the Thane of Fife have a wife, and we'll know where she is now, or we'll hope that she's not at the door. I will take what I can get, and I will laugh at myself, and when I get too old to dream and laugh, I'll remember that line from Lillian Roth: "I'll cry tomorrow." Another professor has begun giving me the eye, and I'm tickled pink. Of course, he has a wife. He's an older man, and therefore I appear young to him and he doesn't like his wife. I'm sure he likes me better. We'll see how it proceeds.

What I'm really looking for is some kind of companionship, someone I can talk to, be with, touch. But first there must be companionship, and then the sex later. Sex without love is lust. I don't approve of lust. Of course, I don't seem to have either love or lust, but Robinson Crusoe was a hell of a long time on that damn island, too, and I don't think he wanted to be there, but he wasn't going to hang himself over it.

I'll take death when it comes, but I won't hurry it along. I'm not afraid of death in the sense that some people are. "The necessary end," you know. Or Socrates: "Think of the best night of sleep you ever had." I think there is nothing after death, and when you think of it this way, you needn't be afraid, but if there *is* something after death, just think of being able to sit in Hades, as Socrates put it, among the great shades of the past, and converse with them. Maybe you could even talk to God. "I would," says Job, "that God would answer me!" All this you would hope. You would hope. But you won't get the answer, and you won't get the wonderful scene in Hades, talking to the great ghosts. No, Eliot was right. "This is the way the world ends. This is the way the world ends. This is the way the world ends. Not with a bang, but a whimper."

I think that reincarnation would be nice, and would suffice, if you'll excuse a play on Robert Frost. I agree with Ben Jonson: "And if I have a seat at this great comedy of life, why will you deny me my pleasure?" I hope I won't be denied, that I'll have a thousand reincarnations, to watch this mad chicanery until the end. I can always *watch*. I am better as a voyeur than as a participant, and I am steadfastly amused. I can always laugh at myself, like the satirists. If you look around life and you panic, you'll lose your mind. You *have* to laugh. You can't be Canute, standing on the shore commanding the damned waves to stand still. You can't be Robert Burns' young lover telling the birds in the trees not to sing so merrily because his love has gone away. You have to sit back and observe. You *have* to laugh. You have to be thankful that you *can* laugh and say, "But for the grace of God, there go I."

This is Jonathan Swift's whole point in Gulliver's Travels. Gulliver is sent to a faraway country, but he hopes that somebody, somewhere, is going to see that it's really England, and that all the people in London might just as well be tied to tiny stakes by Lilliputians. But for the grace of God, there go they. Or Jonson's play *The Devil Is An Ass*. The whole point is that there are more asses than the devil, and they walk the streets of London every day. They come right into my classrooms; I always get them. But there are a whole lot of fools in the world, and they are a riot, they are funny. You must enjoy them.

So life is not a tragedy, it's not even a tragicomedy, it's a satire on itself. God is a satirist, and he has a sense of humor. Is God dead? Have we lost God? Naaaaaah! Naaaaaah! He may be out on a long martini break, but he has his walkie-talkie with him. Don't be silly, he's there, working his usual forty-hour week, watching over "a tale told by an idiot, signifying nothing," as Shakespeare said in *Macbeth*. Or as he said in *Lear*, "We are as flies to the gods. They kill us for their sport." That's us, puppets on a string, while all the time Satan is increasing in power, and isn't that a lovely thought?

Postscript: A Late-night Telephone Call from Esmerelda Wilson

I've just called to tell you about Inge. I'm so sorry to bother you, but I thought you'd want to know. Oh, my, how to start? You knew that she left the campus a few months ago? Well, she turned up in a wee little town in Michigan, teaching the Bible as literature and a course in contemporary poetry, from Whitman to Rod McKuen and *not* excluding Edgar A. Guest. She must have been desperate, to take a job like that. Anyway, she called me a few weeks ago—she was obviously drunk —oh, my, how she babbled on!—and she said she'd had to face the fact that John Aldrich had never had the slightest feeling for her, that it was all a fantasy affair. I remember her exact words, because they were highly dramatic, as usual. "Esmy," she said, "I created a myth, and I watched it die."

But that isn't the reason I called so late. I just heard from Ann: Inge took sleeping pills. At least, they found her lying in her room near the empty bottle. Her breath was coming very very fast, and she was unconscious. They rushed her to the hospital, and she babbled something about Aldrich being dead, God being dead, and everyone being dead. She said she couldn't see the point.

It's hard to imagine Inge attempting suicide. All that vitality. All that energy. All those quotations and their exact sources. Well, they pumped her out. She'll be fine. She'll be fine now.

SNOWFLAKE, 22
Senior, Theological Seminary

You're wondering about my name. Well, as you can see, I'm a flower child, or at least I used to be, and it was stylish for a while to drop our straight names and take some poetic name like Snowflake. I guess it just stuck, and you'd have a hard time finding anybody on this campus that even knows what my real name is.

I guess that's a blessed relief to my parents. We get along now, but nobody's kidding himself. I was the black sheep from the day I was born, and I'm still the black sheep. We all love each other, I'm sure, but on other levels there's a lot of resentment and animosity and shame. I've done things that my parents could never understand or accept, and their life-style is so alien to me that I can't relate to it at all. So we have kind of an armed truce; they don't trust me, I don't trust them, but we still pretend we're a family, and even write each other once in awhile.

Before we go any further, I want to explain one thing: This is not a story of shame and degradation, at least in my eyes. I don't say that I've been perfect, but I don't apologize for my life-style, and I don't accept the establishment attitude about us hippies anyway. So I'll be happy to tell you what happened to me, but don't get the idea that I'm apologizing or begging society's forgiveness. I love all the people who make up sociey, no matter how awful they are, because after all, they're all humans. But I don't intend to lick their boots or change my life-style to fit theirs. The American life-style is a thorough bummer, and it produces sick, sad people. Well, I'm not sick and sad, no matter how much trouble I've had. I've always had a nice time. I still do. When I was little, I was just a crazy kid, and I liked everything I did. I liked the people most of all. I still do.

I was one of those military brats you've heard about.

My father was a navy officer, and we lived all over the place, wherever the navy, in its wisdom, decided to send him. I was brought up in Coronado, Corpus Christi, Pensacola, Alameda, Washington, D. C., and about six other places. As soon as ,I made friends the navy transferred us. and I had to make new ones. Living like that does one of two things to you: It either enables you to go through life making friends easily and quickly and fitting into any new group, or it can really screw your head up and make you insecure. I think I belong in the first group. So I can't really fault the crazy navy life. A lot of my friends blame the navy when they get into trouble. But I think that's stupid. I don't believe in blaming others.

I told you I grew up as the black sheep in my family, but 'it wasn't necessarily because I was a bad person. It was much simpler than that. My father was the stubbornest man who ever lived, and I simply inherited his stubbornness. I refused to believe every word that my mother and father told me; from about the age of five, I decided to find out things for myself. I respected my parents, but I didn't take their words as gospel. And as I got older, I discovered that my value judgments were very different from theirs, and I believed in mine, and the friction with my parents began to get bad. Like when dope came in, I didn't give a second thought about whether it was legal or illegal or good or bad. I just *did* it—because I had to try everything for myself and make my own judgments—and I enjoyed it.

My father's still in the navy—he's a captain, and before he retires he'll be an admiral. He's a perfect officer: dominant, efficient. omniscient. He knows *everything*, and he's superior to everybody in the world below the rank of captain. He has completely absorbed the phony rank-consciousness of the U.S. navy. To my father, everything is rank. A dumb jerk wearing the stripes of a rear admiral—and I met quite a few dumb jerks with admiral's stripes in my life—this idiot gets my father's full respect. But if he runs into a really sharp young ensign, a brilliant, quick, intelligent young man, my father treats him coldly.

All civilians rank below my father, and minority civilians rank the lowest. Like we'd see an old black lady in the street, and he'd joke about it. He wasn't really being malicious, he was just showing that he felt that he was of an entirely different class. He'd see somebody down and out on the street, and instead of expressing sympathy he'd say, "Look at that bum! Disgusting!" These distinctions bothered me from a very early age. Because my father was secure in his fancy uniform with all the glory of the United States Navy behind him, he thought the rest of the world was dirt. It took me years and years, but finally I realized that he was just plain ignorant.

He almost succeeded in destroying my mother, but he didn't destroy me because I was just as stubborn as he was. My mother just couldn't handle him. The whole navy life is like a typical corporation, with the peck order and all that crap. My mother just wasn't made for that kind of life. She is a very outgoing and creative lady. She liked nothing better than to go out in the woods and show me and my two sisters all the secrets of nature. She had a degree in botany from Collegeville, but this didn't help her much as a navy wife. Sometimes my father would go to sea for eight- or nine-month tours, and that's when my mother found her solution: alcohol.

I've always thought that if my father could have accepted my mother's drinking and not made an issue of it, it would never have become the huge issue that it became. My father was controlled in all things and he was not much of a drinker. I mean: If he was at a party and an admiral offered him a drink, he'd take it, but he'd just sip it. He was the same way about smoking. When everybody else smoked, he smoked, but when everybody quit, he quit. That's fine; that's his thing: Big self-control. But this gives him a stern view of everybody else. If you don't have his self-control, you're weak and stupid. So whenever my mother would take maybe one drink too many when they were out in public, he'd take her home and lecture her on what an embarrassment she was to him. Just when my mother was starting to have a good time, he'd haul her away and read the riot act. As a result, my mother went underground with her drinking, and that's when it really got bad. Now right here you have a great example of the difference in life-styles between generations. Like in my group, nobody thinks twice about getting high. Of course, if you're a sadistic drunk, or a fighter, we don't want you around. But otherwise if you want to get high. that's right on! Far out! Nobody gets embarrassed, and if your boyfriend gets drunk and puts on a party hat and does the funky chicken and his pants fall down, why fine! Why get uptight about it? So drinking doesn't become a problem with us. You can get drunk, release your tensions, and let it all hang out.

If it had been acceptable to my father and his social set for my mother to get a little high once in a while, I'm convinced her problem would never have developed. But not only could she *not* get high—she couldn't even *discuss* it with him. So naturally her drinking increased. She had vodka hidden all over the house, and she'd withdraw into her bottle whenever there were the slightest tensions. I can remember plenty of times when my father just destroyed her with his arrogant tongue, and she'd retreat to the bottle. It's really awful to hear someone clobber a person who's much weaker. He'd just leave her for dead, sobbing for hours. The big superior captain! Then he began to neglect her, and so she began to neglect herself, and all of a sudden she turned into a dumpy middle-aged lady long before her time, and this made her drink even more heavily, because she couldn't relate to herself anymore.

It got really bad in the early years of high school. Mother would nod out in the afternoons, and she'd say things and not remember them, and she'd get real uptight at us girls for the least little thing. She got to be pretty well known around the neighborhood. Like sometimes kids would come home from school with us, and she'd be laying down sleeping on the couch, and we'd go in and ask her some foolish question, and she'd kind of half wake up and say something incoherent, and fall back asleep. We used to get a real kick out of it. We thought it was really funny. I suppose I should have been embarrassed, but my friends and I didn't have any respect for my mother; she was a tragicomic figure to us.

When I was thirteen we were living in Alameda, California, and I began traveling with a pretty fast crowd of navy kids. One night we went into San Francisco to a bar. I was thirteen. When the waiter came over and asked me what I'd like, I said, "Straight gin," and he served me. That was my first time.

Not long after that I got a phony ID card, and from then on I did quite a bit of drinking. Not sloppy drunken drinking, but drinking to get high and to have fun. It was a social thing among us navy brats. You looked extra hip if you could handle liquor. It was accepted behavior. And there were great scenes. We went to see Ramsey Lewis, Ian and Sylvia, The Big Three—that was Mama Cass's group—Bud and Travis, lots of others.

When I was fifteen I got picked up for underage drinking in a San Francisco bar. Some bartender was trying to be a hero, get brownie points. It was no big deal. I didn't even freak out about it. The old police lieutenant who wrote me up was obviously an alcoholic himself. He wound up putting down twenty-two as my age, so I just stood there and let him do his trip, and pretty soon my father came and took me home and bawled me out, and that was it. So my first experience with the law was not unpleasant. Far out!

In my junior year we lived within walking distance of school, and I used to go home for lunch. My father was at sea, and my mother was always drunk. I'd walk in and yell, "Hi, mom!" She'd give me a vague answer, and I'd know that she was juiced already. So while she was nodding out downstairs I'd slip to one of her stashes and take a nip of vodka. It felt good. I did it just to get high. It gave me a nice feeling of freedom and relaxation.

There were only a few times when I took a little too

much, and I'd get embarrassed at school, or feel sick. I had friends that would actually get drunk at lunchtime and come back into school in terrible shape. But I didn't do that very often. Mostly I drank just because it made life more exciting, and it was fun to tell people about it. It gave me some distinction among my peers.

When my father came back from that tour, my mother was in the worst shape of her life, and still he didn't realize what was going on. Or he realized it and didn't say anything. I guess he was too busy trying to break me, the way you break a young horse. My two sisters did everything he told them, like slaves, but I went my own way, and we had some terrible brawls over it. We even had brawls when I was completely in the right. Maybe another daughter would have given in and apologized to her father, but when I was right, I was *right*, and I wasn't going to apologize or pretend I was wrong. There was one horrible example in my senior year. If my father's any kind of a real man, he must die of embarrassment when he remembers it.

Normally, I had to be in around midnight or one, but I had been in a high school play and on the last night of the production we were going to have a cast party. Now anybody who knows anything about cast parties knows that they don't even get moving till two or three in the morning, and if you're going to a cast party you don't have a chance of getting home before four or five A.M. I explained all this to my mother, and she said she understood; and besides she knew the guy I was going with and respected and admired him, and she knew everybody else who'd be at the party, including several teachers, so she told me to go ahead and not worry about what time I got home. Of course. she was a little drunk at the time, but then she was always a little drunk, so I thought everything was cool.

The boy brought me home at four in the morning, and my father was standing on the lawn. He says to me, "Get in the house!" He says to the boy, "You get out of here and don't come back!"

My mother was waiting inside, and I said, "Mother, tell him I had your permission."

My mother said, "You didn't have my permission to stay out *this* late." I could hardly believe my ears! I looked at her closely, and I could see that her eyes weren't focusing. She was so drunk she could hardly stand up, let alone come to the support of a daughter. She was just too spaced out to get it straight. I wanted to turn to dad and tell him that she was drunk, but I knew I couldn't. She was in a stage where she had to be pathetically submissive to him, and she'd say things and forget them, or she'd go along with whatever he said, no matter how ridiculous it was.

Now he'd made up his mind that no daughter of his could stay out till four in the morning, regardless of the excuse, and there was no way that I could shake him. I told you he's stubborn. Even after he heard my explanation, he kept on insisting that I was a loose girl, and he was ashamed of me.

We screamed and argued, and finally I went into the bathroom, to start getting ready for bed. He came right in after me, still screaming. I said, "Okay, okay! I'm home now! Let me get some sleep!" But he kept right on. My mother came in, holding onto the door for support, and I said, "Mom, will you *please* tell him that you gave me permission? For the last time, will you *tell* him?"

She said, "I didn't give you permission," and she walked away.

My father said, "See? Your own mother says you're a liar," and then he really took off. He said I was a bum, and he said I must be doing awful things at night and he was thoroughly ashamed of me. He went on and on and on, and he really pissed me off, and finally I got so mad I called him a bastard; and all of a sudden I found that we were tugging at each other and wrestling, and he was hurting me with his grip. "You're a bastard!" I said and he hauled off and punched me in the face with his fist. Far out! What a scene!

I fell to the floor, but I didn't cry. I said, as calmly as I could, "You—better—never—touch—me—again!" He must have realized that he'd done a bad thing because he turned around and walked off.

In my senior year we moved again, this time to Corpus Christi, and I had to make another set of friends. When I first went to class the boys surrounded me, they wanted to get to know me, but the girls were more reluctant. So I began hanging with the boys, but only until I picked up where they really were at. Then I realized they were mostly phonies. They had a social scene going with some drinking and some grass, but it was all very secret, and they were very uptight about it. Well, I drank routinely and I smoked grass routinely, and I wasn't going to be hypocritical about it like these jocks. I hate hypocrisy above all else. So I cut out of that scene.

I began to make friends outside the school with people who were kind of hip and crazy, and that's how I met good old Sunflower, my lifelong pal Junie, a real crazy hip artist type who did all the things that I did, and then some. Junie is terrific! She can find a whole volume of information in a blade of grass. She can freak out on a whiff of sassafras. She was the first person I ever met who literally and actually loved everybody, and she taught me to see the good in all people, even in criminals and politicians. Junie changed my life completely around. She wasn't named Sunflower yet, and I wasn't Snowflake yet; that all happened later.

After a while I took up with this boy Chris Vogle, and we went together for a long time. There was only one problem: He was a bastard. Chris Vogle had everything going for him, but he'd always blow it. He came from a rich family, he was handsome, he was smart, but he was just a born intentional loser, and really selfish and stupid in his own way. Like he was conniving. He was a sponger. He would rip off anything he could. He'd use up ten dollars' worth of energy to con you out of a quarter. I used to give him everything I had, money, whatever, and I'd say, "Wouldn't you rather earn your own money?"

He'd say, "Hell, no. Money's money, whether you earn it or find it or steal it."

It was really a half-assed relationship. Like we went

together for a couple of years, but he'd never admit to anybody that we were going steady. He'd always pretend like I was just one of his *many* girl friends. But I did love him, no question about that. I loved him a lot because underneath that awful exterior I could see that he had a lot of good qualities. I just hung around and hung around waiting for the good qualities to come out. They never did.

My mother had graduated from The College, and all my life I had known that's where I was going. I didn't mind. The College is in a beautiful setting, and I had been to Collegeville a few times and liked it. It was a square town, but that didn't bother me. I knew I didn't have to live a square life. I wasn't too happy about leaving Chris, but he had been acting weirder and weirder, and so I enrolled as a freshman in The College. I had been jotting down my thoughts from the age of five, so I decided to become a writer. I majored in English, and from the outset I knew I would have no trouble with the courses. The grades would come easily. The only problem was that after I'd been in The College for about two weeks, I realized that Chris had made me pregnant.

Maybe I was just dumb, I don't know. I'd been having sex since the age of fourteen, but no big deal. Like the first time I ever did it, it was pleasant, it wasn't a back-seat rape, or anything like that. It was nice and easy, very cool. So I was never uptight about sex, and never compulsive about it. Before I started going with Chris in my senior year, I'd had sex with maybe two or three boys. So maybe I didn't know enough about precautions.

I figured I'd work it out somehow and I stayed in school and kept going to class. The girls in the dorm were really good to me. They seemed to like me, and they tried to give me their moral support. At Christmastime my parents came to visit me, and I had to be real careful, like I had to wear loose clothes, because I was showing by then. But they didn't seem to notice.

At the beginning of the spring term, I started calling

welfare agencies and telling them what my problem was.
Eventually I got hold of a family service agency, and they
gave me some good advice and told me how I could
finance the whole trip. They gave me the name of a family where I could stay, where I could work as a live-in
housekeeper and cook and babysitter until my own baby
came. After that, my baby would be adopted by a good
family, and I could go back to school.

When I had this all worked out, I called my parents
and told them. My mother cried. My father sounded all
broken up. We had this big long conversation about
who was the father and why didn't I marry him. I told
them that Chris was the father, and that I loved Chris
but he was a jerk, and that I would never dream of marrying him. They said that people would talk, and I said
I didn't give a damn if people talked. They told me about
a friend of mine who'd gotten pregnant and then got married and everything worked out fine, and that really
bothered my head, because they could respect this other
girl just because her old man happened to be worthwhile
enough to marry, but they couldn't respect my own feeling
against marrying Chris. They figured it was a blessing
to get married and a curse if you didn't.

I was also bothered by the fact that they just couldn't
hide their shame over the phone. They couldn't seem to
get it into their head that a *baby* was coming along, their
grandchild, from their own daughter, their own flesh and
blood, and they should be able to get into that. But they
couldn't. Far out!

Later on I realized that I had done a very heavy
thing to them. I had totally screwed their heads. They'd
have loved it if I'd come back on my hands and knees
asking them for their help. But I had worked everything
out. I didn't need their money. I didn't need them at all.
This deprived them of the pleasure of bearing the big
load and making me feel guilty. It must have been
tough for them. They couldn't even tell me what to do
about the baby, because I had handled everything myself. So there it was: the square parents and the black
sheep daughter, all over again. I was only eighteen

years old, but I had completely severed the silver cord. From that day on, my parents had no further control over me. And they knew it. They didn't like the hippie scene I got into, they still don't like it, but they can't do a thing about it.

I lived with my foster family for a couple of months, and I ballooned out and became *so* healthy. Everything went easy, even the delivery. After I came out of the ether, they brought the baby to me. It was a boy. I thought I'd be all broken up about losing him, but I didn't feel it at all when they took him away. A few weeks later there were private court proceedings, and I had to sign a silly piece of paper giving up my son, and I was surprised to find that my hand shook, and I almost started to cry. But I didn't. I don't cry much. There wasn't all that much to be upset about. Why cry? It takes a lot to make me cry. I get tears in my eyes sometimes, but don't worry—you're not gonna see me cry. I'm too stubborn to cry. No, I've never seen the baby, but I'd like to because I think he's probably a cute little fellow.

That summer, Chris came out to Collegeville and we took a little house in the hills together. For a while, it was nice, and I began to entertain the illusion that maybe his good side would win out. But then my mother and father stepped into the act. Maybe they were trying to entice me away from Chris, or maybe they were just being good, I don't know, but they offered to pay my way on a European tour for a month. I said, "Far out! I'd love to." The idea was so cool.

Chris was excited for me at first. He said, "Groovy! Far out! Go and have a good time!" But the night before my plane left, he says, "Don't go. I want you here with me."

I says, "You're crazy." I says, "How come you wait till the night before I leave?"

He says, "I just don't want you to go. I can't promise that things will be the same when you come back."

I said, "Well, you're a really selfish bastard!" and I left.

It was a wonderful trip. I lived in hostels and communes, and I visited about eight countries. But there were no letters from Chris, and I began to wonder what was happening in our little place in the hills. When I came home, I found out. The place was trashed. It was a wreck. My Siamese cat was running around almost starved. I freaked out. The cat had torn down all the curtains in its misery. I've always loved animals, and I just sat down and cried. My head was wrecked. I looked around in all the trash and junk and I found a couple of notes saying things like, "Chris, sweetie, I brought your lunch over. Love, Betty." Stuff like that. I thought, Oh, no!

I walked all over Collegeville trying to find Chris, and finally I found him at a friend's house. I walk in the door, and he sees me, and he says, "I'm getting married in a week." I just reeled back! I said, "Huh?" It was so heavy I couldn't comprehend it, I thought I must be dreaming. They let me stay over with them that night, in a room of my own, but I couldn't sleep at all. Like I felt if I went to sleep something horrible would happen, and I felt really evil vibes around me. I just blew some kind of psychedelic circuit in my mind. *Chris was getting married in a week.* There was just no place in my head for that piece of information to fit.

I sat up all night; I felt the presence of all the ghosts that existed between me and Chris, and then I saw the sun coming up, and the higher it came up in the morning sky, the freer I felt, and the next day I said, "Goodbye," real nonchalant and calm. I don't know how to explain it, but I felt happy. Nothing hurt anymore, and when I walked away I didn't even cry.

(Just in case you're wondering, I was right about Chris all along. He's been married three times in three years, he's fathered about five illegitimate children, he's been in and out of court, and he's wrecked his body in accidents and by taking hard drugs. So I did the right thing when I decided not to marry him in the first place.)

Well, this was the first real hippie summer for me and the first real hippie summer for Collegeville. I was in on the beginning of it and I loved the whole scene. The hippie movement started out to be love and brotherhood and trying to do good things for each other, being kind and loving, turning each other on, not ripping each other off. We were true flower children; we believed in love, do your thing, flowers, peace, gentleness above all. We even gave ourselves new names, and that's how I became Snowflake and Junie became Sunflower. We loved everything about the movement.

There have been changes since then, of course. There are people who profess love and peace inside, who come on like real hippies, but they're really angry inside, and they're really bums—I mean, I love them, because they're my fellow human beings, but they're really downers, bummers. They haven't got anything I can relate to, and often they take advantage of the real flower children. There was very little of that in Collegeville back then.

The dope scene was just starting out in Collegeville then, too. I'd smoked and I'd done acid before, but this was the first year when there was dope in large quantity. We stayed high all summer. It was so pleasant, so nice. It wasn't like alcoholic highs. You didn't destroy your insides with grass, and you didn't wake up with your head splitting in half the next morning. I laid out of school in the fall semester, and just stayed stoned along with everybody else. It was *lovely*. There was very little pressure from the establishment in Collegeville. They hardly knew what was going on, and nobody seemed to care. How it changed in a couple of years!

I liked *everything* about dope, but mostly the way it opened the doors in my head. It allowed me to see things from another point of view. Now I realize that dope is just another way of seeing things, and you have to tell yourself that it's not the only way. That's why I'd never make dope a way of life. But it is spiritually helpful, you *do* get revelations, and you also learn a lot about the people you're turning on with. Or you can just have fun, giggling and playing with dope. So it's enjoyable.

But you can't make the mistake of deluding yourself into exaggerating what dope can do for your life. The truth is it really can't do *anything* important for your life. You have to assign a value to it, and really, the value's kind of small. If I could never drop another tab of acid or take another toke of hash, I'd barely miss them at all.

After I got over Chris, I began going with a long-haired boy, a navy brat like me. We had a nice thing going. He asked me to marry him, but I decided I'd rather just live with him, and for a while we had a cabin in the hills. One day an old friend of mine asked me and Ben to split to Phoenix, Arizona, and get a dope partnership together, so we just floated off to Phoenix in our little car.

For a while, it was a fine trip. I was Ben's chick, and he was dealing dope. The guy who supplied Ben and his partner was a Chicano. He swam the stuff across the river at night, and he'd drive around with carloads full of dope, and he was a real heavy. One time he brought some stuff to Ben, and he had a baggie full of pure heroin, and like just having it in the apartment vibed us all out. Like we didn't like it. We were curious about it, but that stuff is heavy! It has really powerful connotations. There was like a couple ounces of pure heroin, and I just looked at it, and I weirded out, man. I went, "Oh, wow, man! *Get it out of here!*"

I don't know why we were so terrified of heroin; I mean the sentences were stiff enough for possession of marijuana. Like we'd pick up the paper and read about somebody getting five years for possession, and one day there was something in the paper about a guy getting one to ten years for murder, and another guy getting life for dope. That tells you where their heads are in Arizona. But we didn't worry too much. Mostly we were picking up stuff in Phoenix and selling it back in Collegeville, where we had a lot of connections.

Morally, I never could look on dealing as wrong. There was a mystical quality about grass three of four years ago. The whole dope scene was really just getting started, and you didn't worry as long as you stayed cool. Sentences were very stiff, but there wasn't much enforcement, and you really had to be a klutz to get caught. Either we'd have had to be turned in by one of our customers, which was not likely, since we knew everybody, or we could get turned in by one of our connections if he got busted and squealed on us. But this isn't likely either, since there's an unwritten code that people in the dope network just don't rat. So we felt safe. We knew that no nark or undercover man could infiltrate our operation, because we just didn't deal with strangers.

Once in a while we had a little hassle, but it never worried us. We got stopped one time in downtown Phoenix because Ben was driving real crazy in his Volkswagen. A cop pulled us over and started hassling us, and finally took us down to the police station, probably because Ben had long hair and I was obviously a hippie chick. They wanted to book us for vagrancy, but we had too much money on us, and we had a legitimate local address. I guess the cop who arrested us thought he was getting into some big shit, you know? But it all fell apart on him, and finally the captain said, "Let these guys go." They impounded our car temporarily, but luckily we didn't have any dope in it at the time.

There was another crazy night when Ben and I were cleaning dope in our apartment above a store. The stuff we were getting from Mexico wasn't clean, it was just loose marijuana, with the leaves still attached to the stem, and lots of seeds. So we'd sit there at the kitchen table and pick all the big stuff out, and make the dope into nice neat lids. We were busy doing this, when all of a sudden we smelled smoke, and we looked out the window and saw that the store below us was on fire. Ben said, "My God, what'll we do?"

We finally threw all the stuff together in cans and put it in the oven, and then we went running downstairs. There were about twenty firemen there, and they began going through the whole house. Thank God, they looked every place but the oven.

After a while Ben and I decided to split back to Collegeville. We just plain didn't like Phoenix, even though we had a good thing going there. We figured we had the connections now; we could make out okay in Collegeville. We left late at night in the Volkswagen, and we had a matchbox full of dope, and Ben had taken some uppers to help him drive. Early in the morning, we were almost out of Arizona, and he'd just swallowed another upper, and I was asleep. We were going through a town on the freeway, and all of a sudden he nudges me and goes, "Wake up! Wake up! Eat the dope! Eat the dope!"

I jumped up, and I saw a cop car behind us with the red light going, and I pulled the dope out of the glove box and stuffed it in my mouth. It was miserable stuff to eat straight. It tasted like a bunch of weeds. It might be okay with mayonnaise, but by itself the consistency is too dry.

The cop said he was stopping us because we didn't have the right plates. We knew the real reason: It was Ben's long hair again. The cop says, "I think you'd better follow me to headquarters." So we figured we'd had it. Following the cop car, I was trying to get the grass out of my teeth, and Ben had two uppers left, so he swallowed them, and by the time we got to headquarters about twenty minutes later we were both feeling no pain.

The cops gave us a long rap, keeping us occupied while they checked the registration, but when they found out that the car wasn't stolen they just had to let us go. They weren't happy about it, but they had no choice.

Back in Collegeville Ben and I moved into a little house, and he kept on dealing, and I went back to school. I changed my major from English to sociology because I love people, and I decided that I wouldn't mind being a social worker some day. Right away they threw a couple of math courses at me, required for a sociology major. One of the courses was statistics, all this sociometric crap. It's ridiculous. You go into sociology out of a genuine concern for people and their problems, but all they want to teach you is how to take data, how to put it all down into neat lines and add it up, and a lot of people like me are just not into that approach. They lose a lot of good sociologists that way.

Anyway, I wasn't enjoying school. Otherwise, life was fine. Ben was doing okay with his dealing, and we had a lot of good friends, and a lot of happy times. But it wasn't very long before we discovered that you had to be careful. The cops were beginning to get hip. Like we met this French dude, and we became real friendly with him and his wife. It got very thick for a while, but then we began noticing strange things were happening. Like one of Ben's associates was busted right after a meeting with the Frenchman. More and more things like this happened, and we also thought it was suspicious that the Frenchman kept trying to get Ben to sell him heroin. We knew he wasn't a user and wondered why he was so anxious to get Ben involved. Heroin was something we wanted *nothing* to do with. Finally Ben just couldn't take any more of these weird happenings. He's a very manly person, and he believes in doing things out front, and he believes in friendship. So one day he put it all together and he said to the Frenchman, "André, I think you're a nark, or you're working for the narks." It weirded André out. He split right away, and he was gone for a couple hours, and then he came back and said, "Ben, you figured it out pretty right. Let's go over to my house for a drink and we'll talk about it."

At the house André told Ben that he'd been making money as an informer, that he'd worked for French Air Force Intelligence in France, and he was putting his experience to work in Collegeville on a part-time basis. He pulled out a file on Ben, and he said, "I'll never use this against you, if you keep your mouth shut about me."

Then he made a great show of pulling out a file on me, too. Well, I'd never actually sold dope; I was just Ben's chick, so it was hard to figure what he had in the file. André wouldn't show the file to Ben, but he said that it had information on me. He also said, "I know Snowflake's pushing heroin, but don't worry, I'll keep quiet about it." Which was a joke. I'd never even *seen* heroin except that one time in Arizona, and I would never get near it in a million years.

Well, Ben didn't have the slightest intention of putting up with this bullshit, but he played it cool. He knew André was yellow, a real paranoid, so Ben let a couple of weeks go by and then he dropped a little comment. "You know, André, there were a couple of hoods around town who wanted to know where you live. They were pretty weird looking dudes, you know?" He told André that the hoods refused to explain why they were looking for him, but that it really looked heavy.

Ben let a few days go by, and then he had some friends make a few anonymous threatening calls to André's wife and his secretary, and pretty soon André was breathing very hard. Groovy! Right on! It was Ben's most amazing head trip! He had figured André out. The poor fellow was terrified. He just took off, and that was the last we ever heard of him.

After a while Ben and I began having our troubles together. I'm an idealist, and I believe that if two people are together they should be *together*. They shouldn't need anybody else. But Ben didn't feel that way. He told me he didn't want to be tied down, he wanted to feel free to see other girls, and this was always coming between us. I told him this was a state of mind, but I couldn't convince him. One night he said, "Listen, Snowflake, it's getting too much like a marriage scene. I don't want to live with you anymore."

I said, "Groovy. Right on." But I couldn't stay in Collegeville because it was too upsetting to be around all these old places, and it tore me up to see Ben with other chicks. So I split.

I stayed on the road for months, living in communes, crashing in pads all over the country. I knew that my best friend, Sunflower, was going to college in a place I'll call Southern State University. So after a while I crashed on her, and she was happy to see me. After a few weeks my money ran out, and Sunflower didn't have much money, so we decided to use the dope connections that I still had from my time with Ben. I made a few calls and found out I could get all the dope I wanted, and that's how Sunflower and I turned on Southern State University.

It was really a nice scene. We dealt only in grass. We got into psychedelics a little, but I never liked selling them because I wouldn't sell anything that I didn't use myself, and I never did psychedelics that much, and I didn't want to spend a long research campaign trying them out to see if they were safe. So we stuck to grass. We knew what it would do, and we knew how harmless it was. We were getting good grass at a good price because Ben had agreed to be my supplier. He was getting it in Collegeville now. His Phoenix connection had disappeared, the heavy Chicano. We heard that the Mafia got him. But by now it didn't matter. There was plenty of grass in Collegeville, and the supply never ran dry.

We had a good market. Grass was pretty rare at Southern State Univeristy. The town was just beginning to turn on, and there was a nice, tight community of heads there, really good people. I guess you'd have to say we were the main dealers in town because nobody else had suppliers like ours. But it never was a big market. And anyway, I never really considered it dealing. I considered it spreading dope around and getting paid for it. There was a very low profit. But we weren't in dealing to make money. We were in dealing as a way of life. Using grass and dealing grass are part of our cultural revolution. It's a highly personal thing to me. I'd turned on for the first time three or four years earlier, and I gradually worked into doing more and more of it. So I had enough experience to know that although grass might be illegal, it certainly isn't bad for you physically. If you believe in the life-style of the hippies, then you do dope and you deal dope as a matter of principle. You can't pretend to be anything but what you are, and if you're a hippie you believe in grass, so why fake to be anything else?

People who get high together become very close; they're a fraternity unto themselves; they have their own rules. It's almost like a religious thing. People who get stoned together are nice people. Compare them to alcoholics, who always want to fight and argue and rip you off. Heads never get that way. They get into each other because grass puts you into a different head, and you become better people, not interested in beating each other, but in reaching out to each other.

If you're in this subculture you really believe in it, and if you really believe in it you see nothing wrong about doing dope or dealing dope. It's all part of the revolution. Yes, I'm a complete revolutionary. I'm not a protest marcher, I'm not a women's liberationist, I don't demonstrate, but in my own life-style I carry out the aims of the revolution, and dope is a part of it. That's my thing, and it's revolutionary for this country at this time in history.

By any normal dealer's standards, the prices that Sunflower and I got were ridiculous. I mean, our profits were next to nothing. But this was consistent with our ideals of dealing. If you're gonna deal, then deal at a cheap price, don't try to get rich off it, because that's not what dealing should be about. Furthermore, you sell only the best dope, only what you yourself would use, and then you take it home and clean it even more, take out the big stems and anything rough. That way you give your customers the best possible deal.

The stuff used to come to us through the mail from Collegeville. It was perfectly safe. You used false names and addresses both ways, and you would pick up the load at general delivery. Later on we refined the system. We had the grass sent to the university to some fictitious name, in care of me. If you get something "in care of," you can't be held responsible for what's in the package. So we'd have it sent to some fictitious name in care of me, and then if we'd ever got caught we'd have blamed it on some student. But we never did get caught.

Mostly, we dealt out of the dormitory. People would come to us and we would weigh the stuff out. But we also did "Thunder Road." That was an old song about Prohibition, and we always sang it when we made our deliveries. We'd bag our lids and load up the Jeep and drive around the city delivering grass. Usually we'd just deliver confirmed sales, but once in a while we'd go to some place where they hadn't ordered, but we knew they'd be interested. It was a cool scene because we had something that *everybody* wanted, and our price was low. Like we were selling for ten dollars a lid, and nobody had ever seen grass in that town before for less than fifteen or twenty dollars. They could roll thirty or forty joints from a lid, so they were getting high for something like a quarter a joint, and that's nice and cheap.

We sold quite a bit to the professors, a fair amount to the graduate students, and we even had a couple of doctors and lawyers on our route. Sunflower had been in town for a couple of years, and she knew all the heads. It was a regular network. Nobody would have dreamed of going to the narks. We were just a couple of young girls having a good time turning on the campus. Just a couple of happy hippies. Funky-artist types. We felt we were bringing cheer into each person's life, and it was fun to be liked and admired by so many people, and *needed*. It was a funny trip, an ego trip in a way, an identity trip. Like dealing is a lonely trip sometimes; you're taking a risk, and it's frightening. But Sunflower and I were doing it together, and it was great. It really blew our minds. Far out! And it was fun to be part of the dealer hierarchy. Like you feel a part of something, you've got this big secret community of interest and sharing. It was a mind-blowing trip for both of us.

When Sunflower graduated we both felt that old urge to go back to Collegeville, even though we liked it at Southern State University and we were having a fine old time. But Collegeville is where it's at, so we packed up and drove back and got ourselves a little apartment. I went back into school and kept plowing away at my studies, and taking more and more courses in philosophy and religion. At first we didn't intend to deal, but there were so many people who remembered me from my days with Ben, and they would come to me and ask me where they could score, so we just fell back into dealing. We had all the connections, and we needed the money. We didn't have any capital, so we mostly acted as go-betweens. I mean, all our dealings were frontings. People would front money to me, or front grass to me, and I'd be the go-between and take a little percentage. I didn't ever go up to anybody and say, "Would you like to buy a lid?" I was just doing good for people.

It only took me a little while to learn that things had changed. Dealing dope was not the innocent, naive thing it once had been in Collegeville. There were people around who would rip you off, and a few who would slit your throat. Once I got burned for $150, and that was probably my whole profit for a month. That never would have happened in the old days. But by 1970 the ripoff artists had gotten into the act. I felt really bad to find this out. It took some of the fun out of dealing, some of the meaning. But if dealing wasn't as much fun, school was really a groove. I got deeper and deeper into philosophy, and then I turned to the religions of the East, and I switched my major into the seminary. I got deep into things like Zen and Yoga, not for any special purpose, but just to learn it. and I enjoyed it. My previous three or four semesters had been all mixed up, and I'd had a lot of bad grades, and I'd been on academic probation most of the time, but now I was getting good grades and really getting into learning. In a way this was one of the happiest times of my life. I was dealing, but not much, mostly just for friends. and Sunflower had a good job as a psychiatric social worker, and we figured that life would flow on pleasantly.

But the trouble was, some of my dope connections began getting crossed. For a long time I'd been selling a large amount of grass to a young married man from the city, and it was a good deal. I would sell to him at a small profit, and then he'd break it up and resell it in the city, and he would make out, too. I had a few other deals like that, wholesaling larger amounts, so it took less of my time and allowed me to study.

Then the young man from the city, Jeff Viyalla, called me and said he wanted to bring one of his customers along to meet me. I didn't like the idea, but dealing had always been a matter of trust with me, and if a good connection brings a friend, well, you figure he knows what he's doing. You figure you can trust his judgment.

Several times after that, Jeff brought this new guy, a dumpy little fat man named Bill Browning, and I didn't mind. But then after a while Browning began calling me himself, cutting Jeff out of the deal, and I'm saying to myself "This isn't right. He's supposed to be buying from Jeff. So what I'll do is I'll jack up my price, and I'll sell to Browning, but I'll give the difference to Jeff, and he'll still make his profit."

So for a while it went along like that, and Browning never seemed to object to the fact that he was paving the same amount as before, even though he didn't have to give any money to Jeff. I thought he was just a jerk. It never entered my mind that he might be a nark or an informer. I knew he had a straight job in the city, clerking in a hardware store, and it just seemed to me like he was too solid a citizen to be a police informer.

After a while Browning began telling me about a friend of his who was dying to spend money. The story began getting stranger and stranger. Browning said the friend wanted to make a big deal, maybe something involving thousands of dollars. It sounded peculiar to me because I was a petty dealer and why would he come to me with such a proposition? Anyway, a big deal can be a hassle. You end up having to go to a dozen places and wait around and hope that your connections show up and it's just really ridiculous, unless you're determined to make big money out of dope, and I never was.

But I bore along with Browning because I'm easy to get along with, I guess. One day we made an appointment to meet his rich friend, and the two of them showed up a few hours earlier than I expected. This was peculiar, too, but I wasn't putting it all together. They came busting into my apartment, acting all weird and excited and hyper. I didn't dig it at all. I was entertaining a date. I told Browning, "Come back to the bedroom with me and tell me what you want."

Browning says, "My friend wants to buy a thousand dollars' worth of grass. Can you get it?"

I said, "Whaaaat?" I should have picked up right away, because *nobody* does business like that. Nobody says, "Give me a thousand dollars' worth of grass." Anybody who comes on and says, "I have a thousand dollars I want to spend on dope," you're supposed to say, "What? Dope? What do you mean? I'm not even *involved* in dope, man. I don't know what you're talking about!" Because you know this is not cool. This could be a nark. The only guys that flash money like that are either narks looking for a setup or dummies that'll get you into trouble anyway. I mean, if a man has a thousand dollars to buy dope, why come to me? You'd go straight to Tucson and score your own and fly it back.

But I've always been so easy to get along with. I hate hassles. I'd rather take a chance than hassle somebody. I guess you could say my heart was pure, because I knew I wasn't a big dealer, I knew I wasn't an important cog in the dope operation, and above all I knew I wasn't a criminal.

I decided to play along for a while and see what happened. So I told Browning I'd go score four kilos for the one thousand dollars and I'd meet him back here later. I borrowed Sunflower's car, and on the way I figured that I'd make about a hundred dollars on the deal—the biggest money I'd ever made off grass.

My first connection didn't have that many bricks on hand, so he took me to a place higher in the network. I walked inside, and I saw more kilos of grass than I'd ever seen in my life. There was like a couch made of grass along the wall. It looked like Fort Knox, only the bricks were grass instead of gold. They were into a shape maybe eight feet long, three feet high, three feet thick, and *pure* bricks. I'll bet there were a thousand kilos there. I wanted to ask these dudes where they got it all, but that's not my trip, so I kept quiet.

That stack of grass absolutely dominated the little house. Those dudes must have moved it out with dump trucks when they heard I got busted. But they needn't have worried—I wouldn't have ratted on them. You just don't.

They gave me a friendly joint, and we all sat around and got stoned for a while. They were a great bunch of guys, kind of a corporation. They were the legal residents of this address, so nobody hassled them, and they were all revolutionaries of one kind or another, with straight jobs as covers. The main good thing they do is that by selling all this dope they manage to distribute a lot of the wealth, money that would never get into the community otherwise. So they're doing good in a lot of ways. I just loved those guys! They're good people! They're not Mafia people; they're just good guys, good citizens. I don't see how *anybody* could look down on them.

I carried the four kilos back in my knapsack and put them in Sunflower's car, and I was a little high from the joint they gave me. It must have been 100 percent pure. When I got back to the apartment, Browning and the strange guy were sitting there. I said, "Come on in the kitchen, and we'll open these up, and I'll show you how good they are." How stupid I was! The minute I saw the stranger sitting there with Browning, I should have cut out. But I was high. My judgment wasn't too good.

Sunflower and her boyfriend were in another room, so the two guys and I opened the stuff in the kitchen, and it was *beautiful!* Perfect bricks, very clean. I was thrilled at the perfection of it, but these two guys were very quiet; they weren't getting into it the way real dope connoisseurs would have. Sunflower's boyfriend had been smoking in the other room, and he came around and admired the stuff. and he tried to get the two guys to smoke a joint, and they wouldn't. That was another suspicious thing, because if they were going to spend a thousand, they should have wanted to try the dope, to make sure they weren't getting burned by a load of Sir Walter Raleigh.

Browning and the other guy were acting so strange, so hesitant and weird, that I began to weird out. I weirded out completely when the stranger said, "Well, I guess I'll go down to the car and get the money." When he said that, I said to myself, "Oh, this is *really* bad." But I still sat there, stoned, just waiting.

Browning stayed in the kitchen with me. I said to myself, Go look out the window! See if the cops are there! But I didn't. Then I said to myself, Take the stuff and make a run for it, before the cops get here! But I didn't. I just let the whole thing flow along. Far out!

A few minutes went by, and then about ten guys in plainclothes burst into the apartment. They never identified themselves, and I could have legally shot every one of them. For all I knew, the whole thing could have been a burn by a gang of thieves. But of course they all smelled like cops. They'd even done it dumb, like cops. So I just went, "Hmmmmmm."

From the beginning, it was an illegal arrest. They didn't identify themselves. They showed no badges. They didn't give us our rights. They had no search warrant, nothing. They didn't say a word, except "Don't move!" And my lawyer told me later it was a simple case of entrapment, and if we had wanted to make a big fight out of it, we could have won the case.

Well, anyway, when fat Bill Browning saw them come in, he put his head in his hands and he said, "Oh, no!" and started to bawl and freak out. What an actor! The cops must think everybody's as stupid as they are.

They took us down and put us in cages, but after a little while they came and unlocked Browning, and one of them said real loud, so we could hear, "Come on, we want to question you about another case." Sunflower and her boyfriend and I just looked at each other and laughed. Browning went away, still bawling and sobbing, and we found out later that he went right back on the street and helped bust a friend of mine that same night. Well, that's one way to make a living. I still have to love informers and narks, because they're fellow human beings, but I don't have to respect the way they earn their money.

We finally got out on bail, after a few days, and then the legal wrangling began. My lawyer asked me if I was willing to tell the cops all I knew about the dope network and I said no, I'd go to prison first, we just don't do things like that. And he said, "Well, I don't think they'll try anything because they realize there's entrapment involved here, and it's a weak case. So let's see what the DA offers."

Well, Sunflower's boyfriend was allowed to plead guilty to using marijuana and he got off with a thirty-day suspended sentence. Sunflower was charged with a lesser count of possession and she got probation, but they kept her car. I was charged with a felony count of possession because of the large quanitity, and because they were really out to get me anyway. Maybe it went back to what we did to their French informant, or to the story that was going around that I was dealing heroin, which was ridiculous. But anyway, this one nark had made a career out of trying to catch me. I found all this out later. But because they'd handled the arrest so stupidly, they couldn't even charge me with selling marijuana, because there'd never been a legal sale; no money had exchanged hands. So my lawyer said they'd hold still for a plea of guilty to a felony count of possession, and the judge would give me probation.

I stayed cool right up to the day of sentencing. Then my lawyer told me that the police were putting a lot of pressure on the DA's office to put me in prison, and by the time sentencing came up I was really scared. My lawyer said he couldn't promise me anything. He said it was possible that I could be sent up for five to ten years. When the judge told me to rise, I felt like saying, "Judge, Your Honor, how can you do this to me? I'm just a poor little college girl. *Boo hoo!*" But it turned out to be unnecessary. The judge gave me probation and a little lecture. I said, "Thank you very much."

Well, I guess I should say that my life has changed completely since then, but it really hasn't. Of course, I lost a lot of friends. Once you've been arrested, everybody's afraid you'll bring the heat on them. I had to break all my connections to keep from getting anybody in trouble. There was a long period of big paranoia, worrying about my phone being tapped, worrying about being followed, because I knew if the cops ever caught me again, it would be instant penitentiary for violating my probation. I wasn't even able to go *near* some of my old friends, for fear the cops were keeping tab, and one of the terms of my parole was that I not go near anyone involved in dope. So I had to change my whole group of friends.

But after a while I calmed down. Some of my older friends would come up to me and say, "Do you know where I can score some dope?" and if I knew, I would tell them. But I would never handle the stuff or take any money, and I still don't. I just do it for a favor.

None of this represents any real change in life-style. I mean, my values are the same as ever, but what's happened to me is that I've learned something about the establishment values, and I act accordingly. I mean, if they want to spend all that money prosecuting nobodies, well, that's their business, but I have to be aware of it, and watch out.

I've been out on probation for a year now, and I haven't bought anything or dealt anything since the day I got busted. If I wanted to, I could jump right back into the middle of dealing again. I still know all the connections, even though I haven't gone near them. It's just not worth it. I still smoke, but I don't buy and I don't deal. It's not that important to me, anyway. If I never saw another joint in my life, it wouldn't bother me in the slightest. I mean, it's a nice high, but I can live without it. I don't want to wind up buying joints from the guards at the penitentiary. That's stupid.

I still dream about being busted. Like in one dream, there's a couple of us dealers there, and it's like a funny TV show. The cops are really klutzes: funny, bumbling idiots. They find all kinds of contraband around the house and they mark it Exhibit A, Exhibit B, and they lay it all out on the kitchen table. Then they walk out of the room to confer, and I eat the stuff: hash and marijuana. So there goes their evidence. Now all they've got left on us is one lid of dope, and they put us in the cop car, and the lid is sitting right on the seat, so I pick it up and empty it out the window. By the time we get to the station, they've got nothing, and we walk away laughing.

The second dream is I get busted, and I start running, and they're shooting at me, but I run *between* the bullets and I get away.

In the third dream we're being busted again, only when the cops come bursting into the apartment, my father is one of them, and he's running the show, as usual, bossing everybody around and looking at me and saying, "There she is. She's a loose woman. Put the cuffs on her!" Then they take me and the stuff down to headquarters, and the chemist walks in and says the evidence is catnip, and I walk out thumbing my nose.

I guess that dream shows a certain resentment toward my father, and I don't deny it. But mostly my parents and I are getting along now, staying at arm's length but at least treating each other decently. They accept my collect calls, so I guess they can't be too mad at me. It didn't hurt when my little sister was busted for possession, too. It helped to teach my parents that maybe I wasn't the only black sheep. Once in a while my father says something about what I intend to do with my life, how do I intend to make a living, but he lets it drop pretty fast. I think he's finally beginning to understand that we're different, and he's having to accept that. He's also learned about my mother's problems, or at least he's admitted that it's happening, and he steered her into AA, and she's improving fast. It's like I always told them: If you bring things out in the open, you can solve anything.

I have another steady boyfriend now; I never seem to go with more than one at a time, and I like the steady trip. He's a college graduate, and he thinks he's going to go back to medical school, and maybe I'll just go along with him, keep up my studies in the seminary, and maybe someday we'll be married, and I'll tell my kids all about college and what a groovy experience it was, and I'll be a doctor's wife, and everybody will respect me for what I am.

Right now I'm just thinking about getting a degree to show my parents that I have some value. Last semester I got three A's and a C in my majors, and this semester I'm doing even better, if you can imagine. Once in a while I get a little restless for the old life; I feel like pulling up stakes and hitching around the country again, but each time I've been able to resist it. My head's strictly into an Eastern religion trip, losing all identity of self. It's a very real rap to me. All the unhappiness that people experience is made from their own heads; it doesn't exist outside their own heads. It's all manufactured right there. You're subject to pain until you realize this. That's the main thing I'm learning. Slowly, slowly, I'm working through all my religious trips, and I'm becoming a truly happy person. I'll be a truly happy person the day I attain complete nothingness. In the meantime I just wish people would let me live, let me do my thing in my own way. I'll never hurt anybody; I'll never bring any harm. Just give me a chance, and I'll love you all.

CONSUELO MARTIN, 21
Sophomore, School of Education

Ruth Francis, M.D., director of the People's Clinic of Collegeville, says:

Connie Martin wandered into the clinic at the request of a hysterical female professor who'd found out she was shooting heroin. But heroin turned out to be a very minor part of Connie's troubles. She wasn't using much dope, but she was picking the wrong companions to do it with, and she got sucked into a lot of trouble.

Nancy Amory, a friend, says:

Connie's a real sweet chick, at least on top, but underneath I'm not so sure. Like when she's high, she turns a lot of people off because of statements that she makes, opinions and things that seem hateful. When she's high, she's the opposite of when she's not. When she's not high, she's quiet and sweet, and she'll let people get away with murder with her, but when she's high she cuts you down; she's always on the attack. She gets *really* nasty. She's lost a lot of friends that way.

I'm good at facts, but I'm bad at theories and interpretations. Like I can tell you all about my life, but I can't tell you why. Most of the theories I have about myself were told to me by other people. I just parrot what they say. I'm at a loss to explain myself. You figure it out. It's too much for me.

Mostly I feel like a middleman. I mean, you think of me as a Chicano, right? Well, maybe I am, because I have a Spanish name and all my people are Spanish-

Americans. Of course, we've been in the United States for a couple of hundred years, but that doesn't keep people from referring to us as Chicanos. I don't get mad about it. People love to have special names for things. But I don't really *feel* like a Chicano. Like my name, Martin. All my Spanish friends pronounce it Mar-Teen, but the Anglos just say Martin, as if I was Irish. So I feel kind of in between.

Am I the Mexican girl Consuelo Mar-teen, or am I just plain Connie Martin, an American chick from Montana? I don't know. You figure it out.

A lot of my people still live in the old hometown, let's just call it Jonesville, Montana. It's a little place of about five thousand population, a really dull place to be brought up in, although I didn't realize this at the time. Now you have to understand something about Mexican families. I don't know if it's because of poverty, or what it's because of, but our families are all mixed up. Like when I was born my parents Martin were just breaking up, so they took me up to my grandparents in Jonesville and dropped me off when I was a baby. So I was brought up by my grandparents Garcia, people who were forty years older than me. But that isn't all. My grandmother Garcia had been married three times, and my grandfather twice, and there were sisters and brothers and half-sisters and half-brothers all over the West. This isn't a matter of morality; it's a matter of economics. A lot of us are stoop labor, or we follow the fruit crops, or we work in mines that sometimes close down, or we go off and herd sheep for a while and then try something else. There's not enough money, so the children have to be raised wherever the money is.

That's the way it was with my real parents. They had three kids on their hands, and their marriage was breaking up, and my dad was going from job to job and my mother intended to go to the East Coast and start a new life, so there was no place for me but Jonesville and the little gray bungalow that my grandparents Garcia kept on the wrong side of the tracks. My two brothers had to be taken in by other relatives, and I've hardly ever seen them. There was no other way.

Well, try explaining all this to a kid. I was maybe two years old, and I grew up with the bitterness of being dumped like that. I grew up wondering who I was, a Martin or a Garcia. I grew up hearing my grandmother say what a *puta* my mother was, for abandoning me. My grandmother Garcia had at least three children that she hadn't raised herself, but she didn't mention them. You can imagine the resentments. Somebody was always dumping a kid off, or trying to get a kid back, or bad-mouthing some other relative because they'd dumped their own kids. It was a hateful, resentful atmosphere. I remember once when I was in the seventh grade, and my grandmother Garcia's real daughter Feliciana came down from Chicago with her kids. Feliciana was one of the kids my grandmother had dumped, but she came into the house all smiles, pretending that everything was fine. She was going to stay a week, but she wasn't there two days before the fireworks began. She looked at me and she said, "Mother, how come you're raising this little brat, and she isn't even yours, and yet you dumped me off?"

That started it. My grandmother Garcia defended me, and there was a family fight, and it wasn't about anything except long, old resentments. It was about a very old case of hurt feelings.

Well, I'm not advertising this as a good childhood, but I really didn't know any better. Like my grandmother never really hugged me, or showed any love. There was never any hugging or kissing, or anybody saying, "I love you." This just wasn't done. We knew we loved each other, but we never said it. Once in a while one of the uncles or half-brothers or aunts would bounce me on their knee, or something like that, but never my grandparents. I couldn't really talk to my grandmother. We didn't have the kind of relationship where I could come home and say, "Grandma, grandma, there's this really cute guy at school, you know. . . ." I wouldn't *dream* of saying that. I don't know why. That's just the way it was.

I guess my grandmother was cold from having a pretty rough life. She'd gone from family to family, raising different kids, giving some away, and bickering all the time. Things like, "Well, you never raised me." Or, "I'm not really your mother, you little brat." Or like my grandmother would tell my real mother, "Well, you know, Berta, Consuelo hates you." My grandmother used to say this all the time. So you wind up with far more hatred than love.

My father—I mean my grandfather, but I thought of him as my father—was just a poor, hardworking Mexican miner. He would come home so tired that he could hardly talk. So I didn't get close to him either. We would just discuss up-in-the-air things. How'd school go, how's work, okay. I really can't tell you what kind of a man my grandfather was. He was always so tired he just went to bed.

There were no rich people up in Jonesville. Everybody struggled. There were three or four black families, and maybe fifty Mexican families, and the rest white. There were a few merchants who might have had a little money, but not enough even to be regarded as middle class. Jonesville was all just degrees of lower class. But since we were all poor, we got along pretty well. The men worked on the railroad and mined. Not interesting things like gold and silver, but dusty things like sulphur and soda ash and chemicals that dry your throat and tear your lungs out. There was some sheep-raising in the countryside, but mostly the herders would try to stay away from Jonesville. Nothing much grew. It was the kind of town that you see on a cross-country drive, huddled back there several miles off the main road, marked by a big cloud of yellow smoke. You see those towns and you wonder how in the world people can survive in them. Well, we survived.

We didn't know any better—maybe that was a help. Like now I realize how dull and boring my childhood was, but at the time I just didn't know. Like there was nothing to do all day long. Like I rode my bike around. Around and around, all by myself, just riding and riding. That would kill the day. Since my father went to bed early, we all did. I was in bed by nine every night. We had no TV. We had no phonograph. We had a radio, but mostly it played western music. So I didn't listen much.

Our house was always neat and clean, but there was nothing to do in it. The big event of the evening was washing the dishes. That's about it. Every other weekend I'd do the floors. That was exciting. And I ironed my own clothes from the seventh grade on, not because I was told to, but because it was something to do. It didn't even seem grim to me, except every two or three years I'd start thinking, wow, I wished I had a brother or sister. I'd say to myself, "I wish I had *somebody!*" And maybe I'd start to cry, but that would be my emotional outburst for another two or three years.

I never knew anything different from the life in Jonesville, and it would only get me down once in a long while.

The social life was limited. For a while we had a skating rink, but mostly Mexicans went there, so they had to shut it down, because there'd always be a fight or some roughhouse. It wasn't what you would call racial trouble because it was all among ourselves. Once in a while there'd be a fight between Chicanos and whites, but mostly it was between Chicanos and Chicanos. I guess we Mexicans were resentful, and a little quicker to use our fists. And anyway, fighting and brawling was better than nothing. Some of our Chicano guys really grew up mad, really mean, and they're in the Chicano movement now, and they're still just as mad, but they're doing something constructive about it.

In general, morality was something that just wasn't taught to us. We were just supposed to have it. The last thing my grandparents would ever have talked to me about was sex. They were so uptight on the subject they squeaked. One of my aunts put my first bra on me; my grandmother never would have done it. I was in the sixth grade, and one night my aunt brought home three bras, from the smallest size up, and she tried them on me, and it was cool. I was wearing a bra! She said it wasn't right for me to develop without some kind of support.

In high school some of the kids were into ripping off, and once I took a bottle of mascara, but I was so scared, I figured *never again!* No way, boy! I just can't go through that again! So I never stole after that. I always wondered how the others did it. I guess it just takes confidence.

I learned a little bit about right and wrong in the Catholic church, going through the Commandments, and being told what I could do and what I couldn't. I didn't like it, but I accepted it. The priest told me that even if I *thought* something wrong, it was a sin. And I didn't think that was fair. It was too much. I went to catechism and the whole bit, and I felt I learned a whole lot of lessons there, believing in God and stuff like that, but pretty soon I discovered I wasn't too crazy about all that jazz anymore. I couldn't see going into the confessional and rapping about a lot of stuff that I didn't necessarily think was wrong. I mean, according to the priest you can't do *anything.* Even if you have a bad thought, you have to go in and say, "Bless me, Father, for I have sinned. I had bad thoughts." Stupid! I figured this is *their* thing, not mine, so I drifted away from the church, although I still believe in God, I think.

The nicest thing in my life was school. I got good grades because I always did my homework. There was nothing else to do; nowhere to go, nothing to do. Homework was a relief. I don't know if I have a high IQ or not, but I always got A's and B's. And I just loved being there. All through my childhood, I couldn't sleep a minute on the night before the first day of school. Three o'clock in the morning I'd still be lying there awake, so excited about the next day.

In my sophomore year I began going with Crispin Gonzales. Crispy was a happy-go-lucky, superfriendly, exciting kid. His father collected garbage around Jonesville, except that he was out of work when I met Crispy. He was a great kid, he *still* is. He makes people laugh, he's always joking around, and he's very well liked. I went with Crispy for six months, and we made out a lot, before I went to bed with him. I was kind of old-fashioned about things like that. We'd been going to bed together for a month or two when I missed a period, and the doctor told me that I was pregnant. He says, "What do you plan to do?"

I says, "I don't know. We'll see what comes along." That's the way I always looked at things.

Well, naturally, it was depressing, especially after I saw Crispy driving around with another chick a few days later. I didn't know *what* to do. One night I was laying in bed crying, and my grandmother came in. We had one of our typical conversations.

"What's the matter?"

"Nothing."

"What's the matter?"

"Nothing."

"What's the matter?"

"Nothing."

I just couldn't tell her. Finally she says, "Are you in trouble?"

I said, "Yeah."

My grandmother was in the room with me thirty minutes, and I cried the whole time, and I never did tell her flat out what the trouble was. She was sitting on my bed, but she wouldn't touch me. But finally she broke down and put her arms around me, and I was really scared, and I still couldn't tell her what was the matter—I mean, I'd have just *died*—and finally she says, "Do you have a problem?"

"Yeah."

"Are you in bad trouble?"

"Yeah."

I never said the word "pregnant" but I guess I got the message across. She just said she was sorry and backed out of the room.

A few days later I talked to Crispy, and I told him

that my grandparents knew. I told him that we should get married, but he didn't have to marry me if he didn't want to. I said maybe I'd just stick around and have the kid at home, you know? But I really didn't have any answers; I was just totally naive.

Anyway, the two families got together, and Crispy and I were married a month later. I finished out my sophomore year, but I missed my whole junior year of school having the baby and all. There's nothing new about this around Jonesville. Lots of kids there get married early, because it's something to do. Like I have a friend back home who's fourteen years old and had her baby last summer. Her husband's in the ninth grade. It gives them something to do.

Well, my marriage was the old story. Crispy was a wonderful guy around others, but no bargain around the house. We lived in a one-room triplex, but that didn't bother me. I had always been poor, and it was kind of fun to have a place of our own, even though it was so tiny. Crispy got a job pumping gas, and I worked nights as a waitress after Maria was born. Our first big fight was when I told him I was going back to school to get my diploma. He just couldn't understand that. He'd dropped out himself, and I guess he didn't want anybody with a better education around the house. I just couldn't explain to him about school. School meant everything to me, it still does. School is a way of being with people, and I've always needed that. And there wasn't a single person in our whole family that had ever graduated high school, and I swore I'd give my grandparents the first graduation ceremony they'd ever attended. I was desperate to break the family tradition; I could see my grandparents at the graduation exercises, the dinner, the whole bit, so proud. I couldn't explain this to Crispy. He accused me of caring more about school than I did about him.

Another thing I didn't like was his attitude about sex. With him, it was jump on and jump off. No romance, no love, no turning me on. After a while I began to make up excuses for not doing it. He'd wait a while and then he'd say, "Well, it's time for my once-a-week." I didn't like the idea that he was going to bed with me just because it was time, it was the once-a-week, so I'd say, "No, forget it," and he'd get mad. But am I right or wrong? You're supposed to do it when you feel like it, right? Not just because a certain time of the week has come around, right? There were lots of times when I just went through the act with him, without any real feeling at all. But a woman can only do that for so long, and then it becomes impossible. You just can't do it. And then your husband begins to tell you that you're cold.

Crispy began dating a sixteen-year-old chick. I didn't know *what* to do! I still loved him—I even love him now, he's the father of my baby—and I tried to show my love. But the boredom was beginning to get to him, too, and pretty soon it was a regular thing between him and the sixteen-year-old. He'd call her up right from our house, and ask her if she wanted to go out, and I'm going, "Hey, wait a minute, man!" You know?

One night there was a dance, a band from Nevada, a big deal, and Crispy said he wasn't going to take me. I said, "You're taking me!" He said, "No way. I'm not gonna do it."

So I said, "Okay, I'll go myself, with my girl friends." So I did. There was a big fight at the dance, and the cops came, and everybody was hassled, and so my girl friend and I drove home, and right down the middle of Main Street we passed Crispy with the sixteen-year-old sitting next to him. In a town that size, he wasn't even trying to hide. He was just doing it right out.

He got home at two in the morning, and I waited up for him. I said, "Well, Crispy, *I'm* married, and *I'm* not out messing around, so why do you do it? I mean, I'm staying home, taking care of Maria. Why can't you?" He didn't say anything, so I said, "Hey, this is the end! No more."

But I really didn't want a divorce, so I hung on for another year. I saw Crispy less and less. He and one of his buddies began turning on to acid, and they were always telling me to try it, and threatening to stick it in my coffee, and I would get all paranoid about it. I said, "Hey, man, don't you do that! When I'm ready, I'll try it, you know? But let me think about it for a while."

Right up to the very end, I kept up the same policy. I never told Crispy to leave, and I never asked him to come back. When he would disappear for a week or two, I wouldn't go after him. But even after our worst fights, I wouldn't order him out. This was something my half-sister had told me on my wedding day: "Never leave your bed, never leave your house, never tell your husband to leave, never ask him to come back. Let him do whatever he does on his own." I went by these rules. I never once slept on the couch; I always slept in our marriage bed. If he wanted to sleep on the couch, that was his business.

No, it wasn't much of a marriage, but I tried to keep it together for the baby. I decided there would be *one* Mexican family that would not send its kids to be raised by others. But then one night Crispy and I had our worst fight. He had just lost his job, and I wanted to go over and see a girl friend, and I asked him if he would babysit Maria. He got bent out of shape, so I just got in the car, and he came out raving and jumped into the car and grabbed the ignition keys. Then he slapped me across the face.

I jumped on him and grabbed his face and tore into him with my nails. I was in complete control, and I decided I wasn't going to be slapped. I knew just how deep to go with my nails so I really wouldn't hurt him, yet I could do some damage. I could feel my nails across his eyes; I could have scratched them right out. I could have literally done a job on his face. I had him down on the front seat, and I kneed him and kicked him and scratched him. I was really getting the best of it. Then all of a sudden Crispy brought up his fist and smashed me. I didn't pass out, but I started to. I went limp, and he dragged me out of the car and into the house and took off.

After a while he came back and I was putting a cold towel on my eye, and he started heckling me. "Do you want another black eye?" I'm not saying a word. His face was all cut and scratched and bleeding, and he kept blaming me for it. But I didn't yell back. Then he went in and picked up Maria and started out the door with her. I said, "Bring her back! You're not taking her away! That baby belongs with me!"

He kept right on going, so I called the sheriff, and after a little while Crispy came back with the baby and started cracking smart with the sheriff. "Why aren't you out taking care of the real crime?" "Let us alone, we're minding our own business. Go take some graft." Crispy's just not bright. You can see that.

I went to the lawyer after that. There was no way I was going to be hit again. No way! I'd known a lot of women whose husbands knocked them around, and I don't dig that scene. So a divorce was the only thing. I still loved Crispy, I'll always love Crispy, he was my first love and the whole bit, but I would never live with a man who punches me. The court ordered him to pay me sixty-five dollars a month to support Maria. What a joke! The divorce was two years ago, and Crispy has paid me a grand total of one hundred and five dollars since then.

I couldn't stand it around Jonesville anymore, so I took Maria and what little money we had and went off to stay with relatives in Collegeville. Nothing much happened; we were just a typical divorcee and her daughter trying to get by. I worked as a waitress, but after a few months they replaced me with an Anglo girl, and then I got another job slinging hash. We were barely getting by. We lived in one room, with kitchen privileges and a bathroom down the hall. My job paid $1.78 per hour and the rent was $90 a month. Mostly, Maria and I ate macaroni, stuff like that. I don't like to cook. It's no fun to cook when you're alone, and my daughter eats like a bird. She loves macaroni, so I give her a lot of it. We have it every other day, even now. It's cheap and I've never had much money. We were making payments on a 1958 Ford, and we were constantly in debt.

One day the boss announced that my job would end in a month, and I didn't know what to do. I was all alone and I was desperate, and I called the welfare people. They gave me all kinds of tests and interviews, and for the first time in my life somebody suggested college to me. The idea had never entered my mind. The Mexicans of Jonesville, Montana, don't go to college; college is Mars. But here was the welfare lady telling me that my tests were very good, there was no reason why I couldn't make it in college, and between the welfare money and the special money paid to minority students, I could get about $270 a month plus expenses. I went home with my head reeling. School was the one consistently pleasant thing in my life, and here was a chance to go to school and feed my baby at the same time. It was like a dream.

Well, nothing is ever as good as it seems, but I was absolutely crazy about The College. I kept saying to myself over and over again, "You're a college woman! You're a college woman!" But I was also a Chicano college woman, and personally I'd have preferred just being an ordinary student. For one thing, I didn't like the Chicano courses that they shoved us into. The Chicano Movement, The Chicano Woman, all that crap. Like, man, I didn't see the point. Chicano kids take courses like that because they're easy A's. They're a gift to us downtrodden minorities. Like in The Chicano Woman, all they taught us is that the Chicano woman never says anything in front of the man, never contradicts him, and all that crap, and like I don't agree with that. After a while I tried to avoid courses like that. I tried to study things that I could use. I wanted to be a teacher, not a professional Chicano, so I tried to take the courses that were useful. But the powerful radical Chicanos keep forcing these subjects into the curriculum, and then all the silly Chicano kids take them to get the easy A's.

After a while I began to feel the pain of being a middleman. Some of the Chicanos put me down because I hung around with whites. One of my girl friends had blond hair and green eyes, and it made my Chicano friends mad. I would rap with the president of the movement, he's a real Chicano heavy, and every word he said

had to be about the movement, and I'd get tired of that.
I mean, I can dig the Chicano movement, but not 100
percent of the time. Like I can see the good in whites,
but maybe somebody from the barrio, he says all whites
are bad, because like he's never met a decent white. So I
just couldn't get along with people like that, because I
relate to all races. Of course, in the official college records
I'm listed as brown. They break students down into white,
brown, and black. They don't have any purples yet, but
I guess they'll get some sooner or later.

I guess my biggest problem when I came to school was
the difference between me and the other students. I was
twenty years old, with a kid, and I had nothing in common with these other chicks. They were so immature and
young. They were all formed into cliques, and they were
trying to turn The College into a big high school, an extension of the high schools they'd known. Well, I'd never
been accepted by an all-chick clique in my life. So I
didn't have much choice. I had to find my friends among
the Chicanos.

I had a cousin on campus—anyway I called him cousin, but he was really a third cousin of one of my step-
sisters—and he put me in a pretty fast crowd. I've always been impressionable, and I've always taken the
easy way out, doing what everybody else does, so naturally I began doing a few things along with them. Like
one night we were all together, and somebody handed me
a joint, and I just took it and smoked it. I don't know why.
I just figured I was gonna smoke. I don't know why. I
just don't know. I handled that J as if I'd been smoking all my life, I took right to it, but to tell you the
truth I'm not all that crazy about smoking. It's a nui-
sance to take the smoke into your lungs and hold it
there all the time, just to get a little high. But I went
along with the crowd. I still do. I have one special
rule, I never roll a J and smoke it by myself. Never!
But if somebody else has got the stuff, I'm not gonna
say no. I don't know why. Like I never drink, but if
somebody passes me a bottle of wine, I'll take a hit
just to be sociable. I'll always say, "Sure, why not?"

My "cousin" Huero always had plenty of grass, and we smoked a lot. It just came natural to him and his group. Huero had always been in trouble. He's about twenty-five and he's been inside reformatories for at least fifteen years, but that doesn't shock me. He's a relative, and I take people for what they are right now, not for what they've been. Anyway, he never did anything all that bad—car theft, narcotics, larceny, silly stuff like that.

Huero was my social contact with other Chicanos. I was lonely, and I had to do something. He'd come over and bring his friends, and we'd mess around and smoke. I didn't know places to go, and I'd never been the type to go anywhere myself, so Huero was good for me. He started taking me into bars, and he and his friends would drink beer and I'd drink cokes and later on we'd go home and smoke some marijuana, or drop some THC or LSD, things like that.

I kept right on getting good grades in school. My girl friend Nancy loved to smoke grass and hash, and we'd go home from school at lunchtime and smoke. One day I'd smoked at lunch, and the English teacher sprang a quiz on us, and I had a little trouble because I couldn't read the questions. It was embarrassing. So I tried to cut down a little after that, but Nancy was always urging me on. Even in the morning, before we went to school, we'd have a *J*. I still didn't like it very much, but I did it. I don't know why. Nancy'd just say, "Let's get high," and I'd say, "Okay."

One day I was hanging around the quadrangle and this guy named Ramirez came up and we started rapping and he asked me when we could get together and do a little scheming. He really looks wiped out, and he says, "Wow, I've got some THC. You want to turn on?"

Normally, I would have said yes, but he was so wiped out I didn't want to fool with him. "No," I said. "I don't think I can handle it right now." I looked at his arm and it was full of tracks, and I says, "Wow, your arm is really messed up, you know?"

He said, "Yeah, that's what smack'll do." All I knew was that smack was heroin, and heroin was supposed to be bad stuff, but in the back of my mind I'd always known that someday I'd try it. I'll try anything once.

Ramirez says, "It's really good, it's really great. I'll turn you on the next time I see you."

I said, "Well, okay."

I saw him several times after that, and each time he'd say, "I'll turn you on someday."

I'd say, "Okay," because it was the simple thing to say.

One day I'm driving home from class, and here comes Ramirez and his friend Manuel, and they have their packs on their backs as usual. They both deal grass and chemicals, and they keep twenty or thirty lids in their packs all the time, so they can sell right on the campus. They're always scheming.

So anyway, Ramirez says, "Hey, pull over!" I pulled over and he says, "Hey, I got the stuff. We'll be over to your house in a little while."

I says, "Well, listen, I gotta go pick up my daughter from the babysitter first."

So I went and picked up Maria and when I got home I was really thinking, What am I gonna do? Am I really gonna shoot up? Like I knew that some people thought, Wow, I'll never do any heroin, man, like that's as low as you can get, that's not for me, and all that stuff. But I also wondered about what it would be like, and I thought maybe I could try it once. My mind went back and forth.

I knew the guys were on the way, and I'm saying to myself, "Wow, I can't believe this. These guys are gonna be down here in a minute. Am I gonna put my arm out for them?"

I sat in my chair, waiting, thinking. I kept telling myself maybe they won't show up. Sometimes I hoped they would, and sometimes I hoped they wouldn't. I cleaned up the place—I keep it immaculate—and then there's a knock on the door, and it's Ramirez and Manuel, and I'm going, Wow, this is too much!

Ramirez comes in and he says, "Hey, you wanna get straight?"

I said, "Aw, I don't know."

He says, "Well, have you got a spoon?"

I put the baby outside to play, and I said, "Yeah, I got a spoon." Somehow Ramirez had known my answer would be yes.

He gets the spoon and he says, "Bring me a glass of water," and him and Manuel took the works into the bathroom. I could hear Maria screaming and playing outside, and I hoped she'd stay put. Ramirez gets everything ready and does a fix for himself, and then he calls me into the bathroom and he says, "Put your arm out."

Manuel grabbed me by my upper arm to block the veins, and Ramirez shot the stuff right into me. He told me to flex my hand. I says, "Wow, listen, don't give me too much. I don't want to OD." I'd heard about that. This was about four in the afternoon, and I'm standing there and all of a sudden this rush hit my head, like waves coming in, breaking across my whole body, and it really felt good, like you know, wow!

After the rush we started sitting around talking, and it was really good, you know? I felt good and I could talk! I mean, on grass I just mumble and stutter and I'm not myself, but on heroin I can talk real good and feel real natural, real fine. I knew right away that heroin was for me.

We played some rock music and rapped and drank Cokes and had a fine time. Later on another friend of Ramirez came over, and they all hit up, and then they did it again. I'd brought Maria in and put her to bed, so she didn't know what was going on. When they left, Ramirez said I might get sick and throw up, and later I did get a little nauseated. I threw up my Coke, and I got sicker and sicker, and I just sat around throwing up for the whole rest of the evening. Around midnight, I crashed, and then I went to bed.

After that we'd all get straight once in awhile, like three or four times a week. But I never paid for it. Ramirez would bring it over and we'd hit up. We were just good friends; I knew his chick and I liked her too. Like sometimes I'd take Maria and we'd go over to Ramirez's house and hit up, him and his chick and me, and we'd sit there and watch the children playing. We'd hit up two or three times a night that way, so like I was getting maybe ten or twelve hits a week, all free. Just friendship. Ramirez was just a guy who liked to turn people on. Lots of times I'd be at his place when somebody new would come in, and he'd always offer to turn them on. I knew that he dealt grass and chemicals, but I was sort of surprised one day when he opened a drawer and I saw all these balloons in there full of heroin, and that's how I found out he sold smack too. But he never sold any to me.

My schoolwork went on just the same. No big change in grades. I was turning on quite a bit, but I wasn't really addicted, at least not physically. I mean, I wasn't tense about it. I knew I could always go down to Ramirez's pad and we would geeve.* I knew I could always cop a fix. So it wasn't on my mind all the time, the way it is with street junkies. I also had another friend that would give me nickel bags, dime bags.** I always used it socially, with friends. There was only one night when I took it myself. I'd been smoking grass with some friends and when I went home I just felt like getting higher, so I did some smack that I had in the house, and it was good! I really got wiped out. I put my music on, laid on the floor and played with Maria, and we had a fine time. Then I put her to bed, and nodded out.

At the end of my freshman year, I shot up with the wrong guy. He was sick, and it turned out he had hepatitis, and I got it too. I was in the hospital for a month, and I missed five weeks of school. But I still passed everything. I got three B's in my major subjects and a C in Spanish, and Spanish was always my toughest course. I told you, I'm not a real Chicano; Spanish is a foreign language to me.

During the summer vacation, I met some interesting guys. Snaky, but interesting. One of them was nicknamed Macho, which means manly in Spanish, and Macho's way

---

* Inject heroin.
** Five-dollar and ten-dollar bags.

of being manly was to steal everything he could find. One day he came up to me when I was sitting in my car and he said, "How'd you like to buy a hot inspection sticker?"

I needed one bad—my old car would've never passed inspection—so I said yeah. I had four bald tires, no directional blinkers, everything messed up, no brakes and the whole bit. I bought two of the stickers for three dollars and then I sold one to my girl friend Nancy for five dollars. So I made out. You've got to scheme to get by. I took her five dollars and I never did pay Macho, so I ended up with a free sticker and a five-dollar profit. Scheming! You have to do it.

When school started, I bumped into Macho on the campus, and he said, "Hey, you know anybody that wants to buy a hot TV?" and I said, "Wow, I sure don't." I said, "How many you got?"

He said, "I got four of 'em right now."

So I go, "How much?"

He says, "A bill."*

I goes. "Wow, I don't even know anybody that wants one, but I'll look around and let you know."

I didn't know that Macho had stolen the sets himself, but I did know they were hot. I didn't have the nerve to ask him how he got them, or where, and I didn't care anyway. That was his business. Some questions you just don't ask.

I got to know Macho a little better, and he introduced me to three of his crazy friends, Jose, Joselito. and Luis. They were all very skilled thieves. They could rip off leather coats right out of a store, right off the rack, and get away with it. They're always styling, they've always got nice clothes, three or four leather coats hanging in the closet, nice boots, the whole bit. Amazing guys! They could walk into a record store and buy one album and walk out with a whole stack. Fantastic guys! They'd come to my house and say, "We got some albums today. Bought one and got five," and I'd say, "That's cool. Wow,

* One hundred dollars.

give me a couple!" Because, like I didn't know how to do things like that, I never even learned to shoplift.

I never really became close good friends with these guys. I mean, I saw them once in a while, and rapped with them, but we were definitely not close friends. I was hitting up all this time, but mostly with other people, and I was sort of mingling around the edge of several groups, but superfriendly with nobody except maybe Nancy. Then one morning Macho calls up and says, "Can I borrow your car?"

As usual I says, "Okay." So I drive it up to him at the dormitory because he didn't have any wheels, and I gave him the keys and asked him how long he'd need it and he says, "Oh, about two hours." He didn't show up till about six o'clock that night, four hours later than he'd promised. I said, "What have you been doing with the car?" And he said, "Oh, we've been driving back and forth to the city all day," but he wouldn't say anymore. When he left, I looked inside the car, and I found all these nylon stockings in it. I couldn't figure this out. It was a long time before I knew what they did with the nylon stockings.

A week later Macho and Luis borrowed my car again, this time at nine in the morning. I went on to school and about two o'clock in the afternoon I come home and I see my door's open and I really flipped out. I knew I didn't leave the door open. When I walked inside, there was a big TV on the floor, big rifles, huge ones, six or eight of them, one pistol, an AM-FM tuner, and pillowcases and bags all over the floor, full of jewelry and things like that. There were leather gloves and a nice looking suede coat, and about twenty-five bottles of booze. I look around, and Jose's sitting there, and Luis is out fooling with my car, someplace.

I said, "Hey, man, where'd you get all this stuff?" But I really didn't have to ask; I knew they'd stolen it. I said, "Shit, I just don't see how you can get away with taking that much stuff." I was really curious, but Jose didn't say anything.

The picture I had was that they would park in front

of a house and then go inside and walk in and out with all this stuff. That's the only way I could imagine it, and I didn't see how they could get away with such open stealing. It was blowing my mind, trying to figure out how they did it. A little while later, Macho and Joselito drove up in Joselito's car, and Luis came back with my car, and we all came inside and sat around and rapped. Finally somebody said, "Well, we're gonna take the stuff now," so they load up Luis's car with the rifles and the suede coat, and they left the TV and a vacuum cleaner and a guitar and some other stuff behind, and they said they'd come back and get it later that night.

I said, "Why don't you put it in the bedroom, I don't want it lying around here in the living room." So they piled everything into the bedroom. Macho and Joselito said they had some more stuff in my car, so they brought that inside too: cameras and lenses and some silver, trays and things like that and a bag of jewelry. And they brought it in and checked it over. The jewelry was Indian stuff, not very good at all. I wasn't too interested in it. There were a couple of solid silver bracelets that I liked, so I said, "Well, I'll take these." It really didn't enter my mind that this stuff belonged to somebody else. I figured, well, gee, this is *already* taken, I'm not stealing it. So I didn't have any trouble with my conscience. I just kept wondering over and over, "How did they get away with this?" There was a watch and I said, "Well, I'll take that, too."

Finally they all left, and the stuff stayed in my house for a couple of days, and I began hoping that I could sell some of it myself, because I was in a real bad financial position. In fact, I was up on the campus trying to get a student loan, and just outside the loan office here comes Macho and Joselito, and they find out what I'm up to, and they say, "Don't bother. You'll just have to pay it back."

I said, "Well, what am I gonna do? Since you guys borrowed my car, it's barely running and I've got to have a car, and they tell me it'll cost a hundred or two hundred dollars to get it fixed."

Macho said, "Don't worry. We'll think of something. Come with us, I think I know where I can get some smack." Honestly, that's all those guys think about, going someplace to score smizz. But we couldn't find any, so I went on home.

That night I was really feeling down. I had all this fancy stuff in the house, but nothing to eat. Nancy called me up and told me to come over, we'd all get straight, so I took Maria and went over to Nancy's, and we went into the bedroom and hit up. We hit up twice more that night before I finally got off. Maybe it was bad heroin, I don't know. Every time Nancy hit up she got off, but it took me three times. No, twice. That's right, I hit up twice. No, I'm a liar: It was three times.

I got to sleep about four A.M., and at eight o'clock I got up and sent Maria to the babysitter. Then I went back to bed, and I was still sleeping when somebody knocked on the door at eleven. I opened it, and Macho and Joselito walked in. "Hey, what's going on?" I said. "I'm still sleeping."

Macho says, "We just came over to see if you wanted to make some money."

I knew exactly what they meant. I was still a little high, and I said, "Sure, let's go make some money."

Macho says, "Why don't we get straight first?"

"Okay."

He pulls out his kit and he's got blue morphine. It looks like blue chalk, but you just dissolve it like heroin. We went into the bathroom, and Macho stuck the needle in my arm and then he pumped the syringe for a really long time, sucking the blood in and out, and that felt good.

I took a shower and got dressed, and then we smoked some grass. I had eight lids of grass in my house; I was keeping them for a friend who was hot, and the friend had told me that I could smoke some of it if I wanted to. So we each did a couple of Js, and then Macho said, "Okay, let's go make some money," and I said, "Okay, I'm ready."

Well, I told you at the beginning I'm only good at facts; I'm not good at opinions or interpretations. So I can't tell you why I went with them. Maybe I was curious. I was always wondering how they got away with all that stuff. Oh, I don't *know* why. I don't know! I haven't really thought about it. My friends keep asking me, and all I can say is I don't know, I just don't.

We went up to the student center and borrowed a friend's car and then we headed for Collegeville Hills. On the way, Joselito says to Macho, "Don't go where we were yesterday. That's too hot."

We drove into a new addition in Collegeville Hills, and all this time I'm saying, "Well, how are you gonna do it? How are you gonna do it?" And they're saying, "You'll see. You'll see." It was really funny. I was *so* curious.

We pull up in front of a nice house and Macho says, "Connie, knock on the door and see if anybody's home. If somebody answers, ask them if they've got a car for sale. They'll say no, and you say, 'Oh, I must have the wrong address. I was answering an ad in the paper.' "

So I go up and knock, and there's a lady there. I said, "Do you have a Ford Model B for sale?" And she says no, and I says, "Oh, I must have the wrong address," and walk off.

We cruised some more, and then we went down this street to a dead end and turned around and came back up the street and stopped at a house with a two-car garage, empty. I knocked on the door and nobody was home, so Macho backed our car into the garage and quickly pulled the doors shut. Nobody was in sight, so Macho and Joselito took these big vise grips and clamped them on the doorknob that led into the house. They jerked hard and broke the spring. It was really funny. I mean, man, I have to laugh telling about it. I was always wondering how they got away with all this stuff, and now I knew. All they did was walk in, and everything they did was behind closed doors. No wonder they were getting away with so much. Oh. what a deal! It was *so* funny.

They also cleared up the mystery of the stockings in my car. They put them over their hands. They said the stockings mess up their fingerprints. Then they stationed me in the laundry room and told me to keep a lookout at the window while they did the house.

Man, my head was really spinning around. I looked at this house we were in, and I realized, man, these people really *have* things. Wow, they must really have it made! I'll bet they even have his-and-her cars. I would really dig living here. Then I flashed that Chicanos might live here, my own kind of people, but then I thought, well, if they live in a place like this, then they must be *vendidos*, sellouts, and if I were a Chicano heavy, deep in the movement, I'd be even happier to clean out a *vendido*. But I realized these people must be whites—no Chicano could ever afford a house like this—and I wondered what was in the rest of the house and what it'd be like to live in a place like this.

I began to think about what we were doing. We were stealing. Well, so what? You have to understand, there are a lot of people like me who never had a TV, never had the money to buy one. So the only way they could get one was to steal it. Like, back in Jonesville, I grew up without a TV, and I'll *never* have one here in Collegeville. I'll never have the money. I know I'm not entitled to steal one, but I really *want* one for my daughter, so she can watch *Romper Room* and *Sesame Street* and things like that. *I want one!* What does Maria have, that poor little child? She colors, and she keeps herself occupied, and I really feel sorry for her, because she's so alone, and I hate to bring her up that way.

Besides, Macho and Joselito had already told me that these people all have insurance, and nobody gets hurt except the insurance company. So what's the difference? I peeped inside the living room, and I saw all this furniture, nice things, a really pretty house, fully carpeted, the whole bit. I thought, well, maybe someday if I had a house like this, how would I feel if somebody slipped inside. . . . But I didn't draw any conclusions except that it must feel awful to come home and find your things gone. I wondered how you'd report it to the insurance company. Would you have to go back to all the stores you'd bought from and get new receipts? I was wondering what the backyard looked like. I thought it must be nice; maybe there'd be a swimming pool and all. Then I saw the cop.

He was driving over the hill in a cop car, headed down our street, and I ran through the living room and hollered up the stairs, "You guys! It's the cops! Hey, Macho, Joselito, it's the cops!"

No answer.

I went back to the window and I saw the cop drive past the house and down the hill, and I knew there was a dead end down there and he'd have to come right back. So I hollered again, "Hey, you guys! He went down the hill. He's gonna turn around and come back! I'm sure he is!" But they still didn't come down.

Well, I might have been a little high, but right at that point I knew that all I had to do was walk out the back door of the house and nobody could ever accuse me of anything. As long as I got off that property, the cops couldn't touch me. But I didn't do it. Oh, I don't know why. I just don't know! My friends keep asking me, and all I can say is I don't know, I just don't. I knew that cop was gonna turn around and come back, and I knew he was gonna bust us, but I just stayed there and waited. I wish people would stop asking me why I acted so dumb. I don't know *why* I do things. I just do them.

The cop comes back and he parks right in front of the garage door, and still I stood there. Then I heard him working on the front door, and Macho and Joselito came running down the stairs, and we were all scrambling, running back and forth, trying to find a place to hide, but of course there was no place to hide. I knew I was busted, just plain flat busted. I stopped trying to even look for a hiding place. I just walked back into the garage and ducked behind the car with Macho and Joselito.

A few seconds later the cop came in with his gun and he said, "Come out with your hands up or I'll blow your heads off!"

So Macho goes up, and then Joselito, and then me. I mean, like I'm a follower. I just do what the others do.

"Put your hands on the car!" the cop said. We were busted. It was unbelievable. Dreamy. I looked sideways at Macho and I said, "Wow!" Like who could believe it?

Pretty soon there's about eighteen cops there, and they herd us into the living room, and one cop starts shoving me around. I go, "Hey, wait a minute!" I says, "I'm being good. I'm not hassling you, so it's not cool for you to be hassling me." I says, "You don't even have to *touch* me."

But I guess he felt he had to tap me along. I guess that's just the way cops are. In the living room they made us lay on the floor for a long time till the detectives got there, and then they drove us to the police station and booked us for burglary. Macho couldn't wait to rat on everybody. He was babbling all the way down about everything he knew. They took him into a side office and he ratted for three or four hours.

Finally we were all in adjoining cells, in a holding block, and I still had two Js in my pocket, and I was thinking, these male cops can't search me, I'm safe till the matron gets here, and I knew they had sent for one. So I'm in the middle cell, and I'm still handcuffed, and I couldn't get the Js out. Then somebody came and undid the handcuffs, and I took the Js out of my pocket and I says through the bars, "Hey, you guys, I got these Js."

They said, "Oh, yeah?" So I flipped the Js into their cells and they each ate one. Funny! I have to laugh when I think how I got rid of that grass.

After a while the detectives came in and said they wanted to talk to me, but I knew I didn't have to say anything, so I didn't. I just said, "Would you please appoint me a lawyer?" They kept after me, but I wouldn't talk, so they took me back to the holding cell, and they didn't let me make a phone call till two o'clock in the morning, about thirteen hours after we'd been busted. I just called Nancy and asked her to get Maria at the babysitter's and take care of her till I got out of trouble.

The next day, in court, the public defender and the head of the Chicano students on the campus and a couple of other people all came in and spoke up for me, and I got out of jail on a $2500 bond that the Chicano group put up. I went straight home, and I found out that my house had been searched from top to bottom. There was a paper on the table, and it was the search warrant, and it listed everything they took. Some of the things they took were stolen goods left over from a few days before, but a lot of it was my personal stuff, too. They took personal letters and some of my shoes, and they also took the eight lids of grass. And they got $124 in cash that I had hidden away, the last money I had in the world.

I didn't know what to do. Finals were coming up, and I desperately wanted to pass all my subjects. Somebody came around and knocked on the door, and it was a Chicano guy and he told me that Jose and Luis had been caught doing exactly the same thing we'd been doing, just about twenty-four hours after we were busted. It turned out that both Jose and Luis flipped out in the cell, and had to be given shots of methadone. Don't ask me why they went out to do the same thing we did the very next day. I told you I'm no good on theories. There was a doctor in the case and he said he thought we'd all *tried* to get busted, because we were doing heroin heavily and the whole thing was too much of a hassle, and we were trying to get caught, subconsciously, or something like that. I don't know how to explain it myself.

Anyway, when I saw that they'd searched my house, I realized that I was in more trouble, and I was afraid they'd come and pick me up and take me right back to jail and I wouldn't be able to take my finals. So I hid out at a friend's house until all my examinations were over. I didn't do so good, but I passed, and then I went down to the public defender's office and turned myself in. It turned out there were three new warrants for my arrest, and the police had been looking for me. I guess they never dreamed I'd be right back in class, taking my finals.

They charged me with some new counts: receiving stolen goods and one count of possession of narcotics for sale. They made five charges altogether, and my lawyer really had to make a big pitch to the court to get me out. He talked about how hard I worked in school, and how well I took care of my daughter, and how I'd agreed to go to the People's Clinic for treatment, and he promised that I would always be available to the court. He also said that I would see a psychiatrist, but I never have, because I feel good mentally, I really feel *good*. I don't need to see a psychiatrist. The head of the Mexican students on campus also spoke up for me, and finally the judge let me out on a $20,000 bond and the head of the students signed for it.

Well, that was all a couple of months ago, and I've been in and out of courts ever since, and my lawyer thinks that after a lot of pulling strings, I'll get probation. But it looks bad, it looks very bad. I'm not a criminal, I've never even shoplifted in my life, I was brought up too strict. How can I be a criminal? And yet here I am, in all kinds of trouble. I mean, I could go to the state penitentiary for years and years! But I don't really worry about it. I don't think about going to prison. At the point when the actual sentencing comes up, that's when I'll start to think about it, because it's something I can't even imagine right now.

The lawyer's working all the time for me, and for nothing. He says the police want me to tell them all I know, that'll make it easier for me, and he set up an appointment for me with the cops. But all I know is what I've told you. I have no idea what those other guys did, what places they robbed, *nothing*. This whole thing happened to me in less than a week, and I barely even knew the guys before this happened. I'm just stupid, that's all. No commonsense. I'm too trusting; that's it right there. And I hate boredom. That's what my girl friend Nancy tells me. She says I got into trouble because I was bored; I don't have enough to do. She says I sit around the house too much, just the way I did in Jonesville. Well, that's all I know how to do, and I'm limited because of my kid. I can go visit friends, but that's about all. I love Maria, so I tend to stay home with her and take care of her. And then I get bored, and then I'm ready to get into trouble, I guess.

I'm always open to anybody's suggestions. That's just about how my life really goes down. I do what my friends do. I believe in that.

I'm sort of from another world. I think that's why I'm led on so easily. I'm the middleman. I don't have a world of my own to cling to. I'm not a white, and I'm not a Chicano. I'm always borrowing somebody else's world, somebody else's attitudes and ideas. Like if I get interested in you, and your whole bag is helping others, doing good, giving to the poor, things like that, why, I'll do it with you. And if your bag's stealing and doing dope and ripping people off, well, I guess I'll do that, too. I don't seem to have a mind of my own. I wish I did.

Like you know I'm so damn goodhearted. I'm one big fat big sucker. That's what my lawyer says. He says, "You're one big fat big sucker. You really are." I was used: They used my car, they used my house, they used me. And I'm not even mad at them: I just can't stay mad at people. Sometimes I see Macho and Jose and Joselito and Luis on the campus, and I smile and give them a big hello. They're all students, just like me, and I know they have their own problems. I don't hate anything or anybody. Nothing bothers me. Like I even feel good now, even though I'm in this trouble. *I really feel good!*

But I'll never do crime again, because my daughter means too much to me. She's made me what I am. If I were free and single, I'm positive I'd be in a lot more trouble. I'm just that way. Maria keeps me straight. I'm getting good grades again, and I'm taking more hours than anybody else in the program. I feel good about school. I still want to become a teacher, and I'm taking a lot of courses in the School of Education. I just hope to God I haven't messed up my chances.

The one thing I can't figure out is heroin. I think about it all the time. I think, Wow, I'd like to hit up! Like man, there's lots of times when it's really on my mind, and I can't shrug that feeling, and I don't know *what* to do about it. If somebody walked in that door with smack, I'd do it with him. I'd shoot it.

I don't know exactly what the attraction is. I do like

the feeling you get tripping with people. You lay back and enjoy the rap and dig the music. I would never do smizz by myself, unless I had some around and I had a fit, then I might do it. One thing, I'll never get addicted.

I know that I have to avoid certain old friends like Nancy. Man, she does a lot of get-highs! If I go down there at nine in the morning to pick her up for a class, we smoke a *J* before we leave, and I don't even like to smoke, so I'm trying to stay away from her.

A couple of days ago Nancy and I were walking around the campus and as we were going past Moore Hall, one of the boy's dormitories, she said, "Why don't we stop and see if Gringo's there? Maybe we can get straight."

I said, "Okay." Isn't it funny? There it is again: Somebody is always suggesting something, and I'm always saying, "Okay."

Gringo's one of the Chicano kids, only he's half white, that's where he got his name. To me, he's a good person. A person that's style is all right, a *good* person. Gringo dresses nice, and like he's got ten leather jackets, man, you know? He makes a lot of money. He's style, and he looks good at all times. He has a private room in the oldest dorm on the campus: Moore. A lot of people go knocking on his door, day and night, but he and Nancy are really good friends, and that's why he'll give us as much smack as we want for nothing.

Gringo's working his way through college by selling smizz, but not to me and Nancy. When we were up in his room, five or six of the other guys came in and they all hit up, and they all paid. But like he charged us nothing. Half the time the damned door was unlocked, and we're all in there hitting up! It's funny! Gringo gave us such good stuff that I stayed and hit up twice. It felt good, but I got sick afterwards.

I know that it would spoil any chance I have to stay out of jail if the cops caught me fooling with heroin while this robbery case is happening, but I don't figure it's much of a risk. I mean, there's not much chance I'll get busted where the dope's at, and I'm not gonna use it any place else. I mean, I'm not gonna take it home. I'm just gonna shoot up and leave. So it's safe enough. And besides—I remember a feeling I had the day that we did the job, that we were gonna get busted, and I think I have a kind of a sixth sense now. So if I go over to Gringo's to get straight, I keep waiting for that feeling, and I don't worry unless I get that feeling. But if I get the feeling that I'm gonna get busted, well, then I'm not gonna hit up no matter how bad I want it. My daughter's too important to me. I'm just not gonna get caught.

Besides, I don't think the cops are working too hard on the heroin problem here in Collegeville. If you want heroin on this campus, you can find it without any trouble. Lots of people know Gringo—he's a sophomore in the School of Economics, and he's pretty famous for his good smack. And there are plenty of other sellers too, and if you don't know where they are, just ask. You'll find out fast. In my personal experience I've met maybe twenty-five kids who do junk, and they're almost all Chicanos. You see them around the campus, nodding out, walking funny. They can get all they want right here.

I've still kept to my rule that I would never buy it myself, but sometimes it's tough. Like all of a sudden I had a terrible urge to see my real mother in New York, and I got court permission to leave the state, and I went to see her, and all the time that I was there I was thinking about heroin, and if I could have found any I'd have bought it. I knew it was wrong, awful wrong, but I wanted it so bad.

I'd have bought it. But I just didn't know where to start, and I didn't dig going into the street for it. My real brother turned me on to some acid in New York, he really digs acid—but I didn't get much out of it, and that's just not my scene.

Mostly, I rapped with my mother. It had been three years since I'd seen her last. Her sixth marriage had just broken up, but she was really cool about it. My mother's a very hip person, except that she doesn't dig the drug scene, because she's had a lot of trouble with her relatives over it. She told me she doesn't date anymore, she just stays home and watches TV. She's thirty-seven years old, and not bad looking, and I'm sure she could date if she wanted, but I think she's just gotten tired of life.

I told her that I was in trouble, but I didn't tell her the whole story, just that some friends had left some stolen goods at my house, and I'd gotten into trouble accidentally. She said, "I'm sure it wasn't your fault."

I said, "That's right, mother. It wasn't."

She told me how she'd been in some check trouble, but it wasn't her fault either, and we told each other that we'd both learned our lessons.

It finally got around to the same sore subject that had been bothering me all my life: Why did she leave me with my grandparents? My mother cried and said that she did it for me; she did it because she wanted me to have a good life, and she knew that they would take good care of me.

Well, I understand, I guess. I have a little girl, and I'd never give her up, but I guess my mother must've been desperate. I understand all this now.

That night I walked the streets thinking about my poor mother and also thinking about heroin. God, how I missed it! I craved it, I needed it, I'd do almost anything for a hit. I walked the streets, and I kept looking at people, and I kept sort of hoping that somebody would say, "Here, girl, have some smizz." But that dream didn't come true. I thought of asking my brother to find somebody in the barrio who would sell me a fix, but I fought it and fought it and I wound up going back home to sleep. I rolled around the bed in my mother's house all night long, and the next morning I took the plane back to Collegeville.

I still walk around thinking that maybe somebody will lay some smizz on me, but I *won't* buy it. I won't. *I just won't.* Gringo has started saying that he can give me some heroin at a very low price, but I turn away. I won't buy it. *I won't buy it!* The first time I ever buy it, that will be the end of my life.

Once there was a time when it wouldn't have mattered. What difference did my life make when I was listening to the radio in Jonesville or running around Collegeville accomplishing nothing? I could have dropped right off the earth and nobody would have cared. But I hope they care now. Or at least they'll care in a few years, when I get my degree. It's still a dream—"Consuelo Martin, B.A." —and I've gotta make it come true.

Dr. Ruth Francis says:

I'm not in the least surprised that she's shooting up, even though it may cost her a chance at probation. It's all related to being young, to being a Chicano, and to being enraged without even knowing it. To a person of Connie's age, the taking of great risks is a way of asserting your independence and showing your contempt for all the people who keep telling you what you shouldn't do. And it's a way of working off the rage of being a minority person and flatly refusing to accept an inferior role.

The prognosis? Well, we've stopped dealing in prognoses here at the clinic. What's the point of giving an accurate prognosis in a case like Connie Martin's? It's so much more important to *change* her prognosis, and that's what we're doing. When she comes around to our meetings and our rap sessions, we try to give her a lot of love. We're throwing all our limited resources into her case, and we feel that we can alter her prognosis from the disastrous one of becoming an addict and a con, to the hopeful one of becoming a happy person. She's got a lot in the balance right now, and she's worthy of all the help we can give her.

As far as the criminal case is concerned, it's not hard to understand. Every Chicano has to feel rage, *must* feel rage. A socially acceptable way to get rid of it is to become active in the Chicano movement, and an unacceptable way to get rid of it is to shoot heroin and rob houses. She chose the unacceptable way, that's all.

Postscript

In Collegeville Municipal Court, Consuelo Martin was found guilty on all counts and placed on five year's probation.

ANITA VANDER KELEN, 34
Former Faculty Wife

Dr. Ruth Francis says:

Anita's the worst liar I've ever met. She's capable of telling the truth, but she very seldom does it. Her childhood headache story makes me laugh. It's so maudlin! But she insists it's true. She *enjoys* being a tragic figure. She's very well known around Collegeville in her role. Her friends—and she has a lot of them—they keep saying, "Oh, poor Anita," and she dines out on that attitude.

She gives you all that business about burning the books, fleeing the Dutch Nazis, and the way she talks, it's as though all the tragedy in the world came down on her shoulders. She's just a poor pawn in all this international tragedy—that's her attitude. She'll say things like, "My addiction is my own fault, and I can't blame my problems on anybody but myself," but she hopes to God you won't believe her.

Well, I've been doctoring her for two years, and that's enough. Do I think she'll kick? I really don't *care* any more! I can't be spending all my time with her. She's lived thirty-four years, so maybe she *will* kick. Most addicts do, if they live.

Mary Ann Weyer, an English professor, says:

I know a grad student who had an affair with Anita Van der Kelen, and he says she's a very sweet woman at heart. I've never seen her that way. I see her as a troublemaking, decadent bitch, a Lady Macbeth. She almost seems to flaunt her addictions.

I really don't think she's trying to kick the habit; I think she's glad to have it. Another addict told me that Anita just uses the methadone program. He said if they'll let her stay on it twenty years, she'll stay on. Somebody ought to kick her heinie all the way back to Amsterdam, wake her up a little.

I've heard all the stories about what goes on among the professors and their wives, and the swinging life on the faculty level, and all the pot-smoking and promiscuity, and the fascinating wild parties. Well, I was into that scene for years, and I can tell you the stories are all wrong. The faculty members are so busy with their scheming little political tricks to get advancement that they have very little energy left for wild parties. This is a pretty social school, too, and people have whole little social hierarchies worked up, and they're interested in climbing from one to the next.

As an assistant professor's wife, I could sit back and look, and not take part in the politicking and the socializing. Thank God, I didn't have to hostess teas and things like that, but I did have to go to them. They were *very* boring. The men would sit on one side of the room and talk about Hegel and Ramakrishna, and the women would sit on the other side and talk babies. There was a little polite drinking, but very few drunks. Associate professors of philosophy and their wives don't get drunk in public!

I don't mean to say it was entirely bleak. There were two or three professors and their wives whom I enjoyed and spent some time with. One of them is famous, you'd recognize his name in a second. They'd come over to our house and we'd play chamber music on our recorders. Music was one thing I always loved. Toward the end of our marriage, there were fewer and fewer of these enjoyable sessions. Bill withdrew more and more into philosophy, and I withdrew more and more into drugs.

Would you excuse me a minute? I have to take one of these pills four times a day to prevent convulsions. That's one thing about heavy drug usage: You're always in danger of convulsions, even when you're on methadone. I'd offer you a pill, but you wouldn't know what to do with it, would you? No, I really shouldn't take them when I'm

on methadone, but I take them anyway. I just try not
to abuse them.

People who know me well say I could easily have been
Anne Frank. Our backgrounds are similar, except that
Anne died when she was a little girl, and I was lucky
enough to go on living. I'll fill you in on the sordid details.

I was born in 1935 in Amsterdam. My father had just
taken his doctorate in biology, and my mother was teaching school, but she had to quit when I came along. Both
my parents were Dutch Jews, both intellectuals, both
pretty radical, and both very interested in Zionism. In
those awful 1930s there was anti-Semitism all over Europe, not just in Germany. Hitler set the tone, and the
petit-bourgeois of all the other countries followed suit.
The Dutch speak piously about Anne Frank nowadays,
but you can be sure they didn't make life too pleasant
for her and her parents when she was alive. My mother
and father always wanted to get away but it was not
easy. When I was an infant, they went to Palestine just
in time to get caught up in Arab rioting, and they quickly
came back to Amsterdam. They figured if they were going to get killed, they might as well get killed at home.

My family always had tremendous energy, and I have
it too, although the dope has worn me down quite a bit.
Even now, I have relatives who are always running to
Israel, living in kibbutzes, doing all sorts of outlandish
things. I have an ancient grandfather who is nearly ninety and does daily calisthenics and once in a while goes
off and climbs a mountain. We've always had a sort
of intellectual energy, too. When Americans were buying
records and playing them, our family was having relatives over and playing chamber music, or reading plays
aloud. I remember it well from my early childhood. It
was one of my pleasures.

By 1938 it wasn't wise to be a radical Jew living in
Amsterdam. When I was three years old, I was packed
into a baby buggy, and the complete Lenin library was
hidden underneath me, and my mother wheeled me
across Amsterdam to a strange house where there was a

big fireplace. She threw the books into the fire one by one, and she was crying. Not long after that, the three of us got on a big ship and sailed to a strange place called Galveston, Texas. My parents spoke no English, and life was difficult. Later we moved to a small town in West Texas where there were only two other Jewish families, orthodox religious fanatics. My parents began a crash course to learn English, and I learned it with them. By 1940 my father was working for a farm co-op, at something like thirty-five dollars a week, and my mother was tutoring in languages. We changed our name to Vander Kelen, a good respectable Dutch name, because my father expected to encounter anti-Semitism in West Texas, and he was right. But what he didn't expect was the reaction of the two other Jewish families in the community. When they saw my mother sweeping the porch on Saturday afternoon, the Jewish Sabbath, they called the FBI. They said, "These can't be real Jews. They must be spies." We were investigated, and we lived like outcasts in that small town for two or three years.

When I was six we moved to Houston. My parents' English had improved, one of my little sisters had been born, and my father held a good job as an industrial biologist in the city. We should have been happy, but I spoiled it all. I began to get frightful headaches, and I was in exceeding pain. I would scream for hours at a time. The doctors couldn't find anything wrong.

The war had been going on for a couple of years, and even though I was just a little kid I was very anxious about the suffering in Europe. I began having anxiety attacks along with my headaches. I realized that someday I would have to die, and I didn't *want* to die. All day long I'd go around worrying about death. I think I know how it started. There was a Jewish agency my parents sent me to every day, and in one of the rooms there were files about Jews who had been killed or were missing in Europe. This was long before it was generally known what was happening to Jews in Europe, and I read those files by the hour, compulsively. I felt I had to read *every file*. The information had come from relatives and other informants in Europe. There were long files on individuals, how people had been killed or tortured, or how they were simply underweight, or suffering from tuberculosis, and long files of names and ages of people who had already died. This was 1941, and already Jews were dying by the thousands in Europe, and hardly anyone knew it except me. This was a big load of death for a kid to learn about.

I don't pretend that I was an easy child for my parents, and they weren't getting along anyway. Sometimes our house would ring with the cries of people in agony. My mother and father would scream at each other night after night, and I would lie in bed and scream about my headaches, and bite on my pillow and try to stuff it in my mouth. By the time I was seven, two little sisters had been born, and my mother and father were fighting and screaming worse than ever, and my headaches were intensifying. One day my mother took me and my sisters on a trip to Nevada, and she told me that it was because she was sick and had to take some treatments. I was terrified. I expected her to keel over and die any minute. Death again! But it turned out that she was establishing residence for the divorce, and when we came back to Houston, I didn't have a father anymore. I had always loved him; I was his baby, and my sisters were my mother's. He and I would take long walks, or read the morning paper over cinnamon toast before the fights would start, and it was a terrible blow to lose him. I loved my mother, too, but she was much more taken up with my sisters. And she was a bitter person. Who can blame her? I understand her. I'm not bitter about her. She's been exceptionally good to me considering the problems I've given her over the years. She's helped me a lot. But when I was little, she only seemed like a stern, Teutonic disciplinarian. She kissed and fondled my little sisters, and screamed that my headaches were a fake.

As soon as she got a divorce, my mother began an almost compulsive campaign to find a husband. She would give parties for servicemen—Jewish only. I remember one night when I was barely eight years old, she had eight or ten Jewish servicemen to the house, and she got really bugged at me because I came in in the middle of the party and complained about the headache. One of my sisters was playing the violin, and I interrupted the concert, and my mother hustled me off to bed and told me to shut up.

I was a precocious child—every member of our family was precocious—and I'd do things like reading under the covers with a flashlight, and my mother would catch me and accuse me of insubordination. But I couldn't help it. I never learned how to sleep. I've had insomnia all my life and piercing splitting headaches that wake me up at all hours. I'm sure my mother loved me, but she had certain preset ideas of how children should act, and I was a deviant. She just couldn't stand my being such a little monster. All through my childhood I was threatened with mental institutions if I didn't toe the line. A normal parent might say to the child that he'd have to stay in his room for an hour, but I was told I'd be packed off to the insane asylum. My sisters were held up to me as constant examples of how children should behave. But then my sisters didn't have headaches.

I guess I was about seven or eight when my mother discovered codeine. She began giving it to me by the shovelful. Codeine didn't completely relieve my headaches, but it quieted me down, and as soon as my mother realized that, she knew she had found a good thing. The codeine kept me out from underfoot. I wasn't a disturbance anymore because she gave me so much codeine that I was like a zombie most of the time. Whenever I'd get in her hair or ask too many questions she'd give me codeine. If I had a headache at bedtime she'd give me codeine, and eventually she'd give it to me even if I *didn't* have a headache because she didn't want to run the risk of being waked up later.

God knows I needed relief from my pain, but I didn't need daily doping, I didn't need all the codeine she gave me. That's why I can't sleep at night now. I never learned normal sleep habits as a child. I could only sleep with codeine.

By adolescence I was bright enough to realize what my role was around our house. My role was *not* to set a bad example for my mother's pets, the little sisters. It's still that way, and I'm still not friends with my sisters, for that reason. No wonder my mother didn't like me. All she wanted out of me as a child was *not* to rock the boat, *not* to set a bad example for my precious sisters. So when I was little she filled me with codeine, and when I got bigger she threw me out. But who can blame her? She'd never known anything but oppression. And her first experiences in the New World were with the FBI, and she began to get a little paranoid. Or maybe it wasn't paranoia, but simply reality. So I can understand my mother and sympathize with her.

But she *did* make it hard. I started going with men at the age of twelve, maybe to get out of the house, and from then on my mother looked on me as a fallen woman. One of our neighbors called her one day and told her she'd seen me holding hands with a boy, so my mother hired a college kid to move in with us and keep an eye on me while she was off at work and couldn't watch.

She became monomaniacal about pregnancy. I don't think she cared about what I might do to my own life if I became pregnant, but she was terrified I'd be a bad example.

I don't really think she'd have cared if I'd slept with every man in Houston, so long as I kept up a good virginal front. But I didn't. I was an early member of the beatnik generation, and my mother hated me for it. She told me that my morals were bad, at a time when my morals were fine. I mean, the kids in my group talked about things like daisy chains and gang bangs, but we never did it. The beatniks were thought to be involved in all sorts of sexual perversions, simply because they looked different, but the fact is that they did their sexual thing just about the same as previous generations.

When I was fifteen my mother just couldn't stand me anymore and she gave me money to live away from home. I've tried to figure out exactly what it was about me that she couldn't stand, but I'm really not positive. Maybe because I was going with men. I was still a virgin, but I was precocious, and she didn't like my precocity, at least on the sexual level. She had so many morbid fears left over from the Netherlands. She claimed that the FBI was still investigating us and that they would never stop. I'm not entirely sure she was wrong. We were *different,* and this has never set too well with the FBI. Throw in a slight history of radicalism, and a foreign accent, and you've got the ingredients that always made J. Edgar Hoover's hair stand on end. So this made my mother tense and nervous and paranoid all the time, and made it harder for her to get along with me. I suppose I was the last straw for her. She wasn't finding a husband, and she had this kid with constant headaches, screaming and running around with boys, and limiting her social life and perverting her beloved daughters.

She wasn't yet forty when she put me out of the house, which left her still young enough to find a new husband It took a long time, but she has one now, and they live together on a little farm in Vermont. She sacrificed me to find that man, and I guess she thinks it was worth it. When she threw me out, I had just entered high school, and she gave me twenty dollars a week plus rent. I roomed with a nice old lady in East Houston, and I didn't mind. I had no trouble getting codeine from our old druggist, I had no trouble with my schoolwork, and I had no trouble with my love life. When I was sixteen, I found my first real lover. The first of several, although I have never been a promiscuous woman.

Once in a while I saw my dear father, and as I approached the end of my high school years, he and I began to talk about my going to college. There really was never any doubt about it. For generations back, my people had been scholars. My people automatically went to college, we took Ph.D.'s the way others take high school diplomas. I told my father I wanted to be a research physician, and he said to go ahead, he would provide the money.

By high school graduation I was the consummate beat-nik. I didn't wear lipstick, I didn't wear stockings, I didn't shave, and my idea of heaven on earth was a hootenanny. I entered college, and immediately fell for a twenty-one-year-old man who could make a guitar talk. I was like a folk music groupy, and when I heard Rex open up on that guitar that he'd handmade himself, I was madly in love, or imagined that I was. We went together for three months, and our courtship was a long string of folk concerts and beer drinking and fun. I thought it was heaven. When he asked me to marry him, I didn't even think. I said, "Let's get married to-night." It all seemed like a dream. I would be inde-pendent of my parents, and my life would be one long hootenanny.

Oh, yes, my first marriage. It was a disaster. We should have lived together first, and we'd have learned about each other. This is why it's so good that the kids aren't getting married today, they're living together in-stead. People are made up of lots of personalities, and some of them can be completely concealed if you don't live with a person day and night. Men can keep the evil side of their personality concealed for months or years, but when you share the same bed and the same house and the same problems, the truth comes out. That's how it was with Rex. He was a glamorous figure to me, ad-mired by all the girls, gentle and kind and interesting, but when we were married he was a raw monster. If I had lived with him first, I'd have found this out.

Since we were both in school, we talked about not getting pregnant, how ridiculous it would be for us to have to support a baby while we were in school, and he agreed, at least intellectually. But it developed he felt far different emotionally. I don't know how to describe his attitude, except to say that it was pure mental ill-ness. When I had my first period after we were married, he flew into a rage. My period proved to him that he was sterile. I know it sounds nuts. Here we were des-perately trying not to get me pregnant, and he freaked out over my having a period. I didn't pick the best of all possible husbands. He was nuttier than I was. He was psychotic on the subject of his "sterility." He created a big scene around the apartment, raving and stomping and crying. First he was angry at himself, and then at me, because I was the one who "proved" he was sterile.

He let a couple of weeks go by, and then one night he raped me. He just jumped on me and shoved it into me and released his sperm so that I wouldn't have time to get my diaphragm on. And I became pregnant. Imagine, after doing this to me he began to claim that the baby wasn't his. He was still obsessed with the idea that he was sterile, and he had tests made to see if his sperm was viable, and he came back to me and said that the laboratory had told him that it was almost impossible for him to become a father. The lab had confirmed his lifelong fear. But he *was* viable, and my baby was the proof.

All through that horrible pregnancy, I took no drugs. This has been my lifelong rule. The last thing I'd ever want to do would be to give birth to an addicted baby, which can happen. It's bad enough to start on drugs when you're a little kid, as I did, but to start when you're born, that's too much of a handicap. So I bore my headaches and my insomnia, and I took nothing, but there were times when I thought I would die. The headaches felt like they were slicing my head in half. I'd wrap a towel around my head with two table knives in the knots, and I'd keep turning the knots tighter and tighter to make a tourniquet on my head, and it helped a little, but not much. I was trying to knock myself unconscious. I guess that's what I've always tried to do.

Dear Rex was beating me up regularly, all through the pregnancy. He didn't have to have a reason. He'd just come up and smack me because he felt like it. He was insanely jealous, and more convinced than ever that the baby wasn't his, and that I was consorting with other men. He'd say, "I'm going out. I won't be back for a few days." That meant that he was going to the nearest window, so he could try to overhear my phone conversations. Of course I had no other men! But he was crazy on the subject, and without provocation. In some ways he reminded me of my mother, always suspecting the worst.

More than once he knocked me cold. He gave me several concussions, and I don't suppose he helped my headaches either. I was crazy to stay with him, but he threatened to kill me if I left, and I feared him. I never fought back. I'm not violent. I knew I would not win a fight with a six-foot man; I would just risk my life and the baby's. I'll tell you how much terror Rex instilled in me. Not long ago he wrote that he wanted to come out and say hello, and the first thing I did was to buy a tear gas gun. I still wake up dreaming about the beatings he gave me.

I gave birth to Isaac at home, and that was one of the few good things that I can remember about the marriage. Babies *should* be born at home. I'd gone folk dancing that night, and on the way home I developed a backache, and pretty soon I realized I was in first-stage labor. Isaac was a beautiful baby, with blue eyes and black curly hair, and he renewed my interest in life. But he also presented a problem. I left Rex when Isaac was two months old, and now I had to worry about supporting both myself and the baby without any help from a husband. I was eighteen years old, and I guess I was too dumb to realize that I was in a bad spot.

I wanted to get completely away from Rex, and after the divorce I took Isaac and moved to the other side of Houston. Father gave me financial help, and I got a part-time job, and I stayed in school. But I had to give up any idea of becoming a research physician. I decided to get a teacher's certificate so that I could support Isaac. I didn't particularly want to become a teacher, but I didn't think I had any choice.

School was easy—I never had any trouble studying, because I was usually up all night anyway, with my insomnia and headaches, and I had plenty of time to study —and there were day-care places and plenty of baby sitters for Isaac. I began to travel with some other early beatniks who were just getting into drugs, but I couldn't get much satisfaction out of anything but codeine. By now I was taking enormous quantities, and still having the pain. I got some codeine from our family doctor, more from the Student Health Service. I've grown to hate the stuff. I would *never* voluntarily take it. It makes you sick to your stomach, and it's not strong enough, it doesn't really do the job. But it's all I could get in those college years. I probably have about the world's highest tolerance for codeine because I took so much. It's really disgusting because codeine has given me cross-tolerances for other drugs, so I have to take a large amount to get anything at all.

The kids I hung around with were into speed-type drugs, but I never could handle speed, I never liked it. My normal metabolism is high; I'm like the rest of my family, full of energy, grinding my jaws, itching to do things, to read every book, and see every sight. So speed just drove me crazy. I couldn't take it.

But I did enjoy grass. After a while we got into a thing where we'd go to Mexico and bring back grass or cough syrup. There was one kind of cough syrup that had dextromathorphine in it, and that was a good trip. There was another cough syrup with dihydrocodeinone, which is much stronger than codeine, in a cherry-flavored cough syrup. When we wore out our welcome at the drugstores in Houston, we could always get the cough syrup down in Matamoros, Mexico. We had plastic containers that we would fill with the cough syrup, and then we'd slip them into the gas tank of a motorcycle. That was a new thing then, but it's common now. It's the first place they look now. We'd go down to Matamoros on two big BMWs, to make a contact on one of the cycles, and bring the stuff back in the other. This way we fooled any possible informants. Sometimes we'd come back with a gallon of cough syrup in the gas tank, and sometimes we'd bring back a couple of keys of marijuana.

It took me seven years to get through college, what with working and pregnancy and all my problems, but at the age of twenty-four, I was the proud possessor of teaching credentials and a five-year-old son. I got a job teaching elementary school—something that I'd always thought I'd like—and hated it. Really hated it! The principal was a miserable jerk who undercut all my attempts at authority, and the students were horrible. They were third-graders, and half of them didn't speak English, and the other half carried knives, and I was scared to try to teach them. Their average length of stay in my classroom was six weeks, and I would have to maintain order among forty or fifty kids who would soon be gone and another crop appear in their place. I would get terribly uptight, and I slowly began to realize that teaching was not the career for me. But what else could I do?

I'd never been on hard drugs. Of course, everybody smoked grass; I'd smoked it since high school. The captain of the football team had turned me on. But grass is nothing. Grass has no connection with hard stuff. I know dozens of people who've smoked grass all their lives and never went on the hard stuff, and I also know dozens who went on the hard stuff without ever smoking grass. That's one of the misconceptions: that the one leads to the other. Not long ago a friend said to me, "What made you take up heroin after twenty-four years of avoiding it?" I had to explain that I had never avoided heroin; it just hadn't come my way, and I had no idea how to find it. But I'd been ready for it for years. I'd thought about it; I knew it brought instant oblivion, and that was something I was seeking.

So when it all happened it was a funny coincidence, or tragic, or whatever you want to call it. I had this apartment in Houston, and there was an extra bedroom, and it was really a large place. Old, but large. One night a friend of mine came over and I gave him ten dollars to go out and buy me a lid of grass. He had a friend with him, a wiggy young man I'd never met, and while the two of them were gone I turned on my radio and all I could get was static. I couldn't figure out what was wrong. I looked in the back of the radio and there was a tinfoil package stuck inside. I opened up the tinfoil, and inside was a set of works and some heroin.

I took it out of the radio, and I confronted the new guy when he came back. I said, "I found your works, and if you want them back you're gonna have to share with me." I was sublimely convinced that I could do it, enjoy it, and never pay the penalty. Just like every junkie. Just like the driving maniacs who say, "I can drive like a nut, because I'm the one guy who'll never get in an accident."

The upshot was that my friend's friend and I made an arrangement. He was new in town; he was a dealer, and he needed a place to stay. I told him he could stay in my extra bedroom, I would give him free room and board, if he would give me all the heroin I wanted. I made him agree he'd never deal out of my house, and never use my phone to deal or make arrangements.

After we made the agreement, he injected me, and it was very nice for about a minute and a half, and then I got sick and threw up. Oh, how I hate to throw up! But I did it all night. I sat on the floor with a bowl till dawn. I guess he gave me a pretty heavy load.

They say that some people get so frightened from that initial sickness that they never try heroin again, but it never entered my mind not to stay on it. Little by little I stopped being so sick, and soon I began feeling good from it. Among other things, the heroin helped me at school. Every morning before I'd leave the house, I'd shoot up, and then I'd drive to school. The National Safety Council says that you're not in control of your car when you're high, but I felt that I was. I was also in better control of my students. I was more relaxed, and they liked me better, and I liked them better, and I had fewer misgivings about their knives and their general behavior. My only problem was that I couldn't get any heroin at lunch, and I'd begin to get antsy during the afternoon. I could have taken some to school with me, but I was terrified that I would be caught. That's one thing about me, those early years in Europe gave me a tremendous fear of the law. There was so much paranoia around me that I ingested some of it, and I made up my mind that no matter what I did with my life I would never be arrested or in trouble with the law. At least I've made good on that.

If you're preprogrammed to think about the horrors of dope and the horrible things that dope fiends do, you'll never comprehend what those two years were like. I had none of the problems associated with dope, and all of the blessings. I had a constant supply, so I never had to become a street junkie, with all the troubles of hustling up dope every day. I hid my works from my son, and I tried not to take enough so that it would be obvious to him what I was doing. My big hit of the day would be just before I went to bed, when he was already asleep. I never had any trouble with tracks, because I always used the same place. I never got sick or abscessed or had hepatitis or any of the other things associated with shooting up. I always used a brand-new needle or a needle that I had boiled thirty minutes. I've always been a very controlled person.

It was very clear to me that heroin was entirely good. It was great for my headaches. If I felt one starting, I'd take a fix and the pain would be gone. I loved the rush, like an orgasm, except that it hits you all over your body, your chest and your head, because the rush starts where the heroin hits your heart, and the feeling's out of sight. After the rush, I'd feel euphoric and relaxed, and I loved that feeling too. I had seldom been relaxed in my life.

It wasn't long before I was shooting up four times a day: a small shot in the morning before school, a big one when I got home, a small one during the evening, and a very powerful hit at bedtime. It was the best time of my life.

But what I didn't realize was that when you're a junkie for any length of time, you begin to lose interest in other things. For instance, the sunset isn't beautiful anymore, it's just boring. I've never known any junkie who didn't feel that way. Junk becomes so much in the forefront of your life that it eclipses everything else.

I was in the early stages of this loss of normal feelings,

but I was too dumb to realize it. As you might imagine, I'd long since decided there was nothing on earth that would get me to marry again, but I was feeling so euphoric on my steady diet of white powder that I began to take a normal interest in men, and even to think of getting married. I was hanging around a beatnik crowd and taking a few night courses, and in general living my life on a cloud, when I met Bill, my second husband. He was a brain in philosophy. He was taking postdoctoral studies and teaching at the same time.

We had a whirlwind courtship, but I didn't want to accept his proposal until he knew all about me. In the three or four months that we went together, I was capable of keeping myself together enough so that he didn't have to know what I was doing, but when it came to marriage I felt that the secrecy was unfair. So I told him I was a junkie. He was disappointed. It bothered him that it wasn't the real me that he'd fallen in love with, but a me that was adulterated by drugs. He approached it from all sorts of deep metaphysical aspects, but it still troubled him.

One night he asked me if I thought I could quit heroin cold, and I said yes. "Then let's get married," he said. Even though I was enjoying the heroin, I felt that the time might be right to get off it. I was beginning to worry that I'd get hooked. I know this sounds silly—I'd been on the stuff for two years—but no junkie ever thinks he's hooked, even after two years, although he may worry about getting hooked in the future. Also, I'd had such an easy heroin trip that I was beginning to get a little paranoid about it. I mean I felt that something was coming around the corner and would catch me any second. It was like that old saying, "Don't look back, something might be gaining on you." I had enough sense to know that you can't have everything on a platter and not have to pay for it in some way. I was waiting for somebody to come and collect my dues, and the feeling was getting very intense.

So Bill came along, and it was perfect. I wasn't in love with him, but I knew he'd make a good father for Isaac.

My son sorely needed a father at that time. I liked Bill
and I respected him, and we had mutual interests. The
future looked good. Bill was just finishing his postdoctoral work, and he had his choice of about ten different
universities. Collegeville offered him an assistant pro-
fessorship, and that's where we decided to go. There
were better schools, there were more prestigious ap-
pointments, but Bill was mad about the setting at Collegeville. He was always an outdoor type anyway, and
Collegeville would be perfect. We found out later that
half the faculty was there for that same reason.

We were married in Houston, and then we drove toward our new assignment. I took my last hit of heroin
the morning we drove away. It was a two-day drive. and
I kept waiting for withdrawal symptoms, but they never
came. For a while I wondered if I'd really been getting
heroin, if it hadn't all been a hoax, but I knew too well
that I was getting the straight stuff. You don't get that
kind of a rush time after time from a placebo. And yet
—I never had a single withdrawal symptom. *Nothing!*
Maybe it had something to do with the fact that I'd been
on codeine all my life, and heroin and codeine are cousins, both of them coming from opium. I've discussed
it with doctors since then, and they tell me they never
heard anything like it, but I swear to you it's a fact: I
shot heroin constantly for two years, and I kicked it cold
without so much as a sniffle.

For about a year, we had a happy marriage. Our relationship was distant, but I didn't mind that because that
was the bargain that we'd made at the beginning. There
were no illusions of a big romantic love. We got along
well and I tried to play the game of being a philosophy
department wife. We folk-danced a lot, we hiked, we
went climbing and skiing. It was not unpleasant. That
old bugaboo that breaks up so many marriages—I mean
sex—was not much of a problem. I'm really very relaxed
on the subject, very well adjusted, much more than
you'd expect the average junkie type to be. I've always
had normal sexuality, even during my worst times. If
there was a problem, it was that I wanted sex the usual

number of times a week, but Bill hardly wanted it at all. He was extremely undersexed, and there were a few times when it troubled me. He'd been a thirty-five-year-old virgin when we married, so you can see how retarded he was about sex. I suppose I should have gone out and had affairs, but I was conventional enough to want to be faithful. I don't think it would have mattered much to Bill either way. But for that first year I played my role.

Just as I'd expected, Bill was a great father for Isaac, and Isaac desperately needed one. He was hopelessly screwed up. I wonder why? He got horrible grades, even though his IQ was 145, about the same as mine. He was always getting thrown out of school, or escorted home for taking a punch at somebody. His maladjustment seemed to trouble Bill as much as it troubled me. We were living in an apartment on the campus, but after a while Bill said that he thought we should move to Collegeville Hills, a middle-class suburb, because it had good schools and the sort of square environment that Isaac might need. Neither Bill nor I wanted to move into suburbia, but we felt it was the right thing for Isaac. Well, it wasn't the right thing for anybody. There was an instant clash.

Bill didn't suffer so much, because he could withdraw into his studies, but I had to live with those damned suburban idiots. Gossip was their main hobby, and we provided them with plenty. Not that we were doing anything horrible; we were just different. For example, Bill went to work on a bike in all kinds of weather, and in Collegeville Hills that made him a loony radical. Look at Professor Collins riding his bike! He must be nuts. Yeah, and when it's warm he wears shorts. Can you imagine a professor teaching in shorts?

They'd stand around their fences staring at us. They hated us for any number of reasons. For one thing we weren't conspicuous consumers, and that was a sin. We had an old car and a camper with wooden slats and four square sides. I didn't rush to the hairdresser's every day —in fact I never went—and I wore old clothes. I wanted to be comfortable and functional, but that was unheard of in our neighborhood.

One day I was invited to a coffee, and I made the concession of wearing nylons, but I refused to shave my legs because I never have and I never will. I like hair. I like it on men and I like it on women. It's natural. At the coffee, the ladies just couldn't seem to take their eyes off my legs. I have excellent legs, and my excellent legs have excellent hair growing on them. The ladies couldn't seem to adjust to these phenomena.

I waited for the conversation to begin, and it didn't take long: sixteen women, all of them talking about the recipe for the cookies the hostess had baked, and their children and their babies (which can be interesting, but not the way they did it, using all the clichés that mean nothing: how to name a baby, how to get rid of diaper rash, whose tricycle is whose, over and over again). I went home and resolved never to go to another coffee. After that I was ostracized by my neighbors, except when some of their kids began to get into trouble smoking dope, and the neighbors instinctively came to me for advice. They didn't know anything about me except that I looked different, and they assumed that this meant I knew all about dope, which I did, but not for the reasons they supposed. One neighbor lady was worried because her son hung out at a hamburger joint and she had a morbid fear that somebody would put LSD in his coke and turn him on. She had all the middle-class attitudes about LSD, that it would destroy her beloved son right on the spot, etcetera. I tried to explain to her that he'd live, he'd survive. She left in hysterics.

One day a delegation called on us to complain that we had too many dandelions on our lawn, and they suggested the name of a herbicide we could use. They even said they would give us some. I said, "Well, I kind of like dandelions. They're nice. They're pretty and they taste good, and they make good wine." So the delegation left in a huff.

Then they began complaining that we didn't rake our leaves. I said, "Why, they're a natural mulch. They're perfectly natural!" They sent two delegations, one to talk to me, and one to Bill, and they left unhappy again. I suggested to Bill that we put up a six-foot fence around our property to spare the neighbors the sight of us, and vice versa, but the zoning code wouldn't allow it.

By this time, Bill was retreating more and more into advanced metaphysics, and leaving the neighborhood problems up to me. We had a little social life with some of the other professors in the philosophy department, but most of the faculty at Collegeville is as square as the people in Collegeville Hills, and I couldn't get much out of them. After a while, I realized I wasn't getting much out of life itself, and I began to think more and more about dope. We'd spent a year in Collegeville Hills, and I hadn't taken anything except my usual codeine, and now I was beginning to get terribly depressed.

I tried to keep up a front for Bill, so he could concentrate on his work and not worry that he was causing my depression. Every night I'd have dreams where I'd be shooting up, and I'd wake up in a sweat just before the rush. I missed it terribly—I started to keep a diary, but I gave it up, because I couldn't think of anything to write about except heroin. I looked back on the entries for a month, and almost every one had heroin in it. I tried to prove to myself that there were millions of other interesting things, but all I had to do to disprove this theory was to look out the window at suburbia. I began taking more and more codeine, telling myself that it was for my headaches, but one day I had to face reality. I was standing in the living room taking codeine pills one after another and all of a sudden I said to myself, "Huh? What are you doing? *You don't even have a headache.*" I realized I was repeating a childhood pattern: taking codeine when I didn't need it. I wouldn't think of going out on the street for heroin, because I didn't want to jeopardize Bill's position. So I suffered along with codeine.

By the time we were well into our second year of marriage I could no longer take the suburbia scene and those dreadful dull social sessions with Bill's fellow faculty members, and I just plain decided that I *had* to have some relief. I knew better than to try to score heroin; Collegeville is a mecca for people who use pot and LSD and psychedelics, but it's not a good place to score heroin. There's not a large supply, and it's very expensive and highly adulterated. But I knew I had to get something. I began going to doctors, trying to find a friendly doctor who would prescribe what I needed. I would go in and complain of my ungodly headaches, in the hope that the doctor would prescribe something that would replace heroin in my life. I told the truth about my headaches, but I exaggerated, and the doctors always seemed to catch on. One by one they'd say to me, "Well, all we can give you is Empirin Number Three because we just can't take the risk of addicting you to stronger drugs."

It took me almost three months to find Dr. Klein. He had a little office on the outskirts of town, and a practice that consisted almost entirely of old ladies. I wouldn't be surprised if Dr. Klein has a lot of hidden addicts on his hands, taking dope for the generalized aches and pains of old age. I don't know for sure, it's just gossip, but that's my guess. I walked into his office and told him I had a terrible headache, and without the slightest discussion he gave me a shot of Demerol, and it felt so *good*. That was the beginning. He gave me a prescription for Demerol, and I took it home and shot it the next day. The relationship went on for eight years, and it never varied. We didn't discuss what I was doing, the doctor and I. If we had discussed it, he'd have had to admit that he knew what was going on.

It was weird. I would go to his office two or three times a week, get a shot of Demerol, and get a prescription, which I preferred, because I could dissolve it, shoot it and get a better reaction. He only turned me down a few times, when I came in too often. He loved the business. He got nine dollars a shot, and it didn't cost him anything like nine dollars a shot, so he was making a nice profit, and it wasn't costing me anything either, because Bill and I had health insurance and it paid eighty percent of the bills.

Once in awhile one of Dr. Klein's nurses would say something like, "You know, you're really getting a tolerance for these things, you're taking too much." One of them said, "You'd better watch out, or we'll be putting you in the hospital one of these days."

But I never brought up the subject of overindulgence with Dr. Klein and he never brought it up with me. It was nice when he gave me a shot, but the best days were when he would give me a prescription for Demerol, Dilaudid, morphine, Numorphan, things like that, because I would rush home and shoot them. I became an expert at dissolving and shooting just about anything. If something wouldn't dissolve in water, I would dissolve it in alcohol. I experimented around. Certain things would jell instead of liquefying, and I had to figure out how to dissolve them so that I could shoot them. I remember a capsule called Mephogran, which was Demerol and Phenergan mixed. Phenergan is a strong antihistamine, but in combination with narcotics it jolts them up, makes smaller doses more potent, and also keeps you from getting sick to your stomach. I used to dissolve Mephogran in alcohol. Dilaudid always mixed very well with water, but some of the other ones were hard to dissolve. Demerol was a bit of a problem. I'd crush it up and put in water and soak it and then shake it very hard, and with some effort the Demerol would dissolve. Morphine was the best, because it came in tablets that were meant to be injected subcutaneously. I found that I could get a good rush from morphine by injecting it straight into the vein. I had to take certain chances with combination drugs, and sometimes I would get slightly sick from shooting them. But beggars can't be choosers, and I didn't dare question Dr. Klein's prescriptions. He had a theory that if he kept mixing up the drugs, I wouldn't get hooked, and I didn't dare make an issue of it, because I lived in terror that he'd cut me off cold turkey.

I went on like this for a few years, and eventually I ruined all my veins by shooting drugs like Mephogran

and Dilaudid and others that were not meant to be shot.
Dr. Klein kept increasing the doses. Toward the end,
he was shooting 250 or 300 milligrams of Demerol into
me, where a normal dose would have been 50 to 100.
He was generous.

In a sense, I had duplicated the old pleasant Houston
scene. I was having my drugs, and I was avoiding the
negative aspects of addiction. I wasn't shooting up with
dirty needles, because I could do it in the hygienically
sterile surroundings of my own house. I didn't have to
sneak around behind my husband, because he knew about
it from the beginning, it was just something that couldn't
be kept from him. He didn't like it, but he didn't try to
stop it. I told him it was because I couldn't stand my
headache pain, but he knew the truth. He was just not
a hassling type of person. He would look at the tracks on
my arms and shake his head, and rush into his study and
open a book. I did most of my shooting at night, and I
would just nod out, so it had no effect on his life. He
could have stood anything, so long as nobody took his
philosophy books away from him. So my habit wasn't all
that unpleasant. I didn't have to go out on cold street
corners to hustle up my junk. Thank goodness. I wouldn't
have been capable of that. A lot of junkies enjoy the
whole syndrome, the stealing and the hustling and the
conning, but all I enjoyed was the junk. I didn't want
the rest of it.

I also realized that this routine was not right, and that
it couldn't lead to anything good, so once in a while I'd
try to kick. Sometimes I'd have withdrawal symptoms
and sometimes I wouldn't, but what always sent me back
to drugs was my terrible anxiety attacks. They could
only be stopped by drugs. I tried natural means, like
leaning on people or taking long walks, but the hysteria
only became worse. I'd always had these anxiety attacks,
and they're very difficult to explain to someone who's
never had them. What happens is you become convinced
something horrible is going to hit you, everything is
wrong, and you become panicky. I'd be walking down
the street, and my eyes would be open wide, I'd be

looking around for danger, and I'd be hyperventilating, and I'd know the end of my life was at hand. I don't know how to describe it to a straight person. Look: You're walking down the street and suddenly you see six huge gorillas coming at you. How would you feel? Well, I felt exactly the same, just as terrified, just as panicked, just as desperate, but *without* the gorillas. That's anxiety. Terrible! You don't know how you can go on living.

With the anxiety came all the phobias: acrophobia, agoraphobia, claustrophobia, so that I was in a constant state of panic. When I went outside, I'd have agoraphobia, then I'd rush home to the house and have an attack of claustrophobia, and I'd be shaking and terrified, and that's when I'd lift up the phone and call good old Dr. Klein.

All this time, Bill kept retreating and retreating. He moved from assistant professor to associate professor, and he had a couple of papers on John Stuart Mill published in national journals. The more successful he became in his profession, the less interest he showed in me and my problem. We had practically no sex life; I did everything under the sun to get him started, but it just didn't work. He was having a love affair with the metaphysicians. For a while I tried having an affair of my own, but that didn't seem to stimulate him either. When my lover moved to Chicago, Bill would give me the money to fly to see him, and even drive me to the airport, and tell me to have a good time.

I suppose I could have taken anything except this indifference. I always expected Bill to show some emotion, maybe to completely blow up, but it never happened. It was just a case of bored, *more* bored, *most* bored. When I threatened to move out, trying to get him aroused, he'd just sit there. He didn't seem to have any energy for me. All his energy went into his work, and into things like mountain climbing and skiing and swimming, but around the house he couldn't raise a finger to help the marriage. So I just gave up. One person can't do it. He wouldn't give. He *couldn't* give.

Dr. Ruth Francis says:

Her values are so twisted, and she's passed them along to her son. The first time I ever smoked pot, it was her son who showed me the technique. He was thirteen at the time, and his mother thought it was perfectly okay. We were sitting around in a circle, up in the hills, and somebody began passing a joint around, and nobody offered to help me till the kid, Isaac, came over and patiently showed me how.

I got a cash settlement. We split everything, and I bought a half interest in a record store with a partner whom I'd known in the old hootenanny days. I kept right on taking drugs, but I tried to regulate my use of them so I could function in the store. I've always tried to be a well-regulated person. We lived in the back, my son Isaac and me and my partner. We made hardly any money, and we were always hungry. Isaac was getting old enough to know the score now, and I tried to keep him in the dark about my habits, but he was just too bright for me. We never discussed it, but I knew that he knew. He told a friend of mine that his mother was a heroin addict, and I didn't bother to correct him. What's the difference? An addict's an addict. I did try heroin a few times in Collegeville, but it just wasn't worth it, and I was getting enough straight dope from Dr. Klein. But Isaac knew I was on something, and we had a lot of arguments about it, without ever mentioning what we were really arguing about, and two days after his fourteenth birthday he moved away with my blessing. He's been gone ever since. He lives with a family near Detroit, and he smokes a lot of pot, but I don't think he's on anything else. At least not yet.

I kept up my interest in the record store for four years, but all that time my main interest was drugs. When I got a chance to sell out at a nice round four thousand, I took it. I'd been hanging around with a real junkie and I lived to regret it. I'd always tried to avoid junkies, and I'd never had any friendships with them. You really can't.

The concept of friendship is meaningless to a junkie. They'll rip you off for everything you've got. But this guy came on very nice, and he had all sorts of ideas in his head to make money, and the first thing he wanted us to do was to go to Tangiers and score some hash for resale. I always liked adventure, and I always liked change, so I agreed to go.

Our first stop on the way to Tangiers was New York City, and we spent a lot of my money on heroin in a two-week binge. Then we went on to Tangiers, to carry out his great scheme. The truth is, he was inept. Your average high school kid would make a better smuggler.

We stayed in Tangiers a week till we scored the hash that we wanted. My friend had lived in Tangiers, he knew the town well, and he took his time about getting the right quality stuff. He did it all alone: It wasn't cool for both of us to be in on the deal. He bought a kilo and a half, three and a half pounds, for sixty dollars. This was expensive for hash in Tangiers, but he wanted unusually high-quality stuff. This was genuine "One-toke" hash; one inhalation and you're stoned, two or three inhalations or tokes and you're stoned for hours.

I had some kind of a crazy dope dream that we would make a lot of money off this hash and then I would take the money and fly back to the States and reclaim Isaac and move to Afghanistan. So I was enthusiastic about reselling the hash in Copenhagen, where my friend had a buyer, but I wasn't enthusiastic about his sloppy method of operation. I wanted to mail the stuff to Copenhagen from Tangiers. The last thing I wanted was to carry it across on the boat to Malaga. But the hash wasn't delivered until Saturday morning late and our boat was scheduled to leave that afternoon, and by the time we'd have got the stuff all packed for mailing, we'd have missed the boat and the post office would've been closed. That was all right with me; why not wait till Monday? But my friend was impetuous and compulsive. And cheap. He said, "We've already bought the boat tickets to Malaga, and we won't be able to get our money back." He said, "Hell, let's take the hash with us to Copenhagen."

I objected, but he said we had to do it this way, and in my dope-addled shape I went along. We took the boat across to Malaga, and the custom people marked our bags with chalk without even opening them, and we were home free. But they hadn't checked the packs on our backs, where we had eleven hundred hash-pipe bowls that we'd bought for a penny apiece, to take back home. I'd had the crazy idea of giving a hundred of the bowls to Isaac to resell among his friends, so he could make a litle money, and the other thousand we would sell one by one in Collegeville. The bowls were absolutely legal in the States, and there was nothing wrong with our having them.

What I didn't understand, in my naivete, was that once your bags are chalked you can walk right out the door of the customs shed. The Spanish customs inspectors don't want to see what's in your packs, unless they specifically ask you, and once they make the chalk marks, you're supposed to leave. But I didn't know this, so I mentioned to the inspector to please mark our packs.

The customs official looked pained, or he misunderstood, or something, and he asked us to take off the packs, and he opened them up and saw the pipe bowls and confiscated them. Hash pipes aren't illegal anyplace else in the world; a pipe bowl is just a pipe bowl, but these guys are different. Now that they had found the pipe bowls, they got all excited and announced that they were going to strip-search us. My friend had the bulk of hash strapped to his body, and I had about an ounce hidden in my brassiere. It was the first and only time I'd ever worn a bra. I had the hash taped between my breasts. The matron didn't ask me to get undressed; she just patted me all over. When she patted around my breasts, I could hear the paper crackling, but she didn't say anything. She motioned me to go, and I was free.

Well, I knew that once they searched my friend and found all that stuff they would grab me again and make me get undressed, so I quickly went to the bathroom and put the hash on the window ledge so I could re-trieve it later. When I came back in the customs shed, my friend had been busted, and then they did strip-search me, but I was clean by then. For that matter, they almost missed finding the stuff on him. He had it on the inside of his thighs and in packets up to his waist, and when they asked him to take his shirt off, a little bit of paper was sticking up over his belt, so they made him take off all his clothes, and then they found the stuff.

He almost cooled things right away because he had some traveler's checks on him, and the inspectors agreed to take one hundred dollars plus the hash and let him go. But just as he was starting to write the checks, five *guardia civil* walked in, and that was the end of that. The *guardia civil*—what a misnomer! They're not inter-ested in guarding the civilian population; they're inter-ested in taking the *turistas*. That's their man occupation. So the customs officials couldn't risk doing business in front of them. They placed him under arrest.

I was miserable. I don't speak any Spanish at all. I went out and bought my friend some water colors and some paper and some books to read, and I found a cheap hotel while I waited to figure out what to do. I still had about three thousand dollars, and my hotel was only ninety cents a day. You can imagine how lovely I felt. I had all our luggage to take care of. I was alone in a country where I couldn't even order a glass of water. I felt I had to stay put in Malaga, so that my friend could find me if he got sprung. I sent word to the jail so that he would know where I was, and I waited.

After a week I had head lice, and sores from the springs that stuck through the mattress. I was followed and in-sulted by Spanish men who thought I must be a prosti-tute because my skirts were short. I let my skirts down as long as I could, and then I started wearing jeans under my skirts, but they still didn't understand. What I really needed was an ankle-length black dress and a crucifix. They'd have understood that.

It took me two weeks to find an English-speaking lawyer, a lush. I had to camp on his doorstep with all his children screaming around me, but I just stayed there until he finally agreed to do something for me. It was a long process, but he finally got my friend out of jail with a combination of bail and bribes. The whole thing cost me every penny. Twenty-nine hundred dollars went to the jailers, and seventy dollars to the lawyer.

That was the last money I ever had. I've had nothing since then, and never will. My friend and I skipped to London, where I copped from a doctor on the Public Health Service. She was so funny. She said, "Make sure after you use the needle, make sure to break it, or else the junkies will get it." I laughed to myself. She gave me Pethadine, stronger than Demerol. Then I used the other half of my round-trip ticket to go back home.

There was more fun and good times to come in Collegeville. I should have learned from the experience in pain, but I came right back to drugs in Collegeville and for the first time in my life I had one of the horrible side effects that beset junkies. I'd always been so careful, but one night when I was skinpopping I must have breathed on myself, and I had strep throat at the time, and the result was a terrible cellulitis. It became generalized through my body, and I got very sick. My fever went up to 104 degrees. I could barely move.

I didn't know where to turn. I called my mother in Vermont and asked for help. I said, "I'm really sick. I need to come home." She said okay. Well, it's amazing that I'm still alive. Somehow I got to the airport and flew to Boston. I could hardly walk. My arm was swollen to double size. It was beet red, and I had to keep hiding it because I was ashamed of it. On the flight I heard heavenly choirs. I hallucinated all the way. In the last half hour of the flight, I passed out cold. My mother met the plane, and they hauled me off, and as soon as I reached the end of the ramp, I threw up. My mother looked disgusted, but she took me to a hospital. The doctors asked me what the trouble was, and I said it was drugs; there was no point in lying. Three doctors looked at me, and they told my mother, "She's gonna die tonight, and we don't want her here. Get her out of here!" I don't know what happened the rest of the night, except that we went to two more hospitals before we reached one where they gave me massive doses of antibiotics and took care of me. My mother took me home and nursed me for two weeks, around the clock, and then I began to recover.

I would like to be able to tell you that I came back to Collegeville with my head on straight and kicked drugs for good, but I didn't. I had been on drugs for thirty-one years. When I came back to Collegeville, I took up right where I'd left off.

That was three years ago, and I guess you'd have to say I'm still on drugs. Drugs and cigarettes and everything I can get into my mouth.

Two years ago, I forget exactly when, I got on the methadone program. I was just fed up with the whole junkie syndrome, but I knew I had to have something. Now I get methadone every day. The effect lasts a little less than a full day. I get it at noon. Some people get take-out methadone, but they don't trust me that much at the People's Clinic. If they suspect that you'll double up on it, or you'll sell some of your supply, they make you come and take it in front of them every day. They give it to me in solid form—like a pink Alka-Seltzer. I break it up into quarters and swallow them.

A lot of people swear by the methadone program, but I'm not so sure. Methadone doesn't tranquilize you or really do anything to you after the first couple months, except to keep you from being able to enjoy any of the other narcotics. It doesn't make you sick, but it makes you lose the ability to feel stuff like heroin. Some people have died because of this; they shoot heroin, and they can't feel anything, and they keep shooting more and more until they're dead. Like I could take $150 worth of Collegeville heroin right now and I wouldn't feel a thing. That's what methadone does. That's why it reduces the crime rate. Junkies get on methadone and they stick to it. Of course it's a habit that has to be kicked, too, and that's the worst feature. One good thing about methadone, it's a preventive for all kinds of pain. Like you never have headaches, you don't notice minor things like colds, and you don't notice any pain at all unless it gets real bad. So it's been good for my headaches.

Now all I have to do is kick the methadone. That's the way the program works. You substitute methadone for heroin, and then you kick the methadone. But I can't. The first couple of times I tried, my old friends would come around and try to sell me dope, because I'm in such a vulnerable position. They wanted to make a buck off my condition. I'd wait about four days, and then I'd be so sick, I'd go crawling back to the People's Clinic for methadone.

I've had to face the fact that I'm thoroughly addicted to the stuff. I've tried to kick three or four times, but I just can't. When I stay off the methadone for a day or two, I begin to get panicky. I get sicker and sicker. I throw up. I get diarrhea. I have cold and hot sweats. Everything hurts, and my skin crawls to the touch. I have anxiety spells, I know I'm about to die. It's a real mess! I've heard of people who killed themselves trying to kick methadone, that's how hard it is. I've heard of suicide, people just trying to get out of their misery.

The procedure for kicking is to reduce the level a little bit at a time, until you're really not getting any at all. But long before I reach that low level I get rotten sick, physically and mentally. That's one reason I'm down on the whole methadone program. It's not designed to help the junkie, it's designed to help society because it reduces the crime rate. It makes you totally enslaved, and it keeps you from having any desire or need to commit crime to get any other drugs. Really, taking methadone is almost the same as taking heroin, but in this country heroin's a dirty word since the passage of the Harrison Narcotics Act, so they give you methadone instead, which is worse, because methadone destroys your liver and heroin doesn't. But methadone's respectable.

The last time I tried to kick it was just a couple of months ago. I got down to 30 milligrams a day from my usual dose of 160. But I was in such bad shape that I was taking more and more tranquilizers, because I just couldn't go to sleep. My sleep has never been ordinary; sometimes I don't sleep fifteen minutes in every twenty-four hours, and some nights I don't sleep at all, I just shut my eyes for a few minutes. So as I cut down on the methadone. I increased the tranquilizers, until I was taking twenty-five or thirty at a time, and sometimes more than that during the night. Tranquilizers like Milltown and Valium aren't made to put you to sleep, and that's why I had to take so many.

I was getting my tranquilizers from good old Dr. Klein. Since I'd started on the methadone program, he'd finally taken me off drugs, but he would still give me as many tranquilizers as I needed. The result was I wound up in the hospital from the effects of the tranquilizers, and when I got better I went right back on my 160 milligrams a day of methadone.

The doctor at the People's Clinic is a tough, practical woman, and she accuses me of wanting to stay on the stuff forever. But I don't. I know I'll have to get off, or my liver will be destroyed, and I'll die, but at the moment I just don't feel like getting off. It's too hard. Sometimes I wonder, "Why don't I just keep taking it till I die?" I mean practically indefinitely. I say to myself, "You've been on drugs for almost thirty years, why not stay on them for another thirty?"

The doctor gets so disgusted with me. She threw me out of her office once. She said she was sick and tired of all my hassles, and she couldn't help me. Her attitude is that I'm hopeless, I'm a terminal case. She really believes that. But I don't.

The thing is, I've depended on drugs for so long. They've given me my only joys. They've made it so that I can't enjoy anything else: my son, a beautiful painting, a sunset, a marriage. I'm fighting very hard to get over this, to regain my joys, but it's almost impossible.

One good thing, my veins are beginning to come back. I'm beginning to see the little ones in my hands and feet. But the larger ones, the ones I used for shooting, may never come back. And my memory is impaired. I'm physically rundown. But I can overcome that.

The worst thing is still the lack of enthusiasm that comes from dope. All I do is read, once in a while go to the movies, and once in a while talk to my lover, Jilly. Jilly is such a wonderful man, just being with him is enough, but I won't be able to hold onto him. I'll lose him. He's seeing me less and less, talking to me less and less, because I'm too dependent on him, and nobody likes that. Why should they? And Jilly hates the stuff I have to take. I'd have a better chance to keep him if I got off the methadone, but it's too late now. He won't wait around. I'm hopelessly in love with him, which is a drag. It's a drag because I'm a drag on him. He's independent; he doesn't need me around his neck. He comes around when he doesn't have any place to sleep. He has a seventeen-year-old girl friend, but I don't dare complain about her because I don't want to lose him. He tells me all about her. He's honest. He met her while I was in the hospital from taking tranquilizers, and they went to bed together the same night, and it blew my mind. His seventeen-year-old girl friend is the free spirit that I used to be and that I can never be again, so I'm slowly losing ground.

Part of my trouble is my age. I don't *want* to get older. I try to pretend that I'm twenty years younger, but I can't. Jilly's twenty-three, a brilliant physicist and a musician and a poet. I try to keep up with his mind, but I can't. Some of my brain cells have been destroyed. I've lost so much of my life, and now I'm thirty-four, and it seems like I should be so much younger than I am.

I may find another man, but it'll never be another Jilly. I put him on a pedestal; there aren't many around like him. He's a born teacher; he sits and talks to me about concepts for hours, and keeps up my interest. At least he used to—he's not seeing me so much now. I know I'll never replace him. I like young men, but the men that I like are getting closer to my son's age. People say that's perverted, or something like that, but I think it's perfectly natural. But it's hard to get a twenty-one-year-old man interested in you when you're years older. Some of them think you might as well be dead when you're twenty-five. The cult of youth. This is an awful age to be old.

Right now I'm living on welfare. I have a single room and my total income is the ninety-six a month welfare sends me, plus an occasional check from Bill or my mother. I could go out and get a job, but I just can't. The methadone keeps me too weird, too fuzzy in the head. I had one job, working in a knit shop, but as soon as they found out I was on methadone, they fired me. Then I tried working at a gas station, but the boss caught me nodding out and sent me home. Now if I wanted to get a job, about all I could get would be a waitress. Imagine, I have the equivalent of a master's degree, and I can't even get a job as a clerk.

So what keeps me going? Well, I don't know the answer. I'm hoping desperately that I can find something meaningful to do with my life because in the last couple of years I've done absolutely nothing, except to live through others, strong people like Jilly. I *hate* doing nothing. I spend my days reading and thinking. What keeps me going? Well, life's been good to me in the past, and I keep hoping it will be that way again. Interesting things have happened to me. I'm lucky. And I don't have any religious beliefs, so I think that once you're dead, you're dead, there's no life after death, and therefore I want to make this one last as long as I can. And also, I keep wondering, what's going to happen tomorrow? Something good? Something to make me happy again? But how long can you go on thinking like this when *nothing ever happens?*

Sometimes I feel sorry for myself, but not often. I whimper once in a while, but when I recognize that mood coming on, I try to get out of it. It leads nowhere. It just costs you your friends. There's nothing people hate more than self-pity. Some of my friends say, "You've been through so much, ever since you were a little child. It's no wonder you're an addict." But I don't accept that line of reasoning. There's a great many people who've been through just as bad or worse and haven't become addicts. I don't use my childhood traumas as an excuse. I have enough sense to know that I have to kick, and the only thing standing in my way is me. If I kick, I can start a new life, even at thirty-four. Don't worry; I'll try again. I'm still fighting. I'm not a basket case.

I was in the bookstore the other day and I got into a long conversation with this spade cat who kept telling me his troubles. I think he was a Black Muslim; he sounded like he had the whole rap memorized, he repeated himself so often. He said that white people can't ever really learn anything, all they do is copy the blacks. He said that blacks built the pyramids, and they were really built from the top down, but white engineers were too dumb to realize it. When I disagreed a little bit, he really began to put me down personally. I'll never forget what he said, He said, "Don't bother tryin' to understand, baby. You're white, and you can never dig suffering. You put us blacks down from the time we're born. You kick us in the legs, and then you blame us for being lame. You're all the same. You're a bunch of white pigs, and you deserve every bad thing you get. Go on back to your fancy house and forget it."

I guess he's still wondering what made me get hysterical.

JENNIFER SCOTT, 18
Freshman, Arts and Sciences

Esmerelda Wilson, Jennifer Scott's English instructor, says:

I ask all my English I students to write journals, and Jennifer's first journal entry told how her mother was coming to visit her, and how lucky they were that they had such a wonderful mother-and-daughter relationship. She wrote that she couldn't understand how daughters could develop such poor relationships with their mothers; it was just incomprehensible to her. I guess she found out fast enough!

Jennifer seems like such a straight arrow, and frankly I was shocked when I continued reading her journals and found out what she was up to. For a long time, I was just very very amazed, but then I became quite pleased about the whole thing. I liked the idea of her asserting her independence, doing her own bag. She wrote in her very last journal that her parents were talking about disinheriting her if she married the man, and she said she hated the idea of giving up her big wardrobe and her ski trips to Europe, but she'd do it for love of her man. I don't know what's happened since then, but I haven't seen any marriage banns posted yet.

I don't know where you'd say I'm from. I was born in Lafayette, Louisiana, but we moved to Indianapolis when I was an infant, and then in my senior year of high school my father was transferred to New York City. So I'm sort of a transit. Because not only did we live in these three places, but we also did a lot of traveling, and I guess you'd say I've really seen the world. My father says that I've seen more of the world than most adults, and I'm only eighteen, and I want to keep on seeing it. I like the feel of going off to Grindelwald to ski, or dropping down to Las Brisas in Acapulco to pick up a tan. Not that we do this all the time, but we do it often enough to keep me happy.

I don't think of myself as a spoiled person, but there's no question that I was spoiled as a child. I had closets full of clothes, and every toy I wanted. I was the baby of the family, and I was indulged. Both my parents had come from a small town in Maine, and neither one had ever had money, and when they became successful, they enjoyed spending it on their baby girl. They still do. I hope they never change.

Dad's an achiever. He lives the American dream. His ambition is very simple: to accumulate fifty million dollars. If you ask him, that's what he'll tell you, and without any shame whatever. Well, he's well on the way—if he lives. He's a business executive, and he became an executive by working harder than anybody else, and now he's in the habit. Sometimes he gets up at five in the morning so that he can be the first one in the office, and there are nights when he doesn't get home till two or three in the morning, or sleeps overnight on the sofa in his office. He's very popular with his men, because if one of them goofs off, dad stays at the office late and does the work. He's insane about work. It's his meat and drink. We take a lot of vacations, but on at least two-thirds of them we pack up and rush back home before the vacation is over, because dad can't stand being away from his desk.

Well, of course, this is really insecurity, isn't it? My father is probably worth four or five million dollars. How can a man with that kind of money be insecure? Well, it's easy. Money grubbing becomes a habit. With him, it's almost a religious thing. He acts as though the devil will take him to hell if he doesn't keep on working, working, working.

Watching him in action, I've learned a lot. I've learned not to be like him. He may be the personification of the American dream, but I think money should be a means, not an end, and to him money is *all* that matters. That's very sad. That comes from stark fright. That comes from remembering childhoods when there wasn't enough to eat, and when his father's house was sold out from under them.

I'd love to think that my parents are happily living the American dream, but I know better. My father's way of life has driven my mother to distraction. He's forced her deep into herself, and that's just not the sort of person she really is. She's a very outgoing, warm person; she desperately needs people, friends, a community of interest. She's not a social climber, not in the least, but she would just die and shrivel up if she didn't have friends around her. Well, how do you have close friends when you're married to a man like my father? When people come over, dad will fall asleep in his chair right in the middle of the evening. Or they'll play bridge, and dad will make the dumbest bids, just because he's tired, or he's thinking about the next day's work. Mother gets terribly embarrassed, and the people don't come back, and she becomes more and more lonely. Dad can find his release in his work, but mother's stuck in the house. It's so sad, because I love both my parents, but especially my mother. I put her on a pedestal. She's always been a Grecian goddess to me. She loves me and my brother so much, and we love her. Of course, she belongs to the generation that doesn't show love. That's not her fault. The love is there; we can feel it emanating from her.

I really don't think I have any hangups worth talking about; I've always been a very straight, square, conventional person. A prude, yes, that's the word. I was always the last person in my group to find out what was really happening in the world, and the first person to decide that I didn't like it. Like sex. I knew nothing about it till I was thirteen or fourteen years old, and that's late nowadays. Part of the problem was that I didn't like what was going on around our house sexually. It's hard to explain, and I hate talking about it. This is the sorest point in my life. Everybody has one thing that bugs him forever, and this is the one thing in my life: my mother's and father's sex. *Ugh!* Just thinking about it makes me want to throw up.

See, they were a very unloving couple toward each other, and I could have accepted this, but once in a while they would have a few drinks together, and then things would happen. Like I'd see my father stick his hand up my mother's skirt, or something like that. When I was very little, I didn't connect this with sex at all. All I knew was that he would put his hand up her skirt, and maybe start to feel her breasts, and then they'd go to bed and I'd hear these grunting and snorting noises in the bedroom. My brother is eight years older, and Kenny always tried to protect me from this. He'd come into my room and start a conversation in a fairly loud voice, to drown out the noises from my parents' bedroom, and whenever I asked him what was going on, he'd say, "Oh, nothing," and try to gloss the whole thing over.

Gah, how I hate to discuss this! Can't we pass on to something else? *Gah!*

By the time I was nine or ten, I had noticed a pattern in the activities in my parents' bedroom. Like mother would keep saying, "Stop it!" or "Cut it out!" or "If you do that again, I'm gonna smack you!" So I realized they were doing something that was unpleasant for her, or at least she pretended it was. I got the distinct impression that they were playing some kind of vulgar game of cat and mouse. And my mother was *definitely* not enjoying it. She didn't want to play the game, but she was *forced* to play it. I said to myself, "What could be going on in that room? *Eccccch!* What are they *doing* in there?"

Oh, it was so vulgar. Vulgar! I was terribly confused and upset by it. It upset me even more when suddenly mother would interrupt and say, "No, no, stop it! Cut it out! Yes, yes, do it! More, more!"

After a while, I became convinced that my father was doing something horrible, but I still couldn't figure out exactly what. But little by little I began to realize that whatever horrible thing he was doing to her, some part of her was enjoying it. That really flipped me out! And

I said to myself that whatever they were doing, you would never catch *me* doing it. Not for anything! I wasn't sure what a virgin was, but I knew I would stay one for the rest of my life. No one would touch me. I was the daughter of dirty people, but I would never be dirty myself.

I've heard about sibling rivalry, and I had some with my brother, although we always pretended to be good pals. I'd find myself inciting little problems around the house, and blaming them all on my brother. I would goad him and goad him till finally he would smack me, and then I would run to my father and complain, and my father would administer punishment. Kenny and my father never got along from the very beginning, and now I realize that I was one of the main reasons. I remember seeing wretched things happen. Once when Ken hit me, I told my father, and my father chased him three blocks and beat him up terribly with his fists. Oh, gah, that was terrible! It was all my fault, because I had been egging him on, and I knew it, but I couldn't stop myself. I hated seeing Ken get punished, but I kept on making scenes.

For almost as long as I can remember, there was hostility between Kenny and dad. You couldn't sit at our dining room table without hearing dad make some comment about Kenny, and usually over nothing. Ken would drop one pea off his fork, and my father would say, "Well, I see we've got sloppy Joe the bartender eating with us tonight." He would pretend that he was being humorous, but then it would turn into hatred, and we'd all get indigestion. Then bang! Dad would blow up!

When I was about eight and Kenny was about sixteen, a horrible thing happened in our house. He caught a disease, and my mother told me that it was just some kind of internal disorder, but later I learned that it was gonorrhea. My father went berserk. There was screaming and yelling around the house for months. My father told me one night that my brother was a bad influence on me, and that I should never grow up to be like him. Oh, it was awful! One night after Kenny was cured, they even got into a fistfight. It was horrifying! They knocked each other all around the rec room, and they both were bleeding and bruised when it was over.

A few weeks after that, I heard the strangest conversation between my parents. Ken was out, and I was in my room, and they were in the living room talking, and I heard my father say, "Marjorie, I just don't know how to change. I wish to God I could. I love the boy, I really do, but I just can't seem to help myself."

My mother said, "Well, it's not all your fault. These things never are."

My father said, "Yes, it is. It *is* all my fault, and I'm so sorry for what I've done to him. Oh, God, how can I show him that I really love him?" And then my father broke down, and he was just racked with sobs. I felt like running down the stairs and trying to comfort him, but I didn't dare. So I just started to cry, and I cried myself to sleep.

You can imagine my reaction to things like necking and making out when I first went into high school. I simply wouldn't allow it! All my peers made out before I did. I just didn't care about things like that. I wouldn't wear makeup or tight clothes because I didn't want to attract boys. I guess I might never have made out at all, except that the girls in my crowd set me up, and after a very shy boy and I made out a little, all the girls congratulated me. It was like somebody else losing her virginity.

By the time I was in the tenth grade, I thought it would be okay to have a boyfriend, because they were nice to have around, but I never connected this with any physical thing. I had no physical desires. I thought that was all disgusting. I knew that I was going to grow up frigid, and I didn't mind.

In the tenth grade, I met a nice boy, and we started going together, and once in a while I'd let him kiss me goodnight after a date. But I absolutely ruled out any use of the hands. We had been going together for three months before he made his big move. We were sitting on a bench in the park, late one night, and he said, "Jenny, I love you, and I'm gonna unhook your bra."

I was petrified! I told him if he unhooked my bra I would slap him and break up with him.

He just laughed. He said, "Come on, come on! We've been going together for three months."

I says, "Forget it."

He reached around and started to unhook my bra, and I did exactly what I advertised: I slapped him and broke up with him. I simply had too much pride to let anybody do a thing like that to me.

Once in a while I'd go to a party and I'd see very unsavory things going on. The boys and girls would pair off, and it would be a case of hands, hands, hands. Disgusting! Once I was at a party where a girl had too much to drink, and she began taking off her clothes. I just got up and left.

Well, don't blame me. It's not my fault. I grew up very modest. Like I never saw my parents' naked bodies. I saw my mother in her bra and her slip maybe six times in my whole childhood. I guess this made me a prude about nudity. I don't exactly disagree with those who run around nude; I think a person should do what he believes in. But nudity makes me very uncomfortable. It may have its place, but I don't think you should show off your nude body to everyone, and besides nudity is so unsexy. The nude body can be attractive, but it can be much more attractive with just a hint of clothing, like a negligee, or a nice clean pair of jockey shorts. That's appealing.

I was also prudish about my language; I guess it was just part of my past. There was a very brief period where I used bad words, to be like the other girls, but then I began to hate the sound of my own voice, and I cut it out. My father had always told me that people who use curse words are stupid because it's a sign that your vocabulary is limited and you can't make your point without saying curse words. Besides that, curse words sound very unfeminine to me. I'm not a hard-hat working on the docks; I'm a girl, and I should sound like one. I don't think these girls on the campus sound like girls when they say "shit." I don't think *anybody* should say shit at all. What good is it? It isn't even a descriptive word; it's just vulgar. Now "fuck" is a little different. I mean, if you want to say fuck, fine! Fuck, I think personally, fuck, unless—well, fuck will only come out of my mouth when I'm very mad, because even though it's not as bad a word as shit, it's still not too ladylike.

One good thing about high school—I solved the problem of listening to my parents' sex. By now, I knew exactly what they were doing, I knew exactly what all their noises meant, and it made me as sick as ever. But I learned to protect myself. By the time I was fifteen or sixteen I just wouldn't sit downstairs and watch TV with them when they were drinking, because I knew that pretty soon my father would start feeling my mother up, and it just made me sick. It horrified me. I'd run upstairs and study.

When I heard the sounds begin in their bedroom I'd put the pillow over my head, or I'd turn the radio up, anything to keep from hearing the noise. I felt it was so—*yuck!* I can't think of a better word to express my disgust. Finally I solved the problem completely. When we moved to New York, I got a fine big bedroom of my own on another floor, nowhere near their bedroom, and I could sleep the whole night without hearing a sound. What a relief! I can't tell you what a sore subject this is for me. Gah!

When we first moved to New York my parents went around and checked the schools, and they decided that I could not get a good education, or a safe education, in the public schools. So they put me in a private school, an all-white school, and I finished out there. They made it very plain that this was not a matter of race prejudice, but simply a matter of getting a good education. They explained to me that there was nothing bad about blacks and Puerto Ricans, but that in general they were under-educated, and they tended to hold back the rest of the students. I accepted this as a sincere and honest argument.

Now that I look back on it, I realize that I was under

a general misconception of what my parents believed. Like when I mentioned blacks or Puerto Ricans at the dinner table, they never got excited about it or said very much at all. They just kept their mouths shut. They didn't commit themselves. Once in a while I'd come home from school and bitch about the awful treatment the minority groups get in the United States, and they'd shake their heads and more or less agree with me, but they wouldn't go any further than that. So I figured, well, they may be conservative Republicans, but on the whole they're relaxed about race.

How dumb I was! There were plenty of tip-offs, but I just didn't notice them. Like one time I heard my mother say, "Why don't we send all the niggers back to Africa?" It was after there was some big riot someplace, and she was exasperated about it, but I didn't take her seriously, because she pops out with things like that all the time, and she doesn't really mean them.

Another time I heard my father say, "The trouble with Negros is they always want everything handed to them on a silver platter. They don't want to go out and work for it." Well, I didn't find this too far out. In fact, I sort of agreed with it, in some instances. In those years, I wasn't too bright about race myself. Now I know different. I know that no black person gets *anything* free in the United States. Like when they released the slaves, they promised them forty meals and a cow, but they never even got that. The way we've treated blacks is not exactly America's finest hour.

When I left home for Collegeville, I thought to myself, "Oh, gah I'm just gonna have to resign myself to it. I'm one of those frigid dames. I guess I'll end up all mixed up and I'll need a psychiatrist, I'm sure of it."

Since I took that attitude to Collegeville, I started out making very few friends of the opposite sex. I'd never been all that attractive to boys anyway. I'm not really attractive to them now. I don't know why. If I knew, I'd change it. I do have brains, and I am ambitious, and both these things seem to turn boys off. It's terribly unfair, but that's the way they are. They want to wow you with *their* intellect, *their* greatness, they don't want to hear about you.

Also, I have a problem about my height. I'm five-eleven. Boys all want to feel taller than you, and if they have to look up at you, they don't like it a bit. Well, I feel the same way. I like to look up to my boyfriends, so that cuts the list of potentials way down. Anybody under six feet can stay away; I don't want those little shorties anyway.

When I finally did begin seeing a few boys in Collegeville, I realized that all they wanted was sex. Well, I valued my virginity. I told myself that when I ever gave my virginity away, it would be a final commitment to a man I loved, and a man who loved me, and never to anybody else. So my early boyfriends and I didn't get along too well. As soon as they'd point to the bedroom I'd jump up and say, "Nope! Bye-bye!"

Whenever I found myself in a compromising position, I'd quickly extricate myself. I'd stop most of the boys before things got too thick, but once in a while I'd get into a bad spot, and I'd have to turn those little devils off. I'd just pull away, and I'd say, "Excuse me, but I'm not in The College for that purpose. I'm here for an education, not for a course in physiology."

Funny things happened. Once I met a guy at a party, and we're sitting on the floor, and I'm in between him and another guy, and they both slowly reach out their hands to take mine, and they wind up holding each other's hands without knowing it! Oh, I loved that! I just cracked up! I saw their two hands creeping around behind me, and coming together, and clutching tighter and tighter, and it was *so* funny! Oh, I just enjoyed it so much. I giggled to myself, and then I just got up and walked out and left them to discover what they'd been doing. I never heard from that boy again.

I met one boy that I could really have liked, but he turned out to be just like all the rest. His name was Jen Williams, and we went out several times, and we got real friendly. One night we were driving around in my old

MG, and I said, "Have you ever seen the Prairie View? I just *love* that place."

He says "No, I don't even know where it is. I don't know Collegeville yet."

Well, the Prairie View was a place where you could go and park and look out over miles and miles of prairie. It was a beautiful place, especially by moonlight, but in my stupid innocence, I'd forgotten also that it was also a lovers' lane. Oh, I'm so innocent! One part of me knew that Prairie View was a lovers' lane, but I never thought that Jen would take it that way. Certainly he *shouldn't* have, because right from the beginning I'd been telling him, "Forget it! If you want sex, you're not gonna get it from me. But if you want to have a good time, and somebody to talk to, and somebody maybe to kiss goodnight, fine." Because I just don't like to lead a man on. Let them find somebody else if they want carnal knowledge.

So we drove up to Prairie View and it really got hairy! We started to make out, and then he unbuttoned the top of my shirt, which upset me. I tried to push his hand away with my elbow, so that I wouldn't make a scene about it. It was the old elbow trick, where you nudge his hand away with your elbow just as if you barely know what you're doing. But it didn't work. The elbow trick seldom works. and you usually have to try something stronger, so I just plain pushed his hand away.

A few minutes later he began unzipping my pants, and by then I was panicky. I said, "Forget it! *Forget it!*" I pushed him away. He came right back at me. We began to make out again, and then he reached for the same zipper. All of a sudden it clicked in my mind: mom and dad! We were making the same kind of noises, doing the same kind of things. So I just reached across and shoved him away with all my strength, and I flicked the key of the car on, and I gunned us out of there about ninety miles an hour.

On the way back I said, "Jen, you just have to forget it. I don't have time for this. I'm not here to look for a boyfriend. I've got to graduate from college and then I've got to go for three extra years to get my degree as a vet. So I don't have time for this kind of thing. Please —just forget it!"

"Don't worry," he said. "I will."

The very next boy I dated took me to a marijuana party, only I didn't know that's what it was going to be. I've always had an intense intellectual curiosity, so I didn't mind trying grass once. I got stoned, but not very. I wasn't the least bit worried about being arrested, because grass is so common on this campus that the cops just don't arrest people for smoking. You can smell marijuana in my dorm anytime you want, and nobody ever does anything about it. As I understand it, the policy in these dorms is pretty well defined. I mean, a cop will bust you for smoking, that's his duty, but there are very few cops around here. Most of the dorms are run by proctors and counselors, and they do all the dope enforcement. If they catch you smoking, they'll warn you, but they'll never really do anything about it. If they catch you dealing, you'll get one free warning. They'll say, "Now cut it out! If we catch you again, you'll be in trouble." So as a smoker you have an infinite number of chances, and as a dealer you have at least two.

I've never become really interested in any form of intoxication, and I never will. I still smoke once in a while but not often. I don't have to smoke to get high. I can get high just walking around. I can get high eating bear claws, like I did today. I can get high enough on oxygen; I don't really need anything else. So marijuana will never really be a big deal to me.

I tell you all this so you will realize in advance that marijuana had nothing to do with what happened to me later. I mean, marijuana was slightly involved, but not really. I did what I did because I wanted to do it, not because I was out of my skull on grass.

Anyway, it began one day at the Coke shop; and I was standing there, and I became aware of this tall black man standing across the room staring at me. I stared back, and he smiled and I smiled, and I liked his looks, and I just figured, "Well, this is cool! This is fun!" He came across the room and I saw that he was at least six-ten or six-eleven, and I said, "Hellooooo up there! How's the weather up there?" I'd read that in a short story by Thomas Wolfe, and I remembered it. Caw told me later that he hated those old clichés about height, but I looked good to h'm at the time so he just laughed.

He said, "Hi, what's your major?"

I told him that I was just hacking around in Arts and Sciences, preparing myself for the School of Veterinary Medicine, and he said, "Cool! Right on! I'm gonna go to medical school myself!"

He had this sardonic look about him, as though he was talking to a four-year-old child and kind of laughing at the whole scene, and I said, "Hey, are you laughing at me?" It was a new experience, tilting my head way back to look up at a man this tall, but I didn't want him to be putting me on and making an idiot of me.

"No, of course not," he said. "I'm not laughing at you. I dig you!"

We talked for a few more minutes and then I had to go. You wouldn't exactly say that lightning had hit me. I mean, I thought he was nice, but not much more. He did give an impression of cool power and manliness, and I thought of him after that as Cool McCool. I knew I wouldn't mind seeing him again.

A few weeks later, a boy I knew took me to a late party at the Alpha Zeta House, and I was pleased to see that Cool McCool was there too. All together, there were about twenty-five or thirty people, about half boys and half girls, and there was some drinking and dancing, and then the pot began going around, and pretty soon the lights were dimmed and everybody started to make out. Well, I smoked two marijuana cigarettes. and I was really stoned, really totally wrecked for the first time in my life, and I did the paranoid scene. I was scared to death that my date would knock me down and take advantage of me, and I was even more afraid that I might enjoy it, so I jumped up and ran out of there fast. I was so wrecked that I tripped over somebody's legs across the door, and I picked myself up and ran down the stairs and ran straight home about three o'clock in the morning.

When I got back to my room in the dorm I was really bugged because nobody had even cared that I left. Nobody had raised a hand to stop me. My date didn't follow me or try to get me back, and now that I was back home he wasn't even trying to phone me. For all he knew, I might have been hit by a truck or raped in the alley on the way home. It was terrible of him to ignore me that way. About the only consolation I had was that I was still a virgin, I was still as pure as the driven snow, even though I'd gotten wrecked out of my mind. I figured it was a close call, and I would be more careful in the future.

When I woke up the next morning, about six other girls on the floor told me that a man named Caw had been trying to reach me and had asked them if I was okay. He said he was worried about me. The girls told me that they hadn't wanted to wake me up because they could see how wrecked I was, and they'd finally told him to stop calling, that I was fine, and not to worry.

I can't explain it, but I was exhilarated by that. I was very touched. Of all those men, he was the *only* one who was worried about me. It felt so *good* to have a man checking to make sure of my welfare, especially since he hardly knew me.

After that I saw Caw a couple of times on the campus, and I felt strongly attracted to him. So when he asked for a date, I said "Yeah, sure." I don't say that I didn't have a few misgivings about dating a black man, but it really didn't make that much difference. He was overwhelmingly attractive, and he was a man with consideration and kindness. That meant a lot to me. Like on our first date, he brought me a sprig of pussywillows, and I thought that was so sweet. This big huge behemoth of a man, and yet so gentle and sweet.

Well, that night we had a fine time over a few beers. From the beginning, I liked his looks. He had a certain type of black features that always appealed to me. He didn't have the broad, flattened nose or the thick, gross lips of a lot of blacks. He had a more Arabian look—thin aquiline nose, a small moustache and goatee, nicely shaped lips, and light brown eyes that seemed to look right through me.

I found out for the first time that he was sort of an assistant basketball coach. He'd been a star, but he'd used up his eligibility a long time before. So now he was helping to coach the team. He told me about his childhood; it was typical. Poverty, a broken home, several stepfathers, a mother who ran around and drank and didn't pay him much attention. He told me that he'd been married once, to a white woman, but it hadn't worked out. He had been in and out of college for about ten years, and he was going to stick it out until he got his MD. I could see from the start what his main problem was. He just doesn't put up with anything. I guess there's no other way to put it: He's a hotheaded black, he's *super*-hotheaded. He sees people in colors, and he always will. He's always talking about black-black-black, and Chicano-Chicano-Chicano. It gets a little old, and sometimes you want to say to him, "Listen, they're all just *people*. Stop being so prejudiced!"

Like he told me how he was out to nail one teacher. He said this teacher was racially prejudiced, he consistently gave blacks a grade or two lower than he gave whites for the same work. "I'll get that son of a bitch," he said, and I knew that he would. One thing about Caw! He has *power*.

He took me home and left me at the front door, and I was impressed by that. Most of the white guys try to make out on the first date, but Caw hadn't even held my hand. I did notice that some of the people in the lobby looked at us funny as we stood there at the door, but I figured they were staring at Caw because he was so tall. I still didn't realize what rednecks we had.

After that first date we started seeing more and more of each other. He called me every day, and he'd ask me sweet little things like, "How you feelin' today?" One night he said, "How'd you like to get into basketball practice?" I said, "Sure, great, I'd love it," and after that I'd go to practice and watch him work out with the men, and then he'd shower and we'd leave together arm in arm.

It didn't take long for my inhibitions to fall away. I didn't see Caw as a black man, only as a sweet, tall person who was nice to me. I even wrote my mother about how I'd met this black man, and what a pleasure it was to be able to go out with people of all colors and exchange ideas and be friends. I told her that he was a lovely man.

My mother replied much more quickly than she usually does. Her letter was full of small talk, and at the end it just said, "Dear, try *not* to get involved with black men, because it can only lead to trouble." But I didn't take that as anything more than another of my mother's glib remarks.

One night Caw kissed me goodnight at the door of the dorm. I didn't think anything of it, but I did notice that everybody watched me as I walked through the lobby toward my room. But this wasn't too unusual. I mean, when I was with Caw, nobody would stare too much because he was so big and they were afraid of him, but they did a lot of looking over their shoulders, and we just got used to it. At first it bugs you a little, but pretty soon you start feeling sorry for the poor people that have to do things like that.

Then one night I found that there was a lot more steam behind these rednecks than I had expected and also that rednecks come in all colors. Caw and I had been out on a date, and he brought me home and walked me down that long corridor to my room, and I hated to see him go, so I turned around and walked him back out to the front door—which is kind of ridiculous, but I just love being with him—and when I turned to go back to my room, I saw these three black girls standing there. I guess they must have thought I was flaunting him, walking up and down the corridor with him, but I wasn't. I just love being with him.

As I started toward my room, I heard the three black girls fall in behind me, and then they began making nasty comments. Every other word was fuck. They called me a white bitch, a white ass, and one of them said, "He must like that white ass," stuff like that. They said, "Keep your white ass away from the black men, honky! You fuck your own kind, hear?" They followed me all the way to my room, screaming insults at me. I thought for a second of fighting, but there were three of them, and I didn't think that was too cool. I sat in my room trembling for a long time, but then I realized that they couldn't help it. There were very few available black men on the campus, and I had taken one away.

When I saw Caw the next night, I told him what happened, and he said that was funny, because something similar had happened to him. Three black girls had knocked on his door and said, "Why are you dating a white chick? Don't you get enough satisfaction out of us?"

Caw told them, "Well, sisters, I guess the answer is no." He said they hassled him for a long time.

After three or four weeks, Caw and I were going steady, and we were seeing each other just about every night. You'd think the kids in the dorm would have gotten used to it, but it only got worse. I'd walk through the lobby, and the black boys would say, "Hey, how about me?" Then they'd get dirty. "What's it like fucking that big cock?" Stuff like that. I don't understand it, but they looked down on me for dating one of their own color. It makes no sense. They'd say things like, "Hey, sister, I got a big cock, too." One of them said one night, "Hey, sister, now you've finished fucking him, how about sucking me?" Ooooooooh! Gross! Repulsive!

I just took my cue from Caw; I tried to stay cool, and I said to myself that I would get used to it, just as he had. But, of course, Caw wasn't nearly as calm on the subject as he pretended to be. I remember one night when we went to the supermarket to get some beers, and a lady about sixty-five was rolling her cart down the aisle, and she saw me and Caw together, and she stopped the cart, her mouth fell open, and she stood there and stared at us. When we moved away, she followed right behind, staring and staring. She did this until we were paying our bill at the cash register. It bothered me something awful, but Caw didn't seem to mind. Oh, how can I tell you this story? It has a horrible word in it. Well, you'll just have to excuse the horrible word because Caw does talk that way once in a while. We were about to leave the store, and the old lady's still staring, and Caw says real loud, but in a nice voice, not annoyed, just quizzical, but *loud,* he says, "My dearie me, I wonder what's the matter with that old honky cunt?"

Not that it was all ugy and repulsive. I mean, sometimes you found out that there were good people on earth. One night I talked Caw into going to a midnight church service with me, and we walked in and sat down several minutes before the service began. As we sat there, a lot of so-called Christians came into the church and sat down too, and one by one they turned and stared at us. This was a church of God, and it was the Christmas season, and yet these people would come in and stare at us and make us feel horrible. One of them even turned around and put his arm on the back of the pew so he could take a good long look and not be too uncomfortable. You wouldn't believe it! Then the whispering began. "Look at that!" "Can you understand something like that?" "Disgusting!" And even though they were whispering, you could hear them clearly in this quiet church.

Well, Caw was sitting there acting like Cool McCool, as usual, but I was getting very annoyed. I was about to take his arm and leave when I saw the minister out of the corner of my eye. He was walking down the aisle, looking at us, and he slipped into the pew and sat down alongside. He took Caw by the hand, and put his other hand on my shoulder, and he said nice and loud, "So *good* to see you here. Thank you so much for coming." Then he went up to the front of the church and started the service, and that was the end of the staring.

After a while Caw and I were doing everything together. We got up and walked at dawn together, and we studied together, and we played together. It was just great! We would see the sun come up and the moon go down every day. It was wonderful. I'd never had a boyfriend like this.

Everything was so easy. He never put any pressure on me. There was none of that childish stuff of feeling me up, pushing me on, putting the pressure on me. It was all cool and relaxed. He learned my secrets, and I learned his. The last one I learned was his age. He told me he was thirty-five years old. I almost fell over. He didn't look that old at all. But it's hard to tell how old blacks are, just like it's hard for them to tell how old whites are. My face must have dropped. I was shocked! He said, "Does it make any difference?"

I was still stunned. I just sat there. I thought, "Oh, Gah, he's older than my brother! My mother would *kill* me!" But I finally said, "No, Caw, it really doesn't." And it didn't. Not when I thought about it. Going with Caw was the most beautiful thing that I'd ever experienced because it was all so easy and comfortable. It just grew naturally, and there was never any feeling that we had to be anything but ourselves in front of each other. We never fought. If we had arguments, they were about social issues, never about ourselves. We were completely and totally happy with each other. He was my knight in shining armor, and I was his little girl. Finally we began talking about it in the open: *our* love.

Then came *the night*. Oh, how it sticks out in my mind! I had already considered giving him my virginity; I'd thought about it a lot, because I don't like to do anything without giving it a lot of thought. The only worry I had was that I'd have all these hangups afterward, guilt and all; the typical virgin scene. But otherwise I was ready to do it.

So on this one night, we were sitting in his room, and I was leaning against him, and he was feeling me up, but I had all my clothes on, so it was okay. After a while he told me that he wanted to marry me, and he wanted to go to bed with me.

I don't know why this didn't strike me as the classic line because word for word it was: Maybe love blinded me. I *knew* that Caw wouldn't lie to me. So I said, "Do you know that I'm a virgin?"

He went, "Oh, God," because he'd never had a virgin, I learned later. He said, "Really?"

I said, "Uh-huh. And I really don't know how to do it and I'm really scared."

He said, "That's okay. Don't worry." He steered me over to the bed, and he laid me down and took off my clothes, very gently, and then he started doing it to me. Agony! Oh, never again! I thought I would die! It hurt *so* much. Oh, the pain! I never did get broken that night. It took two nights to do it.

Not being stupid, I went to the Clinic to get on the pill. It was so embarrassing! This loud-mouthed nurse said, "Yes, and what can I do for you?" I whispered through clenched teeth, "Birth control pills." I was purple with embarrassment. There were all these people standing around, waiting. I was *mortified*. They sent me from nurse to nurse and doctor to doctor, and I had to keep telling them what I wanted, and some of them said, "Speak up, what do you want?" Maybe it's a plot to embarrass you, so too many girls won't get on the pill. Anyway, I finally got the prescription.

The doctor told me to wait till the Sunday after my next period to start taking the pill. They tell all the girls that. Can you imagine? They want everybody in the college to be on the same cycle. Don't ask me why. It puts you on a weekly cycle, so that you're not menstruating on a weekend. Everybody menstruates on a Monday-Friday basis. I don't understand it either, except that it enables the men to know that weekends are safe. If they're dying to have intercourse, no girl on BC pills can turn them down on grounds that she's menstruating. It's weird, it's a male plot!

Anyway, Caw and I slept together regularly after that, and we made plans to get married. We knew that the first thing we had to do was to tell my folks everything. So I got on the phone and talked to my mother, and the minute the conversation began I could tell that she knew. My brother Kenny had gone to The College, too, and he had plenty of friends there, and he was living not far away, and somehow he'd found out and tipped them off. I learned all this later. Anyway, the phone conversation was really strange. My mother wasn't really talking to me. Finally I said, "Well, what's *wrong?*"

My mother started crying. I thought, oh my God, now I have to put up with this. She cried and told me that I would just have to stop dating a black man—and the worst thing was that she didn't have the slightest idea I wanted to marry him. She was shocked out of her skull that I would even *date* him. How could I tell her that Caw and I were serious?

She said, "Jenny, if you keep dating him, you're gonna lose all your girl friends, and some black girl is gonna knife you in the back." That gives you some idea of her hysteria.

After she finished all her screaming at the long distance rates, my father got on the phone, and he hollered at me for at least half an hour more. He is not the hollering type, but he was doing it this time. I realized they were panicked. They wouldn't even let me talk! My father said if I didn't fly his way, he would see to it that I didn't fly at all. He would cut off everything: no more school, no more clothes, no more ski trips, no more anything! He said, "You'd better fly straight! Go out and find yourself somebody white. Aren't there any nice doctor's sons on campus?"

I finally got a word in edgewise. I said, "I thought you raised me to be color-blind, to think of people as people." My father said, "We did *not* raise you like that."

I just blew up. I was shattered. "Well," I said, "What *did* you teach me?"

"We taught you that a white man is a white man and a black man is a black man, and they belong in their own society."

I said, *"You did?"* Oh, I was just pushed all out of shape. I couldn't believe my ears. I was hysterical. I thought I would have a nervous breakdown right there on the hall phone.

My mother came back on, and she was snorting and

huffing as though she couldn't get the words out, and she finally said, "That black boy's just trying to get into our society. He's just trying to get a white girl into bed That's what they live for. That's what they're trying to do. They want to make every white girl pregnant, to further their race."

I blew up. I said, "Oh, you think I'm gonna be just like Kenny, don't you? Don't think I don't know about it. I know he had gonorrhea! And I know you think I'm just like him, falling into bed with everybody and getting pregnant right away. Well, I'm not! Don't think I'm that stupid! I'm not gonna get pregnant, *because I'm on the pill now!*"

I didn't realize what I'd said till after I'd said it. In so many words, I'd told my mother that I was sleeping with a black man. She just sort of whinnied, like a dying horse, and my father came back on the phone. I could imagine mother lying there in a dead faint.

Well, the whole horrible conversation went on for an hour, and I was out in the hallway on the wall phone, trying to get them to listen, and crying hysterically, and they never heard a word I said. Finally, just to get it over with, I said, "Okay, okay! Fine! I'll do *anything* you say. Okay! Fine!" And I hung up.

I ran back to my room and threw myself on the bed and I cried and cried, and then I began to think rationally, and I said to myself, "No, this is *not* the way it's gonna be done. This thing is gonna be done *my* way, or I'm not gonna be able to live with myself. My parents'll only be around a few more years, but Caw will be around forever." I decided to quit school, if necessary, and get a job, if necessary, and marry Caw no matter what the odds. I went to my desk and wrote them a letter. I said "If this is the way you want it, fine. I don't want anything from you at all. But I'm going to do it *my* way, because you're wrong. *You're just plain wrong!*"

I ran out and mailed that letter right away, and in those few hours I realized that I had grown up more than I had in the previous eighteen years. I went back to the dorm and called Caw, and his voice just relaxed me beautifully. He said, "I have faith in you. Everything will be fine. Now you have a big test tomorrow, and I want you to go back in and study, and forget about your parents."

I did exactly what he said. As long as he had faith in me, I could do anything. A week or so later, I got a letter from my mother, and in it she referred to me and Caw as "a love affair." I don't know why this should bother me, but the phrase "love affair" has dirty connotations to me. Like in all the dirty books, they talk about "love affairs." I don't know why, but the phrase just bothered me to death. So I was very annoyed by my mother's letter. There were two pages of idle gossip, and then, "You're putting a lot of pressure on your father, and I want you to know we don't condone your love affair. We think in the long run you will be sorry for this unfortunate affair."

Well, I tried to ignore the letter. The last thing I wanted to do was hurt my parents. Especially I didn't want to hurt my father, and it troubled me that my mother said I was putting a lot of pressure on him. But there was no other way. I had to live my own life.

Three weeks later I got a call from my parents, and one thing led to another, and pretty soon I blurted out that I was going to marry Caw. My mother begged me not to do anything till they could talk to me. She said she'd buy me a Porsche 914 if I would just hold off, and I said, "Fine." But in my heart I knew I was not bound by a bribe like that. They begged me not to do anything until they could come out and see me, and I agreed.

For the next few days, my brother got into the act. He pretended to have business in Collegeville, and he stayed at the motel near The College, and he put a tremendous amount of pressure on me. I was a nervous wreck, with his phone calls and all. He would call me and say, "How's the nigger?" One night he came over and had a few drinks with me, and when he was all tipsy, he said, "That black bastard better stay in line, because if he doesn't, we're gonna kill the son of a bitch."

Right at the start of spring vacation my parents arrived. I had moved in with Caw to spend the holidays with him. I didn't see any sense in lying about it. I didn't want to hurt my parents, and I knew that this would hurt them, but I figured it was better for them to know the whole truth. I hate hypocrisy. I loved Caw and I wanted to stay with him, to sleep in his bed, so I did.

I went over to my room in the dorm to meet my parents, and before they had been there five minutes my mother said, "Jenny, your bed doesn't look like it's been slept in."

I said, "Mom, I'd rather not discuss where I'm sleeping."

She said: "Let's go out to dinner!"

I said, "Well, I'd like to, but I have a lot of things to do, so I can't stay too long. I have to meet Caw." Which I knew would hurt them, but I felt my alliance was as much with Caw as with them. So we went to dinner, and it was *not* pleasant. My father said nothing to me but snide remarks. He and my brother would be snickering behind their hands. I said something about maybe getting a teacher's certificate, in case the vet school didn't work out, and my father said something like, "What the hell's the difference? The way you're living your life, you're not gonna amount to anything anyway." There were remarks like that all through the dinner. When I finished my dessert, I slammed my chair back, and I said, "Well, I have to go see Caw. Goodbye!"

The next day I met my parents and my brother at the motel. My mother said, "I don't like the way you're flaunting this thing in front of me."

I said, "What do you mean?"

She said, "Living with him while we're here."

I said, "Mother, do you want me to be a hypocrite and put up a big front and try to deceive you? Wouldn't you rather see me as I really am?"

My mother said, "No, I wouldn't. I don't like what you've become."

"Well," I said, "You can go on thinking that I'm pure and white and that I do everything exactly the way you would do it. Go ahead and deceive yourself."

She said, "Well, it's not easy to deceive myself when

you're living with that big buck nig——" She caught herself. She put her hand on my arm. "Let's not argue anymore," she said. "We'll straighten this whole thing out together. Don't worry, dear."

They announced that they wanted to meet Caw, and we decided to set up a big confrontation. They rented a double room at the motel, and we were to meet there the next day. I told Caw all about it, and he said it was fine with him. I begged him to be on time, because he has a bad habit of being late, and he said he would be there five minutes early.

I arrived first, and then my brother came in, and for a while it was just him and me. He said, "I hope you know what you're doing to mom and dad. You're gonna drive dad to a heart attack, and you're gonna turn mother into an alcoholic." I thought, My God, remember when you got gonorrhea and they both almost had nervous breakdowns? You've completely forgotten that now, haven't you? Isn't it comfortable that now I'm the bad one? But it also hurt me that he'd say something like that because I just love my parents so much, and the last thing I wanted to do was hurt them.

After a while my parents came in, and the four of us sat around making small talk. Pretty soon it was three o'clock, the time we were supposed to meet, and then it was five after, and ten after, and three fifteen and then it was three thirty, and dad said, "Well, Goddamn it, where *is* he?"

My brother said, "He probably runs on CPT."

"What's that?" I said.

"Colored People's Time," my brother said, and he and dad snickered again. I could have *died*. I was so hurt, but somehow I managed to ignore what they were doing. Then there was a knock at the door and Caw came in.

He was wearing a full-length robe, I think they call it a dashiki, and an African suede hat, and he was twirling a cane, and wearing sandals, and looking *so* cool. You can imagine the effect. He came in looking down on all of them. My father is six feet tall, and my brother's even taller, but Caw looked down on them like gnomes. Caw looked so regal, he looked like the king of an African tribe. Anybody with any real sense of values would have recognized that this was a *very* superior human being.

I looked around. Their eyes were bugging out. My brother's mouth hung open. I guess he thought maybe if things got bad, he could punch Caw in the mouth for violating his sister, but when he got a good look, he became very meek and docile.

Caw says, "How do you do, folks?" in this deep bass voice of his. He says, "I think I know who you are. I've heard so much about you. I'm Caw." He sticks out this hand the size of a frying pan, and then he says very nonchalantly, "Say, there's a football game on. I wonder if you all would mind if I just caught the second quarter on that TV set?" And without waiting for an answer, he turned on the set, got himself comfortable in the biggest chair in the room, and began watching. My parents sat goggle-eyed. I tried to give Caw a look, but he was watching the game intently. My brother's mouth still hung open. My father looked like he was gonna have a heart attack right in front of us.

After about five minutes, Caw turned to my father and he said, "How about that, dad? Wouldn't you like to watch the game? It's a great game!" My dad started to shake his head no, but when Caw kept staring at him, he moved over and watched a little, and when he thought Caw wasn't looking, he'd give me these evil, awful looks. My mother stayed on the sofa, and she kept looking at Caw sideways, but she wouldn't look straight at him—I guess she was afraid she'd turn to stone. I mean, how can you look directly at somebody who's not human? She'd glance all around the room, as though she was studying the decor, or looking out the window, and on the way she'd let her eyes rest on Caw for about a fifth of a second. Dad's sitting very rigid watching the game, and I'm going crazy. I must have smoked close to a pack of cigarettes—and I don't smoke!

Caw was the centerpiece, cool and calm as can be. The only thing he said for about fifteen minutes was, "Well, this game is exciting. We'll just have to wait till half-time to talk, right, Mr. Scott?" My father grunted something.

I thought I would come completely unglued. I was just shaking. I was ready to kill Caw.

After about ten minutes more, my mother said, "Eh, Mr. White, we do have quite a few things to ask you." Caw didn't even turn his head from the game.

"Yeh," he said. "I'm sure you do." He turned back to the game.

I'm sitting there saying Hail Marys, the first time I've prayed in five years, because I needed all the help I could get. Thank God, half-time came. I got up and turned off the set, and for about ten minutes—well it was probably a minute, but it seemed like ten—not a word was spoken. Caw just sat there taking everything in, looking from one to another, smiling, Mr. Cool McCool himself.

Finally my mother said, "Well, Caw, where are you from?"

"Hazard. Kentucky," Caw said. "Po' folks' country."

"And what are you studying?"

"Well, I hope to study medicine, but if I don't make that, I'll try music. I just take things slow and careful, see what happens."

They asked him where he got his name Caw, and he explained very slowly, as though he were talking to idiots, that his full name was Calvin Andrew White, and his initials were C.A.W., and that's how he got the name. "You understand?" he said, and my parents nodded.

Then my brother asked a few smart-alec questions, but Caw fielded them perfectly. What none of my family realized was that Caw can out con my father and out bullshit my brother; he can handle them both the way he handles a basketball.

After a while they had a little debate about big business, and Caw told my father that most of the big American corporations were rapacious, which you just don't say to my father. My father jumped in and said that his own corporation was huge, but it certainly wasn't rapacious, because it contributed to urban welfare and all sorts of public projects. "Well, that's cool," Caw said. "But that doesn't keep them from being rapacious."

I jumped in and changed the subject. We began talking about race, and my father kept saying how liberal he was, how he had nothing against the colored race—that's what he called it, and I could just cringe because I knew Caw hated the word "colored"—and my father kept saying this over and over in different ways. He actually said, "Why, we even had one to dinner in the executive dining room." Caw was taking all this in and not saying anything.

"No, sir," my father said. "Never think for a second that I hold your race against you."

Caw said, "Well, that's mighty good to hear, Mr. Scott. I'll never think it for a second."

My father said, "But I don't understand one thing. Why are you so willing to take on the added problem of having a white girl friend, with all the other problems you people have?"

"I don't follow you," Caw said.

My father said, "Why don't you just make life easier for yourself by going with a colored girl?"

I kept waiting for Caw to say that he loved me, and that he intended to marry me, and that was why he was going with me, but instead he kept coming back with logical arguments, like we're all the same under the skin, and we should be color blind, and people should go with each other regardless of race. He threw in the Constitution and the Bill of Rights, and several quotations from Montaigne and Max Lerner, and he cited the cases of friends who had married white girls and had fine relationships.

It kept going around and around, so to show my true feelings, to show everybody exactly where I stood, I walked over and sat on Caw's lap, and I told my parents and my brother that they might as well know the whole truth, which was that Caw and I were going to get married very soon. There was dead silence. Finally my mother said, "Jenny, would you mind going out to get me a package of cigarettes?"

Now this didn't catch me by surprise, because earlier my mother had asked me, "Do you think Caw will have any inhibitions about talking to your father and me alone?" And I had said, "Of course not." I'd talked it over with Caw, and we'd agreed that they might try to get him alone to threaten him, or maybe even to buy him off. And Caw and I agreed that if they tried to buy him off, we would take the money and run. So I was ready for my mother's little trick.

I went out and got her some cigarettes, and I deliberately stayed away for almost an hour. When I came back, they were all sitting there calmly, and I could tell by the way they were talking that nothing exciting had happened. I was surprised about that, but then I realized that they must have gotten to know how much character Caw had, and that they must have realized that they didn't dare offer him money. We made small talk for a few minutes, and then Caw and I got up. "Thanks for a lovely afternoon," I said, and went away congratulating myself on how well everything had gone.

When we got out of earshot, I said, "Quick! What'd they say?"

Caw said, "They didn't say nothin'. We just sat there and talked football and stuff like that."

"So everything's okay?" I said.

"I guess so," Caw said.

Well, that was a month ago, and it's been a very strange month. Something weird is happening. Caw and I still see each other, sometimes we study together, sometimes we sleep together, but it's just *not* the same. Our relationship has become much less intense. He seems so preoccupied with his studies, and I respect that because I know college is tough for him.

The main problem, I think, is that Caw's just too much of a ladies' man to be tied down to one girl. I see him looking at other girls all the time, and he'll say something to me like "Look at that chick! She really struts it, don't she?" And once or twice I've seen him in deep conversation at the café with white girls. Nothing special, but it's just a feeling I have. I feel that as much as Caw and I love each other, nothing is going to come of it. He's just too oriented to other women.

There *are* men like that. They just can't be satisfied with one woman, sexually or otherwise. They can love lots of women at one time. Caw just *loves* women. I mean, he just *adores* them, and vice versa. It's a huge attraction between him and every other woman on earth. Well, it wouldn't have made a very good marriage anyway, because I've got to feel that my husband gets everything he needs from me, and not just part of it.

Lately I've been remembering a few things that happened when we first started going together. Like I had to break him loose from another girl—he kept right on seeing her till I put my foot down. And I've suspected him of going with others since then. He's just too damned attractive to other women. They mob him. They send him notes. They're always trying to get to him, and I've had to tell him, "Look, *forget* those other women. It's got to be me *all the way,* or forget it." And he says, "Okay, baby," and then I see him on the campus with some blond-haired chick backed up against a wall, laying his line on her.

The other day I made him promise that when he steps out on me for the first time, he'll tell me. Well, he hasn't told me yet, but I can feel it coming. I said, "Caw, the first time you go out with another chick, you let me know, and I'll let *you* know that we're finished. When you do that, it'll all be over."

He said, "Cool, baby, cool. I'll let you know."

It'll be any day now, I know. I'm ready. It'll hurt me, but I'm preparing myself emotionally. Caw and I will always be a beautiful memory, but I'll get over it, and I'll have these beautiful, beautiful memories to console myself. It'll tear me up, but I'll never forget, and I'll never say I'm sorry.

CARROLE D'ANGELO, 28
Senior, Performing Arts

HAMLET. Ay marry; why was he sent into England?
FIRST CLOWN. Why, because he was mad: he shall recover his wits there; or, if he do not, 'tis no great matter there.
HAMLET. Why?
FIRST CLOWN. 'Twill not be seen in him there; there the men are as mad as he.

Hamlet, Prince of Denmark. Shakespeare

Riva Ronson says:

I took a couple drama courses with Carrole D'Angelo, but I can't honestly say that I know her. Nobody does. Like wow! she's *so* far out! I mean, she doesn't do really overt things, but there's a look in her eye, kind of faraway. I mean, like: You *know* that she's a little different from the rest of us. But what the .fuck—we *all* are! So welcome to Carrole D'Angelo! Welcome to the crazy campus of the crazy college. We're all nuts here; how can you tell one nut from the other? One thing about it: If you're really weirded out—and Carrole D'Angelo is *really* weirded out—well, The College is the place to be.

Intellect is everything. I worship at the shrine of intellect. When I was a child I never saw anything else. Both my parents are brilliant. My father deals in art, and he's known internationally. My mother is an MD. They're the kind of people who play chess and bridge instead of watching TV. When I was growing up, the typical conversation was about ten miles over my head, and I don't think I really ever caught up.

In high school I took stock of myself one day, and I didn't like what I saw. I was pleasing my parents, pleasing my friends, pleasing my teachers, and I wasn't pleasing myself. My IQ was only 125, and I was always ashamed about that. Music seemed to be the only thing that I really enjoyed, but I was working like a slave to keep my other grades up. I had almost nothing to do with boys, except for one boy who had an IQ of 160, and I was too nervous even to talk to him. When he finally said something to me, I was up all the next night, half asleep, half awake, so pleased to have exchanged any words with him. I still remember two questions he asked me: Do you believe in free love? Do you believe in mercy killings? I was thrilled! I told him I didn't know what free love was, and I didn't know if I believed in mercy killings, and then I collapsed in nervous giggles.

I was really an awful person in those high school years, and I'll always feel guilty about it. I was completely self-centered and hypocritical, egoistic. I cared about nothing but my own self, my own needs. When I realized that I was getting good grades to impress others with my intellect, I stopped getting them, and then my younger sister stepped in and started getting all the attention. Around our family, she began to outdo me. She became the bright and witty and intelligent one, and I couldn't stand it, and I hated her, and it's still slightly that way.

I made a fakery out of myself. I believed only in me, above everybody else, and I wanted to be prettier, smarter, better, stronger than the others. It was all for self, for personal vanity. I attached terrible importance to appearance. I spent my money on clothes, to create this big image. And all the time my sister was moving in on me and excelling in the things that really mattered in my family: intelligence, knowledge, accomplishment, and she took the play away from me.

In my senior year of high school my average was a C, but my parents had a lot of influence, and they got me into Mount Holyoke, which is one of the finest schools in the United States, and not an easy one to get into. I was thrilled, but it didn't take me long to realize that Mount Holyoke was a mistake. I felt so intellectually inferior. I just wasn't bright enough for Mount Holyoke.

I wanted to be a writer, or something in the arts, but I had too much trouble keeping my grades above the probation level. I was doing too much work for too little results. And I had no social life. One of my classmates told me that I unwittingly drove men away because I was too bright. Imagine! I had to laugh. At the time, I was about to be put on academic probation. Then I fell in love with someone who loved me less; I can't tell you the details, because my shock treatments wiped it all out later. I don't even remember the boy. But I know I loved him. I think he played guitar. I don't think we had any dates. I think I just looked at him, but he didn't look back.

One day I just said goodby to Mount Holyoke, and I went as far away as I could: to San Diego. I loved that town! It's air-conditioned, and the people are easygoing, and there's a genuine artistic impulse. Unfortunately, it took me awhile to find this out. At the bus station I met a man named Hogan Whitley, and I was thrilled when he seemed to take an interest in me. He was about thirty years old and I was only eighteen, but he was so sweet and pleasant that I allowed myself to be led to his apartment. I was dying to enter the artistic mainstream, and I pulled out my pastels and started to work on a portrait of Hogan. Then he borrowed my paints and did a quick landscape with a lake and evergreens, and it was *awful,* it was phony, my little sister could have done it, but I didn't want to insult him. Anyway, he was nice.

The next day I went out to look for a job, and when I came back to the apartment it was empty except for the basic furniture. All my paints were gone, my jewelry, my typewriter, my guitar. Hogan was standing there and he said very calmly, "I hocked all the stuff today," and handed me the pawn ticket. I yelled something, but I forget what. I didn't have much of a vocabulary in those days, so I probably just hollered something like, "You cad, you!" I went to the pawn shop and unhocked everything, and brought it all back to the apartment. I told Hogan that if he hocked it again I would go to the police.

That night, I was walking around town, seeing the

sights, when I met another man in the Plaza. He told me he was selling encyclopedias to put himself through a theological seminary, and I found his story very interesting. We made a date to meet the next night, and then I went back to Hogan. Hogan and I slept together, and it was my first sexual experience with a man. The next night I went out with Kennard, the theological student, and ended up sleeping with him. When I went back to the apartment, Hogan asked me what I'd been doing, and little by little he wormed the whole story out of me. He looked repelled and repulsed. He said, "Now I wouldn't touch you with a ten-foot pole!"

Looking back, I don't know exactly why I lost my virginity this way. I just don't know. Maybe it was simply a case of the opportunity presenting itself. I hadn't had many opportunities in high school or at Mount Holyoke. So when handsome men presented themselves twice, I went to bed with them twice. In two nights.

Anyway, I had a big fight with Hogan, and moved into a place of my own. I got a job in one of those instant cleaning and laundry shops that cater to the sailors who come into the port. I still hadn't met any genuine artist types, but one day I was walking near the post office when I saw what looked to be a mob of people wearing my kind of attire: berets and sandals and easygoing clothes. They were carrying signs, and I saw that they were protesting the arrest of some people who had put on a peace demonstration. When I found out what was going on, I was exhilarated. I had already been to a few peace meetings, but I had never done anything actively on my own. The kids around the post office told me they were going to sit in, and I asked them if I could join them, and they welcomed me. I was flying! I was ecstatic. Everybody was beautiful, everything was beautiful, life was a wonderful thing, and I loved the world! Maybe this is the manic state, I don't know. Maybe I was clinically insane, I don't know. But I felt wonderful at the time. For one of the few times in my life, I felt that I was a part of mankind, and that I was doing something genuinely worthwhile.

After a few hours the police came, and they announced that we would have to clear out or go to jail. I really didn't know what to make of this; I was still so manic. Everybody started telephoning to see if they could raise bail money in advance, so I put in a collect call to my mother in Detroit. I told her that I was demonstrating for my ideals, and I said there was a chance I would be arrested, and I asked her if she would back me up. The answer was no. My mother acted as if it was an outrage, as if I had a terrible nerve to ask her such a thing.

After a while the cops took us to jail. There were eight of us girls in a cell. To me it seemed like a Hilton hotel because we were there for a good reason. We were comrades together, and I was so happy to be able to do something positive about my beliefs.

Well, all my real troubles began in court. I knew that we would be charged with loitering, but I couldn't figure out whether I was guilty of loitering or not. I felt exactly like Socrates. My answer was simply, "I don't know."

We were all brought into court together, and I was amazed to see my mother sitting in the front of the courtroom. One by one the girls went up and pleaded guilty and paid little fines and were released. When it was my turn, the judge said, "You are charged with loitering. How do you plead?"

I said, "I don't know."

The judge said, "Well, you'll have to plead one way or the other."

But I had thought it all out, and I realized that my plea could not be other than "I don't know." Because *I didn't know!* How could I say guilty or not guilty, when I didn't know?

The judge said, "Now, come, come, young lady. We must have a plea, one way or the other. Either you're guilty or you're not guilty. Now which is it?"

I said, "Judge, I honestly don't know. Nobody knows what truth is. Nobody can say something is so or it is not so. You are making a personal accusation against me, that I loitered, but I can't tell you whether I was loitering or. not, and neither can anybody else. Was I loitering? *I don't know!"*

It's funny, I remember those exact words, and yet I remember so little of everything else. I do know that I had carefully premeditated my position; I wasn't being psychoneurotic or neurotic or psychotic. I was telling the court *exactly* what I believed. My courtroom behavior was impeccable. I didn't raise my voice or create a scene. I simply kept saying, "I don't know." I was in a very high state of mind, euphoric, exalted by the fact that it was me against the power of the state, and I was holding my ground. But I don't think that my euphoria showed in my behavior, except that maybe my eyes were a little brighter than usual.

I don't know exactly what happened in the courtroom after that, but my friends tell me that in a case like mine the judge would automatically enter a plea of not guilty on my behalf. I guess that's what happened. Anyway, I was found guilty of loitering, and I vaguely remember being in the judge's chambers with my mother. They were talking about my need for psychiatric help, and I didn't mind a bit. I was very interested in psychology, and I thought the whole process could be interesting. This was the beginning of the trap, but I didn't realize it.

I was on one year's probation, in care of my mother. Doesn't it all remind you of Russia today? In Russia, if you speak out for your political beliefs you wind up being judged a mental case. That's the way it used to be in the United States, and maybe it still is, for all I know.

Anyway. my mother brought me back home, and a few days later she took me to see a psychiatrist who was seventy-five years old if he was a day. We talked for a while and he asked me why I'd been demonstrating, and I told him. He looked puzzled, as though he couldn't understand my behavior, as though anyone who sat in or demonstrated had to be crazy, *prima facie.* Nowadays you can sit in and demonstrate and throw rocks and raise all kinds of hell and they just think you're a little bit ahead of your time intellectually, but ten years ago it was proof of insanity.

I just couldn't relate to this old duck, I really couldn't relate to *anyone* at that stage of the game. I was going through life with a consistent set of thoughts in my head, but these thoughts had very little to do with everyday reality, so maybe I would appear disoriented to anyone, and maybe I *was* disoriented. I know I was heavy into philosophy, but in a childish way, the way a lot of kids are when they first get involved in it. Metaphysics becomes the world; you'd rather read Schopenhauer than Pearl Buck, and you think it's terribly important to figure out how many angels can dance on the head of a pin, and the meaning of meaning. You get over this stage, all young students do, but I hadn't yet, and I know I must've sounded strange and disoriented to this old psychiatrist.

But I also know I didn't belong in a mental hospital, and I was shocked to hear him tell my mother that I was going to have to be put away. I burst out crying, and I'm not much of a crier. I'm not a tough egg, but I'm a cold egg. Commitment to a mental hospital was totally unacceptable and unbelievable to me. I'm sure I was aberrant by the doctor's standards and my mother's, but I certainly wasn't nuts.

Believe me, it's a terrible shock when something like this happens to you. They drove me to the hospital and I cried all the way. I couldn't assimilate the idea that my own mother would help to put me away. I have no memory whatever of going into the hospital, being assigned to a ward, getting treatment, or anything like that. My mother told me later that I was in for three weeks, total. That's all I know.

When I got out of the hospital, I began a period of wandering around, trying to find myself, trying to forget what had happened. I felt that I was under an evil star, and I hated to stay in one place for very long, for fear that someone would pick me up and recommit me. For a while I lived in Chicago, but winter came and it was even worse than Detroit, so I took a bus east to Boston. I loved Cambridge, and I audited a couple of courses at Harvard, but then I began reading about all the wonderful things that were happening in Greenwich Village: the flower children, the peace movement, the first beat-niks and hippies; and I packed my bags and went out to the highway to hitch. What a start! I was standing there hitching, and the first car that stopped to pick me up got hit by a second car, and I panicked and ran into the fields. Hitching was technically illegal, and I didn't want to be arrested and put back in the hospital. Every-thing I did was aimed at not going back to the hospital. I called a cab, and went to the bus terminal, and took a bus into New York.

I moved right into that crazy scene of Greenwich Village, but I lived a completely withdrawn life. I don't really understand why. I'd come to New York to meet all these wonderful arty types, but now I was afraid to say hello. I sublet a single room and worked as a waitress. I went to art galleries and museums. I had absolutely no friends. I was neither happy nor unhappy, I just existed. I read, I listened to music on my radio, I walked the streets, but mostly I sat in my room. Life dictated to me; I didn't dictate to life. I took what came along, and I kept to myself. No, this wasn't normal. I realize that now.

One day I got a telegram. My parents were coming to visit me. I had about one week to get ready, and I used that week to rush out and make three friends, so that I would look more normal to my parents when they arrived, so that they wouldn't send me back to the hos-pital. The big day arrived, and I went back to my room-ing house to wait for them, but I'd forgotten my keys and I was sitting on the front steps waiting, and I began sort of daydreaming. I saw an ambulance pull up, and I saw myself put into it, and then I saw myself carried into a white room, and then I felt a needle enter my spine; and then I woke up and it was nighttime and my mother was standing by my bedside. I was in a hos-pital. The daydream was real.

I asked my mother what had happened, and she said I must have fainted on the front steps. When they'd found me I was lying at the foot of the steps with a big bump on my head, unconscious. I've since realized that I was suffering from some kind of terrible tension and disorientation over the fact that my parents were coming, and it had simply overpowered me.

The next morning I was transferred to the mental ward, and for the first time I realized that I was in the famous Bellevue. It was my mother's doing. Or maybe I had done something irrational, I don't know. Maybe I cursed my mother, or something like that. I have a vague memory of a psychiatrist asking me some questions, and I pulled the sheet up over my head, and he said something about, "Only ostriches stick their heads in the sand," so that was probably the turning point. But there might have been much more, I just don't remember. Anyway, I was put in the mental ward.

I had never seen a rat in Detroit, but now I saw plenty. The ward was overcrowded, and patients slept on cots in the hall. You stood in line for your food. Cockroaches were everywhere. At night I'd sit on my bed and watch the rats begin their nightly rounds. They were big, long, thick-bodied things, and I was fascinated by them. It was like watching a circus.

My poor mother brought me candy and things like that. She stood by me. She did all she could do. I couldn't figure out what was wrong with me, or why I was in the mental ward. I remember one day saying to myself, "God? Are you playing a joke on me? Is that what this is? A big horrible joke, and I'll wake up? And I'll laugh, too?"

After a few more days, my mother and father brought my clothes, and we flew back to Detroit, and I was put into the same private hospital that I had been in for three weeks before. This time I stayed for three months, but I don't remember anything that happened there. Maybe they gave me shock that time, maybe they didn't. I don't remember.

After I got out of the hospital, my parents suggested that I go back to college, but I still felt dubious about the whole thing. I was really looking for *la vie Bohème*, but anyone who has been to Detroit knows that *la vie Bohème* just doesn't exist there. So I wandered over to Ann Arbor, the university town, and I began to meet a few intellectuals. Then I woke up one morning and found myself married to a sculptor. He was about ten years older than me, and not actually good looking, and there was absolutely no physical attraction, but I admired his intellect and his talent. That was enough, or so I thought at the time.

We moved into a little cottage just outside of town, and for a while it was idyllic. I would stand and look over his shoulder while he worked, or I would model for him. When his friends came around to drink and talk, I sat in the corner like a little idolator, and kept my mouth shut.

My husband had a drinking problem, concealed at first, but little by little getting worse. When he drank, he became enraged, and he would lash out at whatever was close. Usually that was me. One night after I had gone to bed, I heard him stomping around the house, and then I heard glass breaking, and I found out that he had thrown a lamp through the front window. I'd never encountered such personal violence, but I told myself that he was drunk and everything would be all right when he sobered up.

But everything was *not* all right. We began having big fights over nothing. We had a battle royal over what kind of milk to buy. He hated the fact that I smoked, and we had a big fight over that. After a while I realized the simple truth: I just didn't like him. Sometimes I got pretty hateful in the arguments, and sometimes I called him some vicious names, but I wasn't acting psychotic. Not at all. I'd had enough of mental hospitals, and I knew that what was troubling me was not my mental condition, but my repulsive husband.

One night we had the battle of battles, and I drank almost a whole bottle of Scotch, which is very unlike me, since I'm not much of a drinker. At one point I found myself going after him with a pair of scissors, but it was only to scare him. I had no intention of doing him any bodily harm. He backed into a corner and told me to quiet down, and began talking to me the way you talk to a psycho. I threw the scissors down and went into the bedroom.

The next morning my mother showed up at our cottage. She said, "I thought it would be nice if you and Marty and I went on a little shopping trip in Detroit. Wouldn't that be nice?"

I said, "Fine with me."

On the way into town in my mother's big car, she happened to mention that Aunt Marguerite was in the hospital, and she suggested that we all go see her, to cheer her up. "Fine with me," I said.

Once we got inside the hospital a couple of big attendants took me by the arm and I was put in the locked ward. When I realized what was happening I went berserk. I had been in the hospital twice before, and both times I had been in just as good mental shape as anybody else, but this time the cure brought on the disease. When they locked that door behind me, I didn't care anymore. I was nothing but trouble for the attendants. I'd throw the dishes. I'd yell and they'd have to lock me in my room. I'd shout obscenities, words that would never have entered my mind normally. I really acted crazy. Maybe I *was* crazy at this point.

After a few days in the hospital they began giving me EST, electric shock therapy. I couldn't understand why, and that's when I *really* began acting insane. They'd strap me up and give me a shot of sodium pentathol, and seven seconds later they'd turn on the electricity and shoot all this voltage right through my brain. At first I was frightened, but then I realized that it really didn't hurt, and I calmed down. But then one day they didn't give me enough pentathol, and I regained consciousness in time to look down and see my feet quivering. The electricity was going through me! I heard someone say, "Give her more pentathol!" and then I blacked out again. After that I was always afraid that this would happen, so I was terrified of EST. I wouldn't sleep all night if I knew the treatment was coming the next morning. They'd come in and give me medicine to dry my mouth, to keep the electricity from burning my mouth, and they'd put these awful electrodes on my head, with some gooey stuff to make it work better, and I just shook and trembled through the whole thing.

Well, this is supposed to help you become normal, but I'll never understand how. The main thing it does is wreck your memory. I've had to regather all my memories since then, and a lot of them haven't come back. They never will come back.

All during this treatment I was indistinguishable from a genuine lunatic. For two or three weeks I was convinced that my mother had assassinated President Kennedy. I figured it out by cryptanalysis. I compared my mother's handwriting, and the number of letters in her name, and the mileage from Detroit to Dallas, things like that, and I proved that she was the murderer.

Sometimes I was just plain violent, trying to fight everybody. I had to be restrained, or brought into padded rooms and tied to a bed. Sometimes the attendants were cruel. One day they tied me down in a bed with one arm under me, and the blood pressure built up in that arm until it was agonizing, and then when the pain was at its height, they yanked the restraints off and gave me a shot in that same arm. It was unnecessary cruelty. There's a line some place in Tennessee Williams to the effect that the only inexcusable thing is deliberate cruelty. Exactly!

My relations with my fellow patients were never good. There was one old lady whom I respected because she had an interesting face and she looked to be above the average patient in intelligence, but just when I'd start to get close to her, she'd go into a spell where she didn't know what she was doing. She'd walk around in a daze, and she'd wander into my room and start putting everything in order. This got on my nerves. I think I took it as an insult. I asked her to please stop it one day, and when she didn't answer me, I did the cruelest, the most animal thing I've ever done. This little old lady was barely five feet tall, and I picked her up and threw her out into the hallway as hard as I could. She landed on her head, and she could have been dead, and all of a sudden I was scared. She turned out to be okay. She got up and walked away as if nothing had happened.

After I'd been in the hospital for almost a year I went into a period where I became emotionally attached to some of the male attendants and then to a few patients. There was a fourteen-year-old boy who shared the day-room with me, and be began to look much older than his years. One night I was upset about something, and I asked the nurse for a shot, and she gave me a little too much sedative, and I felt sick. I got out of my bed and walked down the hall to the men's sleeping area, and I walked to the bed of my fourteen-year-old friend, and I said, "Bill, I think I'm going to faint."

He said, "Sit on my bed." I sat down and one thing led to another, but never anything but mouth contact. That was terrific as far as I was concerned. But the next day I saw him in the dayroom, and he said, "Forget that it happened."

A little later I noticed this handsome boy, maybe fifteen or sixteen years old. He used to sit in the dayroom and tap his feet, as though he were impatient. I would sit across from him and tap my feet exactly the way he did, to put us in touch. It wasn't talking, but it was communication with a fellow human.

One day I was walking down the hall, and this boy suddenly grabbed me, and it was almost like an attack. He said, "Kiss me, Carrole!" And he began making mouth contact with me. Then he let me go and ran. It bothered me for quite a while, the violence of it.

When the doctor said that my condition had improved, who should start showing up on visiting days but my dear husband. Now I want to be honest about this. I'm perfectly willing to accept the idea that I was mentally ill, although I'm not sure that I was as mentally ill as they thought I was, and I suspect that it was the treatment that was causing my worst troubles. I'm not prepared to argue that I didn't need help. But I wasn't *completely* hallucinating, and I'm not completely hallucinating now when I remember the things my husband did to me in the hospital.

He'd sit on the end of my bed, and he would seem absolutely oblivious to anything I'd say, as though I didn't have to be listened to because I was crazy. He'd make passes at me, and when I'd resist he would act as if I was a silly schoolgirl. Like one night I told him he didn't appeal to me physically, and right away he reached over and grabbed me and started kissing me! It was as though I hadn't said a word, that my own feelings didn't matter.

Finally I told him to stop coming, that he was just upsetting me, retarding my cure. But he kept on coming. We'd fight from the minute he came in. It was crude, like a girl fighting off a masher. And yet he wouldn't stop.

One day the doctor told me that I could have twenty-four-hour leave in the custody of my husband, and I welcomed the opportunity. Anything was better than staying in this hospital day after day. Marty picked me up in the morning, and we began to walk into town. Well, this was my first trip outside in a year, and I wanted to see the city, I wanted to see the cars and the action. But Marty announced we were going to walk on a side street where it would be more quiet. When I complained, he actually started manhandling me to make me go where he wanted. "We're gonna walk *this* way!" he said. He had to have his own way! He wasn't treating me at all like somebody who's been in the hospital and needs patience and kindness. He was treating me like an animal.

Finally we got to his apartment, and I realized that I felt completely distant from him as a person. I tried to explain this to him, and I told him that I was seeking the free, untrammeled life of the soul, a free and easy beatnik way of existence that would satisfy me completely and forever. I told him that I would never again be interested in anything else.

He didn't like that at all. He couldn't accept a different life-style. He was an artist himself, but he abhorred the Bohemian life-style. When I told him that he should stop wearing the same dumb old tweed clothes all the time and smoking the same old dumb pipe all the time, he acted as if I was crazy. He said it wasn't how you looked, but what was in your heart. I said that how you look *reflects* what's in your heart. I told him he should wash his hair and let it hang naturally, and stop using greasy kid stuff and combing his hair straight back. He looked so out of it! He told me that the way he looked was none of my business, and he suggested I just keep my mouth shut.

A few months later I was released from the hospital, and I brought suit for divorce. It took seven months, but finally Marty realized there was no hope for our marriage. There were some papers submitted to the court by one of my doctors. and I got to look at them, and one of them said that I suffered from schizo-affective depression, whatever that is.

I moved back in with my mother and father and tried to regain my health. I had lost twenty-five pounds in the hospital and I was nothing but a bag of bones. I'd been in the hospital against my will, and one of my ways of getting back at them was to refuse to eat. Now my mother fed me some good food and put me on some vitamin supplements, and pretty soon I was my old self again, physically.

I hadn't thought about college in years, and then I heard a couple of speeches by the radical lawyer William Kunstler and a man named Rich Rothstein. Suddenly, I felt all my old socialistic ideals flowing back in me. I felt exactly as I had felt before the trouble in San Diego, except that I was in much better control of myself. I knew that everything Kunstler and Rothstein said was true, and I knew that I had to do something better than sit around my mother's house and eat her food.

I developed a plan in my mind. I decided on the person I wanted to become. I wanted to be a degree person, a person with a college degree, but I also wanted to be a non-degree person, a person who takes life easy, and rides with whatever comes along. It's hard to explain, but I wanted to have a degree and yet live as if I didn't have one. I want the pride and the assurance of having a degree as a tangible sign of my worth, so I'll know I am somebody. Oh, it's all mixed up.

All I know is I wanted a degree after my name, even if I never used it. I wanted the world to know that I'm *somebody*, that I'm Carrole D'Angelo, B.A., or M.A. In the back of my mind I knew I wanted to earn the respect and admiration of people like William Kunstler, as well as the people below his level, the people with whom I would have to work for the rest of my life.

I also realized that college would help me restructure my life. It would give me certain places to be at certain times. It would force me to act in a disciplined manner, and it would give me an instant identity that no one could take away. The college would be a place where I could find myself again. I wanted to find the self that was—before I told the court "I don't know."

I enrolled in The College. At first it was strange, but after a while I realized that being a student is an assurance in social situations. My problem was that I hadn't been in social situations, and I didn't know how to handle myself as a completely independent person. So it was a relief to be able to say, "Oh, I'm a student." It gave me a frame of reference for myself.

Well, I've been here for three years now, and I'm just a few months away from getting my bachelor of arts degree. Socially, I've changed very little, but I think I've developed myself intellectually. I still have almost nothing to do with anyone, sexually or otherwise. I go for months without sex, and then suddenly I'm into bed with somebody, and this usually throws me for a loop, and then I abstain for months and months. It bothers me that I do that, and I don't understand it. I do know that I'm still emotionally immature—I'm emotionally about eighteen—because I've worked out so few things emotionally.

There's only one thing that I'm certain of: Nobody's gonna put me back in a hospital. You won't see me acting in an antisocial or strange manner. My awareness of the possibilities is very acute. I approach every stranger as someone who could put me back in the hospital.

I have my defenses up against everybody because *I'm not going back.*

It will always be a question in my mind: whether I would have wound up in a mental hospital anyway, or whether they should not have thrown me into the hospital that first time. I'll never know. I'm certain that I had mental troubles, no doubt about that. But were they bad enough for hospitalization? I think there are lots of people walking the streets who are in far worse shape than I was when I was first committed, but on the other hand I think I needed *some* kind of treatment. I don't think it hurt me. I think I'm the better for it. I hope so, anyway.

I do know that I have to keep my life simple, I have to keep it stripped to the essentials. I live in a small furnished room, with a pallet in the corner. I have a one-burner electric stove, and I do all my cooking on it. I eat no meat, no chemicals; I eat healthy food only. In a typical day, I'll have nothing but greens and vegetables. I don't take vitamin pills, because they're synthetic, and anyway I get vitamins in the greens and vegetables. The mainstay of my diet is raw cabbage and raw rice. I don't have much money, and my parents have stopped helping me, and I find the macrobiotic diet to be cheap and fulfilling. Macrobiotics means great life-giving; the word comes from the play *The Lower Depths* by Maxim Gorky.

I spend most of my spare time in the movies. I don't think of it as a dream world at all. The movies are no less real than life. I mean, who's to say? Maybe what's up there on the screen is as real as what's happening out here. Nobody knows.

I don't worry about the future, but if I had to announce my plans I would say that I live to find out *new* things. I want to live to think, and then to live according to what I derive from my thinking. I want to be free and live within the arts. The cinema has become the big thing in my life because it combines the three major arts of literature, graphics, and music, and I'd like somehow to work with film. Maybe I'll be a director, maybe I'll be a producer, maybe I'll collect tickets at the door. But I'll do *something* in film.

When I graduate I'll probably go out to Berkeley and take some courses there. Berkeley attracts me. I like the people there. They don't waste their time fooling-around the way these people do at The College. Berkeley people are involved in *everything,* and that's important to me, since I'm much older now and I have very little time. They do what they damn well want to, and I like that. What did I say? Oh, yes, I said, "They don't waste their time." Yes, that's right. There's a lot less wheel-spinning there, a lot less purely social roaming around. The people at Berkeley are less hypocritical with each other, and they say what they think. I went there last summer, and it was so free, so independent. You could *feel* the idealism in the wind. Everyone was so politically active. If they didn't like something, they marched, they demonstrated. I like that. They're direct and open and honest.

So I'll go there, and I'll take some courses, and I'll work out a plan for my life. Here's something by Paul Klee, from his diaries:

In the spring of 1901 I drew up the following program: First of all the art of life. Then, as ideal profession, poetry and philosophy. As *real* profession, the classics. And finally, for lack of an income, drawing illustrations.

That's the way I want to order my life, along lines like that, to lay it all out in advance and then follow it strictly. That's exactly the way I began adult life when I went to San Diego, and that's the way I'll continue it eventually.

I just got a little sidetracked.

RIVA RONSON, 20
Junior, Performing Arts

Laurel Milne says:

Riva concentrates so much on schoolwork and memorization, and for such *long* periods of time, that she has to space some other things out. Like she has to pretend that certain household chores don't exist. The other day I taught her how to leave the note for the milkman. She didn't even know that the note existed! She'd complain good-naturedly when we didn't have the right dairy products in the house. I guess she just thought the stuff came down from heaven and once in a while Jesus fucked up the order. So I showed her how to write the note and leave it in the bottle, and she was amazed. She said, "Oh, it's so *simple!*" She was relieved to find she could do it herself, in emergencies.

We finally got her doing a little cooking, but it still terrifies her. She's afraid the kitchen will eat her up; it's a menacing place to her. Once she took a pan of rice out of the refrigerator to reheat it, and then she forgot it was on the burner, and when she came back the whole kitchen was smoky. I asked her what happened and she said, "Oh, I just totally spaced it out, I guess. I got busy learning a part."

This spaciness can be worked out of her, I'm sure, especially since she's beginning to realize the problem herself. Like she's now beginning to get the idea that she *can* cook, she *can* clean up after herself, she *can* do her chores. We had a meeting on the subject the other night, and at first it must have been hard on her. Like I came out frankly and said, "Bonnie and I are making the place run, Riva. You've simply *got* to do your *full* share."

It made her feel shitty. She went right into the kitchen and did the dishes, and she dropped about three of them from nervousness, and Bonnie and I felt so bad, we went out and helped her. But that's wrong! That's treating her like a kid! Cute little spacy Riva, *anything* she does is cute and nice. That's a dumb attitude on our part.

Once I said, "We're not even sure you *like* living here," and that was a mistake.

Riva just bawled. "Don't *like* it here?" she said. "Why, this is the finest home I've *ever* had! Oh, how could you say a thing like that, Laurel?" She said that she'd been upset for a month, ever since I'd made some little offhand comment about moving away when I dropped out of school, and she said, "Oh, Laurel, I'd just *die* if you moved away. I love you so much!" Of course, that ended any possibility that I might move out. I mean, she needs me, I could never leave her. I mean, she's such a thoroughly *good* person, and she believes in the fundamental goodness of others. She never thinks bad of anyone. She's just an incredibly beautiful beautiful lovely lovely person who wishes the best for the whole world. I don't see how I could *ever* leave her. Whether she does the dishes or not. . . .

Bonnie Leblanc says:

Riva's a contradiction. As far as schoolwork's concerned she's the most mature of the three of us. She's a straight A student, 3.8, 3.9 average out of a possible 4.0. But in other ways she's the least mature. Like we had to talk to her about drugs. The only drugs she'd ever had were hash and marijuana, and she was dying to try chemicals like LSD, MDA, THC, DMT, but we were kind of scared to expose her to them, because it's scary enough to see her on grass. She gets *so* stoned! Amazing! Even on wine or beer—she gets completely ripped! She's quite capable of getting a contact high in a room where people have been smoking dope; she'll walk in, take two deep breaths, and fall to the floor in a fit of hysterical laughter absolutely out of control, and then she'll act real spacy. Imagine what would happen if we turned her onto something like Orange Sunshine! It might kill her, and we love her far too much to take any chance. Lately she's been talking about giving up everything like that, even grass. Normally I wouldn't recommend quitting—I mean, there's a lot of pure pleasure to be had in grass and hash and even psychedelics—but they're not for Riva. There's something inside her—I can't explain it—that makes them dangerous to her. Like she's unstable, or spacy, or something. I'm glad she's quitting; I hope she stays off for good.

You remember me, Riva Ronson, the spacy one? Bonnie and Laurel are my roommates, and they say I'm spacy, and they know me better than anybody, so I guess I must be. There are times when I wonder if it's the whole world that's spacy and I'm the only one that's A-straight. I mean, it's hard to figure. Am I weird, or are you fuckers out there weird?

I can tell you all you need to know about me in a few sentences. I'm a twin, and my twin brother is the meanest bastard on earth, even though I do love him in some ways. My parents—you can see them anytime in that painting by Grant Wood called "American Gothic." I've lived all my life in Collegeville Hills, and I'm just your typical suburban girl, clean-cut and wholesome and refreshing except that I smoke dope and fuck. I desperately want to be an actress, and I'm studying drama, ballet, speech, and a few asshole required subjects like French and English, and I also take private lessons on the recorder.

That takes care of the surface. Underneath the surface, I've got my troubles and my hangups, but I'm working on them. I'm just like Bonnie and Laurel; I love my parents, but they really fucked me over. Not that I blame them. They were fucked over themselves. Listen to this. My father had a leg shot off in Guadalcanal, not the whole leg, but two inches below the knee. This wouldn't be so bad; lots of guys had legs blown off. But the navy doctors were so sloppy about treating him; they left him in such pain that he's been a lifelong addict of drugs: Darvon, morphine, codeine. Mom would have to give him shots, and he'd get completely zonked. Oh, Christ, those were terrible Goddamned times. He'd completely weird out when he was punishing me or my twin brother. Like he'd shake his finger at me, then he'd thump me on the chest, and pretty soon he'd just weird himself out completely and go crazy and start hitting and hitting. Then he'd holler, "Don't you dare cry!" Sometimes the only way I could get out of it was to say, "I've got to go to the bathroom," and I'd run in there and lock the door and cry.

You can't know what it's like to be raised like that unless it happens to you. He was always either hurting or high, you know? Sometimes mom would have to drop all her housework and run the store for weeks at a time, while daddy was zonked out. You don't make a good living running a hardware store that way. I mean, if you concentrate on the job, you can have a successful operation, but all we ever had was a hand-to-mouth life because daddy was so fucked up that he really couldn't do a good job in the store. This seemed to affect him, and he'd act as though we were all looking down on him and thought he was trash, and then he'd try to make *us* feel like trash. He made me feel like a dummy from the day I was born. And naturally my twin imitated his father, and that made two people trying to make me feel like a jerk. I'd get all A's and one B on reports, and nobody would even mention the A's. They'd say the B showed how dumb I was. Like I had to take swimming lessons when I was about three, and after just a couple of lessons my father took me to the pool and insisted that I show him what I'd learned. Well, shit, I hadn't learned a fucking thing. I was scared to death of the water. But he had that funny gleam in his eye, and he said, "Go on, Riva, swim across the pool! You can do it!"

I just weirded out, and I wouldn't even jump into the water. Finally he said he would stay on the other side and catch me if I got in trouble. I jumped in the water, and I paddled madly toward him, and when I started to sink I held out my hands to grab him—and he backed away! I churned ahead another couple feet and grabbed for him, and he backed away again. This happened several times, until I finally went under and started inhaling water, and then he grabbed me and smacked me on the back a few times. When I was breathing okay again, he acted as though I smelled. He sat me on the edge of the pool, and he said, "Just sit there. Just be a lump." And he and mom and my brother Olin swam around and had a happy time. Do you understand that? I don't very well. Why did he treat me that way? I was just a little kid. It really fucked me up, you know? It was just an ungentle way to treat a kid.

Later on, I realized he was always turned on or in high pain, but I didn't realize anything when I was three. I just thought he hated me. That began a lifetime of avoiding him. Of course, there was one time when he couldn't be avoided: mealtime. Our suppers were really weird. If we'd accidentally knock something over, like a saltshaker, he's get uptight. He'd jerk us right out of our chairs, so the chair would topple over from underneath us, you know? And like sometimes he'd go just crazy beating us up. He'd wind up taking his belt off and lashing us on the tail. Then he'd scream at us, really lose control, and tell us not to cry, and hit us harder if we made a sound.

Everything was extremely uptight. Like it did weird things to my psyche. Like even when I was a little kid, I was paranoid, you know? I was always reading weird books, murders and mysteries and things like that, and watching weird mystery shows on television and in the movies. Ugh! I don't think I'll let my own kids do that.

My brother and I became the original Charles Addams monsters. We were so weirded out that we didn't do anything in a normal way. Like my brother would pee in a milk bottle and lean it against somebody's door, so they would get urine all over their rug when they opened it. Lovely things like that! We made little bombs out of .22 shells and matchheads and caps, and we'd throw them out in the street so cars would drive over them and the drivers would think they had a flat. Wow! They'd jam on their brakes and almost lose control, and it would weird them out completely. We also distributed tacks across the street, but we quit because it didn't produce many blow-outs. When we were about eight, we let all the air out of a neighbor's tires, and we were caught. Oh, shit! First my dad thumped us and then he whipped us. Then he made us take money out of our allowances to go buy rice, and he spread the rice in a corner of the kitchen, and he made us kneel on it. It doesn't sound like much of a punishment, does it? Well, try it some time! My knees were raw, and when the time was up, my father asked if it hurt. I said, "No, not much," and he made me go back and kneel on it for another hour. I was bleeding. I think I've still got some grains in my knees.

When my brother and I were around twelve, the whole thing got so bad that mom said we just had to do something. Up to then she'd been quiet. I'd never been able to understand why she wouldn't step in and keep my father from beating us, and I decided it must be weakness, she must be copping out just because she had to live with him. But later on, I realized that it must have been strength. Just think how much strength it would take to watch somebody you really love beat up somebody else you really love. What kind of choices do you have? Do you leave him, and wreck up the kids for good? And wreck him up too? The truth is, it's because of my mom that I'm not more wrecked up than I am. She had a difficult childhood herself. Both her parents were alcoholics, and they embarrassed her to death all through her childhood. It gave her a kind of strength. Even though she wasn't stepping in to stop my father, I knew I had mom to lean on. There were a lot of things I never told her. like the disgusting things my brother was doing to me, because they weirded me out so much, I didn't want anybody to know. But in the back of my mind, I knew that if I ever really needed mom, she'd be there.

She finally said that we couldn't go on like this. So we went to the Veterans Administration Hospital to talk to the doctor who was prescribing all the drugs that were fucking up my father's head. What a dumb thing to do, to go to see the very man who was causing the trouble! We should have gone to a psychiatrist, but my mom's pretty weird about shrinks and things like that. So the VA doctor said, "Well, I wouldn't worry about it. I was whipped till I got big enough to manhandle my mother. A little whipping never hurt a child." I thought, Wow! He was really trying to defend himself for what he'd done. He'd turned my father into a beast, and so he had to pretend that it was all very natural for my father to be that way. No big deal—it wasn't *his* knees that were full of rice.

Laurel Milne says:

Riva's parents are really awful, the awfulest. They're pure nineteenth-century, pure wheat-farm conservatives. They try to run her life; they won't let her loose from the stranglehold. What Riva needs is to go through a period of hating her parents and *admitting* it, like the rest of us, but instead she keeps on excusing them and pretending that she loves them dearly. They're so cruel, but she forgives them for all the shit they do to her. She says, "I *could* hate them very easily, yes, but I can understand why they do what they do. They can't help themselves," and all that bullshit. She'll go on and rationalize everything, and she'll say, "I really love them, and they really love me," and blah, blah, blah. And this keeps her hate down, keeps it under the lid of the boiler, just the way I used to do before I took my acid trip. This is a *very* dangerous procedure.

It's so hard to understand. I can't ever hate my father or blame him. There's no doubt that a lot of my mental fuck-ups come from the way he treated us, but there also were times when he was really good, really nice. I really liked him, I really love him a lot, and I really respect him, too. Like sometimes he'd be really loving, you know? And zip! He'd start to beat us up. But still I loved him. I remember doing things with him. He wasn't always tense, just most of the time. I remember sitting on his shoulders a lot. He'd carry me that way. I remember holding his hand in the park, things like that. No matter what happens, I'll still love him.

One good thing he did was keep us in the same house in the same neighborhood. Every now and then he and mom would get the impulse to move, but they'd always beat it down. There's a security that comes from staying in familiar surroundings, even when your whole life is fucked up. When your head is falling apart, when your family is disintegrating, when everybody you love is just totally fucked, it's nice to look around and see the same four walls and the same neighborhood. It keeps you from falling apart.

Laurel Milne says:

The first time I saw Riva perform, I couldn't believe it. She was such a different person, so *complete,* so *whole.* She walked out on the stage with this serious look on her face, and she said, "I'm Riva Ronson, and I'm going to do some selections from Dylan Thomas and Brendan Behan." She didn't seem to be talking loud, but her voice had real resonance, so different from her everyday voice. Like she was somebody else.

She recited beautifully, and I lived through every word with her. When she finished, everybody clapped real loud, and you could hear more clapping coming from the other performers backstage. She told me they pushed her back on for curtain calls, and she came out backward and all embarrassed. But she had such a happy little smile. It made me cry. And I felt good all over. The goodness in her just melted me, and I couldn't even talk for a long time. What an actress she'll be!

When I was in the seventh grade, I decided that I wanted to be an actress. It happened in a funny way. I was rooting around in the basement, in an old steamer trunk that my parents had, and I found some faded pictures of my father in a stage play. I really weirded out! I mean, who would ever suspect that this prosaic hardware store owner had ever wanted to act? I asked him about it, and he tried to shrug me off. Finally he said,

"Oh, I was in a couple of high school things, no big deal." But I could tell there was more to it than that. It's funny, you yearn to know *everything* about your parents, but you only find things out by accident.

One night I said, "Come on, dad, I know you must have been an actor. Tell me something from one of your plays." He'd had a few drinks, and probably a few pills, too, and his face was kind of red and glowing, and he stood up in the living room in front of me and mom and Olin, and he began this fantastic feverish delivery. I don't remember it exactly, but it was something like, "Willy was a salesman, boys, and for a salesman there's no rock bottom to the life. He don't put a bolt to a nut. He don't tell you the law or give you medicine. He's a guy way out there in the blue, living on a smile and a shoeshine. And when they start not smiling back, that's an earthquake. Nobody dast blame this man boys. Willie was a salesman. A salesman's got to dream. It comes with the territory."*

I just freaked out! The way those lines rolled out of him, the way his face assumed somebody else's face, the way his voice tones even changed. I knew instantly: He had *trained!* He had *studied!* And now he was running a fucking two-bit hardware store. How he must have ached!

My mother won't talk much about it, but she's let enough slip for me to put a few things together. My father was a very promising actor and it's all he ever wanted to be. After the war, he went back into acting, and he had some good parts in stock productions. One of them was the role of Uncle Ben in *Death of a Salesman*. But he was already on the morphine, he had trouble remembering lines, and rather than face the embarrassment, he just dropped out, married mom. and came back to Collegeville, his hometown. God, how it must have frustrated him! Sometimes I think that every thump on the chest, the whipping across our bare asses, was just

---

* Slightly misquoted and truncated from Arthur Miller's play *Death of a Salesman*.

my dad letting out his frustration. I don't blame him. I would have weirded out completely, you know?

I didn't know when I was a kid how sons try to imitate their fathers, as a sort of protective mechanism. I mean, if a son is afraid of a father, the best way to suck up to his father and get inside his father's protection is to be a little carbon copy. That's exactly what Olin did. Normally, twins are very close, but the only closeness Olin and I had was when we were little tiny kids. From about six or seven on, it was nothing but fighting. I mean really hair-raising fighting. The fights would start over ridiculous things, just absurd ridiculous things, you know? Like one time we were watching TV in the living room, and my brother brought in one cookie for himself and one for me. I ate it and I really dug it, so I went back into the kitchen to get another one, and as I reached up for it, he grabbed the bag out of my hand and he goes, "No!"

I said, "What do you mean, no? I want another cookie."

He goes, "No!"

I goes, "Why not?"

He goes, "Because you've had too many already. You're getting fat."

At that time, I was probably the thinnest I've been in my life. Like I was around five feet and I weighed about seventy-five pounds. So I tried to get the cookies from him and it just developed into one of the most phenomenal fights, you know? I wound up unconscious on the floor with a bloody nose. All I remember is kind of falling to the floor and him kind of running out the door real fast, looking real scared, and then I just kind of passed in and out for a while, I guess, you know?

He didn't seem to know how to act except hatefully. One day I had a friend over, and Olin walked up to me and tried to pick me up, only he did it by putting one arm under my chin and the other under the back of my head and hauling me out of my chair by my head. Ha-ha, some affection! God! He held me like that for a while, and I was struggling, but he was strong. I had a horrible cold in my nose, and I couldn't breathe. When I finally got loose, man, we started chasing each other around and fighting and just sick you know? Then he ran into the kitchen, laughing and sneering. Oh, he was—oh, he looked like a fiend, you know? I just *hated* him. Oh, did I hate him! I decided to kill him. So I grabbed a bread knife and I ran after him, but I just couldn't catch up, and I remember standing there in the middle of the living room looking at the knife in my hand and thinking, shit, this is sick. What a silly thing to do! But I'd have killed him if I had caught him earlier.

My friend Sally was there that day, and she tried to calm me down. I was in a state, you know? I mean I was catatonic. I was sick, insane, you know? I put the knife down and I can still remember the way I walked. My legs were stiff. I could hardly make my knees bend. My fists were doubled up tight. My shoulders were up around my ears. My teeth were clenched. I was snorting instead of breathing.

Sally just kept sort of gaping at me and telling me to settle down. She kept saying "You'll have a stroke! Just settle down. Settle *down!*" I was possessed with a sick, uncontrolled fury, and believe me, this happened regularly.

I remember another time when we were having a fight, and Olin picked me up and threw me into a chair, and he said, "If you make one move, I'll kill you!" I can remember the look on his face and it just drained everything out of my body. I couldn't have moved if I'd wanted to. He pulled out his pocket knife, and my sixth sense told me that he meant business. So he stood over me for maybe fifteen or twenty minutes, just staring, waiting for me to move so he could stick the knife in me, you know? Then he went over and turned the TV on, and I still knew that if I moved, he'd get up and kill me. I don't remember how it all came out, and anyway I can't describe the paranoia that went on in that house. I've suppressed a lot of it, you know? I do remember that he sat through a whole television program, maybe thirty minutes or an hour, and like I didn't move for the rest of that afternoon. I didn't move more than a few inches until I heard mom coming home, and then I just got up and walked away. I didn't say anything: I knew he would kill me if I did. He'd been staring at me like a fiend. He always looked like a fiend, like a demon. He wasn't human. And *I'm sure I looked exactly the same to him.*

Like I was thinking about the paranoia. In those days, I was horrified to be in the dark, and I don't mean scared, I mean *horrified*. Even up till like maybe my senior year in high school, it would take me hours to go to sleep. Every little noise I heard was somebody coming in to murder us all. I was even afraid to go into our cellar. I never, not *once* in my childhood, *never* went into that cellar slowly. I ran down the stairs and up the stairs at top speed, to get out of the dark. You know, that's sick! And one day I was thinking about that, and I remembered that Olin always did exactly the same thing. We were both paranoid. It's unfair of me to say he was cruel and I wasn't, because we both were. Like one time, it was during the day, we were having a really heavy fight. Oh, shit, it was a real motherfucker. We were in the kitchen trying to rip each other apart, and he ran to the head of the stairs, and I stuck my foot between his legs and I tripped him and I pushed him down the stairs. That's a really heavy thing to do to somebody. I could have killed him.

But of all the things we did, the cruelest was to tell dad on each other. Like I can still remember that the greatest thing in life was to catch my brother in a no-no. And then I'd go, "I'll tell dad on you." Like that was the worst thing we could do, far worse than throwing each other down the stairs, and whoever had been caught would go, "Oh, no!" and plead. But I'd allow him to suffer, you know? Never knowing whether I was really gonna tell dad or not, you know? And like he'd just cower in a corner, and I'd just enjoy it so much. That's a really sick kind of pleasure, but, well, both of us grew up just weirded out, battling.

*   *   *

I can remember complaining to my mom only once, and that was in junior high, and all she said was that I should try to understand Olin, that he had been through a lot of shit and that dad treated him far worse than he had treated me, because dad wanted him to be masculine. "You should try to understand both your brother and your father," my mother said. "Try to understand how horrible they must feel to do such horrible things."

So I looked at things this way until I left home, and I think that's what really scared me. Although there were times when I just felt like killing myself. I just felt like going down the garbage disposal and having somebody turn it on, you know?

Growing up like this, you begin to accept the abnormal as normal. I mean, if Godzilla had walked right through my bedroom, I'd have been terrified and I'd have weirded out, but at the same time I wouldn't have been completely surprised. Do you understand? Terror became a whole way of life. Like when I was about ten I had a bedroom of my own upstairs. That was about the time that dad was most heavily into drugs. Like, he'd come up from the store and mom would give him a needle because he wouldn't be able to stand the pain, and he'd go to bed. My brother and I weren't allowed to say a word. We weren't allowed to breathe. We couldn't talk, or watch TV.

Well, anyway, it was at that worst of times, and I woke up in the middle of the night and I was really thirsty, so I went downstairs to the kitchen to get a drink of water, and while I was walking across the dark living room, I heard this noise at the door, and I looked over and there was the shadow of a man and he was turning the doorknob trying to get in. Well, he piddled around, and I don't know how long I stood there, but I just stared at him in the dark. I mean I was scared to death, *but I wasn't surprised!* I thought maybe I should go get dad, but then I remembered that dad had said, "If anybody tries to get into this house, I'll shoot first and ask questions later." I knew dad would kill the man, and that would be a bummer; and I thought, well, the man could come in and kill us, but I didn't do anything about it.

I must have stood there watching him for four or five minutes, and then I went back upstairs and into bed to sleep. I don't have the slightest idea what happened after that. Did the man get in? I don't know. I never told my parents about it. Now I don't understand how I could be so horribly paranoid of the dark and yet so calm about somebody breaking into our house and maybe killing us. But I *was* calm. Like I remember my palms were very sweaty and when I went back to bed I made sure that I did it very quietly so the man wouldn't hear me or see me. But that's *all* I did. I didn't wake mom or dad.

I guess it's because my whole life up to then consisted of fright. Like seeing a shadow come across my room in the middle of the night, I'd get really freaked because I just *knew* it was a man, ready to come in and murder me. And when there was a *real* man at our door, it had become a commonplace to me. I'd been through it all before.

A few years later there was a horrible murder in our neighborhood. A father who lived down the street freaked out and killed his wife and his four children. He killed them with a knife, so they wouldn't wake up. And then he put a gun in his mouth and shot the top of his head off. Our family knew that family very well, and everybody was upset except me. I mean, I wasn't happy about it, but I took it right in stride.

That particular incident was *mild* compared to the stories I used to write in junior high, you know? I would turn them in and weird my teachers out. They were freak stories, just horrible. I've blocked most of them out, but I can remember one about this freaked-out man who murdered a bunch of men and then murdered his little brother and like he did it in the grossest way. He dis*membered* them. Oh, God, I don't want to think about it! It was just really a gross sick story, and then the next year I wrote some really weird awful stories about basically the same sort of thing. Whew! I was always writing these morbid, horrible stories and I'm fortunately out of that stage now. You know, like I've grown out of my paranoia a little bit. I'm not quite as sick as I used to be. But the extreme paranoia lasted right up until I left home to go to college.

The other part of my childhood life was spent trying to be loved. Trying to get approval, you know? Trying to make sure that dad loved me, trying to make sure that mom and Olin loved me, you know? Even while Olin and I were fighting all the time, I really *wanted* him to love me. I would do absurd things for him, so that I could get his love; I would bribe him, utterly ridiculous little bribes, like I wouldn't tell dad on him for some terrible thing he did to me. Or like with mom, even after I knew I was going to be an actress, I kept telling her that she was right, I *should* be a teacher, and that's what *I* wanted to be, because *she* wanted it. I needed her love, and I was afraid to tell her I didn't want to be a teacher, you know? I was afraid she wouldn't love me, if I told the truth. A lot of things like this went on, and the result was that I was one thing on the inside and another thing on the outside, and I was always torn between the two things. The real me—and my image, you know?

Politically, I let my parents do my thinking for me up through the eleventh grade. Like nothing was going in my head politically. They'd read me selected things from the newspaper. I wouldn't read it for myself. They told me what to think. They were extreme right wing. I didn't care. The right wing and the left wing were equally meaningless to me.

I even spoke my parents' language. I didn't cuss till about halfway through the eleventh grade. Then I began getting into cussing, and it really weirded my mother out. Like I'd get mad and I'd say, "Oh, fuck!" and my mother would just flip. She'd come running out of the kitchen, "Don't talk that way! Only women of the gutter talk that way!"

Long before I ever smoked my first joint, both my parents were very uptight about me and dope. The school was giving lectures for parents, and these stupid cops would come and exaggerate the dope menace. One night my parents came home, and I told them, "These talks are making you more and more uptight." My father screamed, *"I'm not uptight!"* and for two hours, till twelve thirty in the morning, he stomped around the living room screaming and hollering that he was *not* uptight. It was all so stupid because I hadn't dreamed of touching dope at that point. But you couldn't convince my parents of that. My mother was as paranoid as my father. She said she wanted me to go to a doctor and have a blood test to see if I was taking dope. I guess she was terrified that I'd wind up like my father.

I didn't know what to think. I freaked out completely about their behavior. I slept a lot, to escape. I'd come home from school and do my homework and fall asleep on the couch. My parents would come up from the store and they would shake me and say, "What are you doing?"

"What am I doing? I'm sleeping. What do you *think* I'm doing?" And they'd get weirded out. In their view of life, decent people don't sleep in the daytime.

My head was really whirling around. I began to have violent thoughts about myself. I wrote weird things in my journal. I didn't even know a Republican from a Democrat, but I began writing about tearing the government down and setting up a dictatorship. I wrote that a dictator would be good because he could dictate good things, and people would stop suffering, and the only way to get a dictator was to violently tear down the government, you know? Like inside me there was all this violence. Like it's amazing, but when I was in the eleventh grade, I started clenching my teeth. It was just a sign of tension, and I still do it. I haven't been able to get out of it. For four years now I've been constantly clenching my teeth, and it's really a drag. I've got to get over it.

Well, there was so much talk around my house about dope that I guess it was inevitable that I would get into it. I had two good friends in my junior year, and one of them happened to be a dealer. He was seventeen, and his name was Sam, and he comes up to me one day and he goes, "God, I have a chance to buy a gram of hash and I don't have enough money."

"I'm not God," I says. "How much is a gram?"

He said, "Well, this hash is *so* good—like two of us could get a lot of highs off it—it's about eight dollars. It's black opiated hash, the best."

"I'll split one with you," I said. Everybody else was doing it; I figured it was about time for me to start. I'd never tried dope, and it sounded interesting. That's the way I do so many things. My attitude is, Why not? I'm curious. I have an open mind.

The next day Sam gave me my share of the hash. It was a little itty-bitty square glob. I goes, "I don't know how to do it." I hated to admit my ignorance, but I wasn't going to blow my four-dollar investment for nothing.

"You mean, you never smoked?"

"Well—no."

"I thought you were a head!"

"Well, never mind. Just show me how to do it."

So right there in school, Sam showed me how. You put a piece of tinfoil over the bowl of a pipe, and you poke about ten little pinholes in it, and you break up the hash and put it on top of the tinfoil, and you light up. You inhale, and you *hold* it! Then you exhale, and—Wow!

I goes, "Well, it seems simple enough. I'll try it for myself tonight at church."

I was still into the church scene, see, but I was beginning to see the hypocrisy of the whole thing. I loved Jesus, and I prayed to God, especially when I wanted something, but I hated the superjocks that went to our church. These assholes would go to a Wednesday night youth meeting with me, but in school they wouldn't even say hello. I hated them. I hated their middle-class attitudes, everything about them. I thought, "What a terrific place to smoke my first hash!"

So at the Wednesday night youth meeting, I excused myself and went into the lavatory of the church and lit up. Too bad I can't say that it was terrific, that I got a real rush, but I didn't get anything. I didn't even get dizzy or high. I found out later that hash often works this way the first time. All I could think was, "Well, shit, I'm doing something wrong. I'll wait and try it with an experienced head."

A couple of nights later I was out driving around with a weird kid named Martin and two girls. Martin was fifteen, and he was a real sex maniac! That kid is *so* lusty, I don't *believe* it! I mean, he's always trying to rape a chick. God, he's lusty! I've never seen anybody that horny, you know? Wow, he's amazing! Like that's *all* he wants to do, rape chicks and smoke dope.

So we're cruising around, and Martin is saying, "God, I wish I had some dope."

I said, "I'm not God, but I've got some dope."

"What? You've got some dope?"

"Yeah, I have some black opiated hash."

He goes, "*Black opiated hash*?" He almost went through the car roof. He goes, "Oh, for Christ's sake, let's smoke it right now."

We tried to decide where to go, and one of the girls was Jewish and she said she would prefer smoking it behind the synagogue. We pulled into this dark spot behind the synagogue and lit up. The girls had a few tokes, and Martin and I kept smoking and smoking and smoking, and then I burst out laughing. It was so *absurd*. I'd be inhaling, and I'd start laughing, and all the hash would fall on the floor. We picked up that hash about ten times. It was ridiculous. Martin kept going, "She's wrecked! She's wrecked!" And the girls kept going, "No, she's this way *all* the time." I really didn't get anything, because I was still too paranoid to let it happen.

When we finally drove away, I was convinced that a car was following us, and Martin was ridiculously wrecked, and so horny, and it was a weird scene with just him and three girls in the car and he's feeling everybody up right while we're driving around and somebody is following us. I threw the pipe and the hash out the window, and we all got pretty spaced out, except Martin. He just kept right on feeling everybody up.

Well, I wasn't all that thrilled about my first experience with dope, and so I didn't do any other dope while I was in high school. I got all involved in an encounter group, and that was my thing for a long time. The encounter group taught me to start thinking about where my head was, you know? I mean, I knew my head was fucked. I had *no* idea of who I was. I was shutting people out because I didn't want to keep showing them my hypocritical front, but I didn't know the real me, so I didn't know *what* to show them, I didn't know *what* to feel, you know? If you don't know who you are, if you don't know what you feel and think, then you can't show your self to anyone else, can you?

The encounter group was weird, you know? Like it wasn't run by a professional, and I have the feeling that it really fucked up a lot of us kids. Like I guess that there were about fourteen or fifteen of us there, and the leaders of the group were preaching revolution, and after I came away from the whole thing I felt all this violence inside of me. Like I think the encounter group brought my violence into the open. At the same time the group leaders gave me a direction for my violence. They gave me a cause. I was wild for revolution.

I didn't know whether I would join the draft resistance or what, but I knew I would do something. I was so excited and manic that I went home and started to tell my mother about the big change in my head. I said, "Mom, I gotta talk to you about the encounter group, because it's *really* important to me."

At the time she'd been working day and night in the store and she said, "Well, I'm afraid it'll have to wait because I'm really sleepy and really tired. I have to go to bed."

I tried to tell her a few things, but they didn't seem to sink in, and she seemed to be more interested in sleeping. I was really disappointed. Of course, I couldn't talk to my dad at that time because he was really hurting. And anyway, he didn't want to hear about the revolution. From that time on, anytime I brought up the encounter group, they would either shut me up or weird out. They were *horrified*. When I blurted out that I was interested in socialism, they went up the wall. They shut me out. When I said I was going on a peace march, they freaked out. My father shouted, "No! No! You're *not!*"

I began going to more and more meetings of the movement because this was the best way to get away from the tension in our house. And I found some really good friends. One night I learned that we had concentration camps in America, and I went home and told my parents, and they blew up. "That's ridiculous! We have no such thing!" I told them that we do, that there are places where they put revolutionaries who haven't committed any crimes at all. There's nothing to call them except concentration camps, just like Nazi Germany. They send you there if they think you might commit a revolutionary crime later. There's one in Utah, there's one near Berkeley, there's one in Colorado. They're *strictly* for revolutionaries. They convict you on some small dumb thing and use that as an excuse to put you in a concentration camp. This is a known fact. But I couldn't make my parents believe it.

We had some awful fights about my emerging new head. I wanted to go to a demonstration for black power. My father said, "Never mind the niggers. Just take care of yourself."

"But, dad," I goes, "the black man is getting a 'lousy deal. I *agree* with this demonstration."

He goes, "Well, go on and march then. If you go, you're a Communist. And if you're a Communist, get out of this house! Get out of this country!"

They just can't understand. They're afraid that somebody'll come in and destroy what they've built, after all their pain and trouble. They've finally paid off a few bills, and along comes their own kid trying to destroy them. My father said, "We brought you up to be a decent person, and now you're turning out to be something straight out of Communist Russia."

My mother goes, "You're becoming a freak. We've created a monster. You're turning into a fiend."

I just freaked out completely. I fell apart. My parents

and I became completely estranged. They looked at me as though I were a microbe, and it really weirded my head out. I thought, "God, they don't *know* me, I can't ever tell them the truth about myself, and wow!" I was always making my mom cry and my father blow up. They told me I was a degenerate monster so many times that I couldn't stand living with them anymore. I was just counting the days till I could get away to college. I mean, what's a monster about me? That I don't live exactly according to their precepts? Is *that* a monster? I don't hurt anybody, do I? Sure, I disagree with their politics. I couldn't see where Nixon did *anything* that was right, *not one thing*. I still feel that way.

For the rest of my time in high school I was really into the violent revolution trip, you know? Nowadays I see the fallacies in it, you know? I see the absurdity of tearing down the government and having absolutely nothing to replace it. I figure that if you tear down a government you have to do it slowly so the majority of people can learn to accept the change, so that they won't just revolt again. If you threw out the whole government and put in something brand new, like a dictatorship, so many people in the United States wouldn't stand for it. They'd revolt. They'd just go, "Fuck this. We don't want this." And they'd just go hog wild. Crime would just soar. I mean, anarchism is a really cool idea, but the people aren't ready for it yet. I think it would be terrific if people could live in harmony without any government at all, you know? But people can't live under anarchy now because there are too many genuine fuckers around who would just take advantage of it. They would say, "Great! No government! I'll *really* fuck people." You know?

At one point I considered joining the Socialist Labor Party, but after reading some of their absurd literature, I realized it was just ridiculous. Just as ridiculous as the revolutionary literature. I said to myself, "Forget it, it's just fucked. It's just absurd, it's a waste. Things will just have to happen slowly."

I figured I had to do something to work off my violence, so I joined the Downtowners, a group of liberals who were trying to do something about the stupid school system in Collegeville. The Downtowners made a whole lot more sense than the revolutionary political group. They were trying to get textbooks changed for elementary schools. They were trying to get books that blacks and Chicanos could relate to. I mean, our first-grade primers are absurd: The mothers are blond, the fathers are brunette, all have white-collar jobs, mothers never work, there are two or three kids of both sexes, and the kids never do anything but play. Little girls go out to play and wind up snipping flowers for their tresses. *Fuck*! What little kid does that? They go out and play around in the mud and climb trees and rip their clothes. That's reality. What kind of a slum kid can identify with books like that? And why bother? All the action in the primers takes place in suburbia, never in the city, never in a slum. The family always has a station wagon, and the mother always wears a watch and the house is always in the fifty-thousand-dollar bracket and sometimes there's a swimming pool in back. And they're trying to get slum kids interested in reading books like this. Then when the slum kids fall behind the other kids, the racists say, "Well, that's just because they're black. Black kids don't learn as fast as white kids."

For a while I really related to this kind of work, really thought I was doing some good, but in my parents' eyes I was still a monster, and it just reached the point where I couldn't stand the split anymore. They looked at me as though I stunk. They backed off and hated me openly. They even encouraged my brother when he bullied me. My surface strength began to leave me, and I had to call on my reserves, and there were so many times when I found myself wanting. My mother was always crying, and my father was taking more and more pills and berating me even though I was almost a full-grown woman. Like suddenly I was all alone. Totally, totally alone. I couldn't talk to anybody. I went around in a daze.

When my father found out about the Downtowners, he became paranoid. "Who runs this outfit?" he goes. I knew I'd better not give him any names. I knew that he'd just get the people in trouble if he could. So I only gave him first names and I said, "Well, I've forgotten the last names."

A few days later he told me that he'd called the Downtowners to check on me, you know? Which was a horrible thing to do because here were my parents, people I'd loved all my life, checking on me as though I was a common thief or something. My father told me that I was associating with horrible, horrible people, and that I'd better get away from them. I just didn't know where to turn, and my head was just totally fucked. I just weirded out completely. I mean they checked, they *checked* on me.

Finally they made me quit the Downtowners, and they monitored every second of my life. College was coming up, and my mother reminded me that I was going to be a teacher, and I should begin planning some courses in the School of Education. I kept my mouth shut until I couldn't stand it anymore, and then I said, "I want to be an actress."

My dad goes, "An actress?" I might as well have told him I wanted to be an aardvark, the way he looked. "*An actress*?" He started to laugh, this cruel, weird laugh. "Whatever in the world makes you think you have the talent to be an actress?"

Oh, Jesus Christ, oh, man, oh! This isn't happening. He isn't saying these things.

He goes, "That's the most ridiculous thing I've ever heard. An actress? Come on, Riva, you know you don't have the talent."

Oh, man! That really fucked me up for a long time, him saying that. He said, "No, forget it! When you go into teaching, you can fool around with amateur productions, and maybe do some readings, and that'll satisfy your impulse about acting."

Then the two of them sat me down and began a long rap about teaching, all of it on the assumption that I *would* be teaching, and there was *no question* about it, and I had *nothing* to say in the decision. My father was saying, "It's not easy to become a teacher. You'll have to go through a lot of agony. But it'll be worth it in the long run." And I thought, Now he assumes that I'm going to go through shit to be something I don't want to be. It just bummed me out completely.

I finally put it all together. Daddy had wanted to be an actor, but he couldn't make it and he couldn't stand the idea that maybe *I'd* make it. It was plain old jealousy. That's probably wrong, but I was so mad that's the way I felt. He was sitting there destroying me with his mouth. It was just as though he had gored me. I was sick to my stomach. Because here was a man I respected and loved and I knew that he must've been a real great actor once, and he loved me supposedly; and now he was telling me I didn't have the talent to make it. I can't even describe what that did to me, you know? Like acting had been my secret ambition for years, and now he was telling me I couldn't do it. When they finally left, I stood there stunned with my mouth hanging open, and mom came back in, and I said, "*Why* does he treat me so bad?"

She goes, "Well, people who've been treated bad tend to treat others bad." Yes, that's the way it must've been for my father. He must've been thinking, "I had to take so much shit, so I'm gonna unload some on others."

And I was there for him to unload it on. Why? But why? Aren't they supposed to love you? I'm not the only one that was treated like that. Why do parents put their children down? What do they get out of it?

Well, something else bad was going on at the same time, only I didn't realize it. I belonged to this half-ass acting group in school, and one of the things that the teacher kept telling me was that you had to suffer to become a great actress. She cited all the great actresses and the hell they had gone through to give them the maturity and the depth to perform on the stage. She'd listen to me read some lines, and then she'd say, "Riva, you just haven't *suffered* enough. You just don't understand."

And then I would sit there and think, "You stupid thing, how do you know what I've gone through? *You don't know*!" But I wouldn't say it aloud because I realized she was trying to help me, she was trying to tell me something basic. You had to suffer.

When the auditions came up for the senior play, I just bummed out completely. I was *so* bad, and the teacher took me in a private room, and she was really pissed, you know? She had worked hard with me, and I had let her down. She goes, "Why don't you just forget it? Why don't you just become a teacher, Riva?" Wow!

I goes, "I want to act."

"Well, vou can't!" she shouted at me. "You just don't have it. Maybe later, after you've suffered a little."

I thought, Oh. you awful dope! I haven't suffered? Why, I've been either depressed or ecstatic all my life. How can you say I haven't suffered? And I was so tired from being up and down all the time and the terrible fights that were going on at home, I was really bummed out.

I went home; I'll never know how. I got there. I was jelly. I went up to my room and I sat there until late at night, until the house was asleep. I could see absolutely no reason for living. I couldn't stand myself, and nobody else could stand me. I went into the bathroom and I got dad's pill jar down, and I began cramming everything I could find into my mouth. I must have taken forty pills. Uppers, downers. analgesics, Darvon, morphine, Dilaudid, aspirin, everything I could find. Then I went back into my bedroom and got under the covers. Ten or fifteen minutes went by and nothing happened, and then it felt as though a horse had kicked me in the stomach. I ran back into the bathroom and leaned my head over the toilet and threw up about fifteen minutes straight. Everything came up. Most of the pills were intact and undigested, and as I watched them swirling around in the toilet water, I said to myself. "You dumb fuck! You can't even kill yourself right." Then I went in and went to bed and to sleep.

The next morning I woke up at my regular time, and there was nothing different in my head except that I felt more fucked than ever. I went to school, and I was walking around feeling really down until the third period when this chick was standing at my desk and I blurted out, "Betty, I tried to kill myself last night." She grabbed me by the hand and led me in to see the principal. For a long time I just babbled away about my troubles. I told her about all the times I was tempted to pick up a bread knife in the kitchen and ram it into my stomach, or the times when I'd been up in a tall building and wanted to jump out, or the times I'd thought about slashing my wrists. I told her that I was really fucked up, and she said gently, "Yes, I know."

She finally said, "I can understand how you feel, Riva, but you have done so many wonderful things, and there are so many wonderful people on earth that you haven't met yet, that it's worthwhile for you to just go on, because you never know what will happen, you know?" And she just talked to me. It was really beautiful, and she made me feel better. She made me see that I was a long way from rock bottom. I mean, I was only a few inches off the ground, but those few inches could save me. She got me started seeing a social worker, and that straightened my head a little bit more. I mean, my head was still fucked, but at least I could stay alive for a while.

Bonnie Leblanc says:

When Riva and I were assigned together as roommates last year, our initial reaction to each other wasn't too favorable. We looked so different, for one thing. I was wearing the clothes my mother wanted me to wear: elegant, chic, stupid things. I felt like such a hopeless drag! Amazing! Riva was wearing old, comfortable clothes, *normal* school clothes, and I was dressed up like Madame Pompadour. I was *so* embarrassed!

My mother and I were in the room, and Riva came in with her parents, grim-looking, antiseptic-looking people with deep lines in their faces, and the parents introduced themselves and then everybody began eying everybody sideways. My mother was acting like a grand dame, which she's not; it's just a nervous thing she puts on around strangers. "Oh, your dress is just too, too divine, my dear"; shit like that. It's just a lack of true sophistication that she tries to cover up with phony language. I was glad when the whole thing was over, and Riva and I were alone.

I was in a hell of a shape by the time I got to college, but at least I had enough guts to tell my mother and father that I could not live at home. I didn't care if I had to get a job as a washerwoman; I was going to live in a dormitory, to have some kind of a life of my own, away from that fucked-up atmosphere. By that time my parents bummed me out completely. I couldn't have lived if I'd stayed with them. I'd have been dead in a week.

When they saw that there was no other choice, they let me apply for a room in a dorm, and I lived there for the first two years of college, until Bonnie Leblanc and Laurel Milne and I took our apartment. For a while Bonnie was my roommate in college, and like I was so overwhelmed you know? Like she was so *in*, you know? And I wore this blotch of an outfit, ripped pants and an old army shirt and these horrible loafers. The soles were coming off and they looked filthy, you know? I never polished them, it was a waste of time. My legs weren't shaven, and I didn't wear hose. My hair was just kind of itself, frizzy and uncombed. My parents were always tagging along after me, visiting me, and being all their normal dopey selves. Thank God, they've cut *that* out! You know, they are *so* middle-aged.

I was terrified that Bonnie would find out what a horrible slob I am! You should have seen the way I'd kept my room in my freshman year, like I'd usually have five sets of clothing littered about the room at one time, at least three or four different pairs of shoes, all of them covered with dog shit.

Well, anyway. Bonnie wasn't at all the way she looked. She had her own insecurities, her own troubles, and if I was a slob, well, she was just as full of insecurity, underneath her lovely hairdo and her big boobs. For a long time we weren't close, even though we lived together. We kept things concealed from each other. Like we were both doing dope you know, but we were keeping it from each other. I hadn't had any reaction to the drugs I'd taken in high school, but in college I really got wrecked. Wow, did I get wrecked! Jesus, I was just totally fucked! I was still fucked up in the head about being told that I could never act, and I made up my mind that I was going to shift over to the School of Performing Arts in my junior year, after getting rid of some required subjects, whether my parents liked it or not, even if I had to stage a complete rebellion. But I always heard my father's voice saying over and over again. "You don't have the talent for it." On top of that, there was a speech class in my sophomore year that just went horribly. Day after day I bitched it up. And if you can't do well in speech, how can you become an actress?

After a while I began talking more to Bonnie, and I began depending on her. I'd come home really depressed and down because I was shutting people out, and because I was seeing myself as a slob, but Bonnie would absolutely not let me shut myself out of her life. She kept coming on with her liveliness and her joy and her wholesome approach to things. She'd say, "You've got to start looking on the bright side."

But even Bonnie wasn't enough. I started walking all over the campus, which was something I did often because it helped, it gave me a chance to think and to sort things out. I walked and walked, and I found myself passing one of the dorms, and I heard a scream, and I just kind of froze. It was a really horrible scene, and people gathered below the window, and the girl was hanging out the window screaming, "Help! Help! Help!" She goes, "Help! Help! Help! *Get him out of here!*" And all the people down on the sidewalk began to laugh. It was dark out. I thought. "What kind of people are these? What kind of people can laugh and sneer at a girl who's screaming?"

I got very upset. Maybe it was ridiculous, but remember I'd always had this terrible paranoia anyway. And the scream was horrifying. I felt that scream inside myself for a long time, and it was something I could really understand and identify with, you know? It terrified me because there was so much pain and horror in it. And here were all these assholes laughing at her. Laughing! I guess they just figured it was some guy hassling her and she was screaming, but to me it was far worse. It sounded as though he was murdering her. Maybe it was ridiculous for me to get uptight, but I did. I walked away real fast, almost running, and I started thinking, "What an absurd world this is. What a ridiculous world this is. It's so *ugly,* so *awful,* so full of cruel and petty people who don't know how to live, *and never will."* And all at once I just stopped wanting to live. I just decided that I didn't want to have anything to do with the whole human race. I don't know, I just sort of freaked out, and it was like the half of me that was controlling me lost control of the other half of me, and everything was disaster.

I decided to kill myself right then and there, but I couldn't figure out how. I didn't want to go back to the dorm and make Bonnie suffer. I started walking down the middle of a busy street, trying to get hit. All I remember is that a bunch of cars kept coming at me and they would honk and they would miss me, you know, and they would look at me like she's crazy, she's freaked out, you know? I thought, "Why *don't* they hit me?" I thought maybe it's just their essential goodness. I thought, "Well, if they're that good, maybe I'll have some afterthoughts." But then I thought, "Well, if they're *so* good, why don't they get out of the car and ask me if I'm all right, you know?" But then I had to take into consideration that they're human, and when humans see something strange, it frightens them. So I walked on, still halfway trying to be hit. Then somebody finally stopped me and said, "Are you all right? You look like you're having a bad trip."

I walked over to the sidewalk. I said, "I'm okay, thanks," and I headed toward the dorm. My head still wasn't straight, but I figured there was enough strength there so that I could work things out. I'd said to myself, "I really don't want to live anymore, I just don't care," but at the same time, I knew that I *would* live, and that this was my last suicide attempt. It was nothing more or less than an extension of the first attempt, you know? It was just basically the same thing that had been happening in my head, over and over. It was the split inside me.

Bonnie Leblanc says:

Riva tried to kill herself last year, but she decided not to do it in the dorm because she didn't want me to find the body and freak out. It shocked me when she told me all about it later because I'd known she'd been depressed, but I didn't know it was so intense because she covers up with laughter and silliness and spaciness, and at first you can't imagine her being truly troubled.

For months I had either been way down or way up, and sometimes I would go from these extremes several times in a day, and just get worn out, just really tired, you know? Like I wouldn't be able to sleep unless I went to bed about two in the morning, and then I'd wake up like eight in the morning, and I'd just be horribly tense and paranoid and I wouldn't be able to function well at all, and I was continually tired.

Well, anyway, I knew I couldn't go on this way, so I went to see a shrink on the campus, and I decided to work at my past, to dig things out, and try to see things in perspective. One of the things that was really troubling me was that I was balling one boy at the same time that I was in love with another. I mean, how sick! When the boy I loved made a pass, I turned him down like a nervous virgin, and then I would go out of my way to jump into bed with this asshole that I was seeing on the side, a dude I really detested.

Laurel Milne says:

Riva's been going through a stage where she fucks people she really doesn't like. I guess she has to get it out of her system. She's really very immature about sex. Like she's never had orgasms. One day she came into the bathroom, and I was sitting there and she walks in and she says in this little-girl voice of hers, "Laurel, do people pass out when they have an orgasm?" That's how little she knew. Like if unconsciousness is your goal in intercourse, forget it! You're never gonna make it!

So I told Bonnie about this conversation and she said we'd better lay all the facts out for Riva, and we did; and now she talks pretty naturally and pretty openly on the subject. Like one day she came into my room and she said, "Laurel, I'm really feeling horny."

I said, "Well, Riva, if you want Michael for a few hours, I'll give him to you. It's okay. He wouldn't mind. He loves you, too. He almost fucked Ginny the other night, and we just felt so *good* about it!"

She says, "Well, thanks just the same, Laurel, but I just couldn't."

I says, "Well, I'd make love to you myself, Riva, if you wouldn't mind my not having a penis, but I know you just want a penis in your cunt, right?"

And she said, "Yes, I'm afraid that's what I want, but I love you anyway, Laurel. Thank you anyway." So cute! That little tiny voice! Oh, I love her so much!

Sex wasn't the main problem in my life but it was one of the first things I brought up to the shrink. We started some free association, and one day an incident from my very earliest life popped back into my mind. It had been completely blocked.

When I was five or six years old, I went to day camp for a while, and there were two janitors who must have been in their thirties or forties, and one of them kept staring at me. One day I was alone in the rec hall, and I heard this man lumbering into the place with his heavy footsteps, and I remember thinking, "God, I've got to get away from here," but my foot was rooted to the ground. This awful man walked over and started stroking my back, and then he put his hand into my underpants. It was horrible. He even had bad breath! He kept his hand there for five or ten minutes and played around and held me with his other hand so I couldn't get away. I didn't know *what* to do.

He said things like, "Do you like this, little Riva? I do this to my nieces all the time, and they *love* it," and I thought, "Ooooh, wow! Disgusting!"

When he was finished he told me not to tell anybody, and I felt really awful. He didn't threaten me or anything, but I was too ashamed to tell anybody anyway. I felt dirty and cheap. For a while, I thought of telling my mother, but I just couldn't.

After that I tried to hide from the janitor, but he always caught me. Ugh, awful! He did this to me two or three times. One day he had his hand under my pants, and the other janitor—a really sweet person, someone I liked and really admired—walked in and saw us. He just kind of looked at us for a few seconds, and the bad guy snapped his hand away quick, like nothing was happening, but oh, boy! How horrible I felt! It was like being caught balling. Anyway, the shrink and I figured that's where I got my double standard, where I can dig one guy and ball another. Like balling isn't something you do with somebody you really like. It's dirty and you do it only with dirty people. So the shrink helped me to find this out.

Bonnie Leblanc says:

For a while Riva was becoming lopsided about school. All work and no play. Everything was classes, private lessons, and rehearse, rehearse, rehearse like sixteen hours a day. It was unhealthy. Acting has become an escape. When you see her acting or just reading a poem aloud for an audience it's amazing! She's a new person, and you see how happy she could really be. But on the negative side, she's been using this intense interest in drama as an escape from her parents for years. I mean, she'd stay up in her room and learn the whole first act of *The Dollhouse* rather than be with her parents. There was a danger that this unreal world would become her only world, you know? Like slipping into schizophrenia. So Laurel and I had a talk with her. We told her she had to change, for her own good, and she said she'd try.

Laurel Milne says:

I think Riva's coming out of it now. The other day, she said, "I want to read something that isn't drama or music or public speaking or ballet," and she picked up a science fiction book and read it all the way through. That was great! She's learning how to be a *whole* person, how not to throw everything into one discipline. Sometimes Bonnie and I say, Well, I wish Riva would learn a little faster, but then we realize it's cool. I mean, Riva's going through it; *we* should be able to go through it with her.

The biggest thing that helped me was moving into the apartment with Bonnie and Laurel at the beginning of my junior year. In this house of love, a lot of my paranoia has disappeared completely and quickly. Like I sometimes walk home a mile or two at midnight, and it doesn't bother me, you know? I'm not so afraid of people. Like I'm afraid in certain ways, I'm afraid that if I trust them too much I might get hurt, but I'm not afraid they'll mug me or rape me. I think a lot of that security is just knowing Bonnie and Laurel and living with them in a normal, happy environment.

They do a lot of dope, but that doesn't bother me. I do a lot of dope myself; when it's around, I just smoke all the time. But when it's not around I can completely ignore it. Anyway. I've decided to give it up. I'm super-sensitive to dope, I just get stoned so fast! Pretty soon I'm completely wrecked. I can get wrecked off an ordinary cigarette, or a drink, let alone grass. When I was smoking dope heavily, I found I wasn't getting enough work done. I was spaced out completely. I'd get so I didn't know *what* I was doing. Me on dope is like somebody else on smack. I'd say, "What *was* it I was gonna do? What was I gonna say? Where *am* I? I? *Who* am I?" I'd stay stoned for *days*. Now that I'm in the School of Performing Arts, over my parents' dead bodies, I've got to cut this out.

I really love those two girls, Bonnie and Laurel, and if you come right down to it, this silly converted ware-

house-apartment is the happiest place I've ever lived in
in my life. It's more of a home to me than anything
else ever was. I love my family, I love my parents and
I love my brother but living with them was so passionate
and heated all the time, it really got tiresome. You get
to a point where you just want to rest. You don't think
you can handle any more. You just want to lie down
and sleep forever, you know?

I've come to realize that there always will be little an-
noyances, even with people you love. Like sometimes I get
uptight about the crashers that come here and stay for
weeks at a time. They're street people and really hard
for me to handle, but Laurel just seems to encourage
them. When I walk in the apartment and there's six sleeping bags on the floor, I retreat to my room and practice
my recorder, instead of facing these crashers and learning
to be with them. I expect I'll get better at this as the
years go by. But even with the crashers, there's more
peace in this home than I've ever known.

The big problem of my life is still my parents. They
only live a few miles away, and they get superuptight
about *anything* that deviates from the norm. Like one
day, my mom calls, and she tells Laurel, "Mr. Ronson is
on his way to see Riva."

Well, at the time Laurel was having a big party, tequila, wine, and dope. So she says, "Riva's not here!
She's in the English building!"

Mom says, "Well, he's already left. He'll be there in
a few minutes."

Laurel goes, "Oh, boy!" to herself and everybody
quick puts their clothes back on and hides the stash box
and puts the tequila away, and my dad drives up and
there's all these people in our apartment and Laurel tells
him we're just having a little party.

He comes inside, and he sees all the bedrolls and he
says, "Hmmm, what's this?"

Laurel goes, "Those are bedrolls."

Then he finds an empty bottle of tequila, and he goes,
"What's this?"

Laurel says, "Oh, that's just an old empty bottle. We were going to make a candleholder."

That night, my father picked me up and took me home for a talk. He said, "Look, Riva, we're helping to pay your way, and we don't believe in crashers and wild parties. We've learned that *you* don't have to live exactly like *we* do, but you can't expect us to support anything we're totally opposed to."

I goes, "All right, no more crashers."

But he went on and on, really uptight. It lasted three hours. He kept saying the same thing over and over, and I would break in and say, "Well, I already told you, it's *all right!* We won't *do* it any more. I'll tell the crashers to leave and they'll go."

The thing about my parents, I *do* love them, and I would dig seeing them about once a month, but I see them too much. Two or three times a month. Way too much! And they're *always* on the phone. Every other week they come up to the apartment. They have enough sense not to drop in on us without warning. Oh, God, that would be a disaster! I can just see it: Our stash box out, and Laurel running around nude with Michael nude behind her, and me coming out of my bedroom nude with a dude. Oh, what a prospect! I don't know *what* would happen. They wouldn't be able to accept it. They'd just freak out. They'd say the same thing over again, "We've created a monster."

I long ago gave up trying to be like them or trying to adjust to them, or accept their ideas. Every time I allow myself to get a little too close to them, something awful happens. Like at home I had this mongrel Schatzi and this cute little kitten Snip, and my father took to Schatzi, but he hated Snip. So without telling me, he takes the cat to the Humane Society. *Without telling me!* My mother calls and she says, "I have some news for you, and I think I'd better tell you right now." She says, "Dad was just in one of his spells, and couldn't seem to help himself." At first, I couldn't believe that he could be so cruel to a little animal that couldn't protect itself. I'm going, "Oh, *sick!*"

And mom goes, "Well, try and understand." and I said, "Oh, no!" and all those memories of childhood came flooding back. I just couldn't handle them. I thought to myself, "I am *stupid,* I am really ridiculously *dumb.* All my life I've been putting up this facade, this front for my parents, just to get them to love me, and this is what they do in return. Dad can dump an innocent helpless kitten, and mom can try to excuse him." And suddenly I stopped trying to reconcile all the things that I've ever done against their morals. and I could feel the split inside me begin to mend. You know, it was remarkable. I connect the beginning of my feeling of peace with that incident. Dad had committed an act that made me realize it was absurd for me to try and reconcile their attitudes to mine. They're just *different* people. And I'm someone entirely different, too. I've got an entirely different life to lead. and I've gone through entirely different things; different influences have been brought to bear on me, so I *have* to live different. I *have* to accept that. So I don't have to be split between living their lives and living my life. Like I'm still really split, but not so badly. I'm still really neurotic, but man, I'm so much better off. Like wow! You know?

Four or Five Things That Happened to Riva on Her Birthday

Some great philosopher once said that each day is a shit sandwich and some bites are bigger than others. Today I got some really, really big bites. I honestly don't believe that each day is a shit sandwich, but sometimes the conclusion is inescapable. Sometimes that's the only possible explanation.

Like I woke up this morning and found that Meshach the cat had shit all over my bed. That is a very gross beginning for a day. The shit was all over my blanket and my mattress pad, and I had to take everything to the dry cleaners. They just loved it when I came in the door with all that stinking stuff. Then I had to go back to the apartment and clean the mattress pad, and I just couldn't do it, so I ran the hot water and put the pad in the bathtub with a cake of Camay.

This went over very large with the roomies. It took the whole three of us to wring the pad out, and by the time all this was over, I'd blown about two hours of my day. That might not be much to some college students, but I have a scholarship to protect and I'm on a pinpoint schedule that keeps me going about sixteen hours a day, you know?

Well, the first thing on the daily schedule was a recorder lesson. I had intended to practice an hour in the morning, but Meshach blew that. I walked in for the recorder lesson, and God, was I bad! *All* my recorder lessons are horrible, but this was a special piece of shit. I said to my teacher, "I haven't practiced too much, because there was a little problem at home."

The recorder teacher, Mr. Davis, is a very weird cat, and he goes, "Oh, you must have had a pretty good weekend, huh?" He goes, "What's the matter with you, you got a dude or something?"

I goes, "Well, no," because I really don't think it's any of his business.

And he goes, "So you got *two* dudes?"

And I thought, Shit, I'll *never* convince him, he thinks I must spend my whole life in bed. So I decided to string him along, shorten the lesson a little bit. So I goes, "Yeah, I got two dudes."

His eyes light up, and he says, "Do they know about each other?"

I said, "Oh, yeah. We're all three pretty good friends."

He still has this lewd gleam in his eye. He's really a dirty old man, you know, and he goes, "You mean all three have a thing for each other?"

I said, "No, they're not homos or anything like that. Just regular people."

He goes, "Well, you know you can't spend your whole life in the sack."

I goes, "But we don't spend *all* our time in the sack."

He laughs, and squeezes my arm, and he goes, "I'm glad to hear it. Variety is the spice of life." And he laughs his head off.

Well, we started the lesson, but he kept talking about my dudes, and once he goes, "At the rate you're going, pretty soon you'll have enough to write a book." I snickered. But really, this shit gets kind of old after a while. Like Mr. Davis seems to think that I'm balling a different guy every night. That's where his head is all the time. He's typical of his generation. He doesn't come out and say words like fuck, but it keeps running through his mind, you know? It's how the French say it—*Idée fixe.*

I had a girl friend who took from him last year and she said it was really horrid because she knew that all the time he was sitting there pretending to listen, he was really looking at her ass. Utterly stupid! I just don't understand grownups. They're always thinking about sex, at least the ones that I've run into. I guess that sex has been crammed in the closet all their lives, put away, done in the dark, as though it's the most evil deed on earth. So a lot of them spend all their time thinking about it. Me, I believe in doing it once in a while, and the rest of the time thinking about other things.

It's all so hypocritical. Like Mr. Davis, I'm sure he's overheard me using bad language, quote unquote, and that makes him think I'm a fallen woman. But I just don't think you can characterize people by the words they use. Mom and dad did this all the time, and they told me that only low women, women of the gutter, would use bad words. I don't understand people who erase all the beauty inside of you, just because you have some imagined flaw on the outside that they don't dig. I don't dig that whole trip.

Well, I spent two years working to get a 3.8 average and win the scholarship that got me into the School of Performing Arts, and now that I'm in I'm finding that a lot of things are different from what I expected. I mean, most of the students and teachers, even the ones that specialize in drama, are really A-straight. Before I transferred to the School of Performing Arts, my preconception was that all the drama majors would be really freaks, just like me. But they're not. Some of them are so straight and naive, they're just weirded out completely. They'd never touch anything like dope, not even to try it out and see what it's like. Dope's evil! Some of them, if they really want to get high, they go out and drink 3.2 beer. Why, you have to *drown* yourself in that shit to get anything at all! They'd do better to pour a little bit of it in a bowl and snort it up their noses. It's so much simpler and easier to do marijuana, and you don't have to keep running to the toilet for the next three days. I know a lot of the drama students think I'm crazy because I do grass and a few other things, but I'd rather be considered crazy than A-straight. I couldn't dig being completely normal. That would mean *no* drugs, *no* booze, dress nice, and that's *not* my bag. I'd rather show a little imagination, get it on once in awhile.

Like, most of these kids, they have no idea how to enjoy life, you know? Like I'll freak out on a cloud formation. I'll say, "Wow, those clouds are really far out!" And these kids will just shrug and go, "What? Huh?" They don't see it. They're literal minded. A-straight. You wonder what they're doing in the drama school, but then you see one of them act, and like wow! Some of them are amazing! Like this one chick, one of the most naive of all, she performs like an angel. I got to know her a little bit and she's really been hurt in her lifetime, and so she turns everything into acting. That's why she seems A-straight. But she's really very talented. She lets it all hang out on the stage, and *nowhere* else. She gets really uptight if people don't come up and congratulate her after every performance. She's got all her emotions invested in drama.

But most of these drama majors really weird me out. One guy I ran around with last semester, he intrigues me, because he's *so* straight. He's so straight he's freaky, he's weird on the *other* side. He's a superconservative dresser, he wears sweater-vest outfits with white shirts. Oh, wow! 1949! Brooks Brothers! He comes from Clinton, Iowa, prairie country, and he shows it. Like I'd freak out on the wind, and I'd say, "Wow, this wind is so wild. Do you suppose it's not really the air moving, it's just something like a really freaked out gravity, trying to force us in its own direction?"

He'd say, "What? Huh?" and I'd say, "The wind! The wind! It's fantastic! It's far out!"

And he'd go, "Well, I don't like wind. It's not good for the crops. It makes it hard for the farmer."

He's here in the School of Performing Arts, and he's still seeing life in terms of what's good for the farmer! What's good for the farmer is good for America. Everything with him is the practical,; there's no spiritual sense, no poetic sense. But then he'll do a reading, and like, wow! You wouldn't believe the beauty of it, the sensitivity, the emotion, the feeling, and imagination. It's almost sensuous. He can't express anything inside himself except in his acting, in his readings. It's really sad. And it's sad that he can't get into how neat red leaves look, and the sound of brooks, and far out things like that. But he's so superprogrammed. He spends his life rehearsing. -

Well, anyway, after I finished my horrible recorder lesson, I was supposed to play duets with another recorder student, a fifty-year-old woman named Lina Ruggles. She's such a funny old chick. I think she has a thing for Mr. Davis, the recorder teacher, but, she'd never admit it to herself or anybody else. She is completely from another generation, and she's always griping at me about my language, so she didn't like it too much when I started telling her how the cat had shit all over the bed.

She goes, "Riva, how many times do I have to tell you not to use that word in front of me?"

I go, "Well, Mrs. Ruggles, I'm not gonna sit around here and try to think of the most esthetically beautiful word when something like that happens. What's wrong with what I said? Meshach *did* shit all over my bed. I mean, I could call it poo-poo, but that wouldn't keep it from being shit."

So she starts giving me this big rap about how it was stupid for me to talk that way because I wouldn't find work later. I would never get a single part. People hated to hear disgusting language like that. She says, "Nobody will want to have anything to do with you."

So I say, "Mrs. Ruggles, *you're* having something to do with me. I'm accompanying you, and you selected me, didn't you?"

"Yeah," she says, "But sometimes I wonder." Finally she says, "Oh, well, let's get started on the damned duets."

I goes, "Now just a minute, Mrs. Ruggles. If I can't say shit or fuck in front of you, you can't say hell or damn in front of me. It's hypocritical."

She goes, "Yeah, I guess you're right. I used to say blast, but Elizabeth Simpson told me it was a bad word. I couldn't say it anymore. It had a bad meaning."

I said, "Oh, yes, Mrs. Ruggles, you do have to watch your mouth. If you go around saying blast, people'll think you're the town whore."

So we rapped on. She said, "It bothers me terribly to hear you say *S* and *F*." She says, "You know, there's a big difference between the words you use and the words I use. Like hell and damn, one of them's a place and the other's a curse. But S and F, well, one of them's a bodily function, and the other's—what *is* the other?"

"You mean fuck?"

"Yes. That awful word. What *does* it mean?" She's fifty years old, and I have to explain to her what fuck means! Can you get behind that?

After a discussion like that I just have to wonder if the whole world isn't weirded out, if we're not *all* bananas. I know that most of us are miserable, no matter what kind of shit-eating grins we keep on our faces. Like the other night I was at a party and I just looked around at everybody, and I thought, Jesus Christ, there's nobody here that's really at peace with themselves. And I tried to think of who I'd met along the way who was at peace with themselves, and I couldn't think of a soul. I'm sure as shit not. Laurel's not. Bonnie's not. Nobody in the drama school is. And certainly Mrs. Ruggles isn't. Like the other day, Mr. Davis comes in and asks her to play one of the fingering exercises, and she practically collapses. After she finishes, he goes, "Well, what do you think?"

And she goes, "It wasn't very good, was it?"

And he goes, "Would you call it a finished performance?"

And she goes, "Well, would you?"

And he goes, "No, Mrs. Ruggles, I certainly would not." He meant she really fucked it, you know? And that's a horrible thing to say to Mrs. Ruggles because she loves music so much, and she doesn't play well at all, and I think she would slit her throat if she knew how bad she was. It's like an illusion that we all have to maintain for her because she's fifty years old and she's come back to college to look for something that doesn't exist in her outside life. So it was horseshit for Mr. Davis to talk to her that way.

Sometimes I think that the only reason she takes from him is because he appeals to her sexually. That's a hell of a reason to take lessons from such a prick. He cuts her down continually. Like she'll be playing, and she'll be having trouble with her rhythm, and he'll stand right next to her and keep saying, "That's wrong. That's wrong! That's wrong!" instead of thinking of some way that could make her change into the right rhythm, to make her see it differently, to make her *feel* it, instead of just attacking her, "That's wrong! That's wrong! That's wrong!"

It's a very negative relationship. But then Mr. Davis is *into* negative relationships. That's why he's always asking me about my dudes. He's more interested in his personal satisfaction, in getting a little reaction under his pants, in getting a little sadistic pleasure out of violating Mrs. Ruggles, than he is in making good students. An ego trip. Like he'll be working with you, and you'll look out of the corner of your eyes and you'll see this look of disgust on his face. He doesn't give a shit about the music. People sense this. I hate to see people exploit others, because it's so disgusting. Nobody should treat other human beings that way. It produces tense students. Would a good teacher do that? Why would a music teacher put students uptight? Can you teach beautiful things in an ugly way? How can you make a person tense about beauty?

I mean, I see the whole drama bit as beauty, as communicating with other people, not as some way to make money or get famous. Like the world is crowded, it's full of people, you're going to be running into people all your life, and you have to know how to communicate with them. Acting, performing, emoting—that's the highest form of communication. And it's really beautiful when you bring it off. Oh, God, I wish I could express what I'm trying to say. There's so much that's beautiful in people, and if you can just communicate with them you can bring it out and show your own beauty, and then every single person is worthwhile, and every single person has something to offer. It's, oh, shit, it's so hard to put. To perform for people, to show them what you have inside you, to let it all hang out right up there on the stage, and really blow their minds, that's a beautiful thing. It's breathtaking. That's why I want to really play well on the recorder. That's why I want to learn all my lines to perfection. That's why I want straight A's in my ballet course, and in my speech courses. I don't care if I become Helen Hayes or Bibi Andersson or whoever, that has nothing to do with it. I just want to be able to do something for people and say, "Look, this is *me,* this is part of *me,* this is what's inside *me,* and if you love *me,* you love *this!*"

Well, I'm supposed to be telling you about what happened today. I went from the music building over to my speech class and I got another bite of the doubledecker shit sandwich. I have a small voice, you know, and I'd been having a hell of a time with projection, and this particular teacher is another asshole like Mr. Davis, a sadistic motherfucker, and he had been on me for weeks about my projection. At my last lesson he'd lent me this cheap tape recorder and told me to go home and do some readings from Brecht and bring them back so that he could check them. He said maybe I could project better in the privacy of my own room. But he warned me not to do any retakes. "Just read right into the tape recorder and don't play it back, and don't correct or improve anything," he said. "Then we'll analyze the problem when you come back."

"What's this really about?" I said.

He said, "Well, Riva, to tell you the truth, I want you to find out how bad you sound."

Wasn't that sweet? Anyway, I did the readings, and this morning I brought the tape into him. He starts playing it right away, and he plays about five sentences, and it sounded like shit. I mean, I had done it exactly the way he had instructed me, and since it was a one shot, there were mistakes and I wasn't projecting at all. He let the recorder run for about five minutes and then he snapped it off, jumped up, and said, "I can't believe it! I can't believe it!" He picks up the whole tape recorder, and he says, "I've just *got* to play this for the department chairman. Right now! I want him to see what I'm up against."

I go, "No, please, *no!*" I *pleaded* with him. You know I didn't just ask, I practically got on my knees and begged him, you know? But he takes the tape recorder out of the room and he runs off to another office and shuts the door behind him.

I was fuming. I mean, it was such a violation of confidence. He had told me that this tape was between me and him, that it would be for *nobody* else's use. And it all seemed so vindictive. I grabbed up my books, put on my coat, walked into the office and ripped that tape recorder right out of his hands and stomped out the door. I hollered, "This hasn't been a good day! The cat shit on my bed this morning! And you're the last fucking thing I need!" I used exactly those words. He had a sort of stricken, sickly look.

I bugged out of that school *fast*, slamming the door behind me, and I was crying like a baby. Shit! I ran toward the apartment, and I remember thinking, "Pretty soon my stomach is going to get upset, so I'd better get some antacid tablets." So I bought the tablets and took some, but my stomach was already starting to rumble. I was just *out* of it. I was angry and confused and dismayed, and I'd *had* it for this day, and it was only eleven o'clock in the morning. I decided fuck 'em all, and I started walking down the dirt road toward the hills, a great place for meditation, and did I need to meditate! I was weirded out completely.

Well, I began to hitch, and for the first time in my hitching career I was picked up by a station wagon, which was peculiar, number one. A middle-aged man was driving, and he had some of his kids with him, and he was a perfect representative of my enemy class, the suburbanites. Suburbanites just don't pick up us freaks. They have fears about us. They call us "hippies." The hippie is something dirty, you know, and he does things that are against the law. At least that's the way suburbia sees hippies. And whenever something goes wrong in Collegeville, they always blame us. It's—oh, shit, it's just prejudice. Like a friend of mine explained this attitude very plainly. He said, "It's a known scientific fact that if you paint a wildebeest purple and return him to the herd, the rest of the wildebeests will run him out, not because he's bad or he's done anything wrong, but simply because he's purple, he's deviant, and their instincts tell them to get rid of him, he's a potential menace." My friend said it's exactly the same with hippies. People get all uptight about long hair and smoking dope and taking pills, but they're not really reacting to the hippies as people. They're reacting to them as purple wildebeests. Irrationally, prehistorically.

Well, I was really surprised this morning to find somebody in a station wagon that was not afraid of a purple wildebeest. It was a terrific, tremendous discovery. God, I was so excited! Like you get tired of being a purple wildebeest, you know? Like I have the feeling that the young kids in our neighborhood sneak around to see me and Laurel and Bonnie, and point at us, and say, "Look at the purple wildebeests." Like when we first went to school we had to start drawing our curtains at night, so that nobody could look in. And one day Laurel heard some kids saying that hippies lived in that apartment up there, and it made me furious! Because these little bastards get in fights and throw garbage cans around and throw rocks at your house and break windows and everything else, and here we are just a bunch of simple purple wildebeests who want to live in peace with ourselves and other people and not fight. But these kids are normal because they get up and scream and holler and shit all over things, and *we're* abnormal. It's pretty strange, you know?

This man who picked me up was a typical station wagon father, and he looked like he would be married to a typical station wagon woman, and two of his station wagon kids were in the back. I was amazed. Wow! Phenomenal! You know?. Most suburbanites would never pick up hitchhikers with their kids in the car, because it would be a bad influence, but this man was different. He told me he picked up a lot of hitchers. I go, "Wow! Wow!" I'm saying to myself, "God, I've found somebody who doesn't hate a purple wildebeest. It's such a comfort."

He gave me a ride all the way into the hills, and I walked up and down in the woods, trying to piece things together. And I finally realized I couldn't hate the speech teacher; it just wasn't in me to hate. The look on his face when I ran out the door kept coming back to me. He looked hurt, pathetic. He looked like he knew he was a failure. I can't hate him. He probably doesn't understand what happened.

I also decided that I would never go back to him, never take another class in speech from him, never take any more speech lessons from him. I'll just find somebody else. I could understand him, and sympathize with him, but I just can't expose myself to that kind of bullshit anymore.

So now that it was all worked out in my head, I hitched back to the apartment, just in time to hear the phone ringing. It was my twin, Olin. Of all the times for him to call. I had been to a family wedding with him and the oldies a week before, and he had been griping about the whole thing ever since. My cousin got married, see, and she's such a tremendous bitch and her mother is such a tremendous bitch. You know, I really can't handle my relatives at all. Like they're always fighting, you know? Life is one long battle. What a fucked up family! Like my two aunts fight each other, and then they team up against my mother, and then my aunt and my mother team up against my other aunt and it goes on and on and on and on. It's so stupid, you know? And they're all so A-straight. Like I went to the wedding wearing a long frontier dress and my really weird bright orange ski jacket covered with grease spots and water stains and pulled threads. It really looks dirty, but I dig it. When I came in wearing that outfit everybody looks at me and goes, "Wow!" And like all of my family, like aunts and uncles and cousins and things they stand there staring me down, looking at the purple wildebeest again. And I thought, wow, I wonder where their heads are, you know? Like they're just a bunch of jocks, and I was sitting there in the church wishing I had a joint in my pocket so I could light up and pass it around and say to all those fuckers, "Here, do you want to do some dope?" but I didn't. Anyway, when the wedding was over Olin started bitching at me, and he bitched until I just fled back to the campus.

Now he was on the phone and he was bitching again. He goes, "Boy, it's a good thing I don't come around that apartment of yours."

I goes, "Why?"

He goes, "If I came around there, I would just go out and join the army and get a gun and shoot all those people around you."

I goes, "What do you mean?"

He goes, "Oh, those hippies, those quitters on life, those freaks, those bums, those friends, of yours. But you wouldn't understand, being one of them."

He went on and on. This always happens. He lives to cut me down. Gripe, gripe, gripe. He's always lumped me with the lowest shit on earth. It's been that way since I was a little kid. I finally said, "Look, Olin, you turd-face, this has been a bad day, and you're not helping it, so fuck off!" And I hung up on him.

Little did I know! I should've jumped right into bed and stayed there for the whole rest of the day, but instead I went back to school, and I ran into Freddie Stanley, a boy I had gone with off and on and liked once in a while. We sat in the middle of the quadrangle and smoked a joint, and he came on pretty strong, and he said something about. "If you don't treat me better, Riva, I'm just gonna kill myself."

Well, like he was pretty stoned, but I never know how to take it when anybody says he's going to kill himself, whether he's joking or what. It always weirds me out. I said, "Don't talk like that!"

Then he goes, "Why do you overreact like that? Did you ever try to kill yourself?"

And I made a mistake. I said, "Yes."

And then he just gapes stupidly at me, like I was something in a side show or a zoo. He just kind of gaped for a while, and then he looked at me like I was dirt. And then he goes, "Wow! To think you'd do a thing like that!" And I realized what a stupid mistake I'd made. I mean really *absurd*. How could I ever trust a person like that with so much of myself, you know? Like I offered a piece of myself and he threw it away as if it was shit, it just repulsed him, because he couldn't handle it, you know?

The way he reacted, it brought back so many bad memories when I did try to kill myself in high school. The way people looked at me after they found out about it. Like they looked at me like, Wow! She's an escapee from a loony pit. Like she tried to kill herself, you know? Like dudes that had never spoken to me would pass me in the hall now and say, "Oh, hello, Riva, how are you?" really sugary sweet with a sugary sweet smile, you know? It just made me want to quit. Or I'd be walking down the hall and I'd see groups of people who'd known me all my life, since the beginning of grammar school, and suddenly the whole group would stop talking as I approached, or they would kind of stare at me, and when they'd realize that I was watching them, they'd look away. Or I would be walking down the hall and I'd catch somebody's eye, and they'd smile embarrassedly and look away and walk in another direction so they wouldn't have to talk to me, you know? And the way Freddie was looking at me and treating me brought back all these sickening memories of all these sickening people, and I realized that he was one of *them*. Before that, I had thought he was a sensitive person, but I guess he's just naive. Wow, it really hurt! I mean, I wasn't going steady with him and I didn't have big designs on him, but he was one of my friends, and I thought he understood a few things.

I got up and left and went on to my afternoon class. I figured, well, you can't hate ignorance. But it doesn't make the hurt any less. I can't change the fact that he treated me like something completely abnormal, something that belonged in a cage. I wonder if he'll ever understand. I wonder how many other people he'll really fuck over with his insensitivity.

Well, shit, I've been meeting so many crummy dudes lately, you know? I'm beginning to wonder if there's any such thing as a good man that's available. Well, yes, there's one, at least. Like a few nights ago I went to a rock concert by myself, and I met this guy named Steve Perkins, and he goes, "Hi, you want to go for a Coke?"

Well, we went for a Coke, and we were just sitting there making small talk, and I was feeling a little bit uncomfortable, I don't know why, but then he said, "You know, Riva, I really want to know you, and I have no idea of how to go about it."

I really dug his honesty, and I dug it more when he said, "Would it be best to just ask who you are and what you're all about, and be completely honest about it, or what?" And then he kind of stopped.

And I said, "Yeah, be honest, you know, because I'm really sick of this crap where people play games, and you can't let people know how you feel, or they'll use it against you to hurt you."

And he goes, "Yeah, I agree. Well, *who are you*?"

We had a really heavy conversation, and we really got to know each other, you know? I told him I really dug kind people and gentle people, and I told him that if people are kind and gentle, then everything else will follow from that, and I told him that I had an energy about life, a passion for life, that just couldn't be dampened no matter how many horseshit things happened to me. I told him that I'd had a lot of troubles, but that I was really alive, and I felt a warmth in just living and being there talking to him.

We rapped and rapped, and we were on pretty much the same wave length, and he walked me home, and kissed me goodnight, and he said, "Well, I'd like to get to know you better." And I said, "Yeah, Steve, I'd like to get to know you better, too."

So he came over the next evening, and Laurel and Bonnie were there, and he told us a little bit about his life. He's from a ranch, you know? And he spent a lot of time out in the woods with nature and things like that, and he has the strength that comes from the land. He knows how to live *with* nature instead of *against* it. I was really digging him, and so were Laurel and Bonnie, and what do you think he says? *He says he hates Collegeville and he's leaving it!* He says he's going back to his ranch as soon as possible. It killed me when he said this. One good dude and as soon as I meet him he leaves.

Well, anyway, after we all finished rapping, Steve and I went in on my bed and made love and it was really neat. He was really tremendous, you know? Then he came over again the next night annd made love again. When he left that night, he said, "Well, goodbye," and I realized that was it. He was leaving the next day.

I said, "Steve, do you *have* to go?"

He said, "I can't stand Collegeville another minute."

So I kissed him goodbye. Shit! I'm in love with him. I finally found a really good person, and I'll never see him again. Jesus Christ. You know, while I was a little kid I used to have dreams about when I would fall in love, you know? Like I'd be watching soap operas on TV, and I'd see myself in them. Like I figured the first time I fell deeply in love I would fall completely apart, I would be a total wreck, you know? Like I would have some horrible fight with my lover, and then we'd part, and we'd keep missing each other for the rest of our lives, and, you know, the day that I tried to make up with him he'd be pissed, and the day he'd try to make up with me, *I'd* be pissed, and we'd go through life like that, loving each other, but never getting together. That's the way I always saw my future love life, and that's the way it's working out with Steve Perkins. I mean, I love him and he's gone.

You go through a few things like this and you wonder if balling isn't useless. You know, it'll take me a long time to figure things out. I mean, so many times you ball just to get the man off your back. And then he's gone, and he doesn't come back. Or he comes back just to ball. Like where does love come in? Sometimes balling just seems to be something that you just want to get over with, so you can start talking, but the man always leaves. It's like oh, well, you start kissing, yeah, and it feels good, and pretty soon you say to yourself, wow, this guy wants to ball, so you wind up balling. Now isn't that a stupid reason to ball? Making love is neat, but balling is just balling.

Well, sometimes I decide never to do dope again and sometimes I decide never to ball again. Love can be really beautiful, but balling is worthless. Wow, I'm really spacing out. Too much work and too much dope. Sometimes I look at myself and I say, "Did I get lost last night to escape? Did I have sex last night to escape? Did I do drugs the last ten nights, or was it the last eleven nights? Do I do all this to escape? And from what?" You know? Well, as I was saying, this whole day was a real shit sandwich, and after I finished my last class I was walking back toward the apartment, and I walked by this cute boy, and he smiled and said, "Hello," and I goes, "Hi!"

Pretty soon he comes running after me and he goes, "Hi! What's your name?"

I go, "Mary," you know?

He goes, "Oh, my name's Greg. Glad to know you, Mary. How'd you like to go out for a beer?"

And I'm thinking, well, maybe this day won't be such a shit sandwich after all. I thought, how many bad things can happen in one day? And I was thinking, Wow, I've never been picked up before. Like I've never allowed it to happen. And it might be fun, a new experience, you know? All this is going through my head while he's saying, "How would you like to go out and have a beer?"

So I said, "Sure," and we start walking off toward the 3.2 bar.

He goes, "Hey, instead of going over to the bar, let's go to my place. I've got some beer there." I said to myself, this guy's trying to get me into his apartment. This might be a new crazy experience.

So I said, "Okay." Oh, man, was this a crazy impulsive thing to do! But it was kind of neat, too.

Well, I don't remember exactly how it came up, but while we're walking he started talking about sex, and he asked me if I used contraceptives. I said, "No, I don't, I just take my chances."

And he stops right there, and he gives me this amazed look, like I'm a fucking purple wildebeest again, and he says, "Man, you're really stupid! You're really crazy! You can't do *anything* without contraceptives. You must be just dumb!"

Well, it was just too much to take. I started to cry and I said, "I'm going home." I turned away and started walking real fast toward the apartment, but he caught up and he said, "Don't be such a baby. I'll walk you home."

So he's walking me home and he goes, "How can you be so stupid not to use a contraceptive?"

Good Lord, what a fucker! I said, "Well, I just don't carry it with me all the time."

He goes, "Well, you shouldn't go any place without foam in your purse." I'm thinking, Wow! Wow! Some fucker! And he goes, "Like, the next time I see you I want you to have foam."

I go, "You're right, you're right," and inside I'm thinking, what a dumb shit you are! What a fucker! It shows you where his head is, it just shows you where his fucking head 's. The bastard! I was so mad!

So now he says, "Have you ever been pregnant?" And I'm saying to myself, what a male chauvinist, he thinks that every chick should be using some kind of contraceptive or she should have one with her so she won't get pregnant by the first guy who picks her up, you know? I'm really getting pissed. He goes, "Have you ever been pregnant?"

I said, "Yes." I haven't been, but I just thought I would bullshit the fucker, just to see how it all turned out.

And he goes, "Were you in love with the guy?"

And I goes, "Yes."

And he goes, "So what happened? Did he pay for it?"

And I goes, "No. There was an awful stink. I had an abortion, and the police got involved, and there was a big fight, and my boyfriend wound up doing one to five in the state penitentiary."

He goes, "Wow! That's a heavy story!"

Well, I finally got home, and I realized how totally, really absurd the whole day had been. This jerk was a perfect ending for the day. The worst kind of male chauvinist pig. He's the kind of fucker I'd really like to get even with. Sometimes I feel this way about all the guys that take me out to fuck. I have this silly urge to carry a rubber along with me and when they're ready to ball, I'll say, "Well, I haven't been using contraceptives, but I just happen to have one on me." You know? I really think that would be funny. Goddamn, I think that would be just the most tremendous trick to pull on some guy, especially if he was a fucker. I mean, he thinks he's getting this lily-white, teen-age virgin, and then I pull a rubber out of my purse and say, "I just happen to have one with me." I would get such a bang out of that! Such a bang! So I went home to my room and tried to get this dumb fucker out of my mind, and there in the middle of my bed was a package. I opened it, and inside was this beautiful royal blue scarf and a lovely copper ring, and a really beautiful cake all wrapped up in wax paper. I'm stunned! Like, wow! You know?

I picked up a card and it says, "Happy Birthday to our Precious Daughter," and all of a sudden I realized, like, Wow! *It was my birthday!* Like I'd completely forgotten! But my mother and father hadn't. And I realized that's probably why Olin called—to wish me a happy twentieth birthday in his own peculiar way, but I cut him off before he could say it. What a spacy group! What a spacy world! And I began to wonder, is life a shit sandwich after all? I mean, how many good happenings equal a bad? How many good things can make up for three bads, for *six* bads? What's the formula? Like just before I got home, the whole world was fucked and everybody was a turd. Love was the last thing on my mind. But every time you do that, love comes right back in, you know? You just can't keep it out. You wind up totally wrong, everything you've figured out is bullshit, and some silly little act of love washes all the bullshit away.

Those beautiful presents made the whole day good. For just a second I thought about all the terrible things that dad and my mother and Olin used to do to me, and it confused me. Why the presents? I couldn't understand.

So I sat down to figure things out objectively. And I realized that my parents are basically very good parents and very good people. The trouble with me is I'd been trying to see them objectively, and you can't do that with somebody you love.

Boy, I know I'm not making any sense. Michael is playing his Goddamn violin in the other room, and I'm trying to explain all this while that noise is grating on my ears. I'd like to go out and tell him, "Knock off that violin, Michael," but then I remember that he never tells me to knock off the recorder. So I'll keep my mouth shut.

Anyway, I'm sitting here right now with tears in my eyes about these presents. Do you suppose it's just another way for them to make me feel bad? No, I don't really feel bad. I feel that there's hope. The scarf is *so* beautiful. It just sets me up, it makes me feel high as a blue jay. There's hope! There's beauty! I mean, you get the idea that life is a shit sandwich, and you start closing your eyes to it, and then you open up your eyes and *there's goodness!* Some stupid little thing like a scarf. Some silly little act of kindness and decency. And the whole frustrating scene lights up for you. Jeez, I don't know.

I think I'm gonna like it here.

Printed in the United States
By Bookmasters